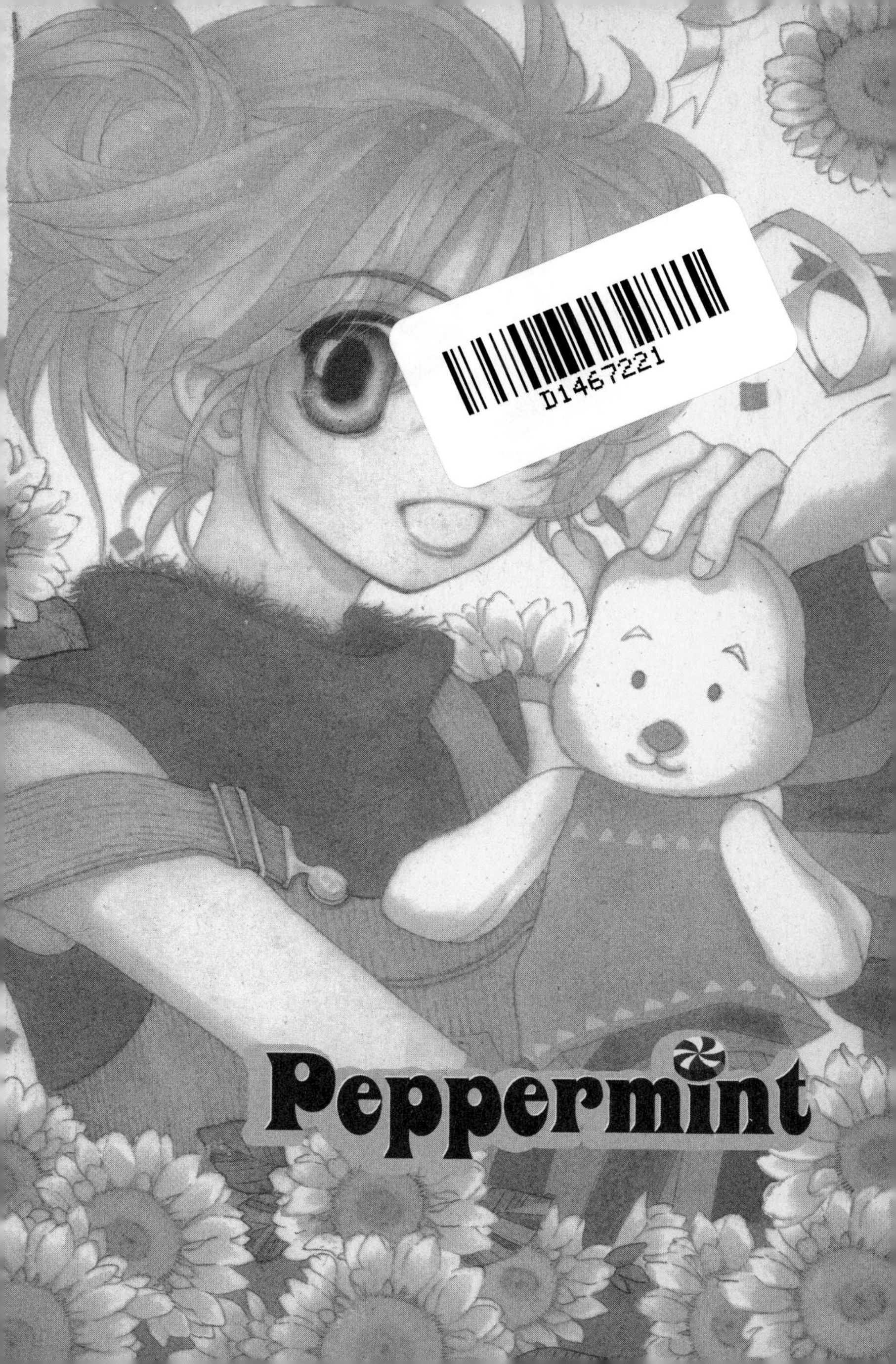
Peppermint

Peppermint

Table of Contents

Peppermint

Volume 1
Eun-Jin Seo

TOKYOPOP®

HAMBURG // LONDON // LOS ANGELES // TOKYO

Peppermint Vol 1
Created by
EUN-JIN SEO

Translation - Jennifer Hahm
English Adaptation - Marc Goldsmith
Lettering - Erika Terriquez
Production Artist - Jennifer Carbajal
Graphic Designer - Al-Insan Lashley

Editor - Julie Taylor
Digital Imaging Manager - Chris Buford
Production Manager - Elisabeth Brizzi
Managing Editor - Lindsey Johnston
VP of Production - Ron Klamert
Editor-in-Chief - Rob Tokar
Publisher - Mike Kiley
President and C.O.O. - John Parker
C.E.O. and Chief Creative Officer - Stuart Levy

A  Manga

TOKYOPOP Inc.
5900 Wilshire Blvd. Suite 2000
Los Angeles, CA 90036

E-mail: info@TOKYOPOP.com
Come visit us online at www.TOKYOPOP.com

ISBN: 1-59816-681-6

First TOKYOPOP printing: July 2006
10 9 8 7 6 5 4 3 2 1
Printed in the USA

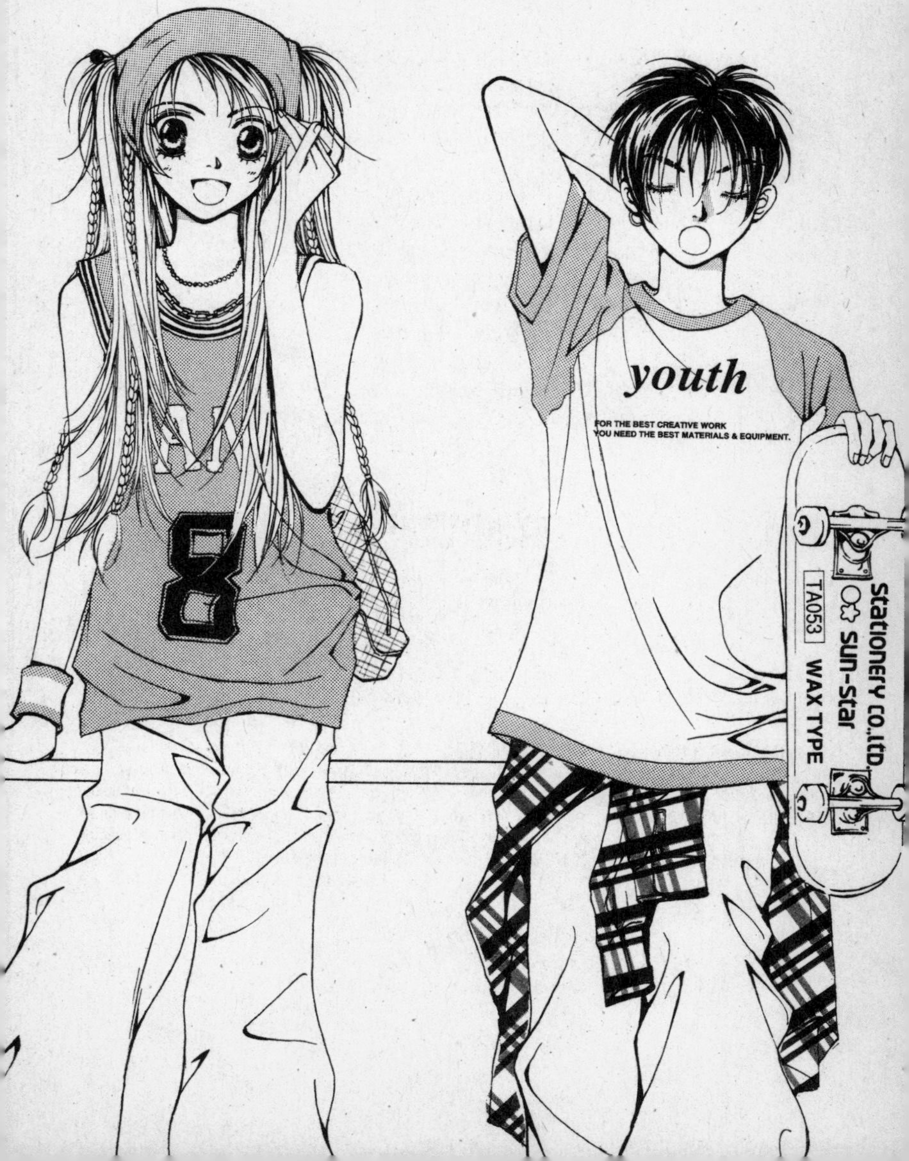
youth
FOR THE BEST CREATIVE WORK
YOU NEED THE BEST MATERIALS & EQUIPMENT.
Stationery CO.,LTD.
SUN-Star
WAX TYPE
TA053

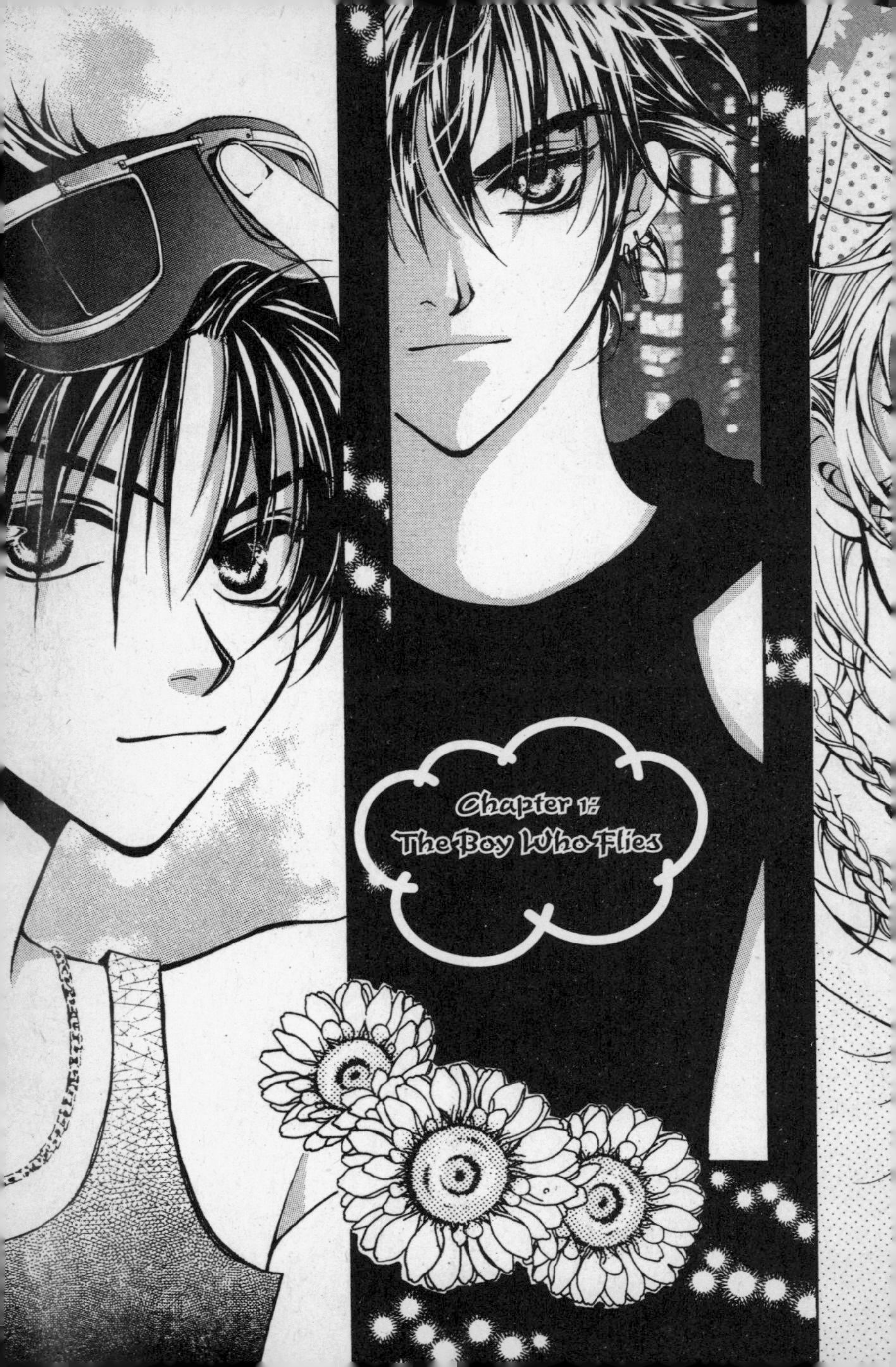
Chapter 1:
The Boy Who Flies

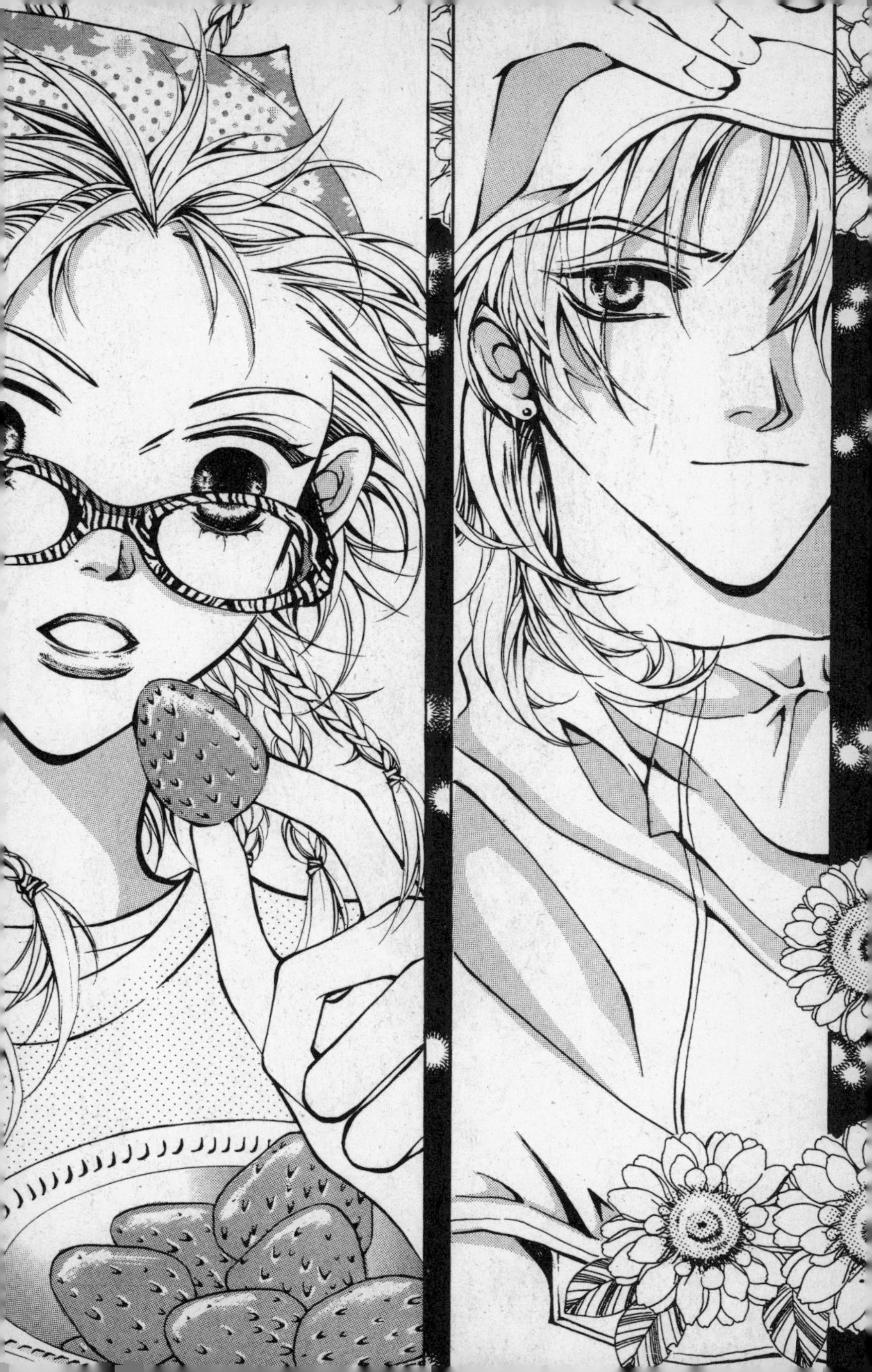

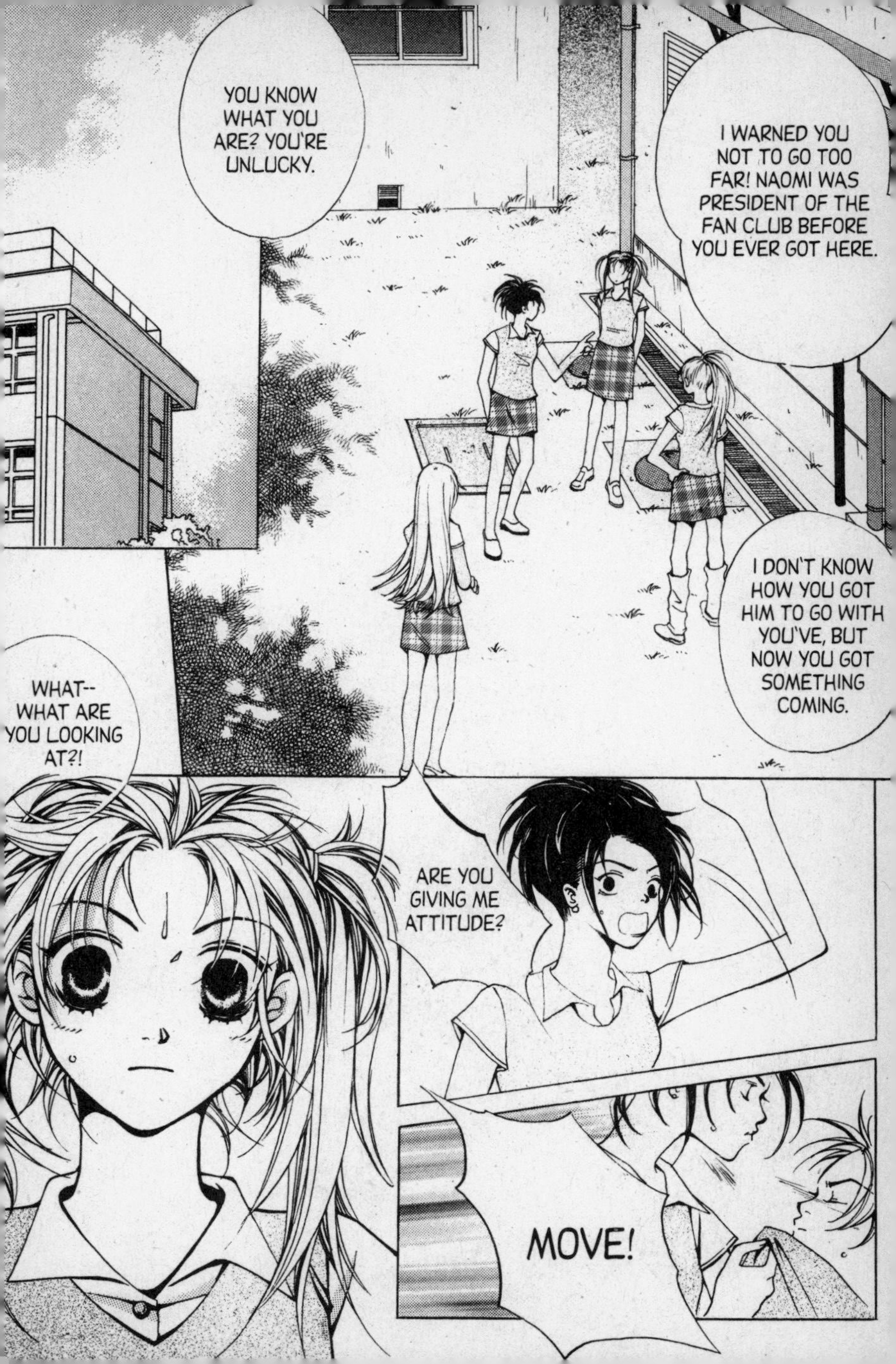
I WARNED YOU NOT TO GO TOO FAR! NAOMI WAS PRESIDENT OF THE FAN CLUB BEFORE YOU EVER GOT HERE.
I DON'T KNOW HOW YOU GOT HIM TO GO WITH YOU'VE, BUT NOW YOU GOT SOMETHING COMING.
YOU KNOW WHAT YOU ARE? YOU'RE UNLUCKY.
WHAT-- WHAT ARE YOU LOOKING AT?!
ARE YOU GIVING ME ATTITUDE?
MOVE!

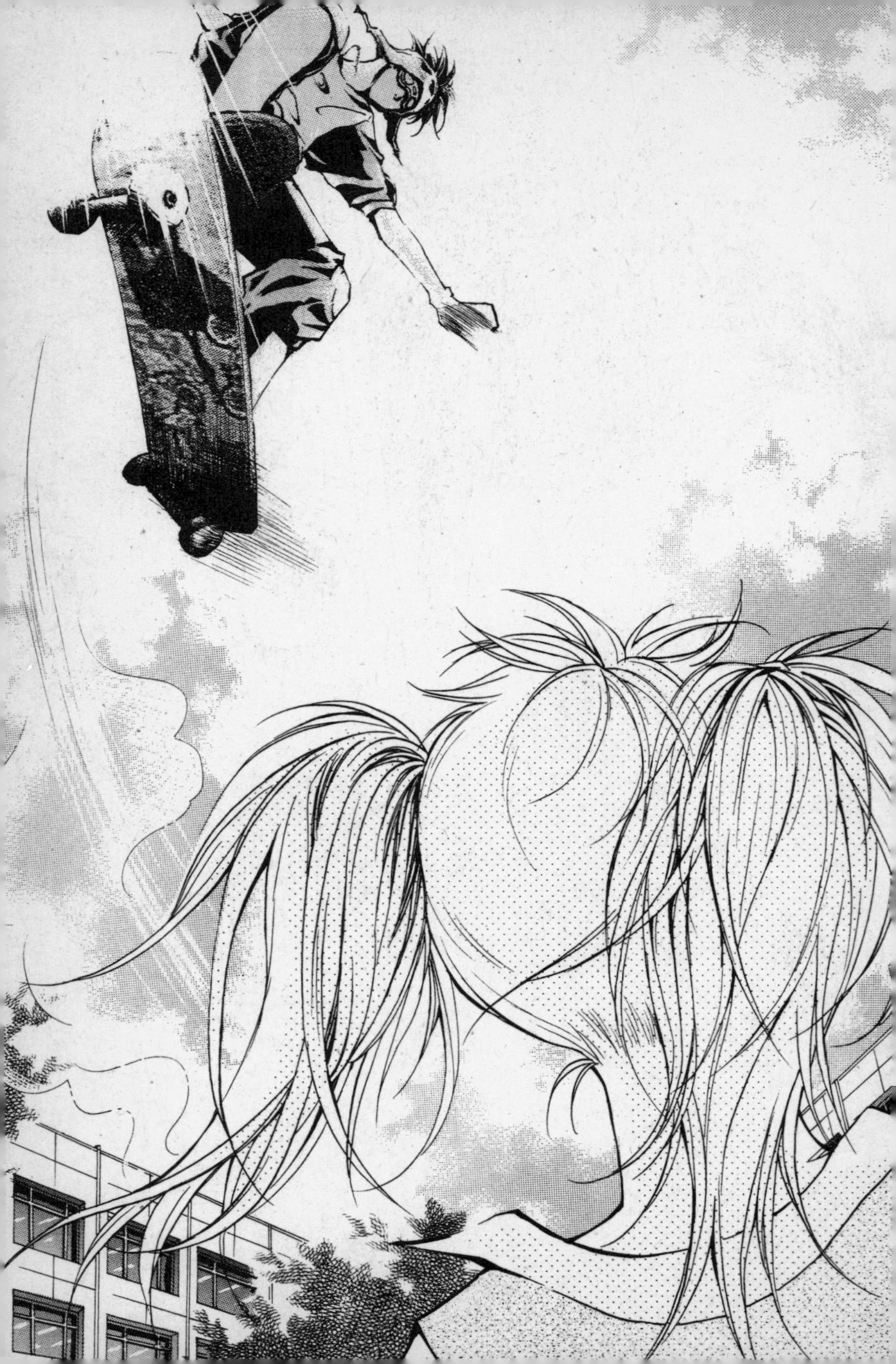

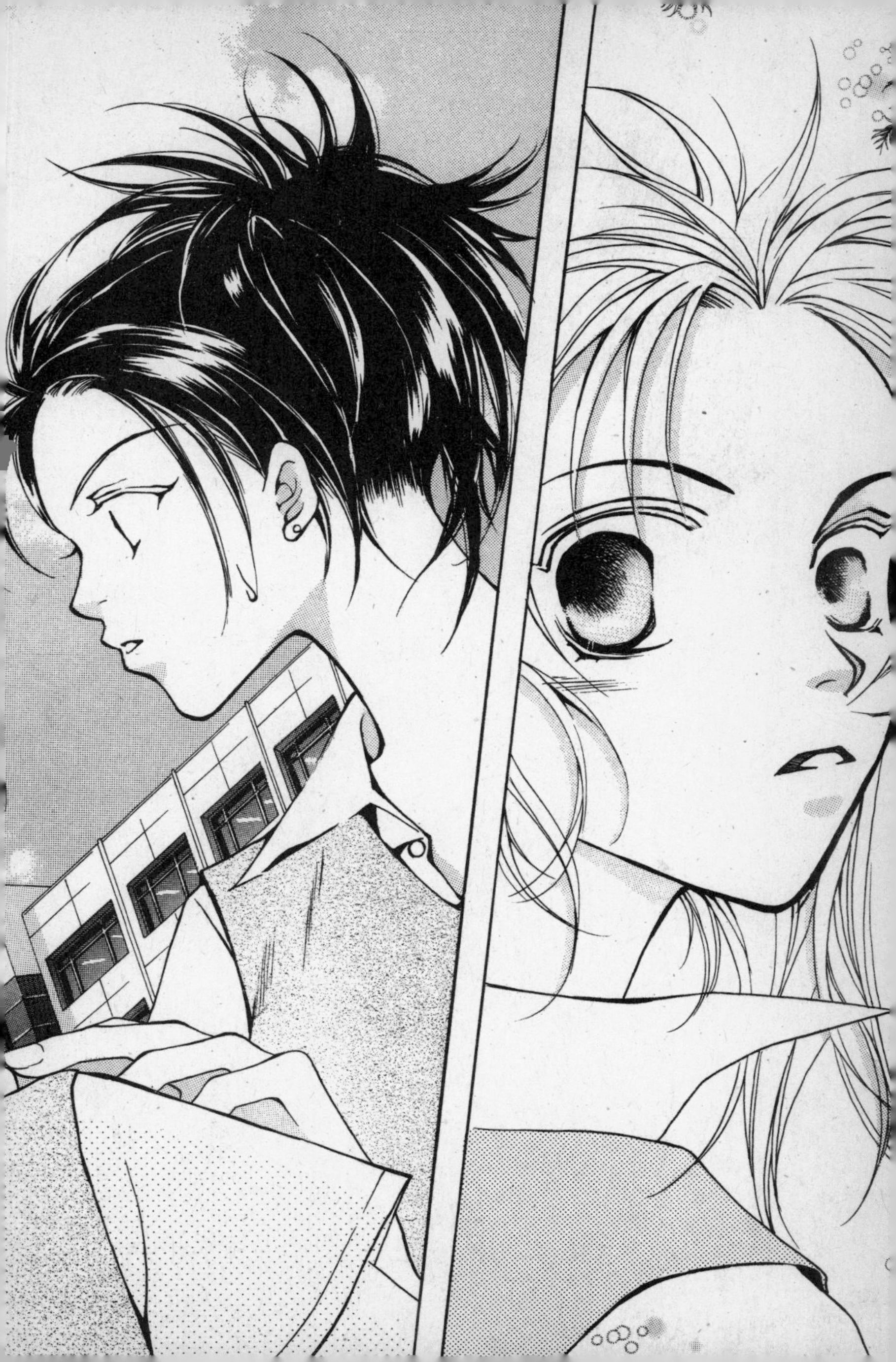

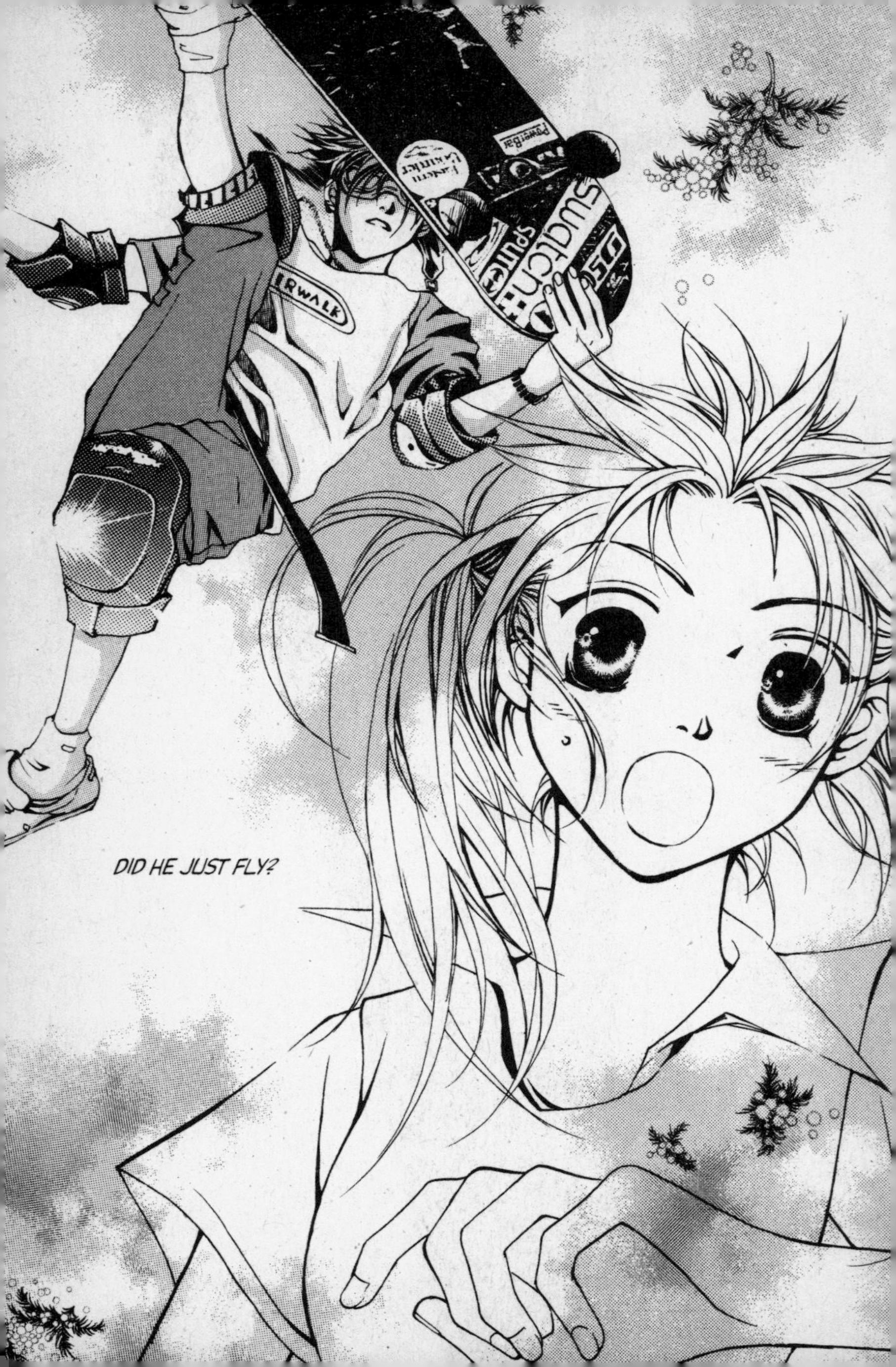
DID HE JUST FLY?

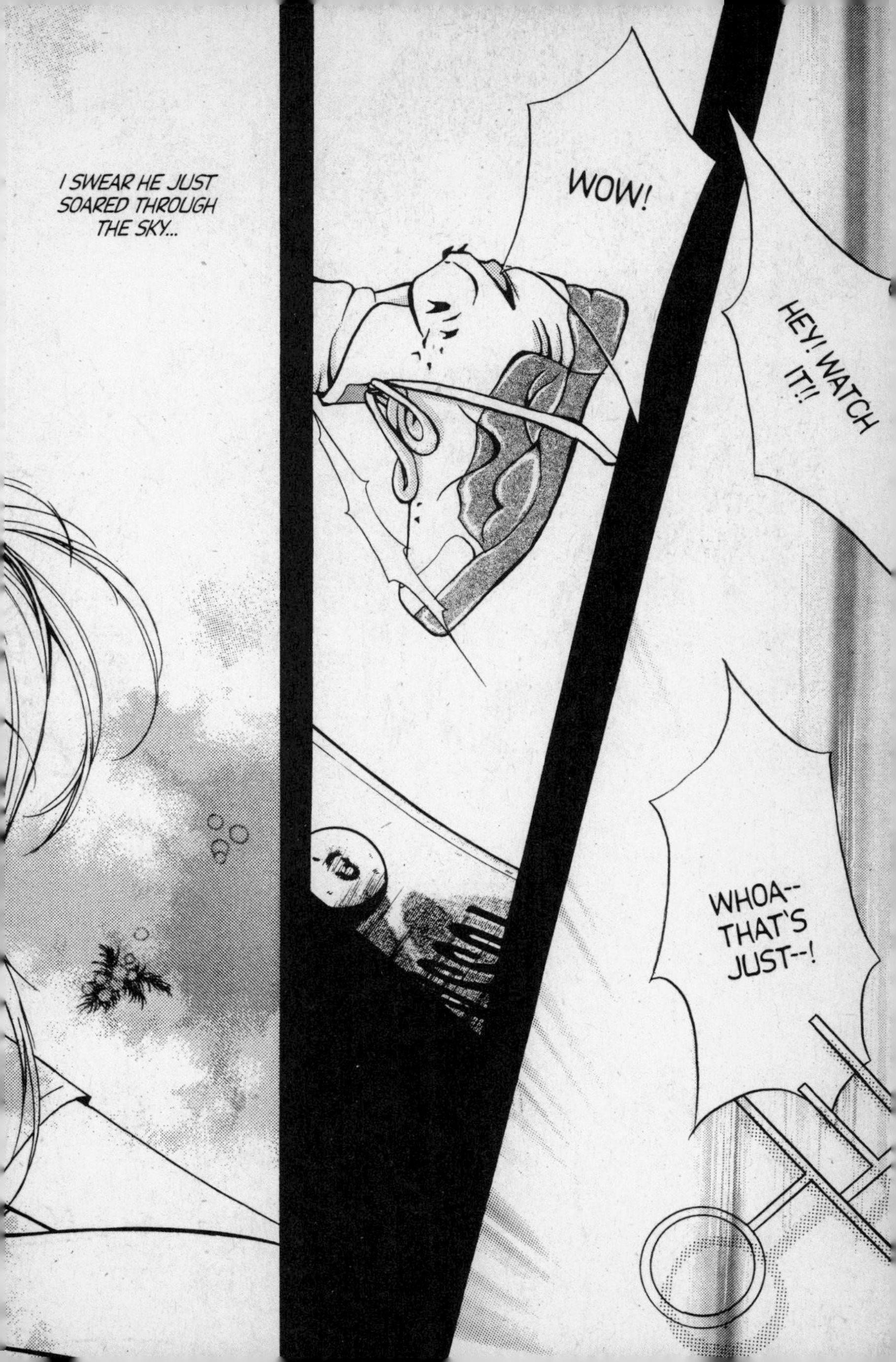
HEY! WATCH IT!!
WHOA-- THAT'S JUST--!
WOW!
I SWEAR HE JUST SOARED THROUGH THE SKY...

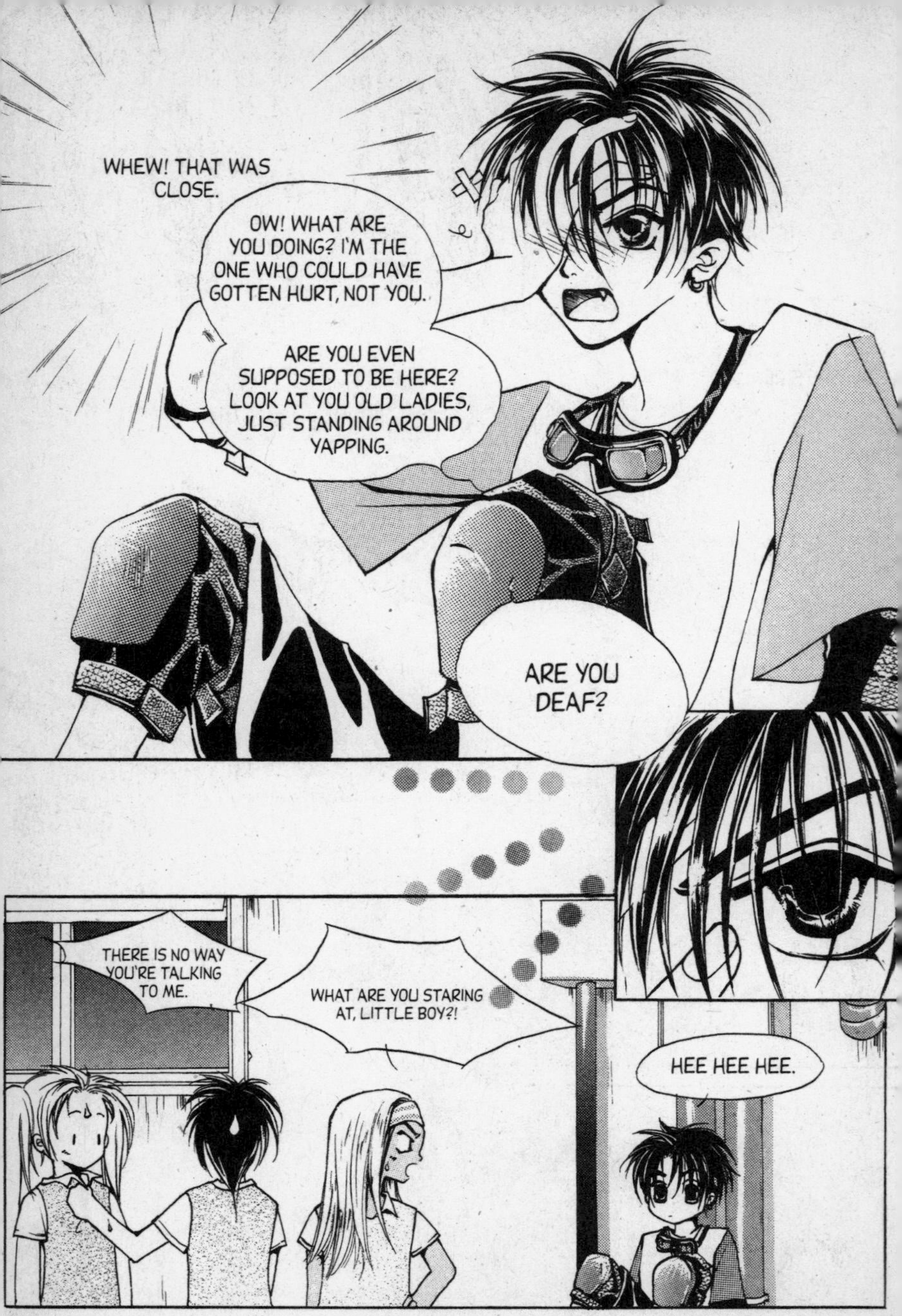
WHEW! THAT WAS CLOSE.
OW! WHAT ARE YOU DOING? I'M THE ONE WHO COULD HAVE GOTTEN HURT, NOT YOU.
ARE YOU EVEN SUPPOSED TO BE HERE? LOOK AT YOU OLD LADIES, JUST STANDING AROUND YAPPING.
ARE YOU DEAF?
HEE HEE HEE.
WHAT ARE YOU STARING AT, LITTLE BOY?!
THERE IS NO WAY YOU'RE TALKING TO ME.

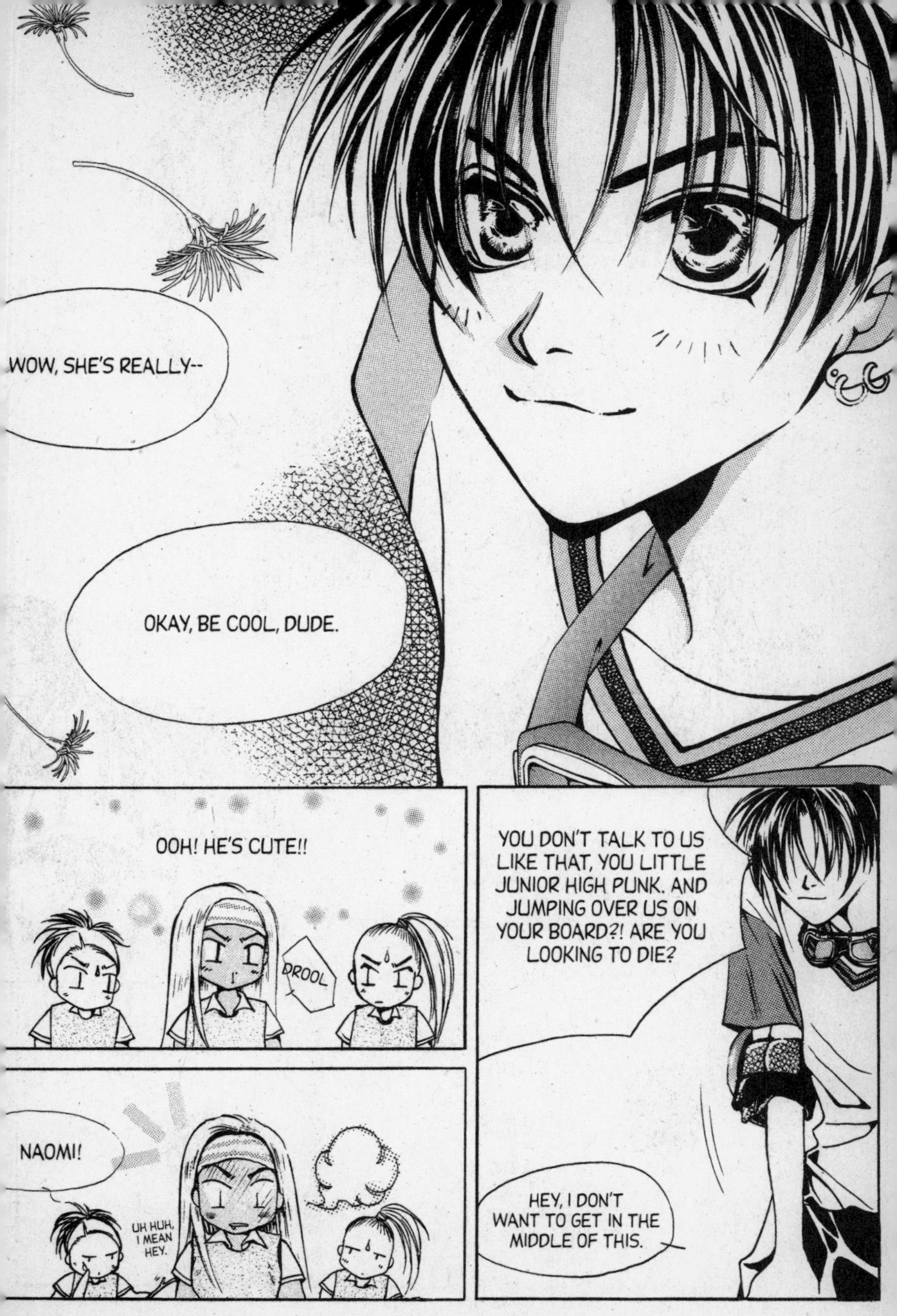
WOW, SHE'S REALLY--
OKAY, BE COOL, DUDE.
YOU DON'T TALK TO US LIKE THAT, YOU LITTLE JUNIOR HIGH PUNK. AND JUMPING OVER US ON YOUR BOARD?! ARE YOU LOOKING TO DIE?
HEY, I DON'T WANT TO GET IN THE MIDDLE OF THIS.
OOH! HE'S CUTE!!
DROOL
NAOMI!
UH HUH, I MEAN HEY.

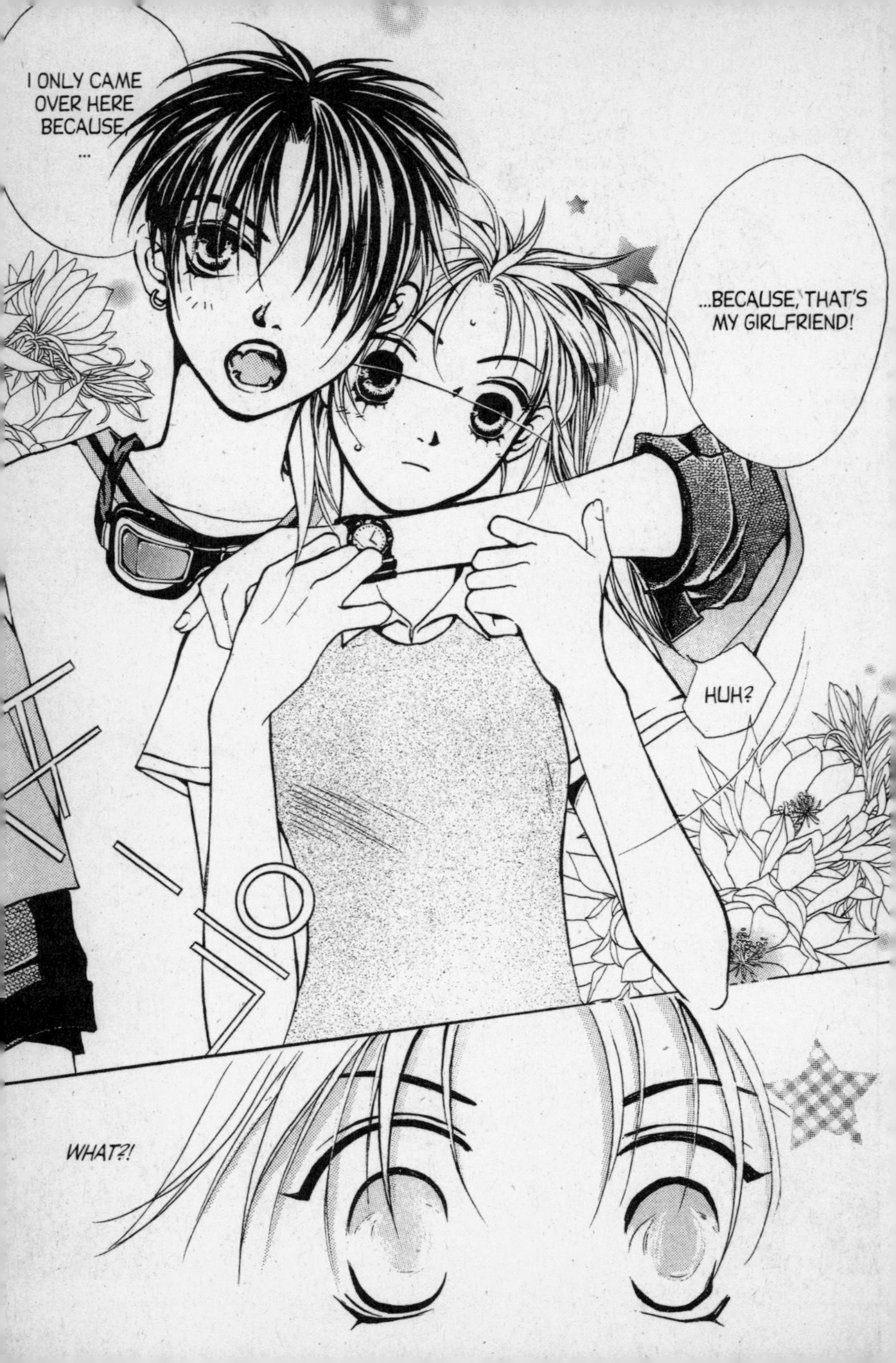
I ONLY CAME OVER HERE BECAUSE, ...
...BECAUSE, THAT'S MY GIRLFRIEND!
HUH?
WHAT?!

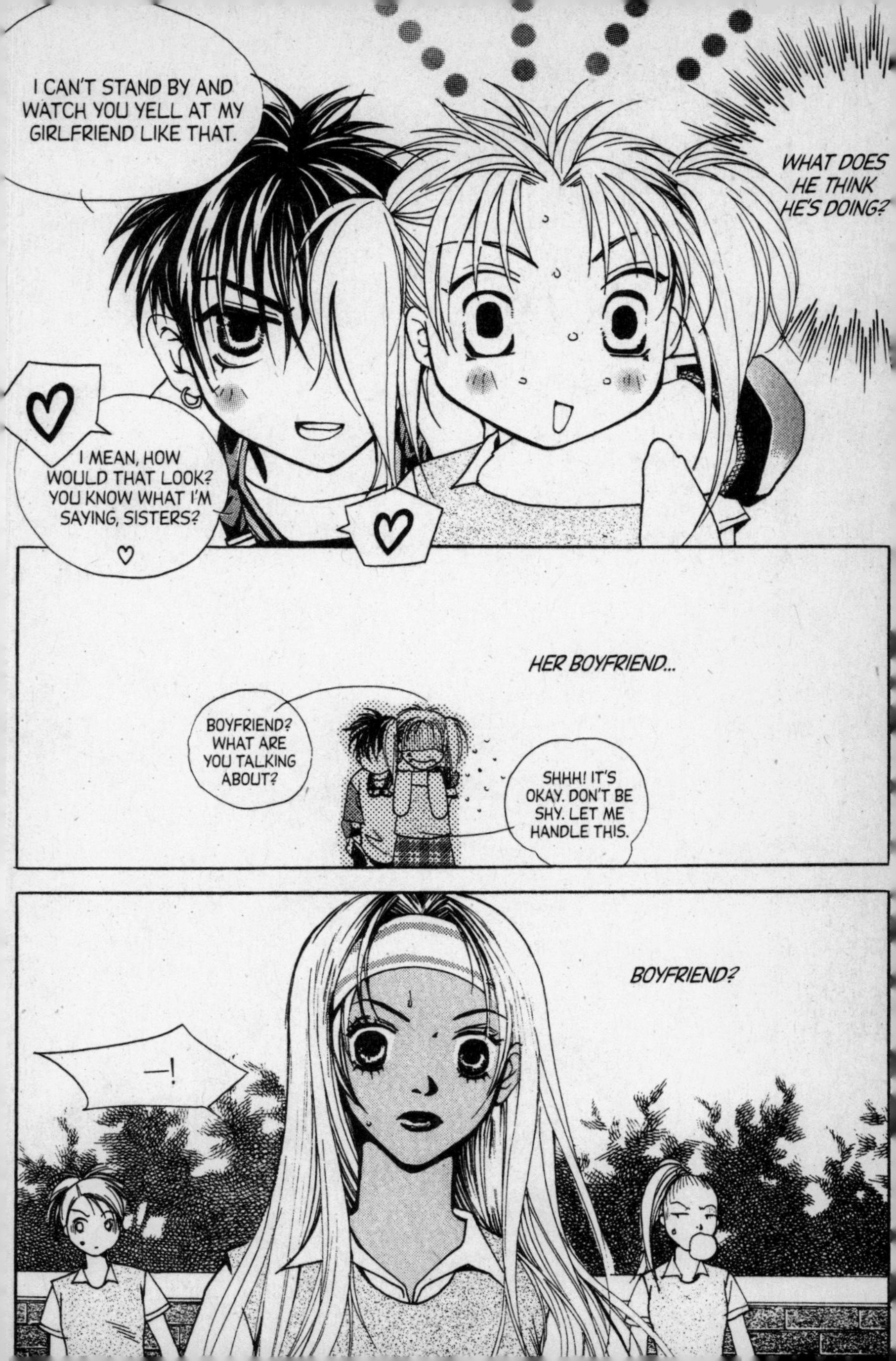
I CAN'T STAND BY AND WATCH YOU YELL AT MY GIRLFRIEND LIKE THAT.
WHAT DOES HE THINK HE'S DOING?
♥
I MEAN, HOW WOULD THAT LOOK? YOU KNOW WHAT I'M SAYING, SISTERS? ♥
♥
HER BOYFRIEND...
BOYFRIEND? WHAT ARE YOU TALKING ABOUT?
SHHH! IT'S OKAY. DON'T BE SHY. LET ME HANDLE THIS.
—!
BOYFRIEND?

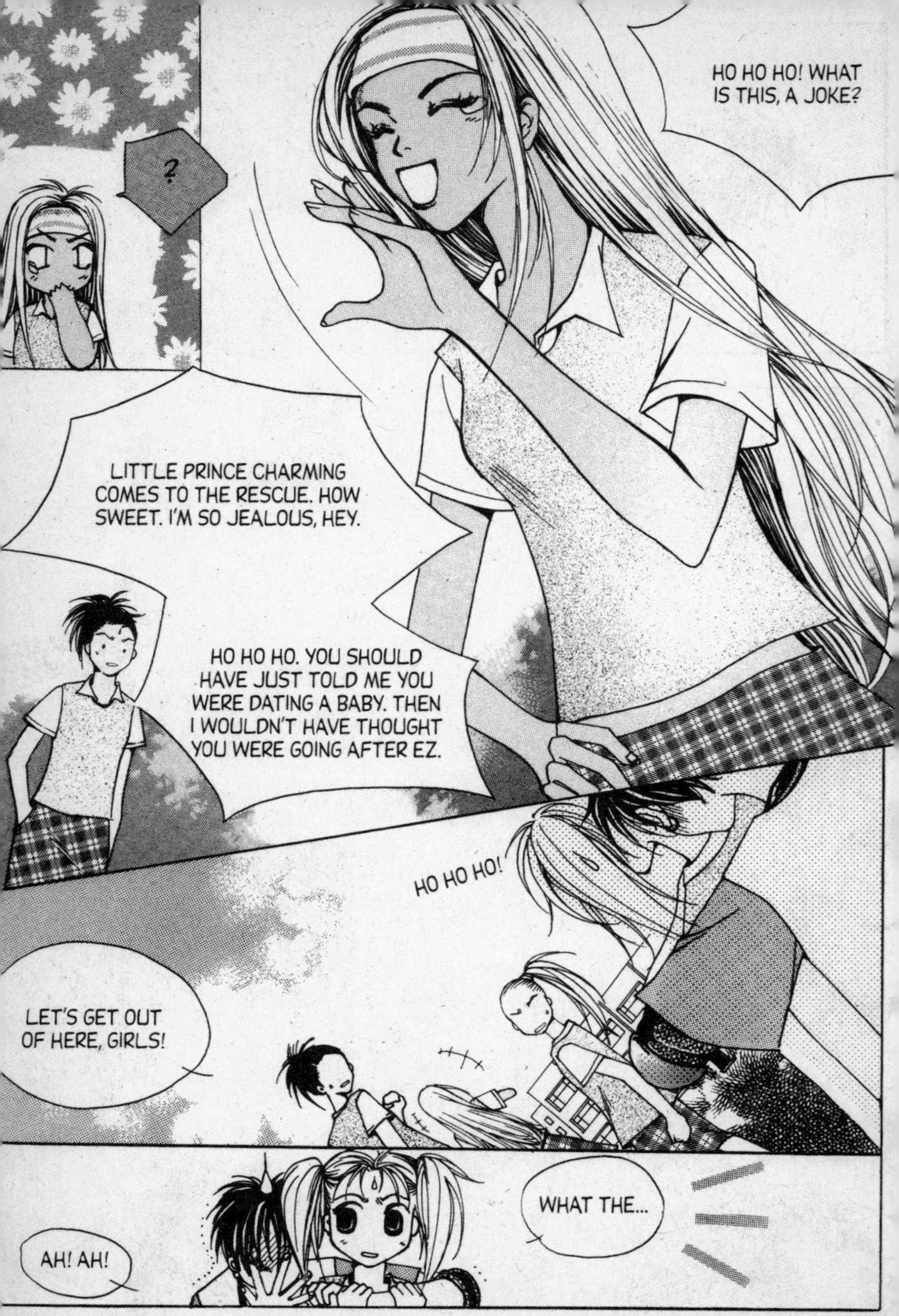
?
HO HO HO! WHAT IS THIS, A JOKE?
LITTLE PRINCE CHARMING COMES TO THE RESCUE. HOW SWEET. I'M SO JEALOUS, HEY.
HO HO HO. YOU SHOULD HAVE JUST TOLD ME YOU WERE DATING A BABY. THEN I WOULDN'T HAVE THOUGHT YOU WERE GOING AFTER EZ.
LET'S GET OUT OF HERE, GIRLS!
HO HO HO!
AH! AH!
WHAT THE...

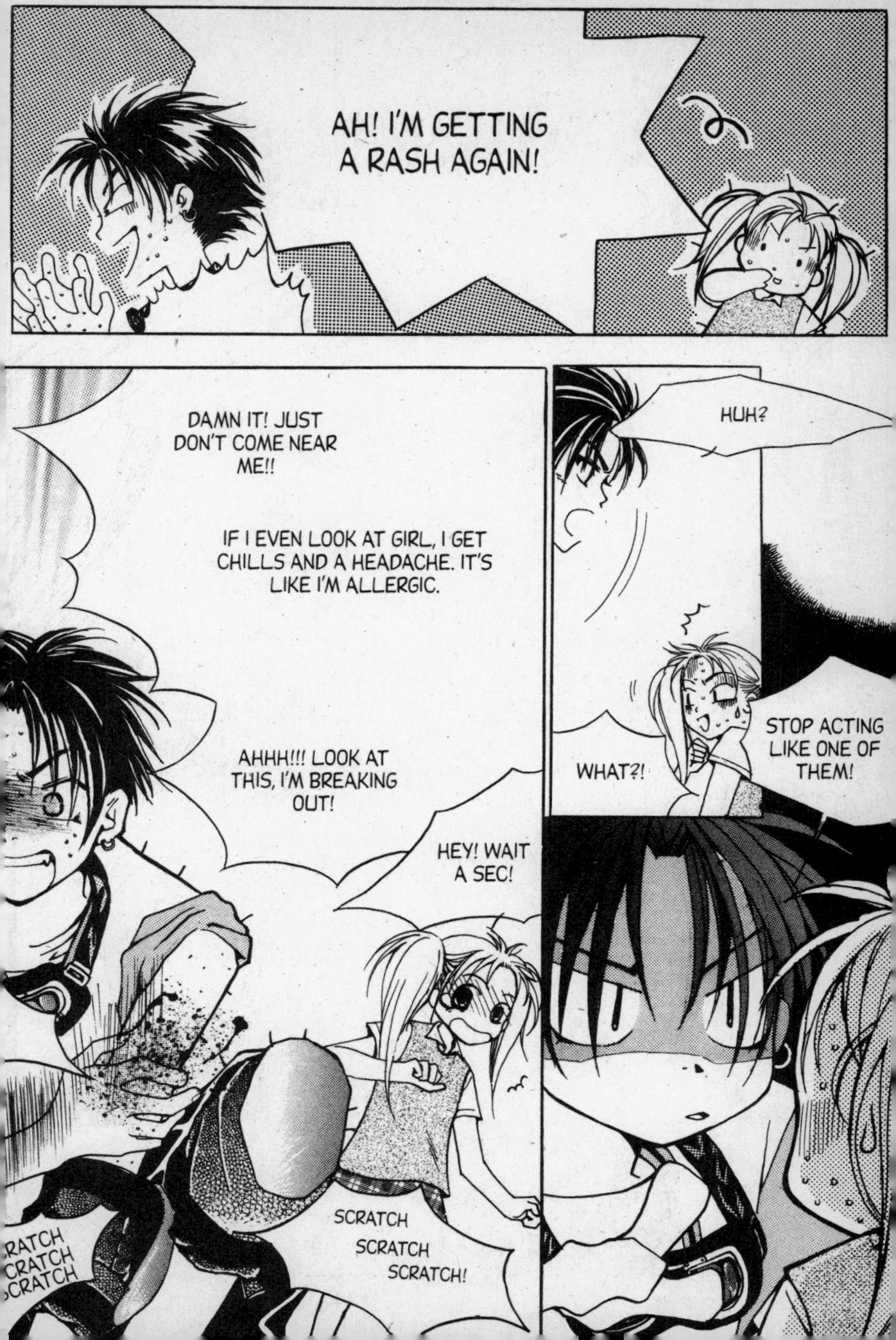
AH! I'M GETTING A RASH AGAIN!
DAMN IT! JUST DON'T COME NEAR ME!!
IF I EVEN LOOK AT GIRL, I GET CHILLS AND A HEADACHE. IT'S LIKE I'M ALLERGIC.
AHHH!!! LOOK AT THIS, I'M BREAKING OUT!
HEY! WAIT A SEC!
SCRATCH
SCRATCH
SCRATCH!
RATCH
CRATCH
CRATCH
HUH?
WHAT?!
STOP ACTING LIKE ONE OF THEM!

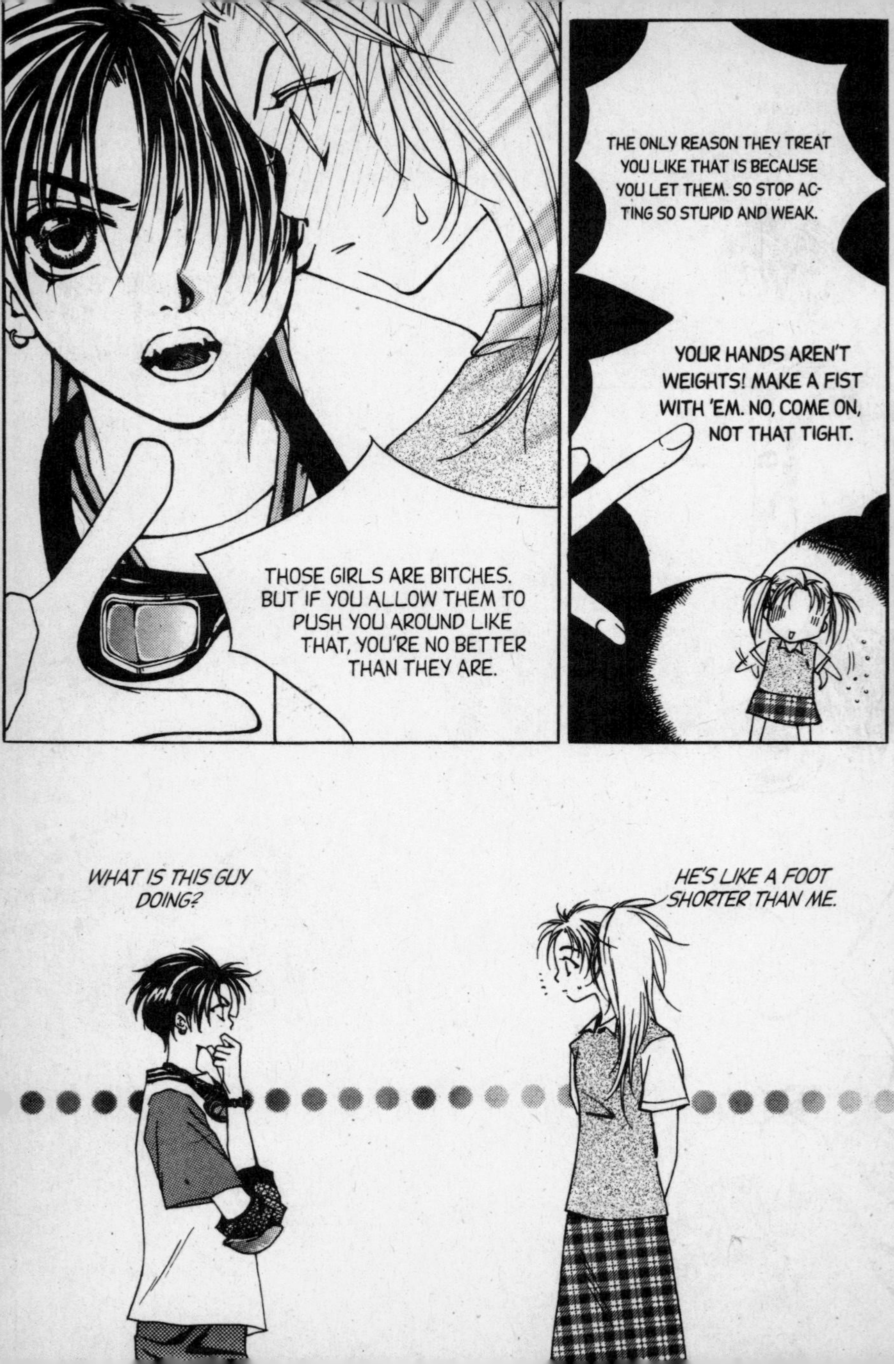
THE ONLY REASON THEY TREAT YOU LIKE THAT IS BECAUSE YOU LET THEM. SO STOP ACTING SO STUPID AND WEAK.
YOUR HANDS AREN'T WEIGHTS! MAKE A FIST WITH 'EM. NO, COME ON, NOT THAT TIGHT.
THOSE GIRLS ARE BITCHES. BUT IF YOU ALLOW THEM TO PUSH YOU AROUND LIKE THAT, YOU'RE NO BETTER THAN THEY ARE.
HE'S LIKE A FOOT SHORTER THAN ME.
WHAT IS THIS GUY DOING?

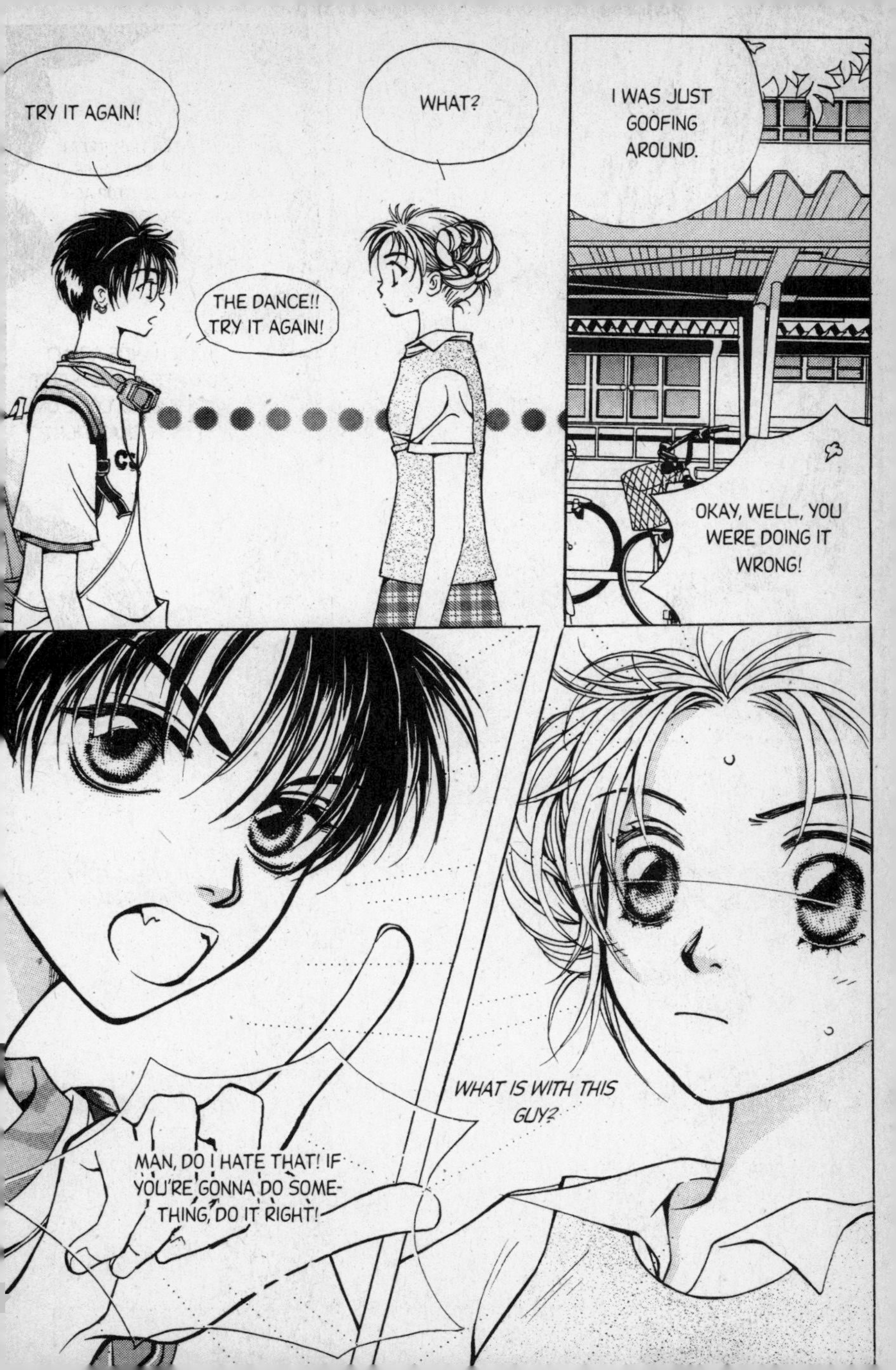
TRY IT AGAIN!
WHAT?
THE DANCE!! TRY IT AGAIN!
I WAS JUST GOOFING AROUND.
OKAY, WELL, YOU WERE DOING IT WRONG!
MAN, DO I HATE THAT! IF YOU'RE GONNA DO SOME-THING, DO IT RIGHT!
WHAT IS WITH THIS GUY?

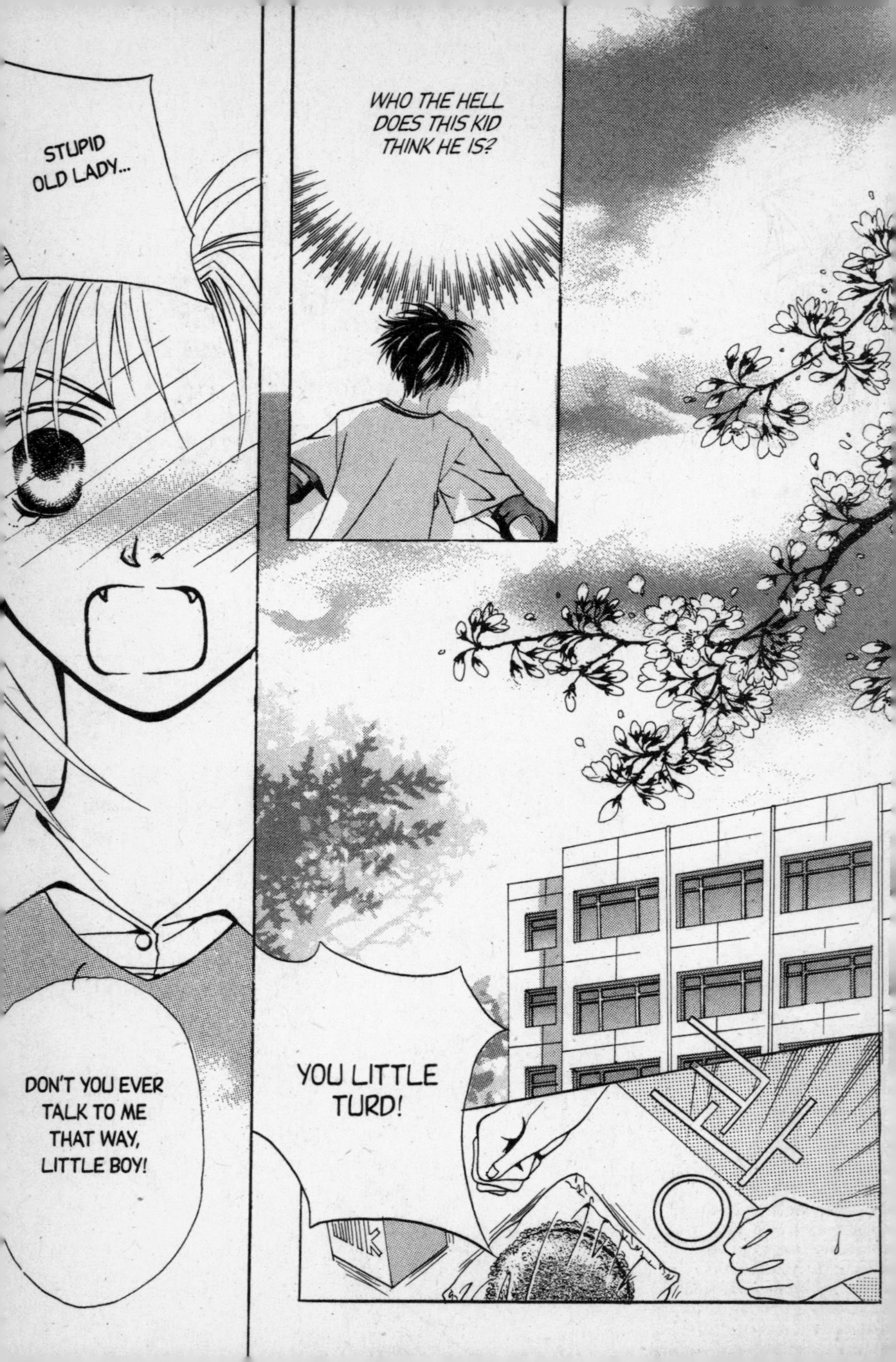
WHO THE HELL DOES THIS KID THINK HE IS?
YOU LITTLE TURD!
STUPID OLD LADY...
DON'T YOU EVER TALK TO ME THAT WAY, LITTLE BOY!

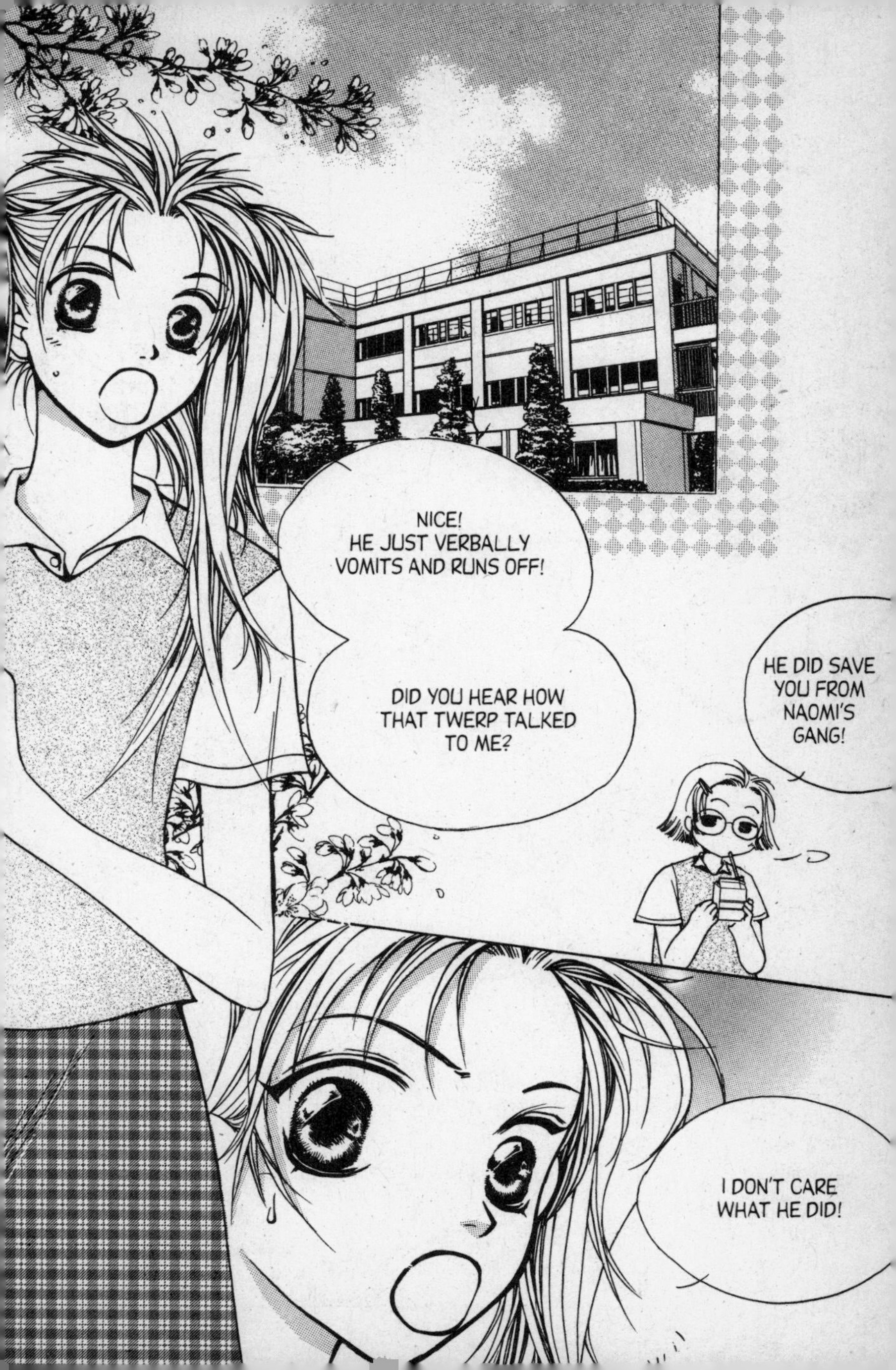
NICE!
HE JUST VERBALLY VOMITS AND RUNS OFF!
DID YOU HEAR HOW THAT TWERP TALKED TO ME?
HE DID SAVE YOU FROM NAOMI'S GANG!
I DON'T CARE WHAT HE DID!

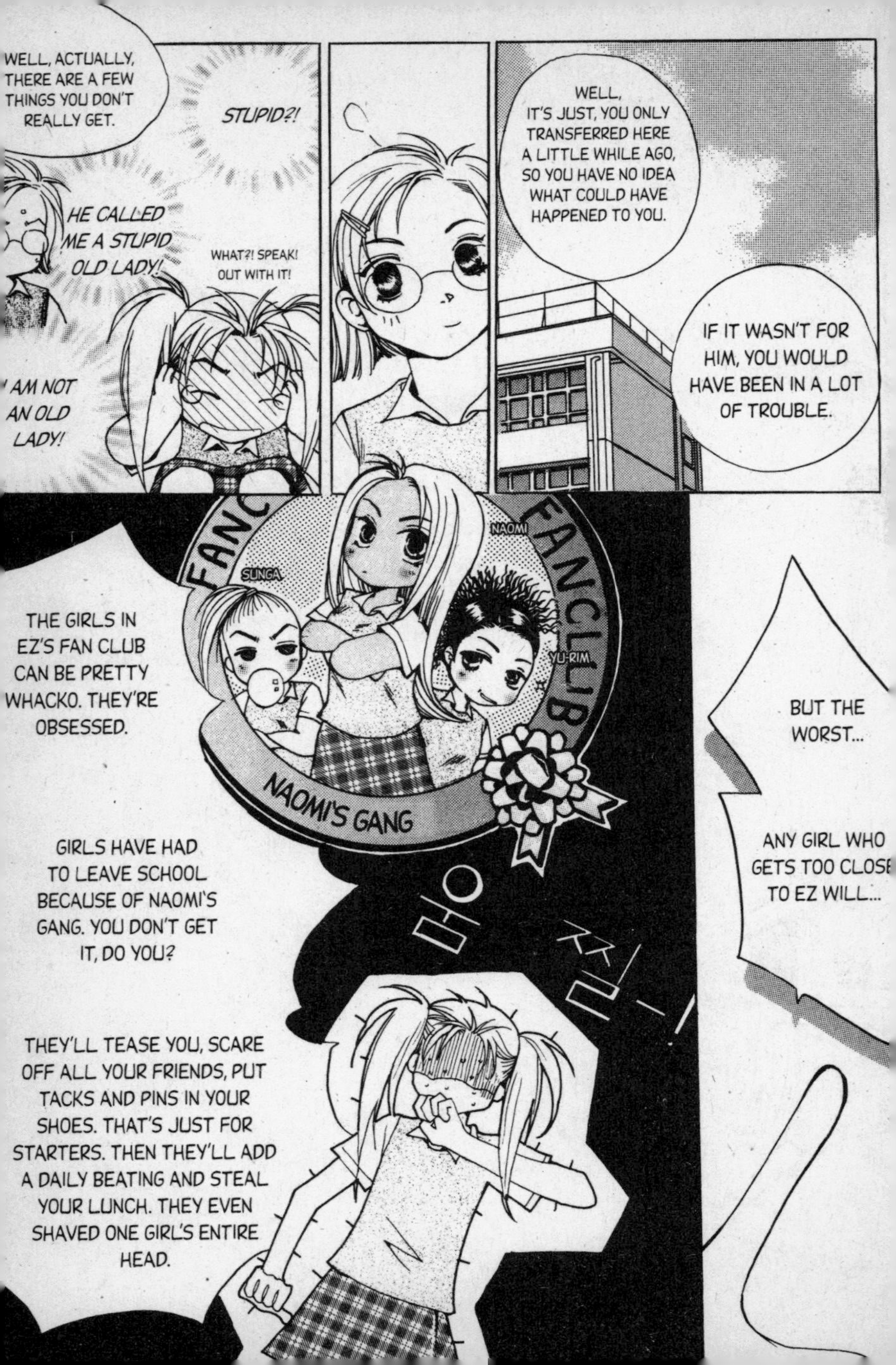
WELL, ACTUALLY, THERE ARE A FEW THINGS YOU DON'T REALLY GET.
STUPID?!
HE CALLED ME A STUPID OLD LADY!
WHAT?! SPEAK! OUT WITH IT!
I AM NOT AN OLD LADY!
WELL, IT'S JUST, YOU ONLY TRANSFERRED HERE A LITTLE WHILE AGO, SO YOU HAVE NO IDEA WHAT COULD HAVE HAPPENED TO YOU.
IF IT WASN'T FOR HIM, YOU WOULD HAVE BEEN IN A LOT OF TROUBLE.
THE GIRLS IN EZ'S FAN CLUB CAN BE PRETTY WHACKO. THEY'RE OBSESSED.
FANCLUB
NAOMI
SUNGA
YU-RIM
NAOMI'S GANG
GIRLS HAVE HAD TO LEAVE SCHOOL BECAUSE OF NAOMI'S GANG. YOU DON'T GET IT, DO YOU?
THEY'LL TEASE YOU, SCARE OFF ALL YOUR FRIENDS, PUT TACKS AND PINS IN YOUR SHOES. THAT'S JUST FOR STARTERS. THEN THEY'LL ADD A DAILY BEATING AND STEAL YOUR LUNCH. THEY EVEN SHAVED ONE GIRL'S ENTIRE HEAD.
BUT THE WORST...
ANY GIRL WHO GETS TOO CLOSE TO EZ WILL...

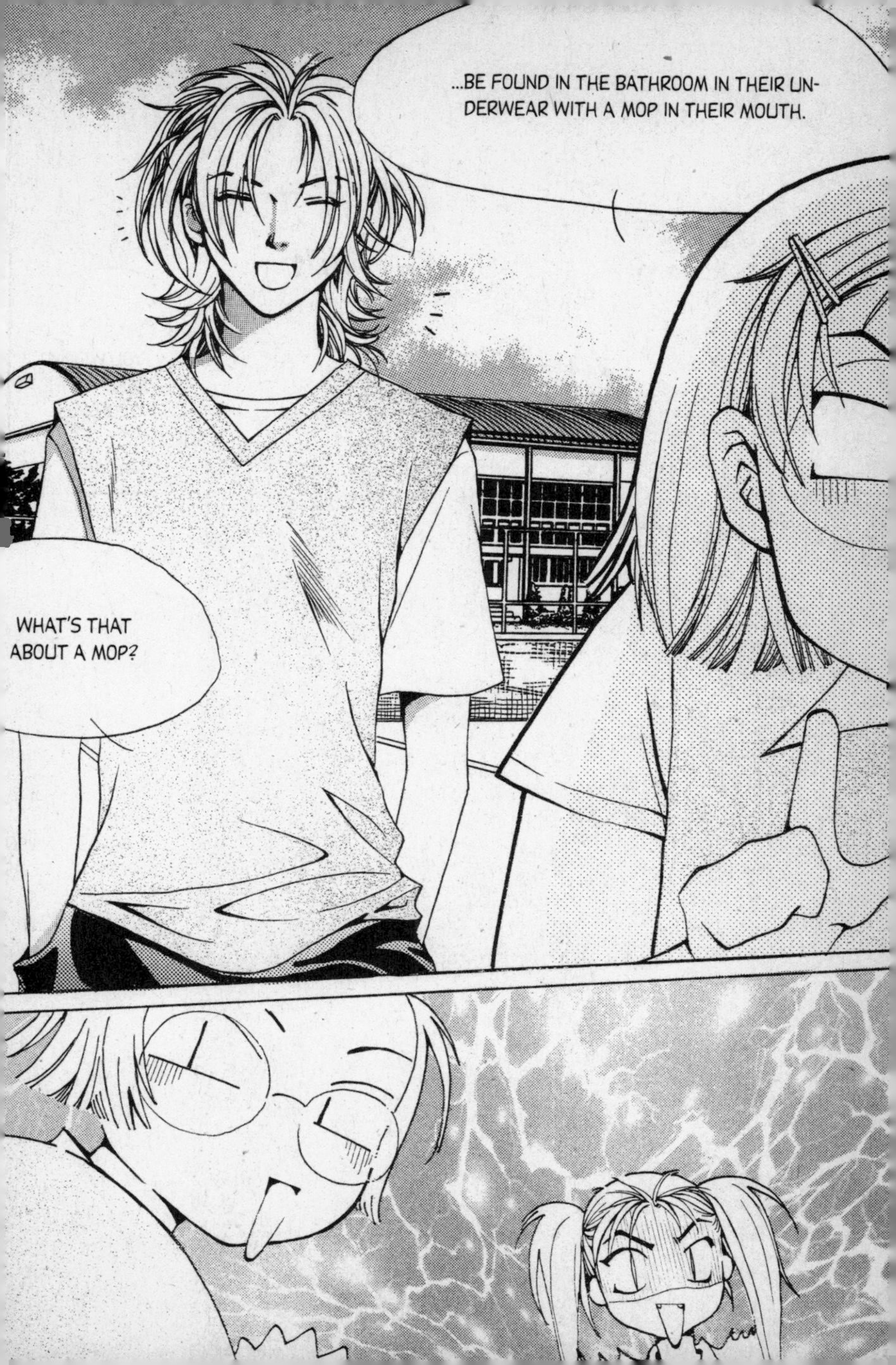
...BE FOUND IN THE BATHROOM IN THEIR UN-DERWEAR WITH A MOP IN THEIR MOUTH.
WHAT'S THAT ABOUT A MOP?

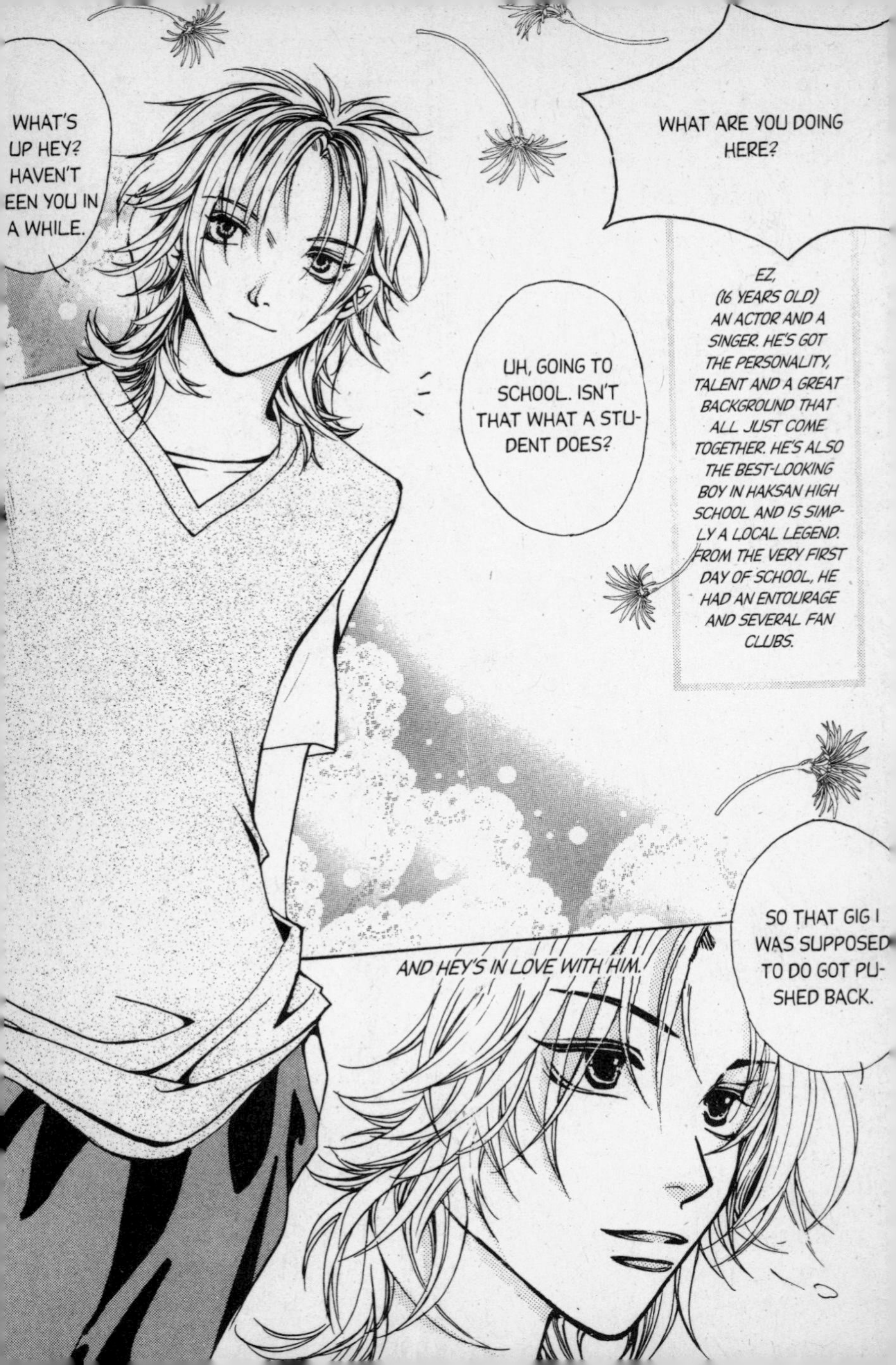
WHAT'S UP HEY? HAVEN'T EEN YOU IN A WHILE.
WHAT ARE YOU DOING HERE?
UH, GOING TO SCHOOL. ISN'T THAT WHAT A STU-DENT DOES?
EZ, (16 YEARS OLD) AN ACTOR AND A SINGER. HE'S GOT THE PERSONALITY, TALENT AND A GREAT BACKGROUND THAT ALL JUST COME TOGETHER. HE'S ALSO THE BEST-LOOKING BOY IN HAKSAN HIGH SCHOOL AND IS SIMP-LY A LOCAL LEGEND. FROM THE VERY FIRST DAY OF SCHOOL, HE HAD AN ENTOURAGE AND SEVERAL FAN CLUBS.
AND HEY'S IN LOVE WITH HIM.
SO THAT GIG I WAS SUPPOSED TO DO GOT PU-SHED BACK.

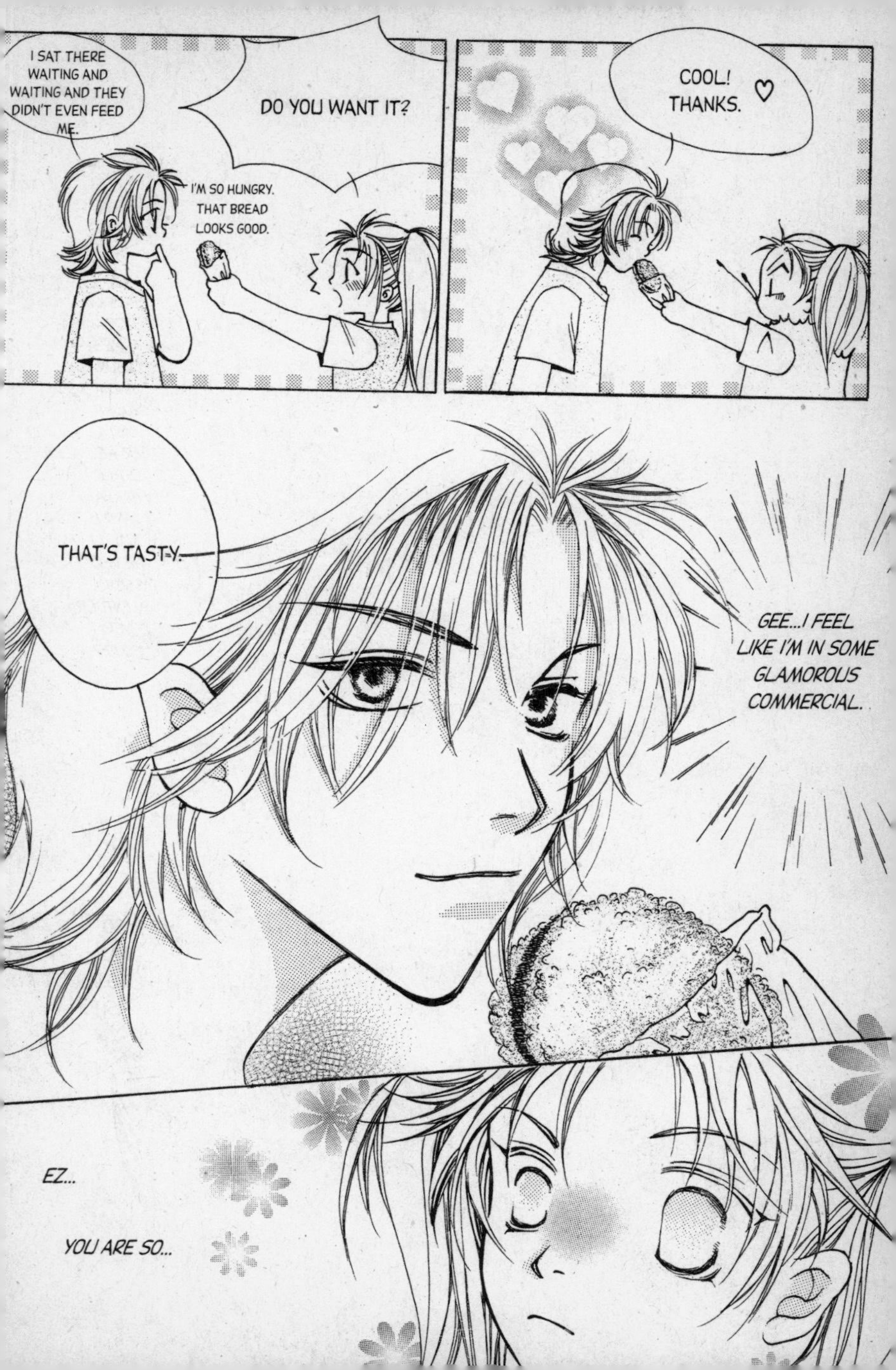
I SAT THERE WAITING AND WAITING AND THEY DIDN'T EVEN FEED ME.
I'M SO HUNGRY. THAT BREAD LOOKS GOOD.
DO YOU WANT IT?
COOL! THANKS. ♡
THAT'S TASTY.
GEE...I FEEL LIKE I'M IN SOME GLAMOROUS COMMERCIAL.
EZ...
YOU ARE SO...

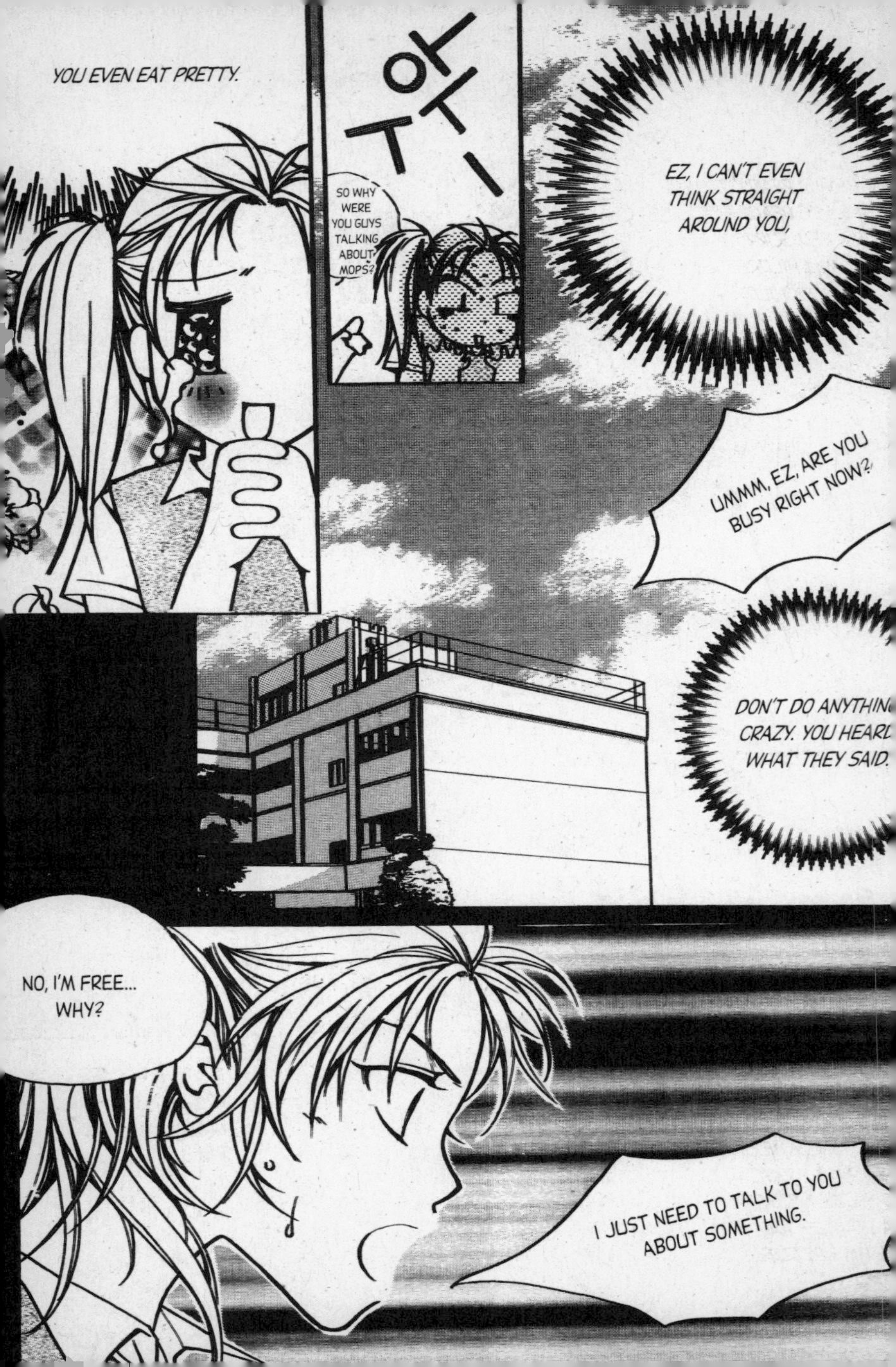
YOU EVEN EAT PRETTY.
SO WHY WERE YOU GUYS TALKING ABOUT MOPS?
EZ, I CAN'T EVEN THINK STRAIGHT AROUND YOU,
UMMM, EZ, ARE YOU BUSY RIGHT NOW?
DON'T DO ANYTHING CRAZY. YOU HEARD WHAT THEY SAID.
NO, I'M FREE... WHY?
I JUST NEED TO TALK TO YOU ABOUT SOMETHING.

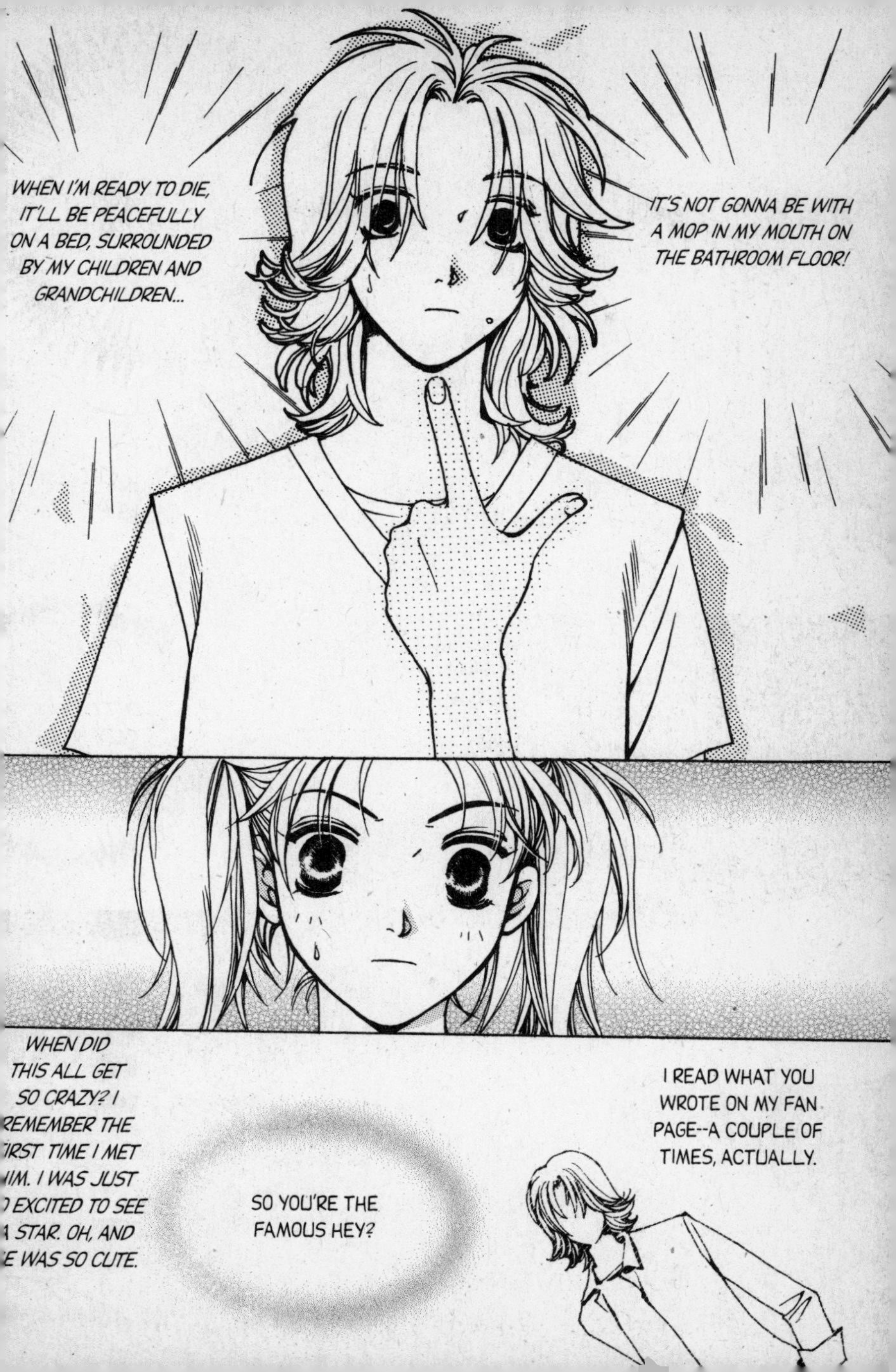
WHEN I'M READY TO DIE, IT'LL BE PEACEFULLY ON A BED, SURROUNDED BY MY CHILDREN AND GRANDCHILDREN...
IT'S NOT GONNA BE WITH A MOP IN MY MOUTH ON THE BATHROOM FLOOR!
WHEN DID THIS ALL GET SO CRAZY? I REMEMBER THE IRST TIME I MET IM. I WAS JUST EXCITED TO SEE STAR. OH, AND E WAS SO CUTE.
SO YOU'RE THE FAMOUS HEY?
I READ WHAT YOU WROTE ON MY FAN PAGE--A COUPLE OF TIMES, ACTUALLY.

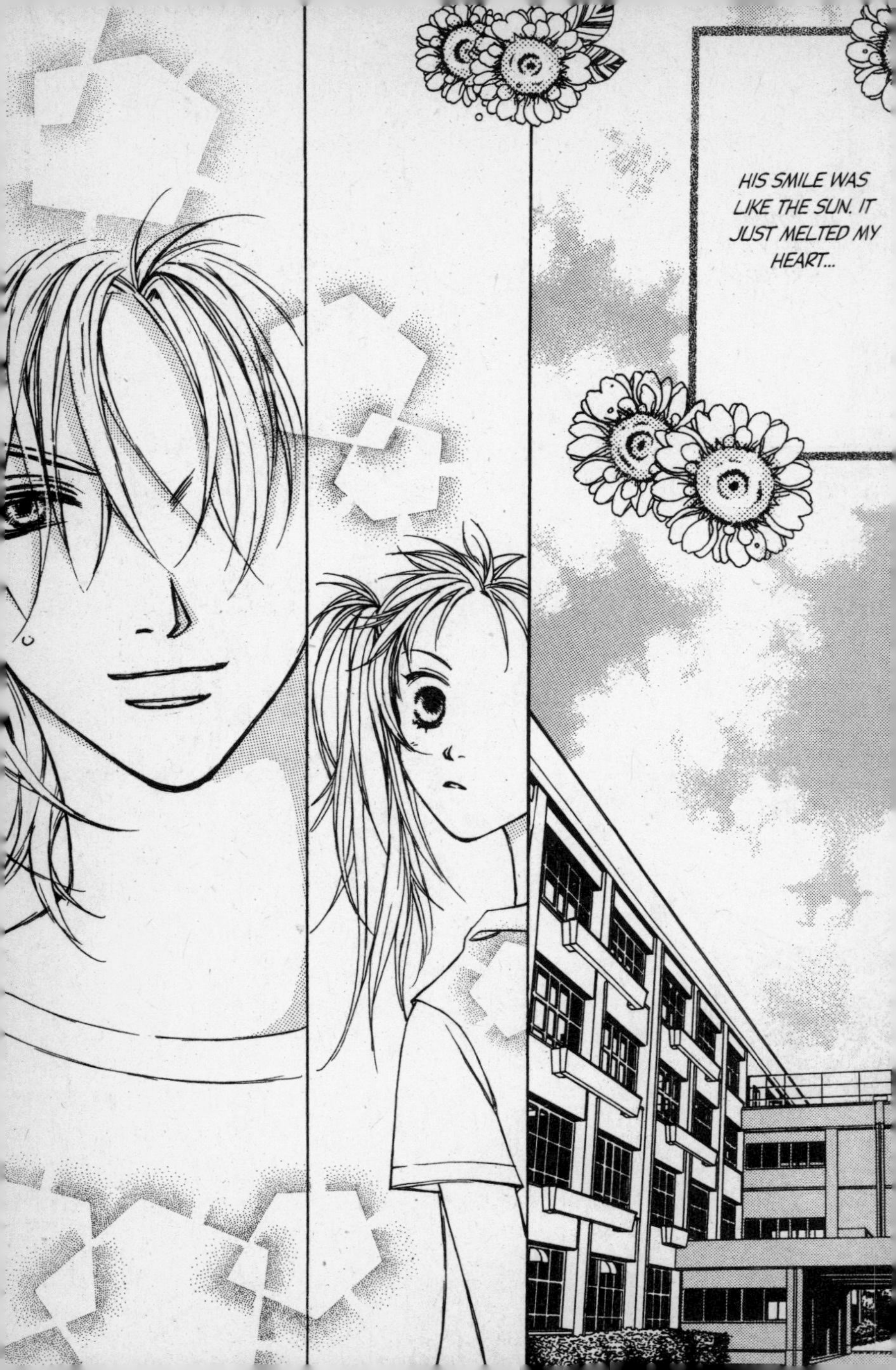
HIS SMILE WAS LIKE THE SUN. IT JUST MELTED MY HEART...

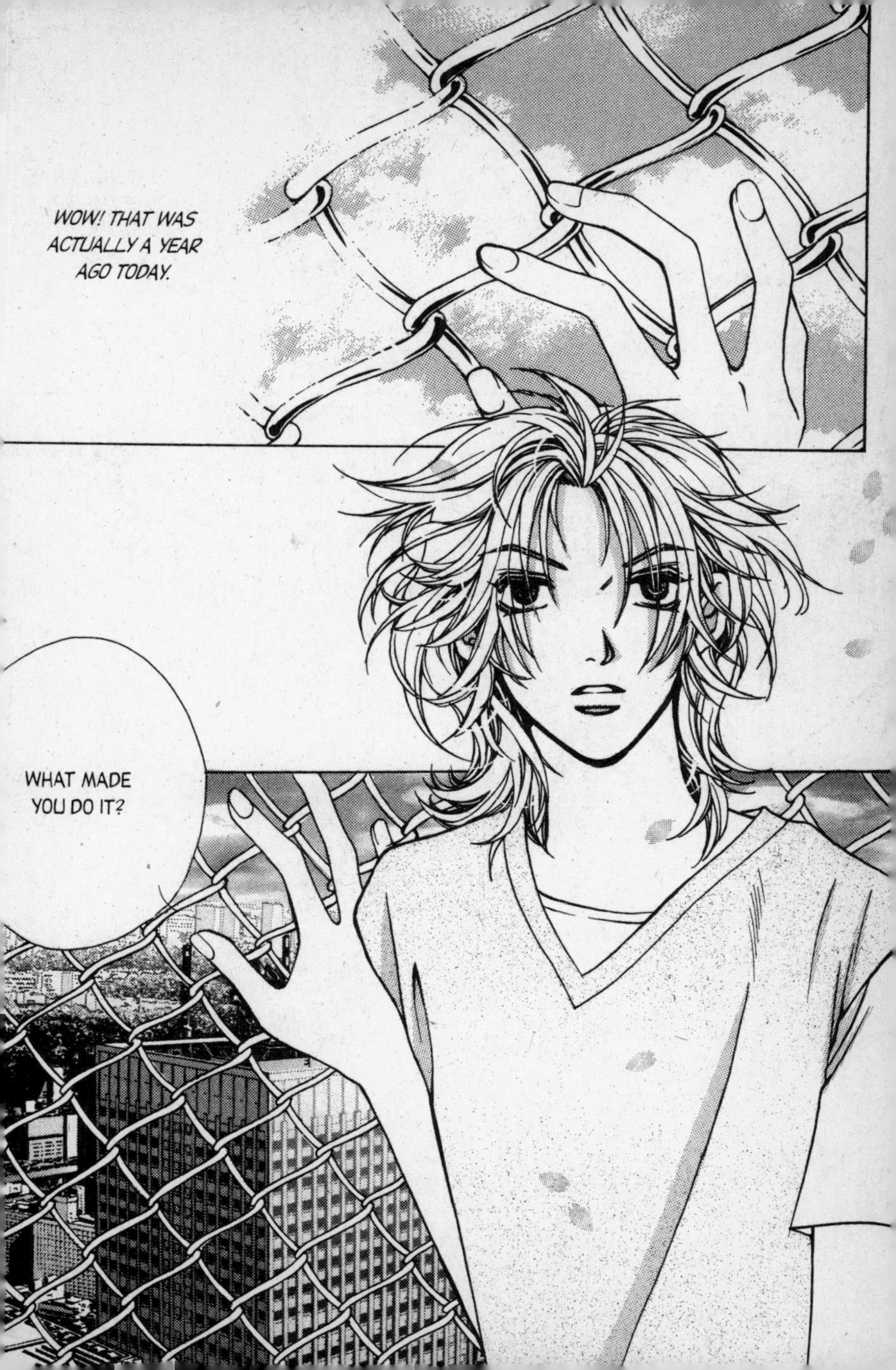
WOW! THAT WAS ACTUALLY A YEAR AGO TODAY.
WHAT MADE YOU DO IT?

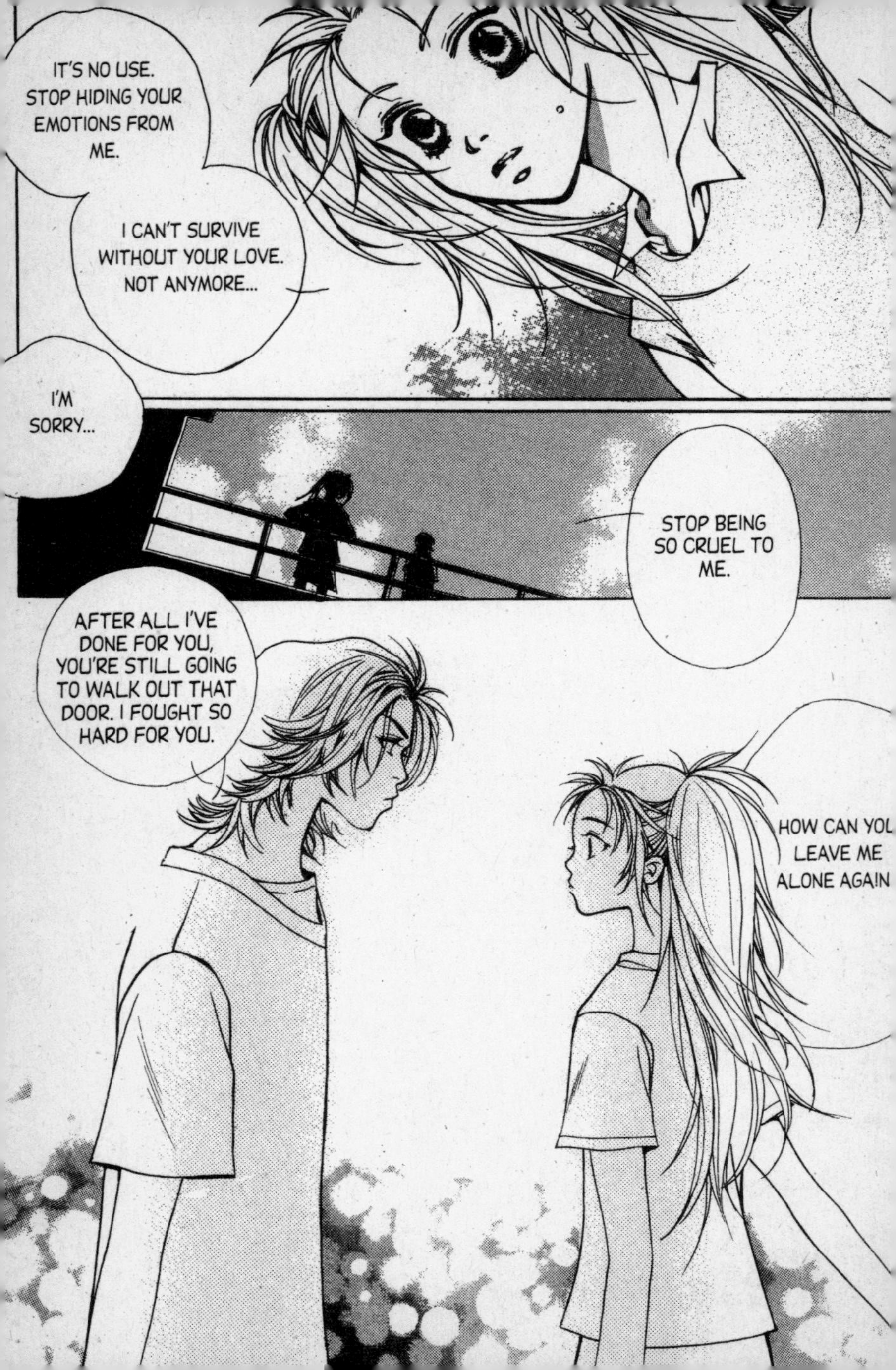

IT'S NO USE. STOP HIDING YOUR EMOTIONS FROM ME.
I CAN'T SURVIVE WITHOUT YOUR LOVE. NOT ANYMORE...
I'M SORRY...
STOP BEING SO CRUEL TO ME.
HOW CAN YOU LEAVE ME ALONE AGAIN
AFTER ALL I'VE DONE FOR YOU, YOU'RE STILL GOING TO WALK OUT THAT DOOR. I FOUGHT SO HARD FOR YOU.

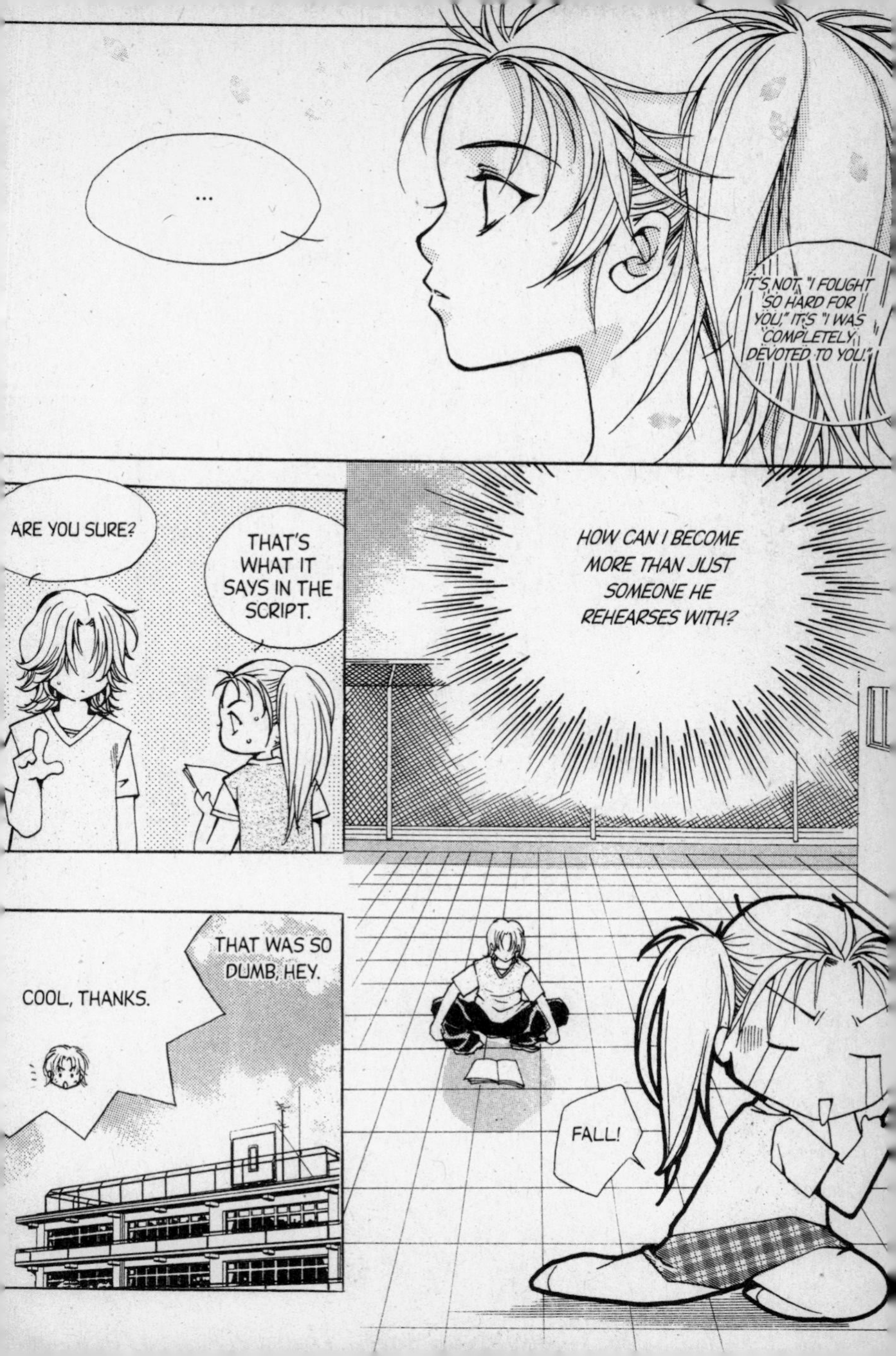
IT'S NOT "I FOUGHT SO HARD FOR YOU," IT'S "I WAS COMPLETELY DEVOTED TO YOU."
...
HOW CAN I BECOME MORE THAN JUST SOMEONE HE REHEARSES WITH?
FALL!
ARE YOU SURE?
THAT'S WHAT IT SAYS IN THE SCRIPT.
THAT WAS SO DUMB, HEY.
COOL, THANKS.

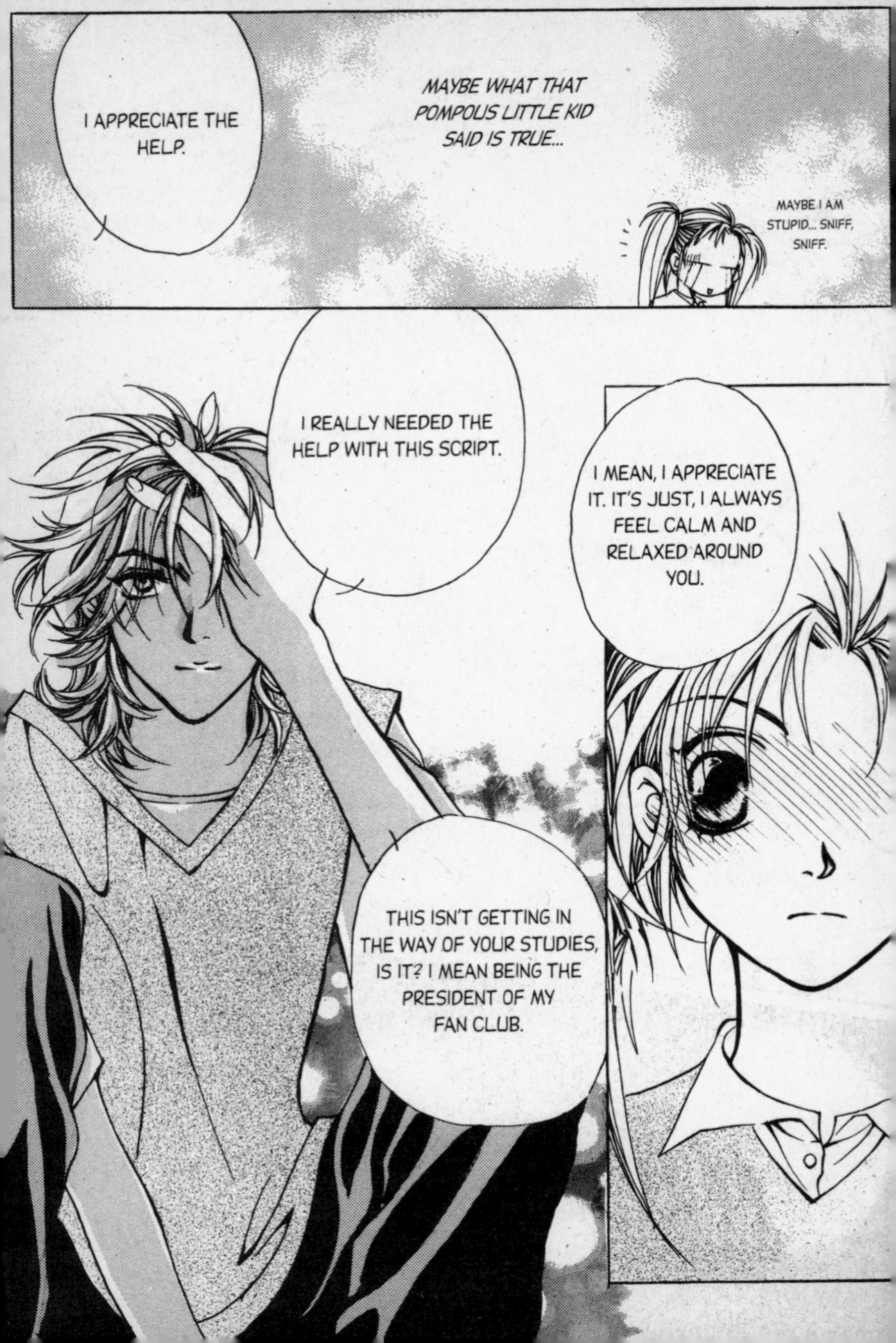
I APPRECIATE THE HELP.
MAYBE WHAT THAT POMPOUS LITTLE KID SAID IS TRUE...
MAYBE I AM STUPID... SNIFF, SNIFF.
I REALLY NEEDED THE HELP WITH THIS SCRIPT.
I MEAN, I APPRECIATE IT. IT'S JUST, I ALWAYS FEEL CALM AND RELAXED AROUND YOU.
THIS ISN'T GETTING IN THE WAY OF YOUR STUDIES, IS IT? I MEAN BEING THE PRESIDENT OF MY FAN CLUB.

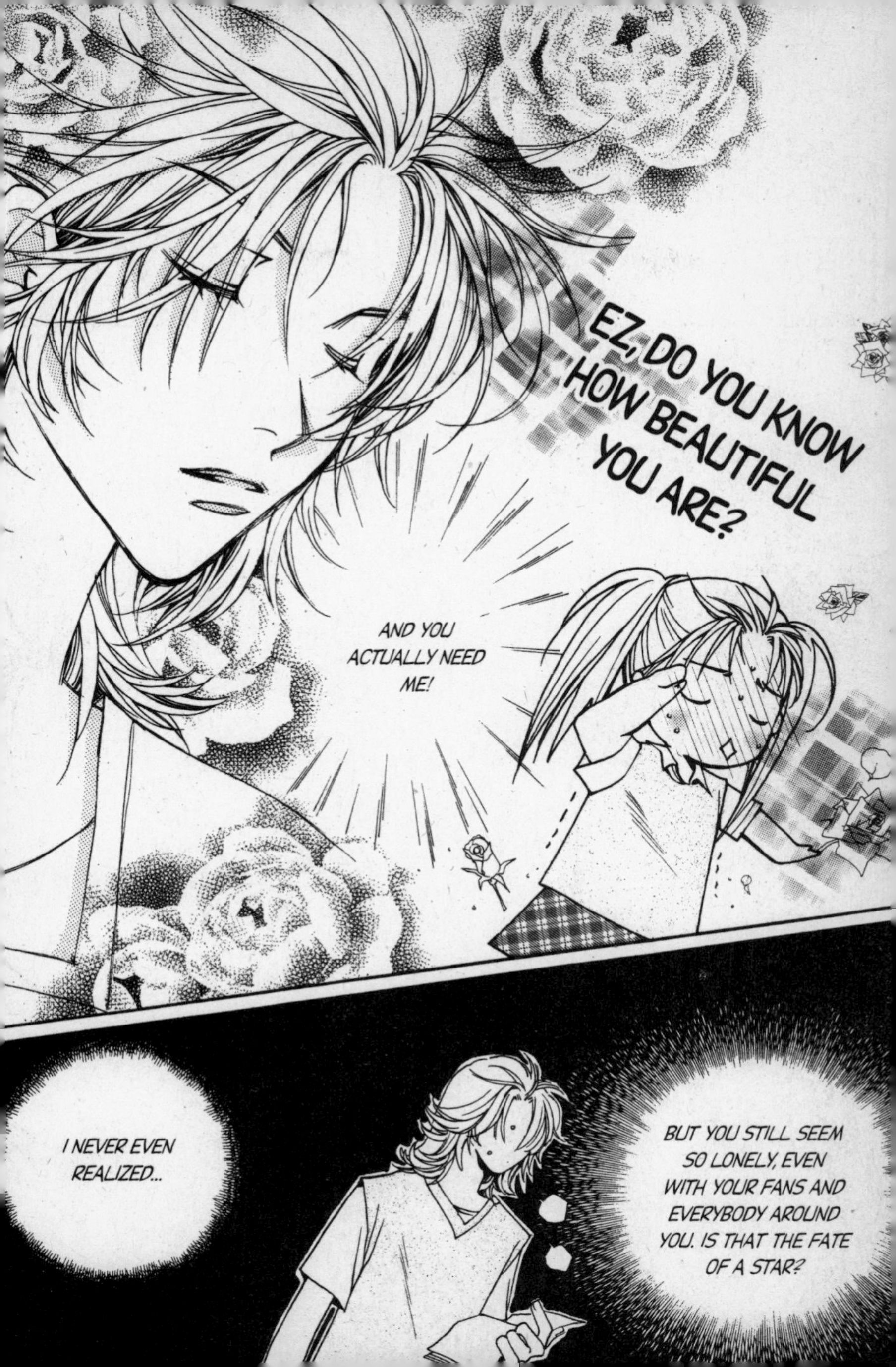
EZ, DO YOU KNOW HOW BEAUTIFUL YOU ARE?
AND YOU ACTUALLY NEED ME!
I NEVER EVEN REALIZED...
BUT YOU STILL SEEM SO LONELY, EVEN WITH YOUR FANS AND EVERYBODY AROUND YOU. IS THAT THE FATE OF A STAR?

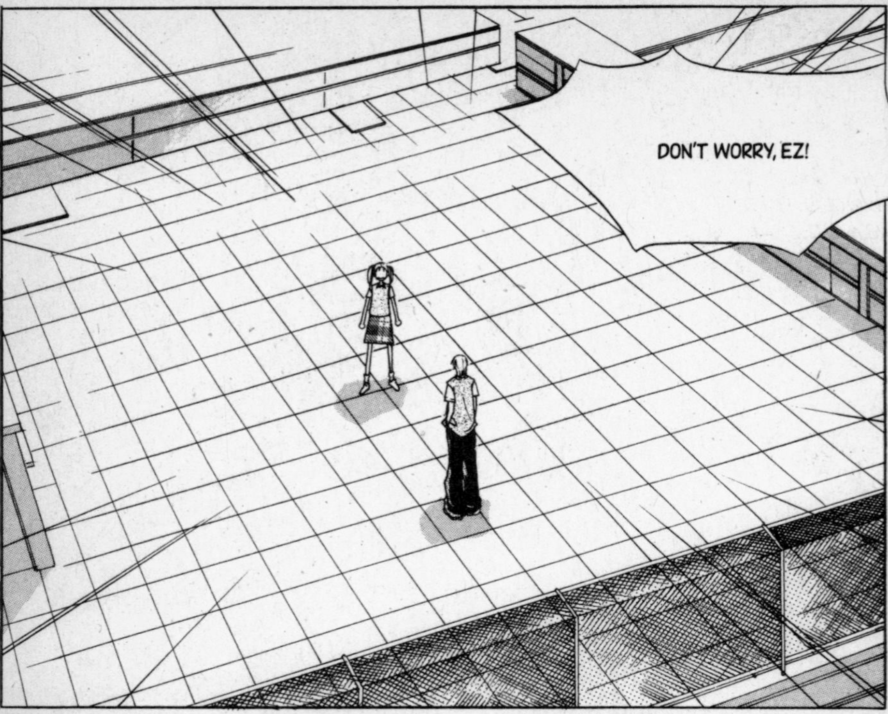
DON'T WORRY, EZ!
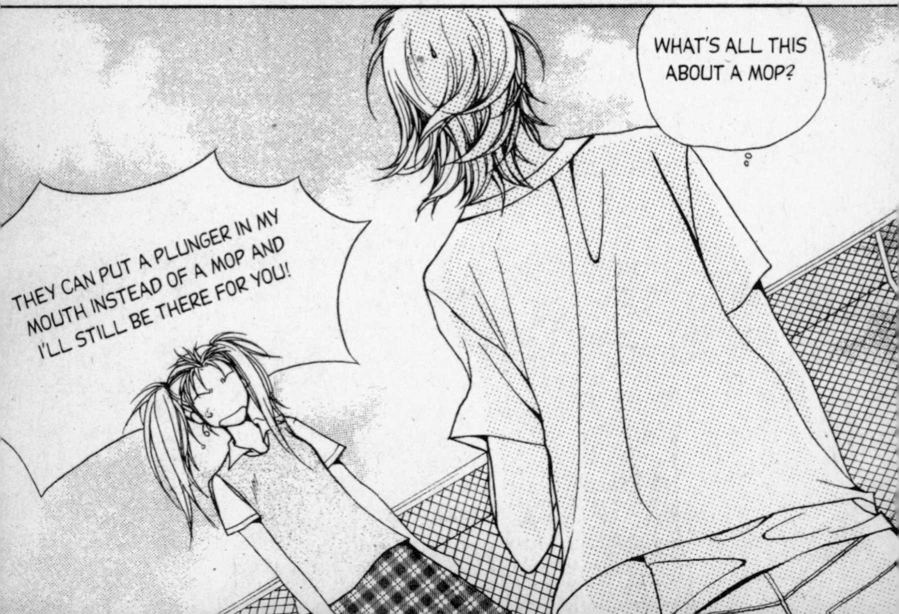
WHAT'S ALL THIS ABOUT A MOP?
THEY CAN PUT A PLUNGER IN MY MOUTH INSTEAD OF A MOP AND I'LL STILL BE THERE FOR YOU!

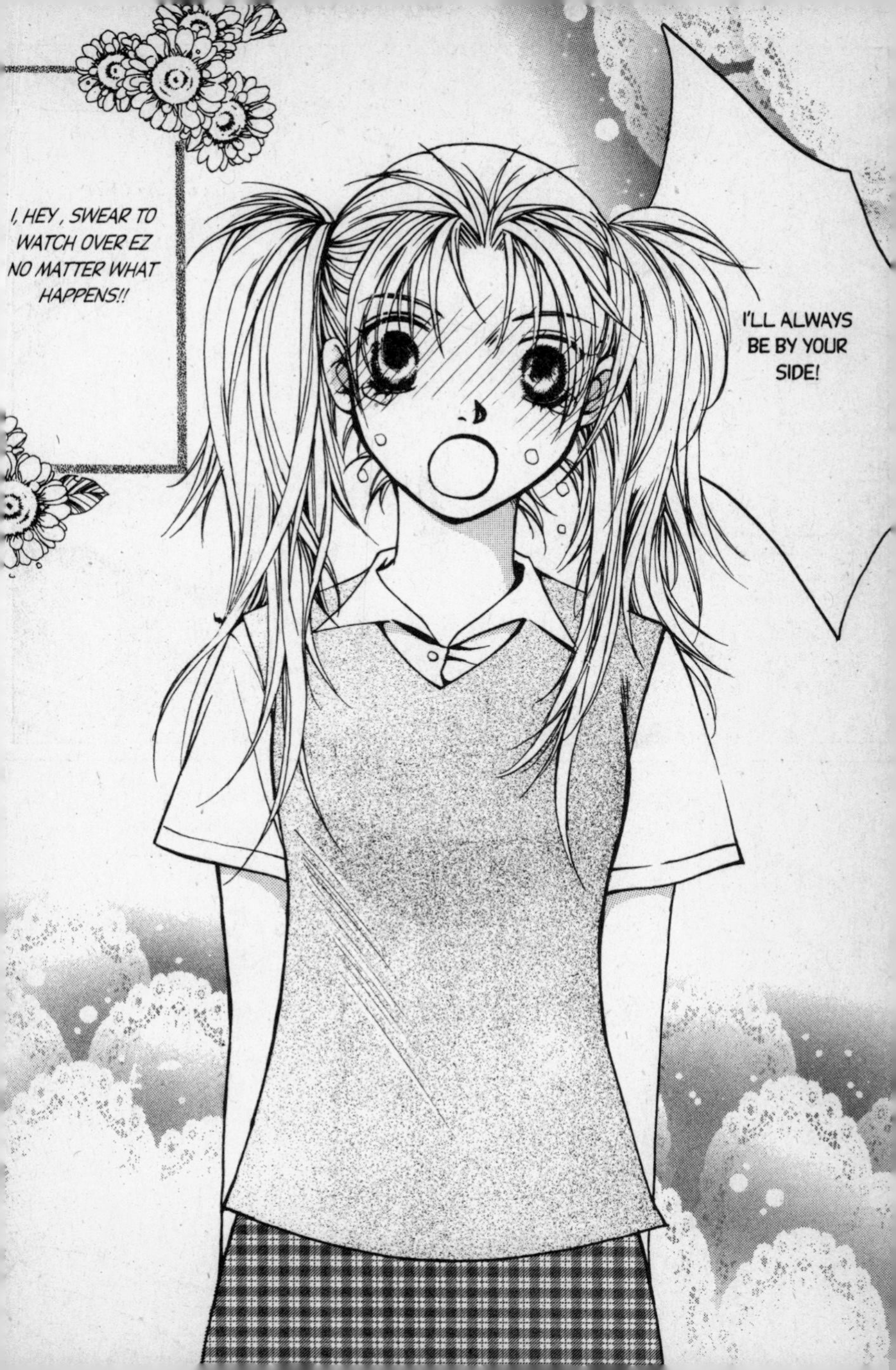
I'LL ALWAYS BE BY YOUR SIDE!
I, HEY, SWEAR TO WATCH OVER EZ NO MATTER WHAT HAPPENS!!

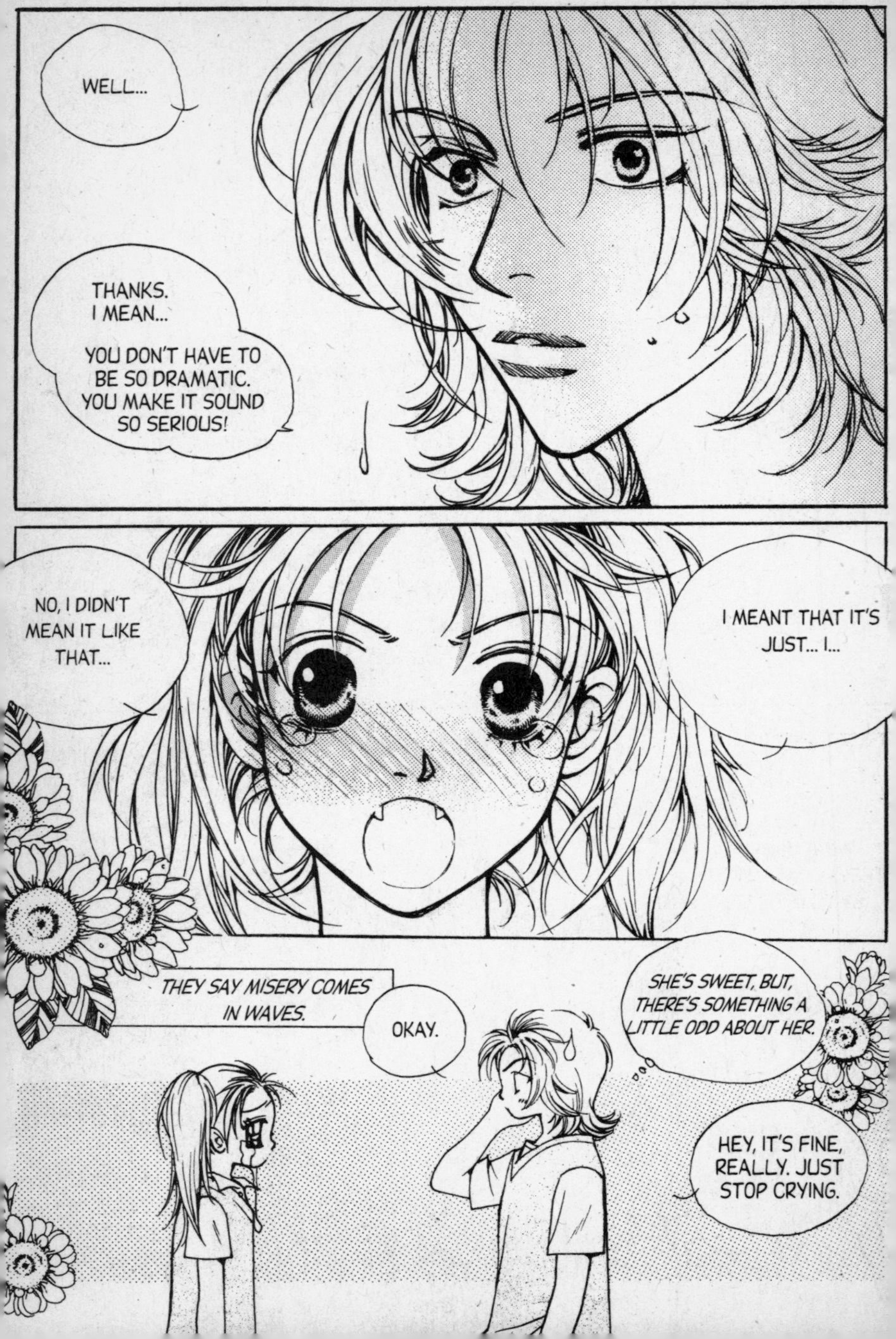
WELL...
THANKS. I MEAN... YOU DON'T HAVE TO BE SO DRAMATIC. YOU MAKE IT SOUND SO SERIOUS!
NO, I DIDN'T MEAN IT LIKE THAT...
I MEANT THAT IT'S JUST... I...
THEY SAY MISERY COMES IN WAVES.
OKAY.
SHE'S SWEET, BUT, THERE'S SOMETHING A LITTLE ODD ABOUT HER.
HEY, IT'S FINE, REALLY. JUST STOP CRYING.

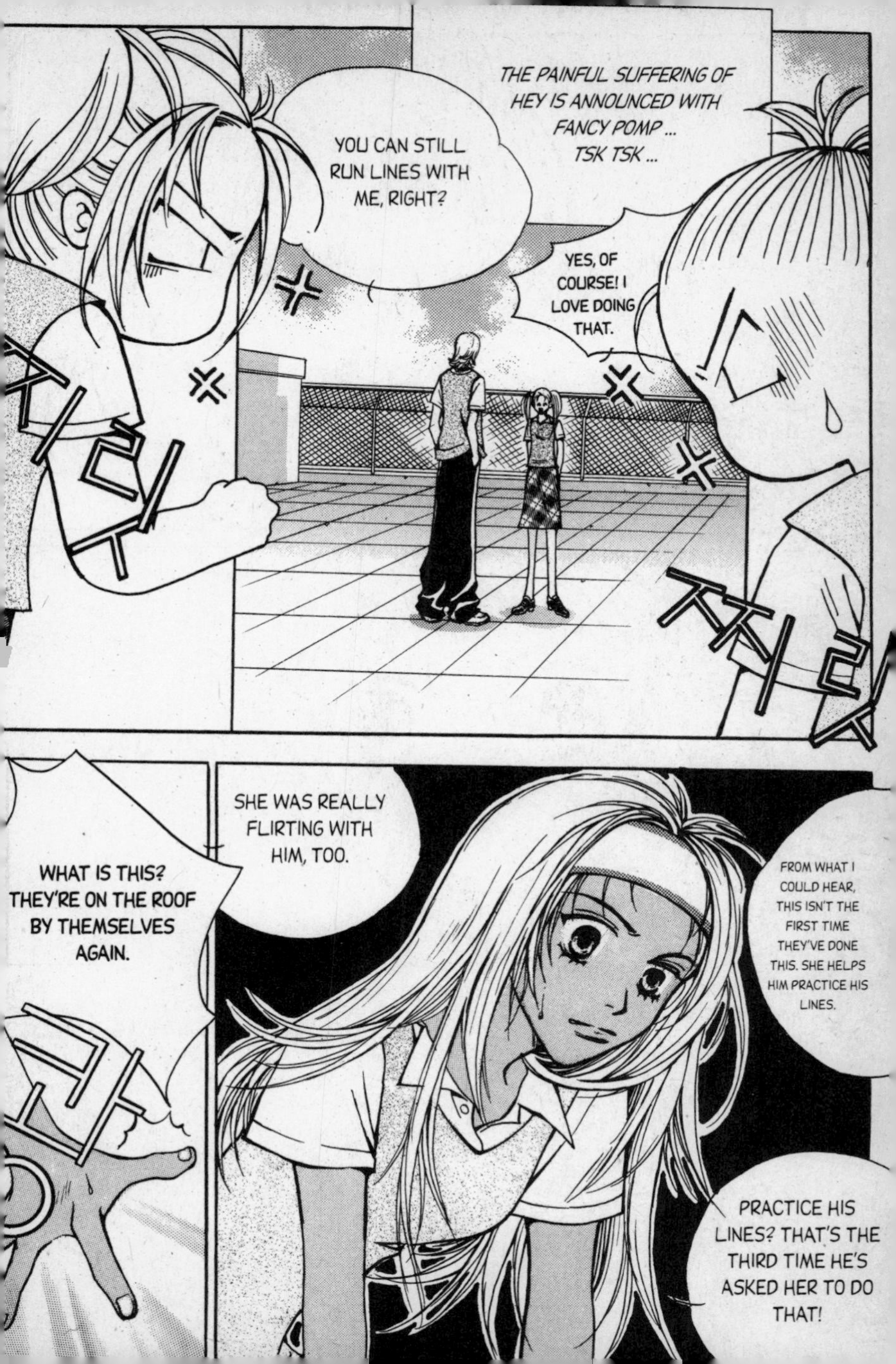
YOU CAN STILL RUN LINES WITH ME, RIGHT?
THE PAINFUL SUFFERING OF HEY IS ANNOUNCED WITH FANCY POMP ... TSK TSK ...
YES, OF COURSE! I LOVE DOING THAT.
WHAT IS THIS? THEY'RE ON THE ROOF BY THEMSELVES AGAIN.
SHE WAS REALLY FLIRTING WITH HIM, TOO.
FROM WHAT I COULD HEAR, THIS ISN'T THE FIRST TIME THEY'VE DONE THIS. SHE HELPS HIM PRACTICE HIS LINES.
PRACTICE HIS LINES? THAT'S THE THIRD TIME HE'S ASKED HER TO DO THAT!

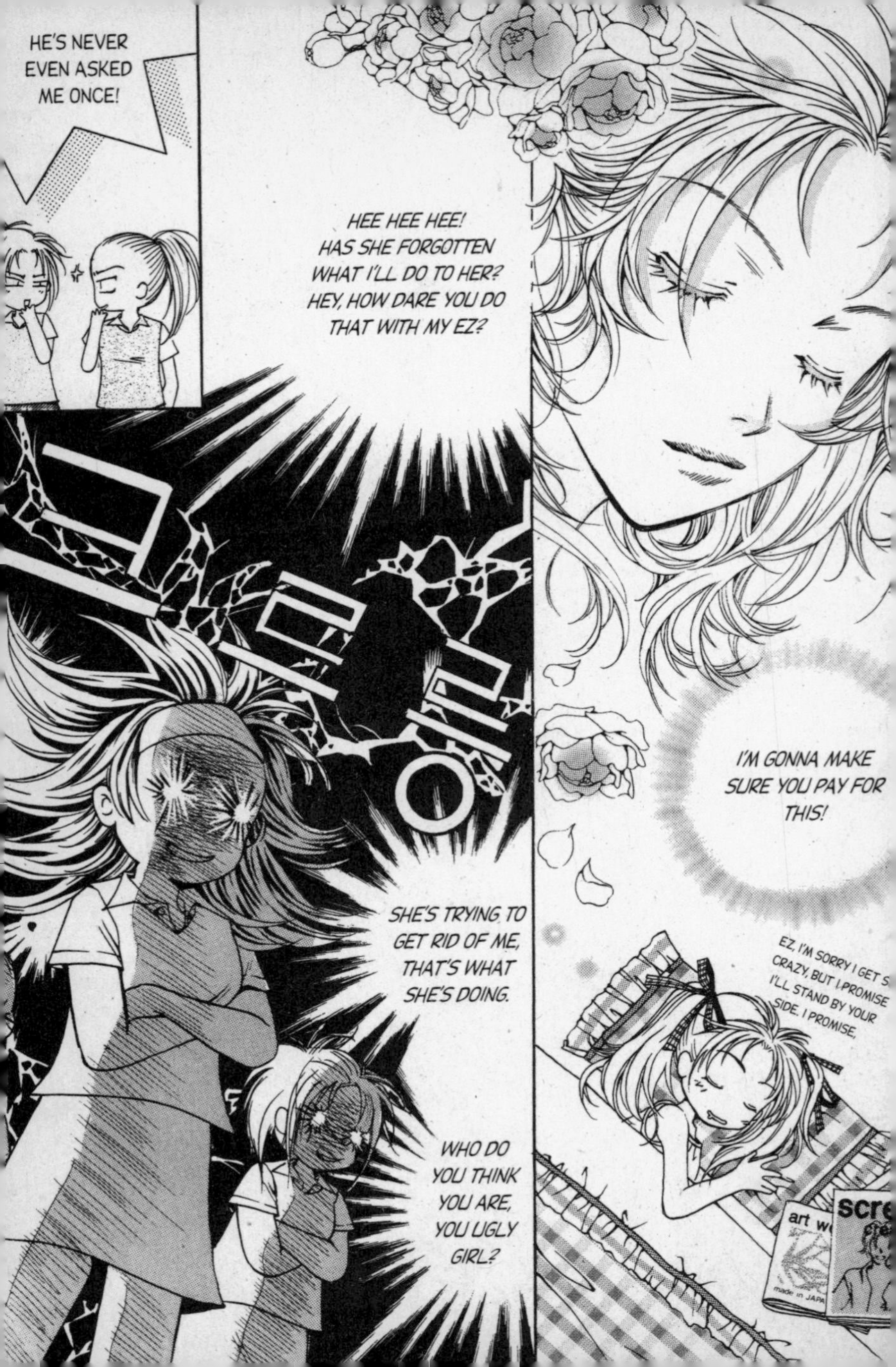

HE'S NEVER EVEN ASKED ME ONCE!
HEE HEE HEE! HAS SHE FORGOTTEN WHAT I'LL DO TO HER? HEY, HOW DARE YOU DO THAT WITH MY EZ?
SHE'S TRYING TO GET RID OF ME, THAT'S WHAT SHE'S DOING.
WHO DO YOU THINK YOU ARE, YOU UGLY GIRL?
I'M GONNA MAKE SURE YOU PAY FOR THIS!
EZ, I'M SORRY I GET S CRAZY, BUT I PROMISE I'LL STAND BY YOUR SIDE. I PROMISE.
art w
made in JAPA
scre

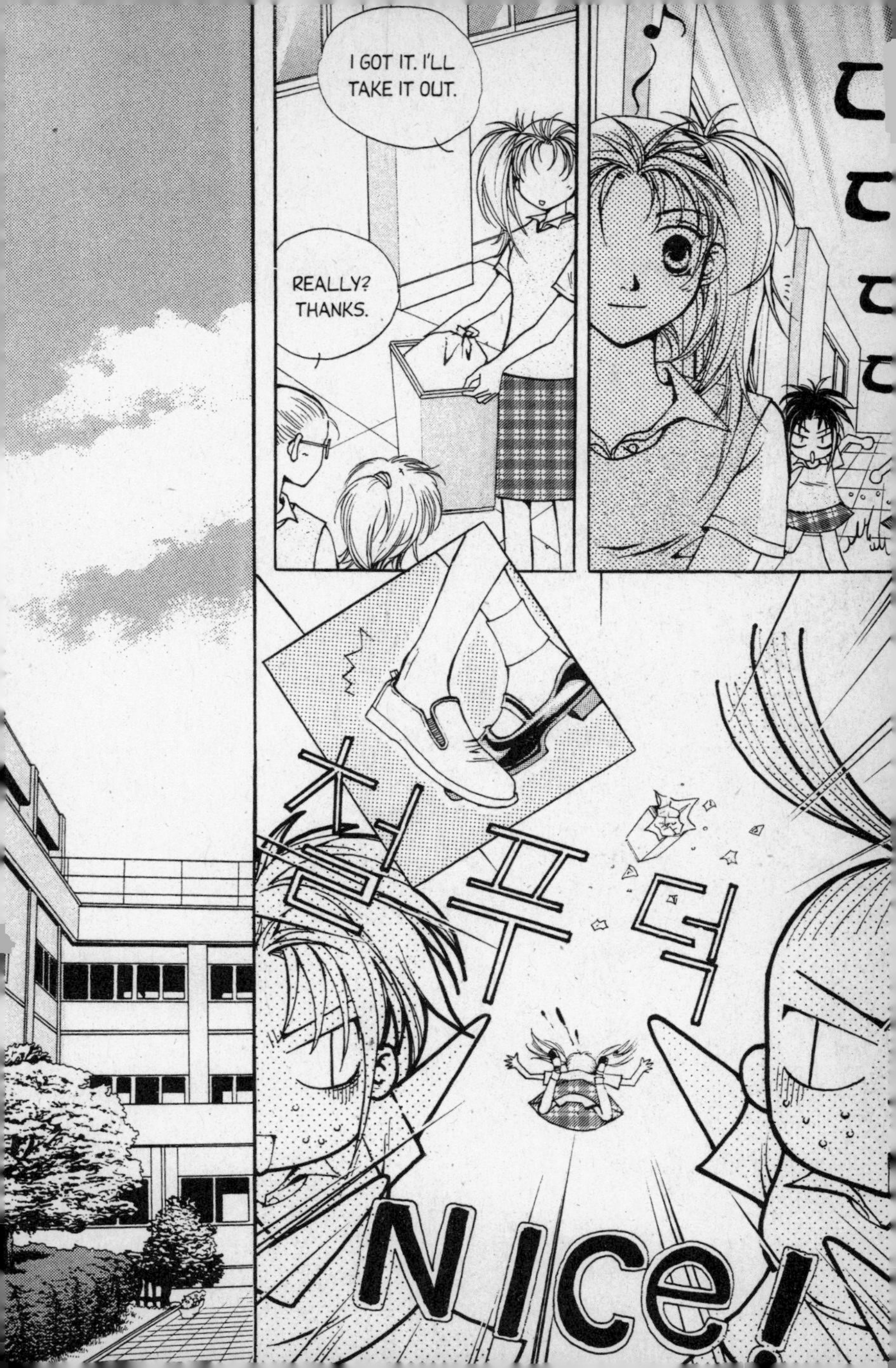
I GOT IT. I'LL TAKE IT OUT.
REALLY? THANKS.
てててて
철퍼덕
Nice!

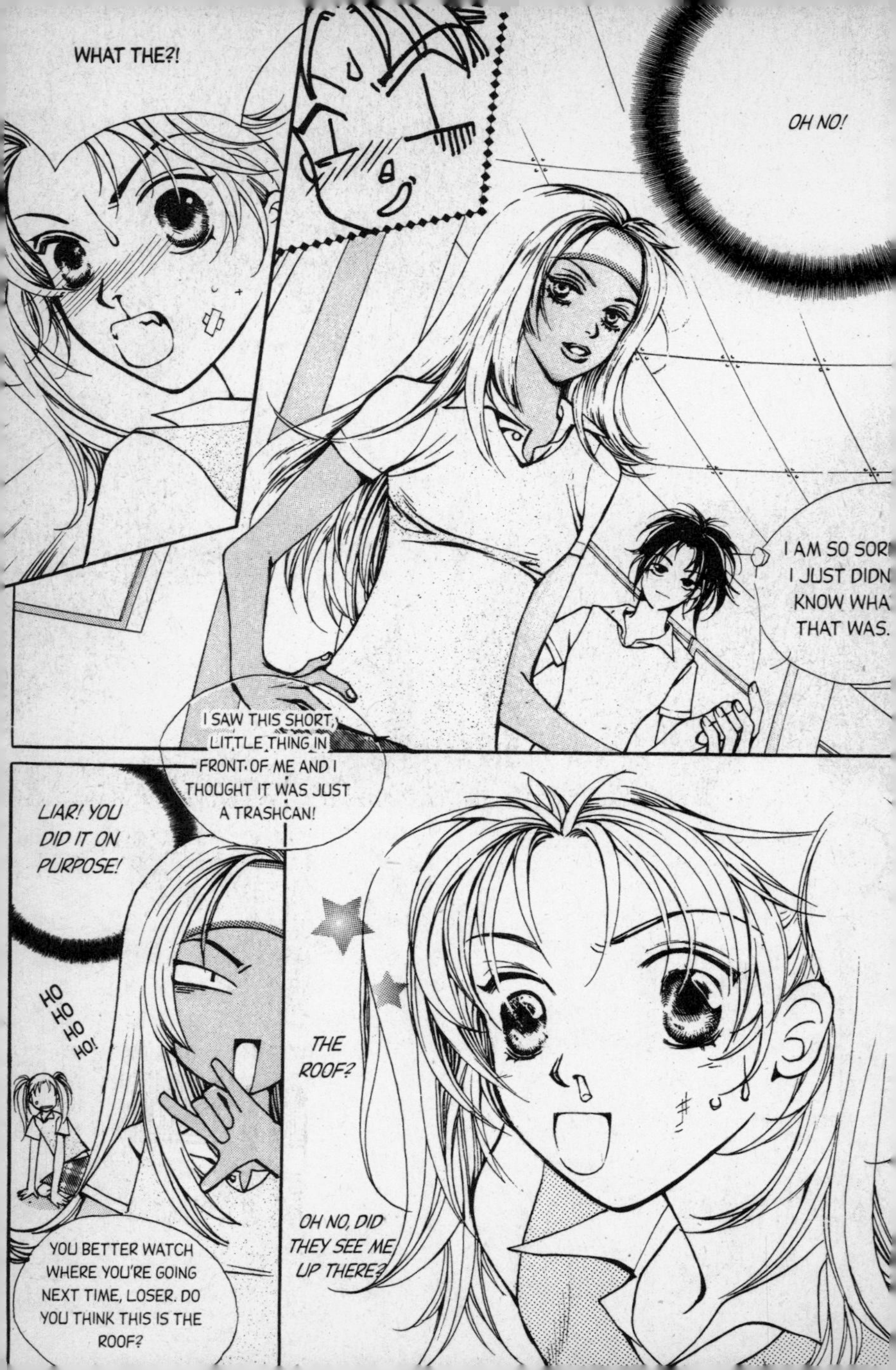
WHAT THE?!
OH NO!
I AM SO SOR
I JUST DIDN
KNOW WHA
THAT WAS.
I SAW THIS SHORT, LITTLE THING IN FRONT OF ME AND I THOUGHT IT WAS JUST A TRASHCAN!
LIAR! YOU DID IT ON PURPOSE!
HO HO HO HO!
YOU BETTER WATCH WHERE YOU'RE GOING NEXT TIME, LOSER. DO YOU THINK THIS IS THE ROOF?
THE ROOF?
OH NO, DID THEY SEE ME UP THERE?

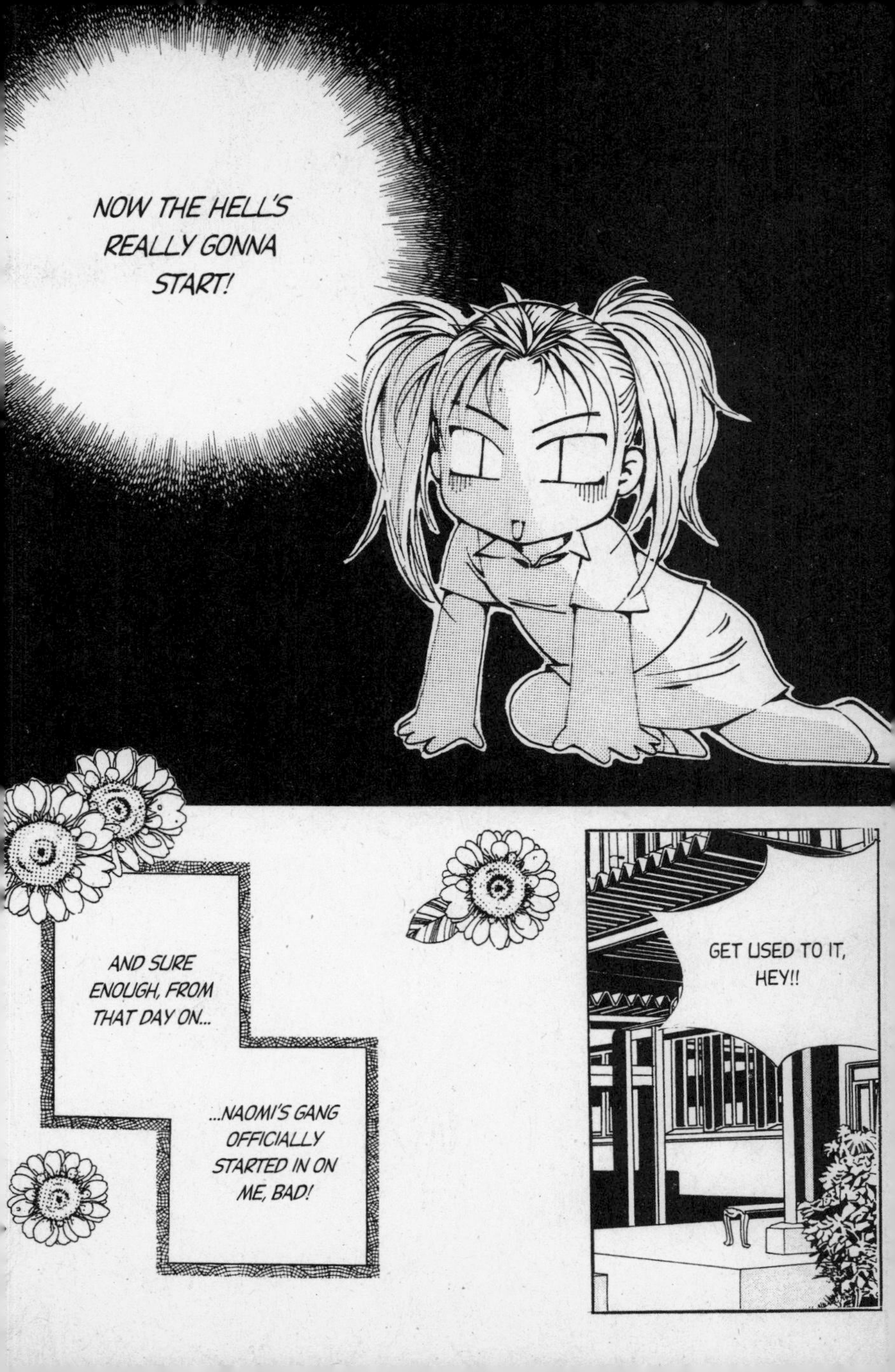
NOW THE HELL'S REALLY GONNA START!
GET USED TO IT, HEY!!
AND SURE ENOUGH, FROM THAT DAY ON...
...NAOMI'S GANG OFFICIALLY STARTED IN ON ME, BAD!

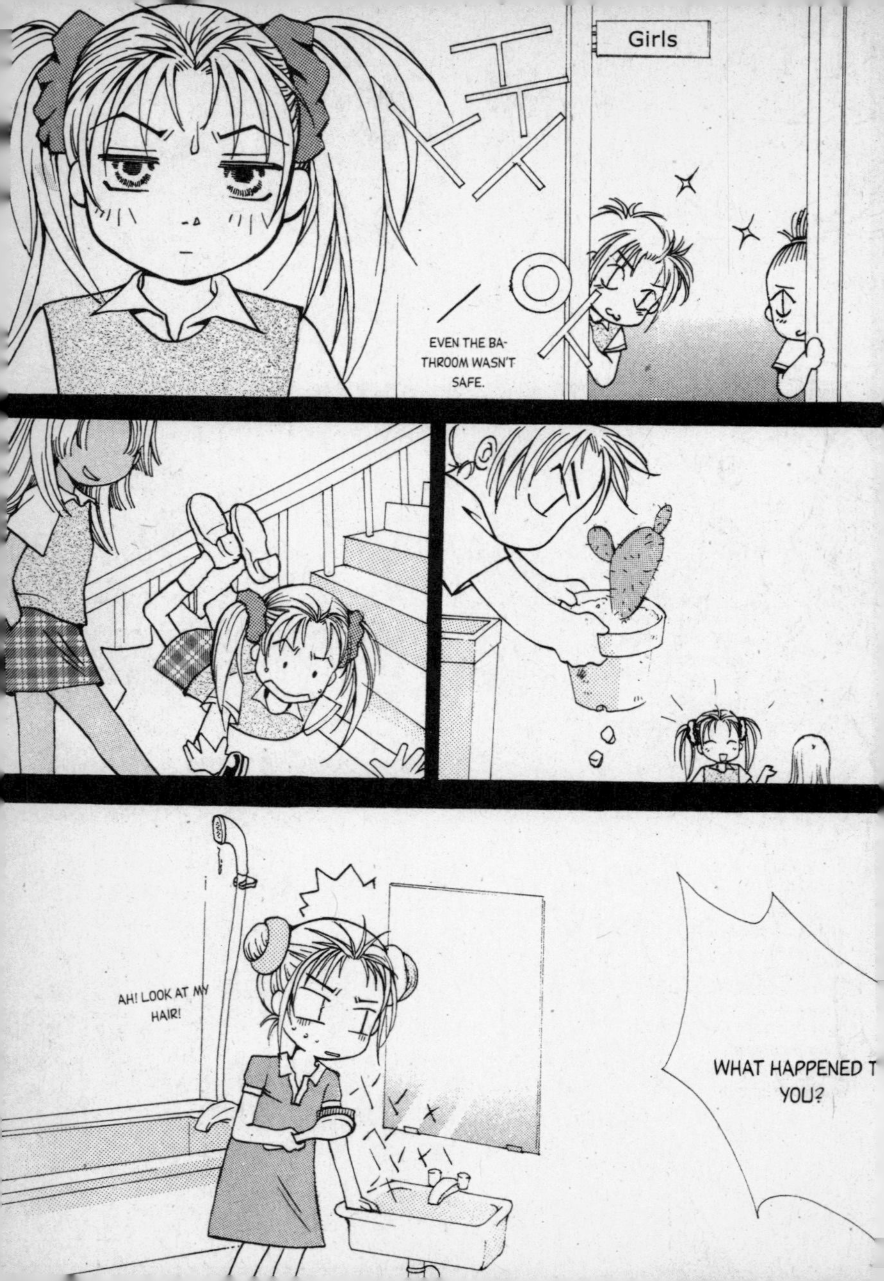
Girls
EVEN THE BA-
THROOM WASN'T
SAFE.
WHAT HAPPENED T
YOU?
AH! LOOK AT MY
HAIR!

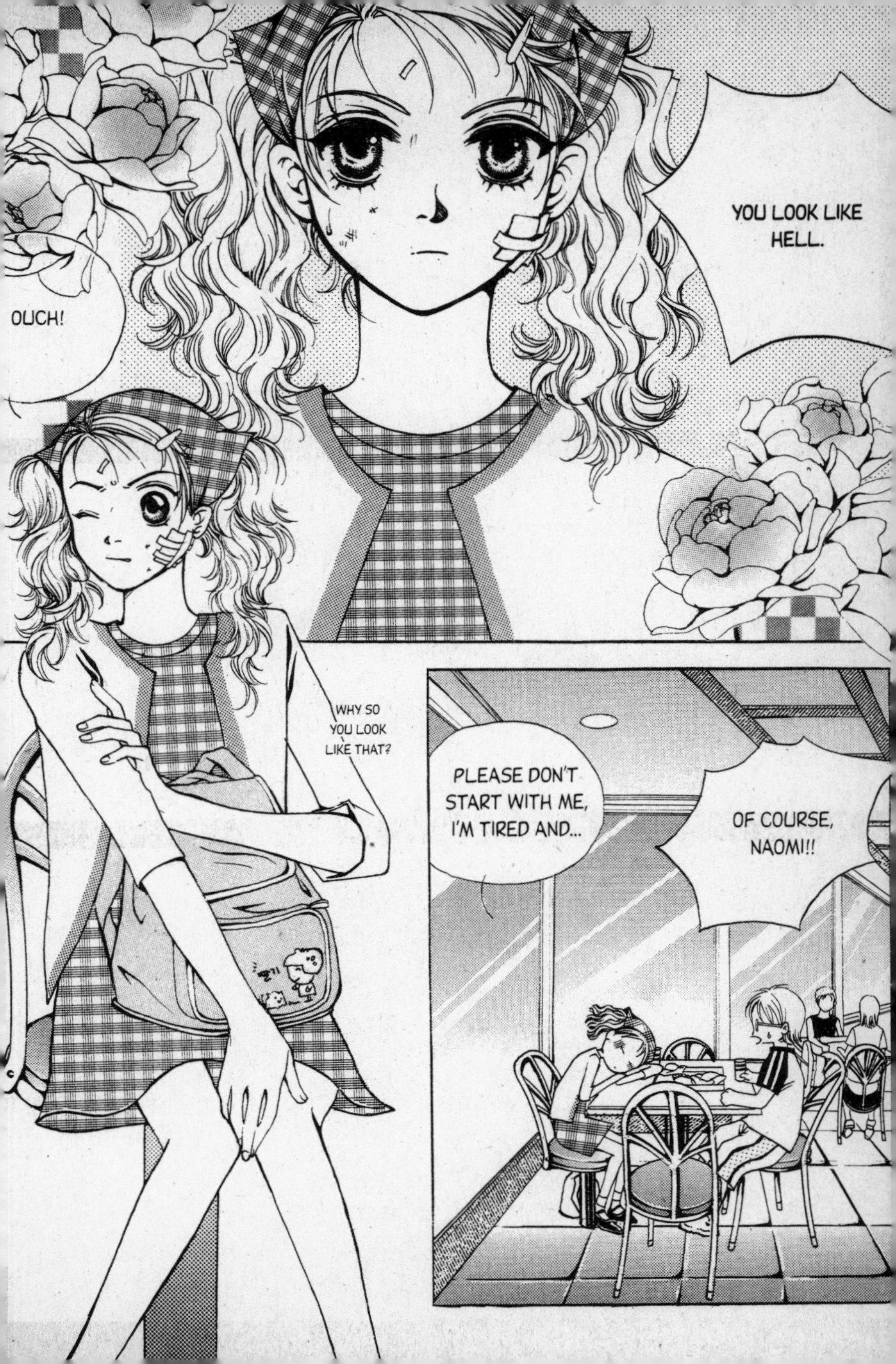
YOU LOOK LIKE HELL.
OUCH!
OF COURSE, NAOMI!!
PLEASE DON'T START WITH ME, I'M TIRED AND...
WHY SO YOU LOOK LIKE THAT?

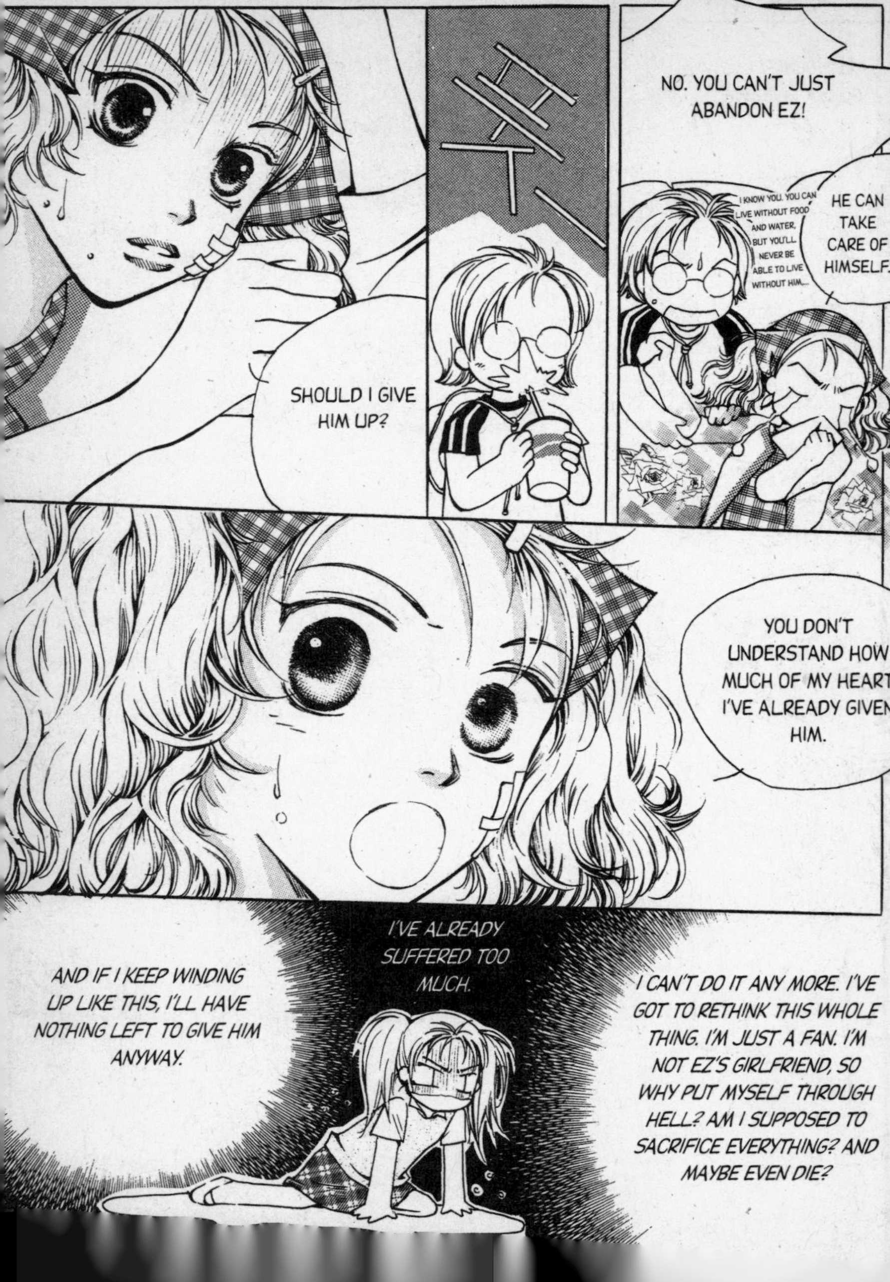
SHOULD I GIVE HIM UP?
NO. YOU CAN'T JUST ABANDON EZ!
HE CAN TAKE CARE OF HIMSELF.
I KNOW YOU. YOU CAN LIVE WITHOUT FOOD AND WATER, BUT YOU'LL NEVER BE ABLE TO LIVE WITHOUT HIM...
YOU DON'T UNDERSTAND HOW MUCH OF MY HEART I'VE ALREADY GIVEN HIM.
AND IF I KEEP WINDING UP LIKE THIS, I'LL HAVE NOTHING LEFT TO GIVE HIM ANYWAY.
I'VE ALREADY SUFFERED TOO MUCH.
I CAN'T DO IT ANY MORE. I'VE GOT TO RETHINK THIS WHOLE THING. I'M JUST A FAN. I'M NOT EZ'S GIRLFRIEND, SO WHY PUT MYSELF THROUGH HELL? AM I SUPPOSED TO SACRIFICE EVERYTHING? AND MAYBE EVEN DIE?

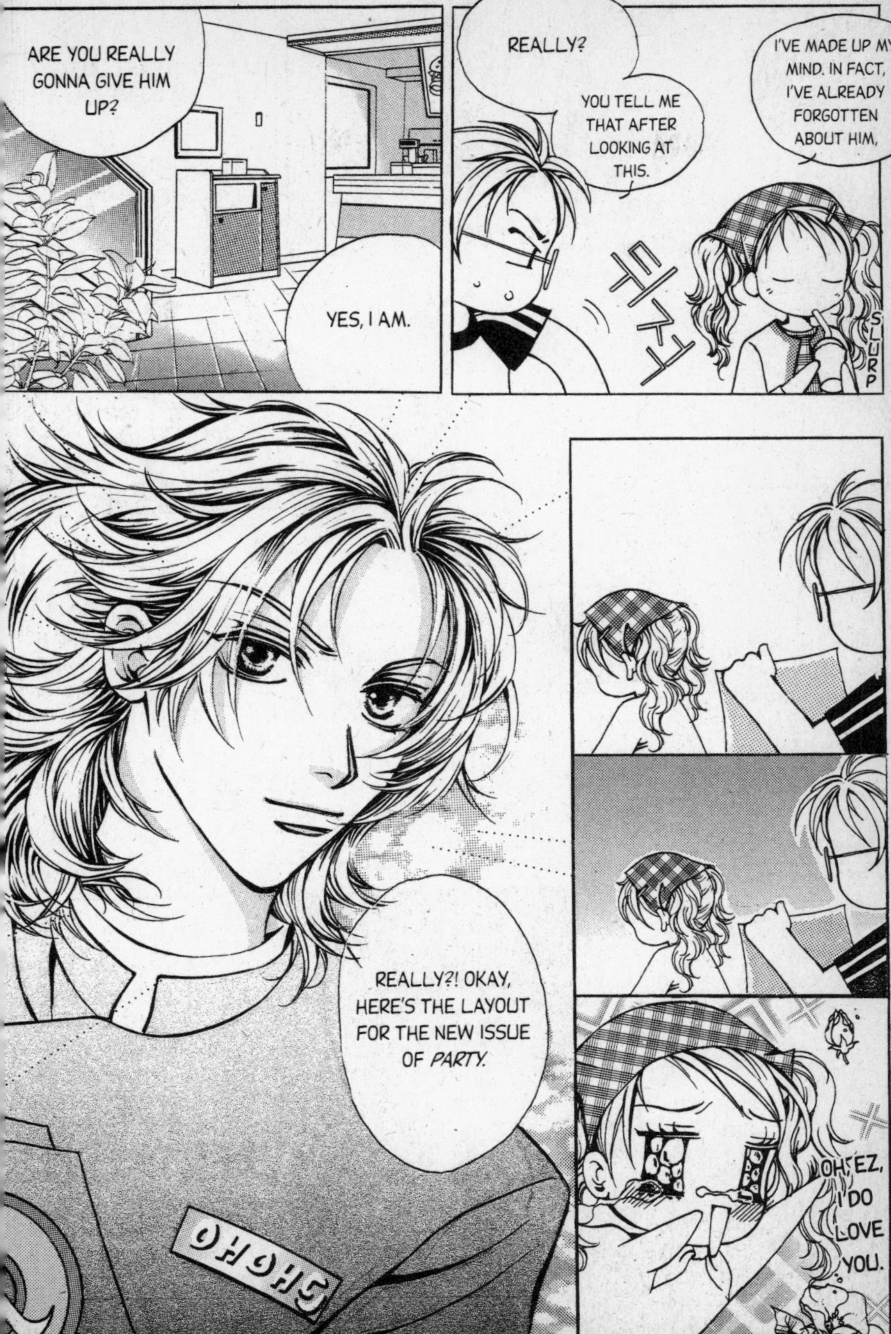

ARE YOU REALLY GONNA GIVE HIM UP?
YES, I AM.
I'VE MADE UP MY MIND. IN FACT, I'VE ALREADY FORGOTTEN ABOUT HIM.
SLURP
딱
REALLY?
YOU TELL ME THAT AFTER LOOKING AT THIS.
REALLY?! OKAY, HERE'S THE LAYOUT FOR THE NEW ISSUE OF *PARTY*.
OH, EZ, I DO LOVE YOU.

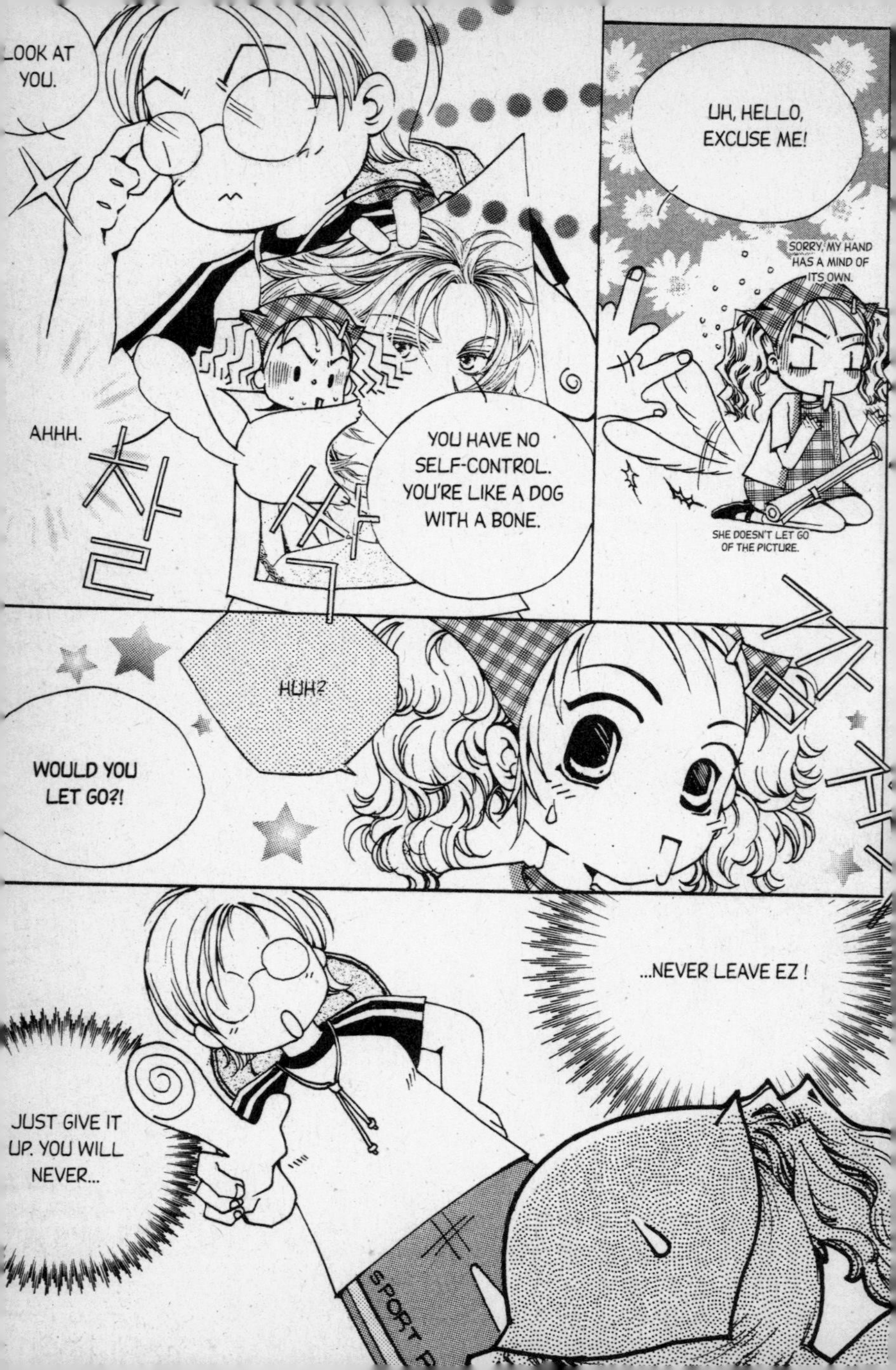
LOOK AT YOU.
AHHH.
YOU HAVE NO SELF-CONTROL. YOU'RE LIKE A DOG WITH A BONE.
UH, HELLO, EXCUSE ME!
SORRY, MY HAND HAS A MIND OF ITS OWN.
SHE DOESN'T LET GO OF THE PICTURE.
WOULD YOU LET GO?!
HUH?
JUST GIVE IT UP. YOU WILL NEVER...
...NEVER LEAVE EZ !
SPORT

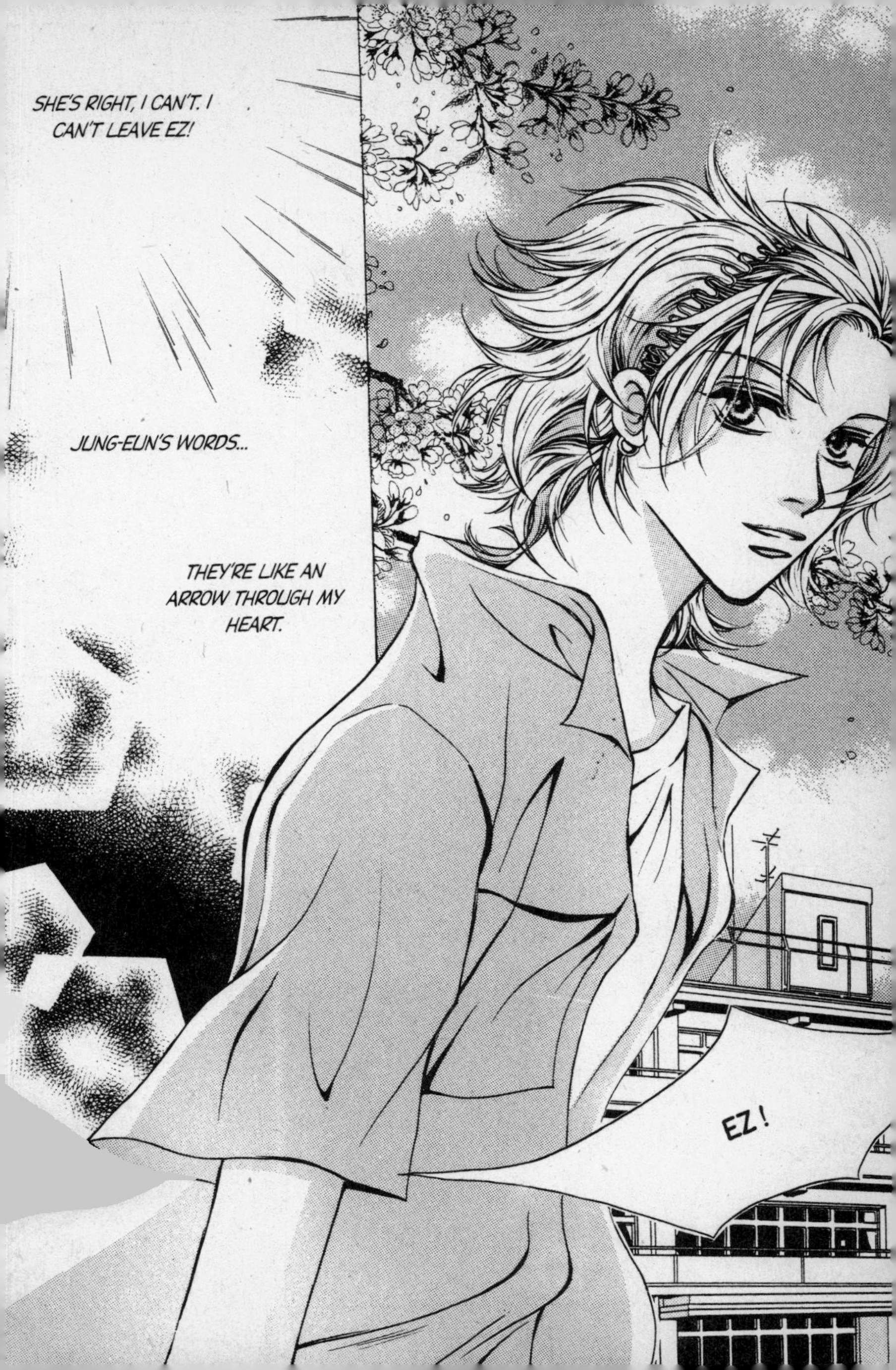
SHE'S RIGHT, I CAN'T. I CAN'T LEAVE EZ!
JUNG-EUN'S WORDS...
THEY'RE LIKE AN ARROW THROUGH MY HEART.
EZ!

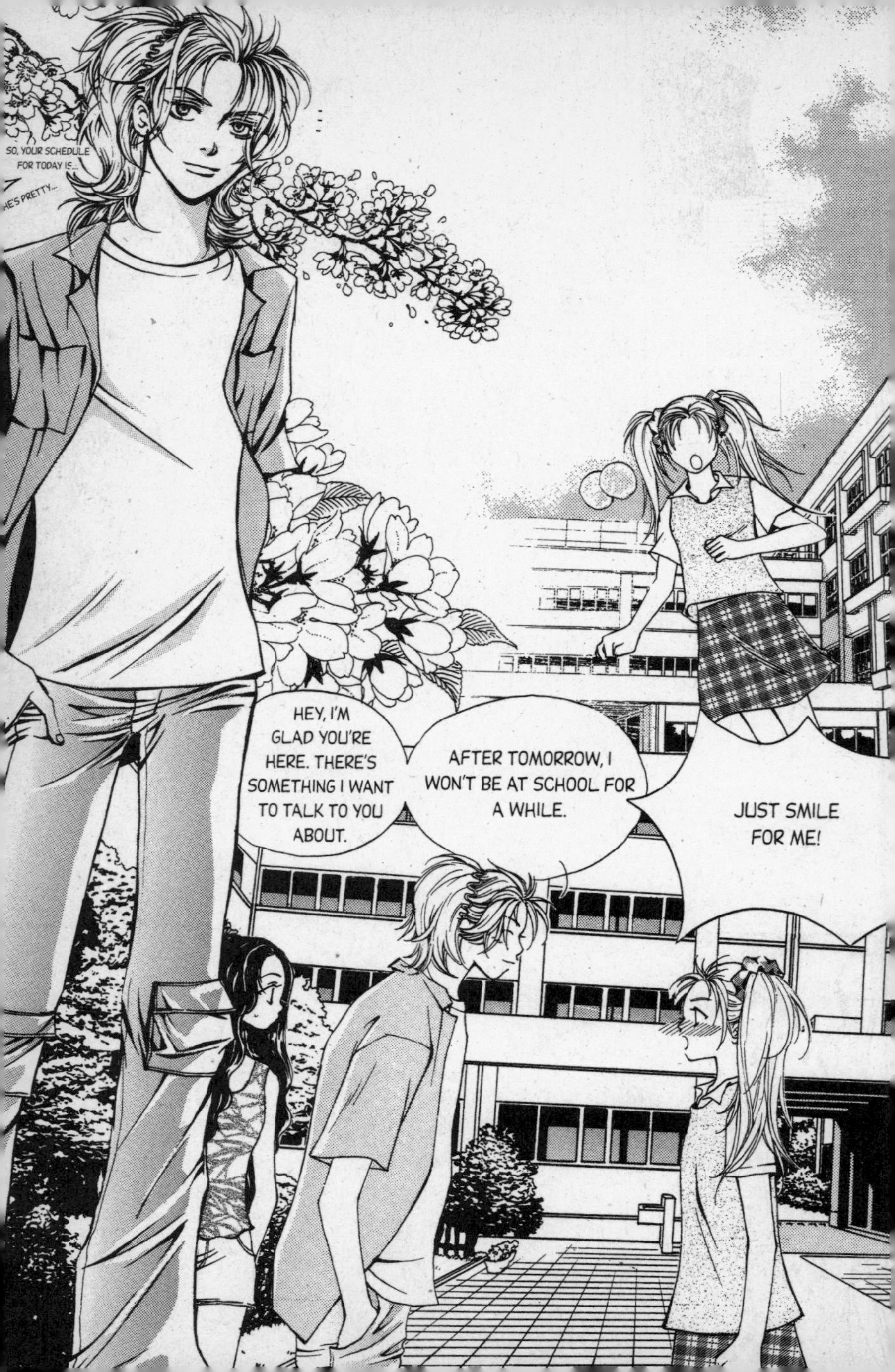
SO, YOUR SCHEDULE FOR TODAY IS...
HE'S PRETTY...
HEY, I'M GLAD YOU'RE HERE. THERE'S SOMETHING I WANT TO TALK TO YOU ABOUT.
AFTER TOMORROW, I WON'T BE AT SCHOOL FOR A WHILE.
JUST SMILE FOR ME!

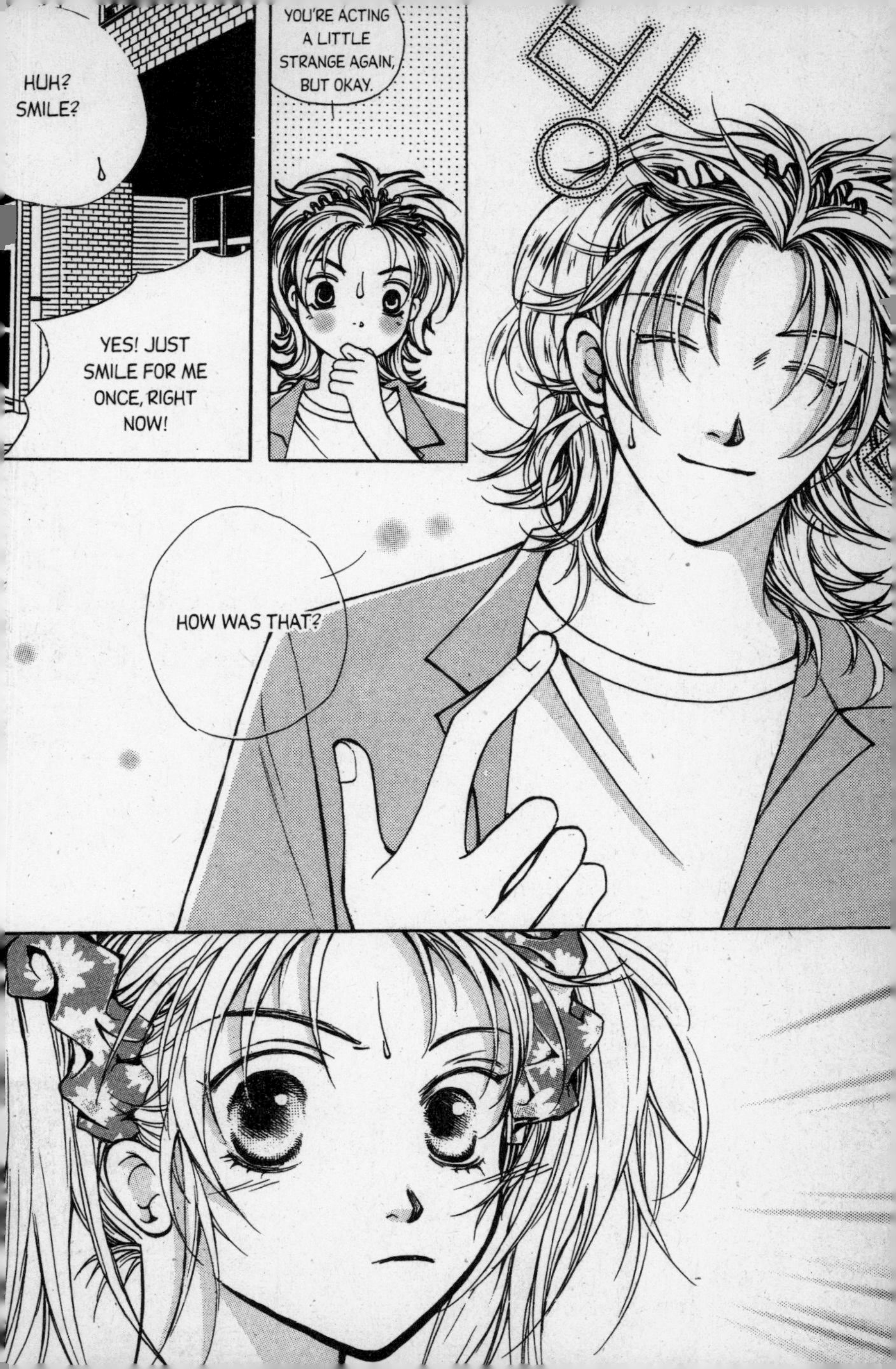
HUH? SMILE?
YES! JUST SMILE FOR ME ONCE, RIGHT NOW!
YOU'RE ACTING A LITTLE STRANGE AGAIN, BUT OKAY.
HOW WAS THAT?

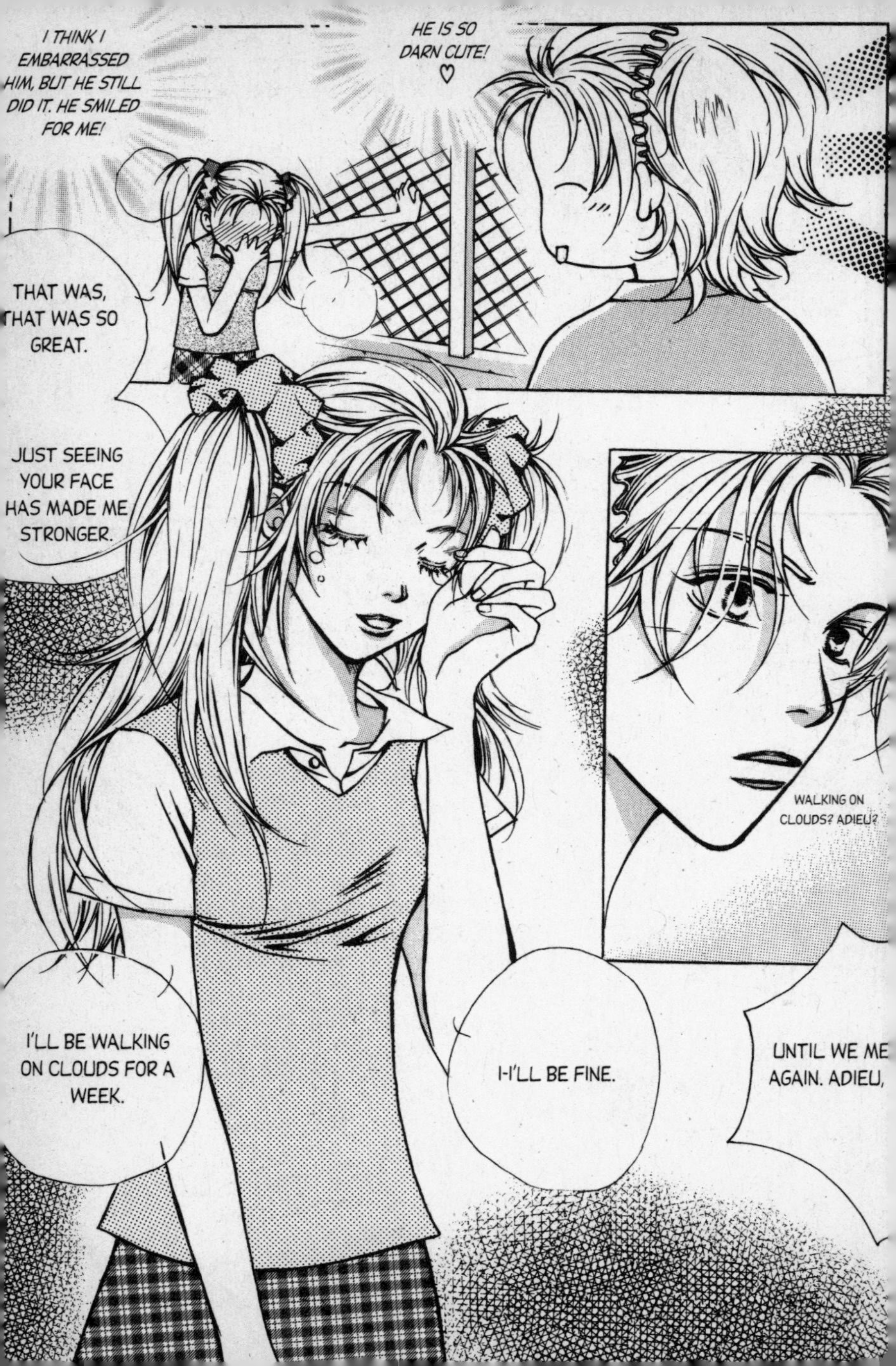
I THINK I EMBARRASSED HIM, BUT HE STILL DID IT. HE SMILED FOR ME!
HE IS SO DARN CUTE! ♡
THAT WAS, THAT WAS SO GREAT.
JUST SEEING YOUR FACE HAS MADE ME STRONGER.
I'LL BE WALKING ON CLOUDS FOR A WEEK.
I-I'LL BE FINE.
UNTIL WE ME AGAIN. ADIEU,
WALKING ON CLOUDS? ADIEU?

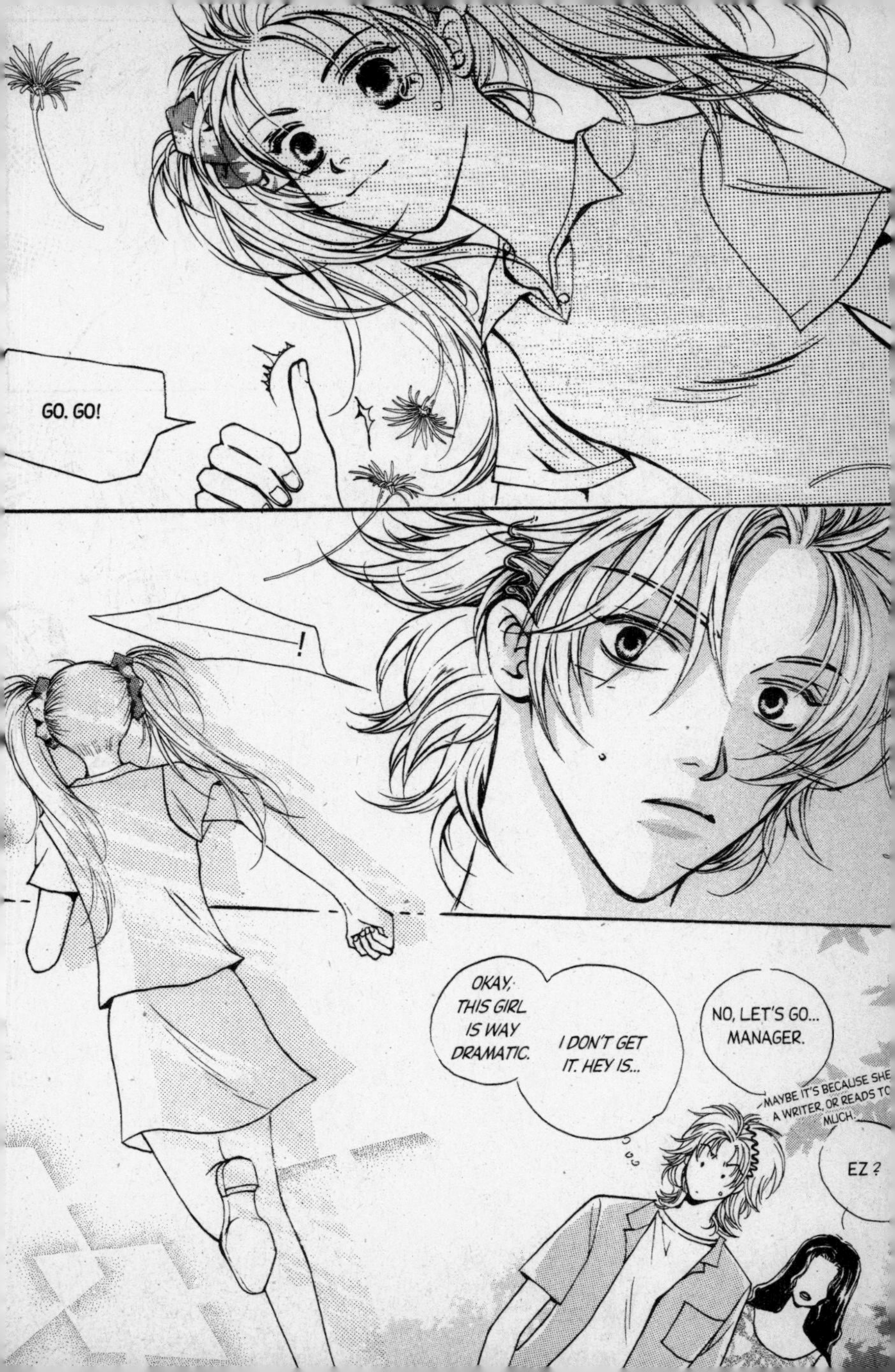
GO. GO!
—!
NO, LET'S GO... MANAGER.
EZ?
MAYBE IT'S BECAUSE SHE A WRITER, OR READS TO MUCH.
OKAY, THIS GIRL IS WAY DRAMATIC. I DON'T GET IT. HEY IS...

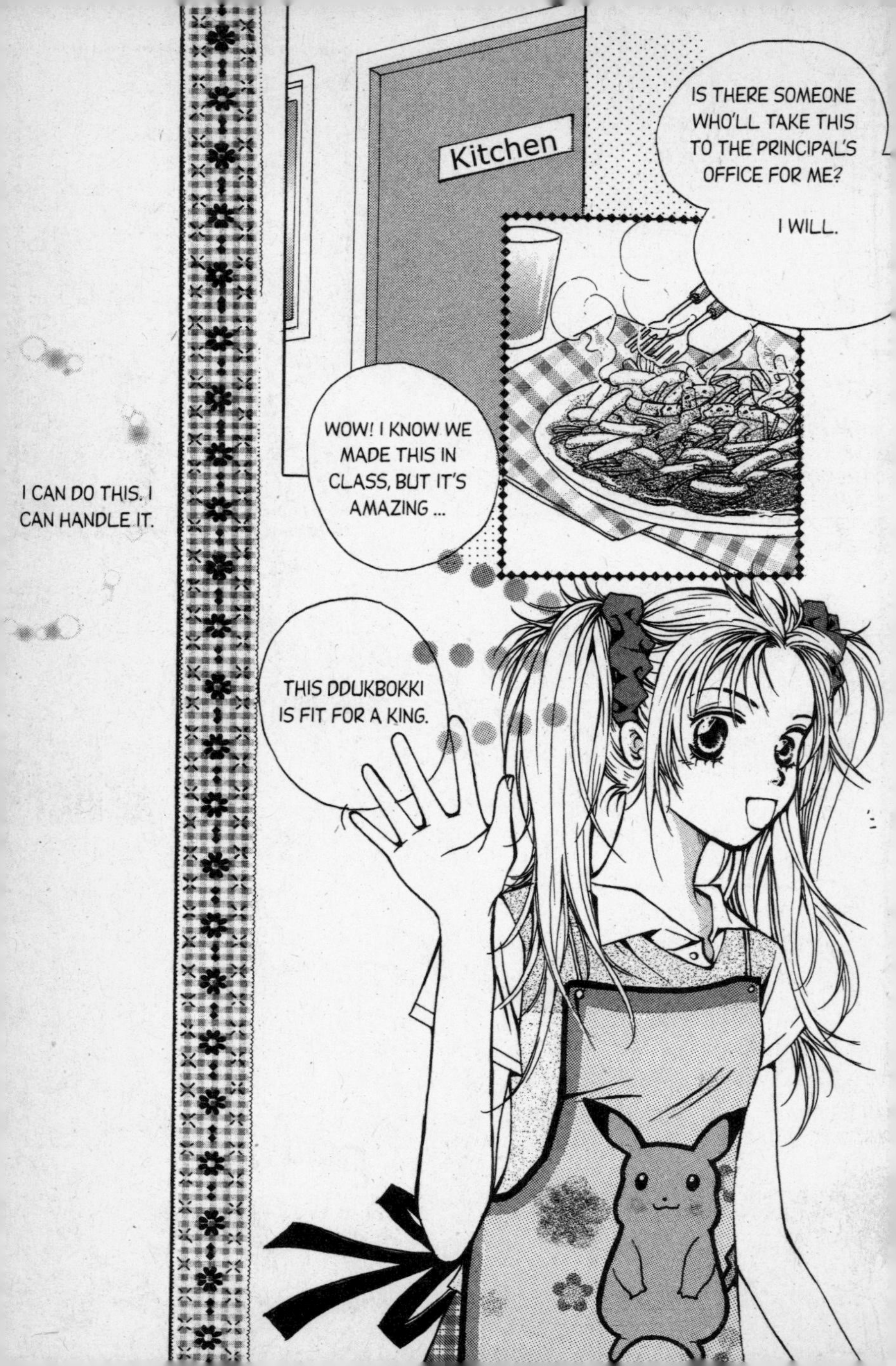
Kitchen
IS THERE SOMEONE WHO'LL TAKE THIS TO THE PRINCIPAL'S OFFICE FOR ME?
I WILL.
WOW! I KNOW WE MADE THIS IN CLASS, BUT IT'S AMAZING ...
THIS DDUKBOKKI IS FIT FOR A KING.
I CAN DO THIS. I CAN HANDLE IT.

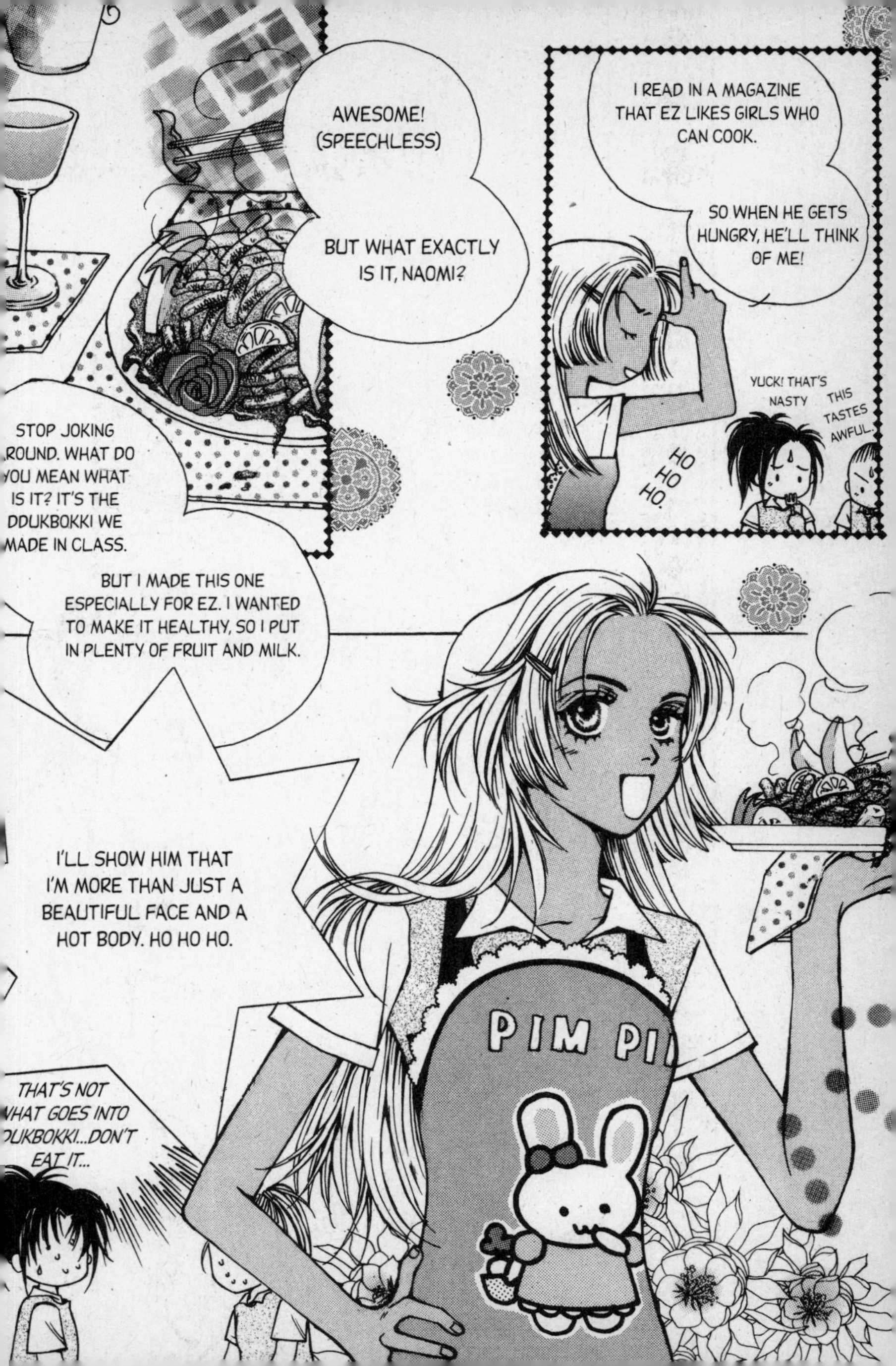
AWESOME! (SPEECHLESS)
BUT WHAT EXACTLY IS IT, NAOMI?
STOP JOKING ROUND. WHAT DO OU MEAN WHAT IS IT? IT'S THE DDUKBOKKI WE MADE IN CLASS.
BUT I MADE THIS ONE ESPECIALLY FOR EZ. I WANTED TO MAKE IT HEALTHY, SO I PUT IN PLENTY OF FRUIT AND MILK.
I READ IN A MAGAZINE THAT EZ LIKES GIRLS WHO CAN COOK.
SO WHEN HE GETS HUNGRY, HE'LL THINK OF ME!
HO HO HO.
YUCK! THAT'S NASTY
THIS TASTES AWFUL.
I'LL SHOW HIM THAT I'M MORE THAN JUST A BEAUTIFUL FACE AND A HOT BODY. HO HO HO.
THAT'S NOT HAT GOES INTO UKBOKKI...DON'T EAT IT...
PIM PI

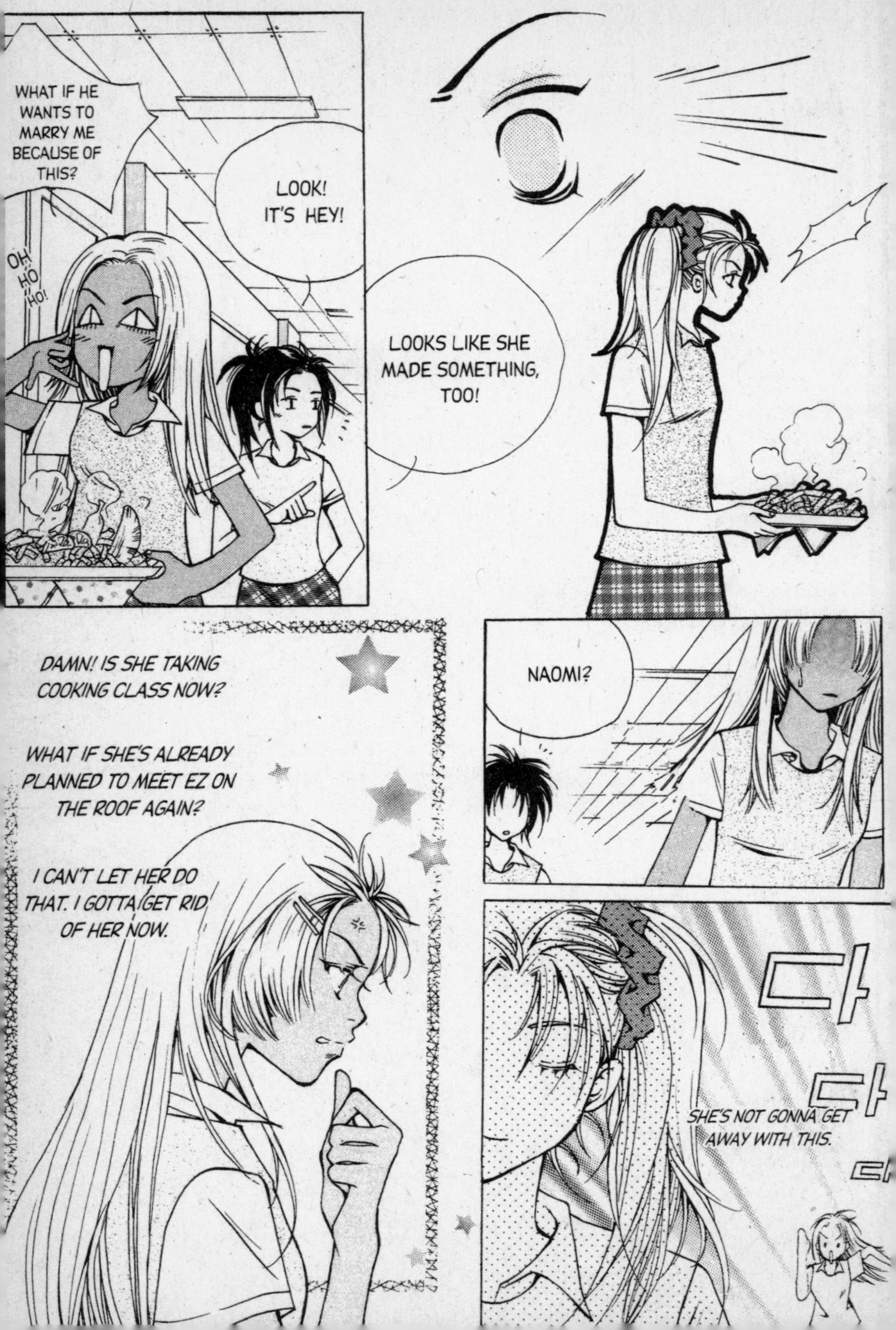
WHAT IF HE WANTS TO MARRY ME BECAUSE OF THIS?
OH HO HO!
LOOK! IT'S HEY!
LOOKS LIKE SHE MADE SOMETHING, TOO!
DAMN! IS SHE TAKING COOKING CLASS NOW?
WHAT IF SHE'S ALREADY PLANNED TO MEET EZ ON THE ROOF AGAIN?
I CAN'T LET HER DO THAT. I GOTTA GET RID OF HER NOW.
NAOMI?
다
다
SHE'S NOT GONNA GET AWAY WITH THIS.

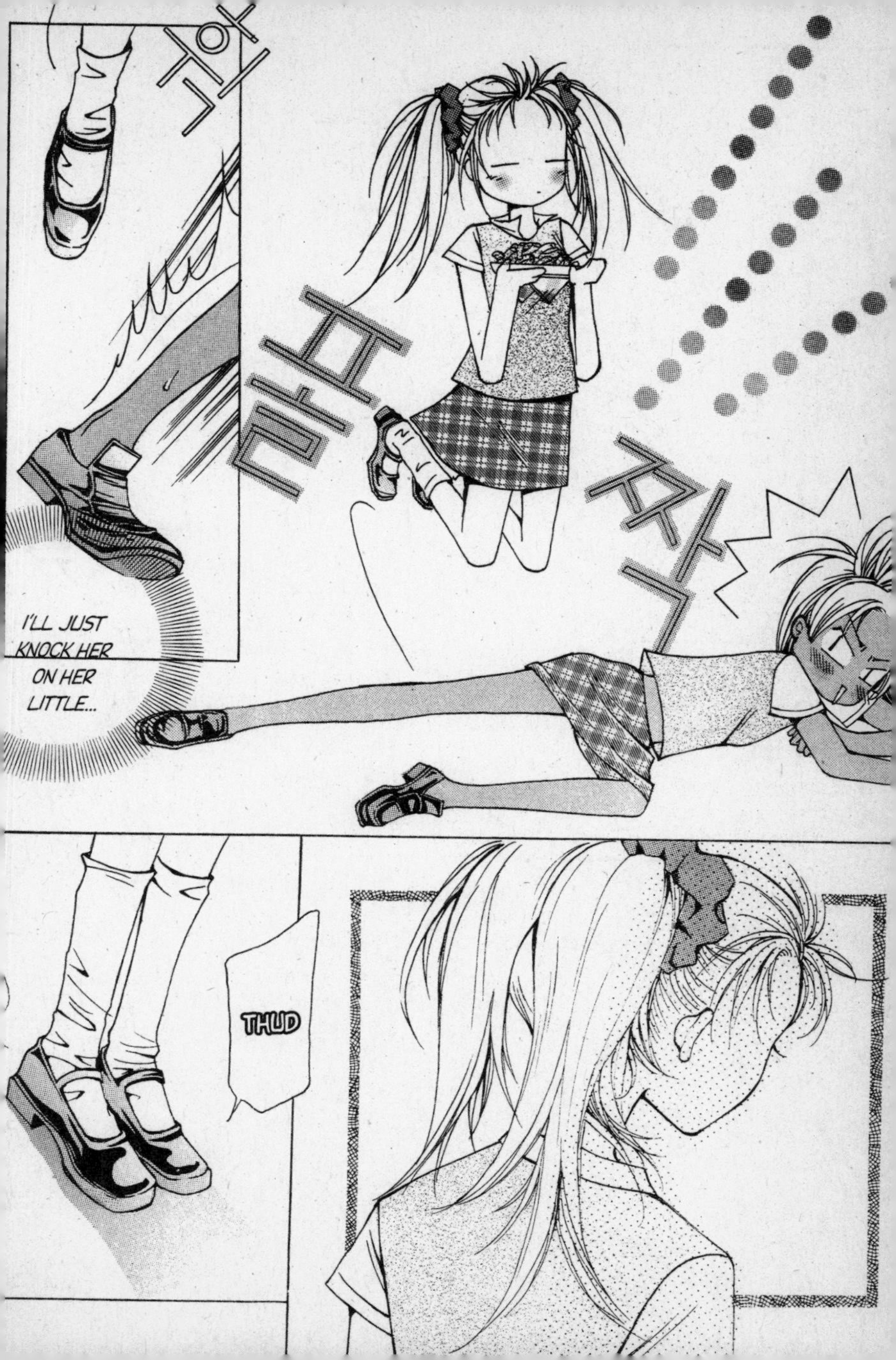
I'LL JUST KNOCK HER ON HER LITTLE...
THUD

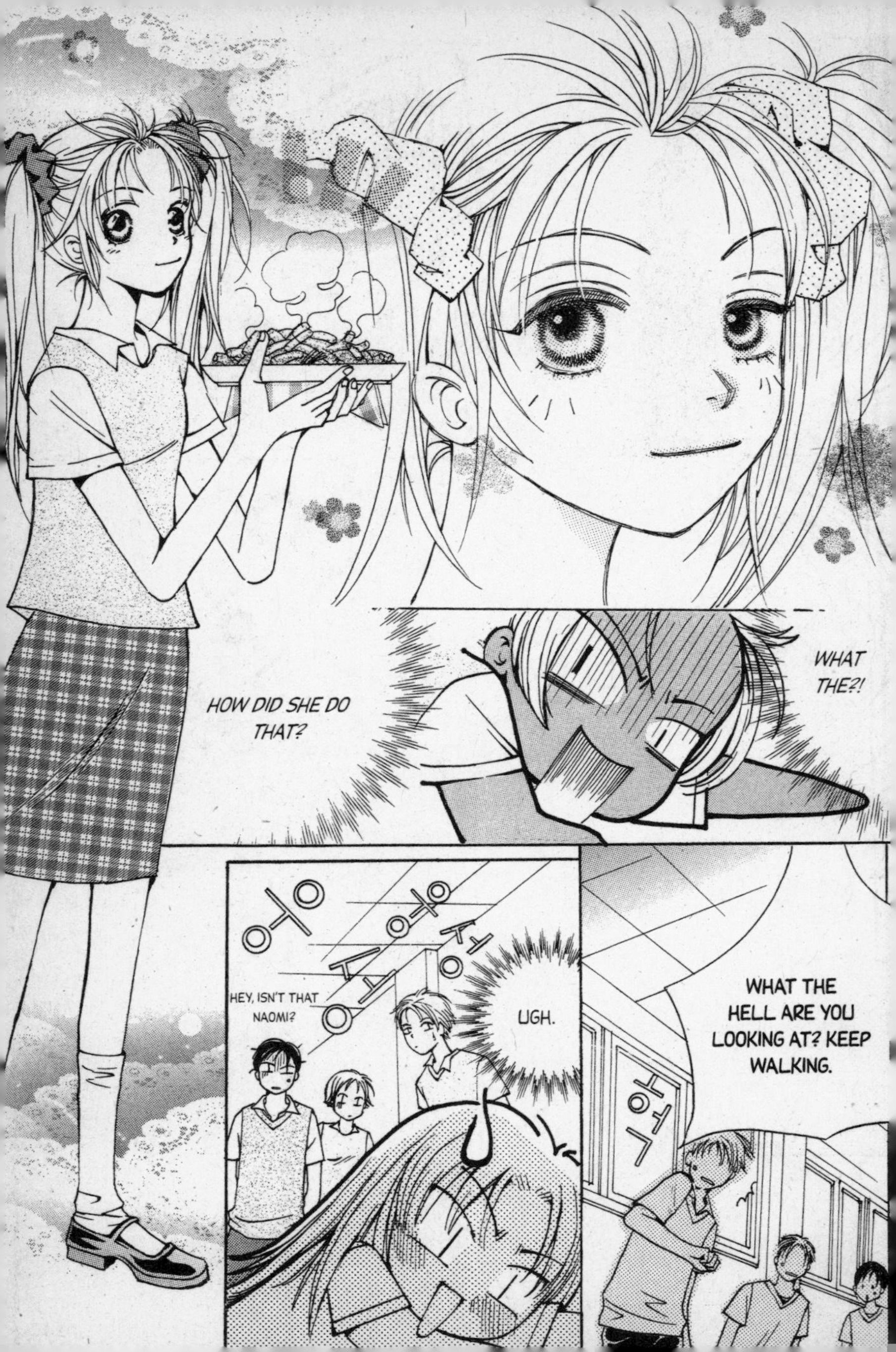
HOW DID SHE DO THAT?
WHAT THE?!
HEY, ISN'T THAT NAOMI?
UGH.
WHAT THE HELL ARE YOU LOOKING AT? KEEP WALKING.

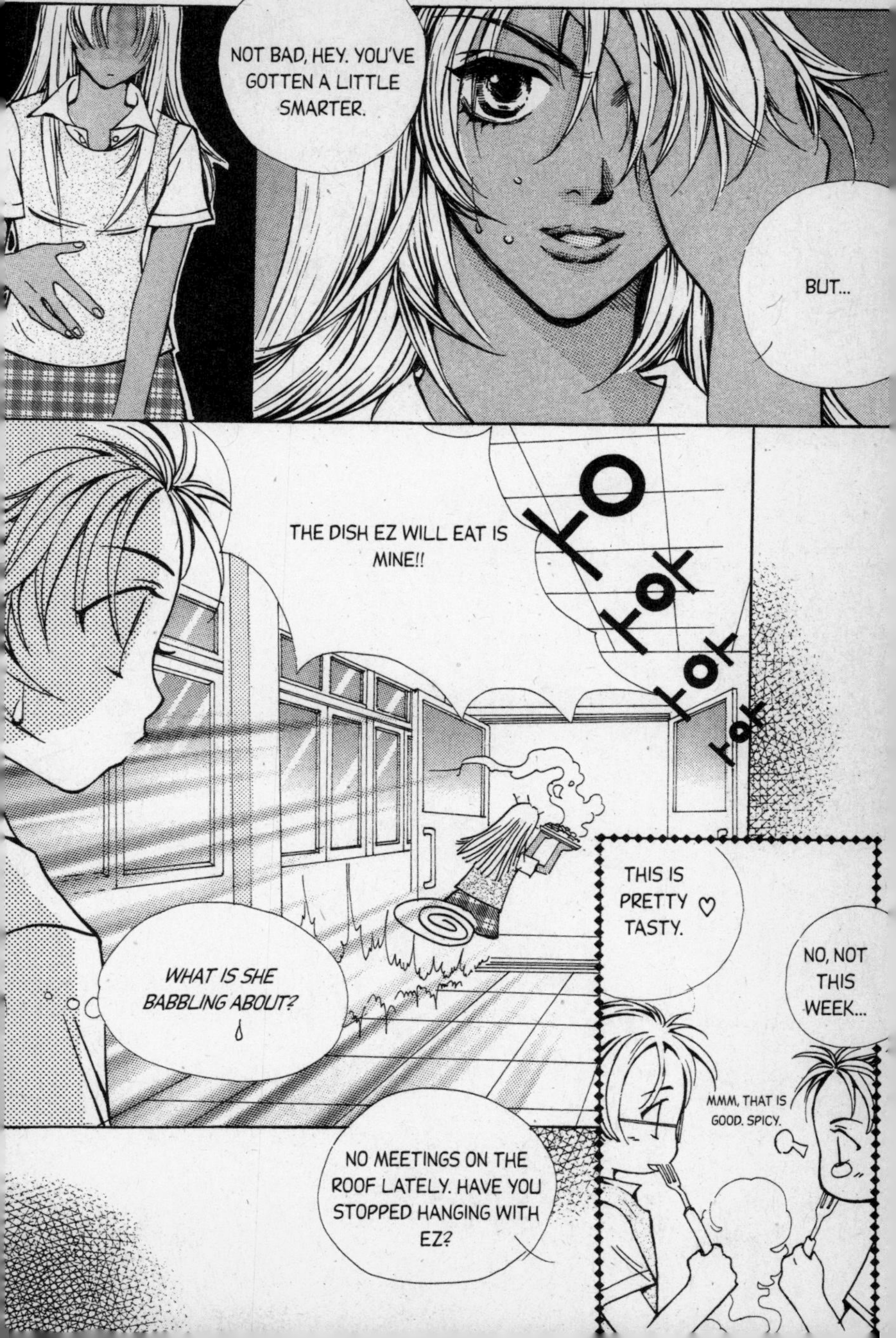
NOT BAD, HEY. YOU'VE GOTTEN A LITTLE SMARTER.
BUT...
THE DISH EZ WILL EAT IS MINE!!
TOK TOK TOK TOK
WHAT IS SHE BABBLING ABOUT?
THIS IS PRETTY TASTY. ♡
MMM, THAT IS GOOD. SPICY.
NO MEETINGS ON THE ROOF LATELY. HAVE YOU STOPPED HANGING WITH EZ?
NO, NOT THIS WEEK...

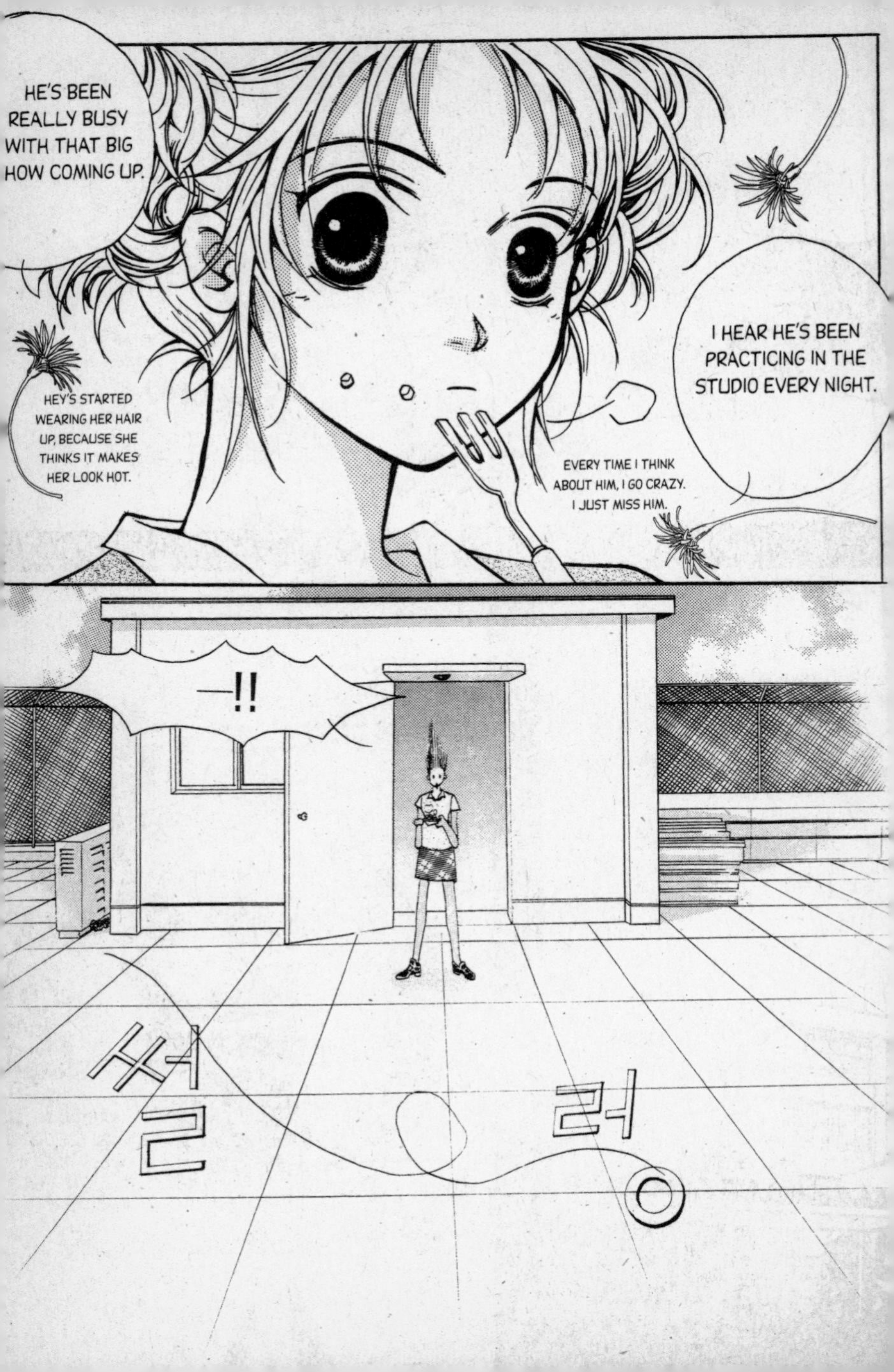
HE'S BEEN REALLY BUSY WITH THAT BIG HOW COMING UP.
HEY'S STARTED WEARING HER HAIR UP, BECAUSE SHE THINKS IT MAKES HER LOOK HOT.
I HEAR HE'S BEEN PRACTICING IN THE STUDIO EVERY NIGHT.
EVERY TIME I THINK ABOUT HIM, I GO CRAZY. I JUST MISS HIM.
—!!

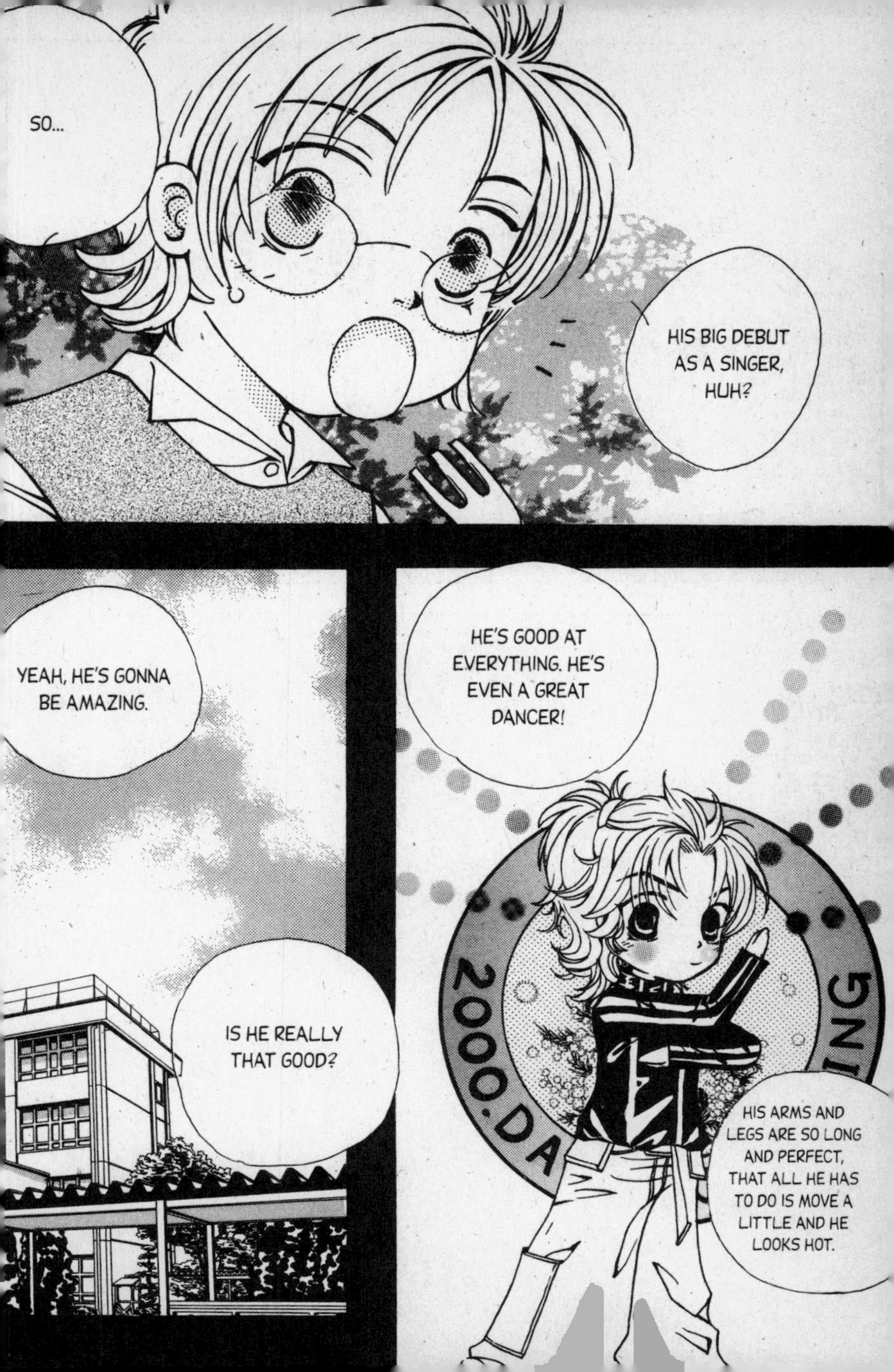

SO...
HIS BIG DEBUT AS A SINGER, HUH?
YEAH, HE'S GONNA BE AMAZING.
IS HE REALLY THAT GOOD?
HE'S GOOD AT EVERYTHING. HE'S EVEN A GREAT DANCER!
HIS ARMS AND LEGS ARE SO LONG AND PERFECT, THAT ALL HE HAS TO DO IS MOVE A LITTLE AND HE LOOKS HOT.

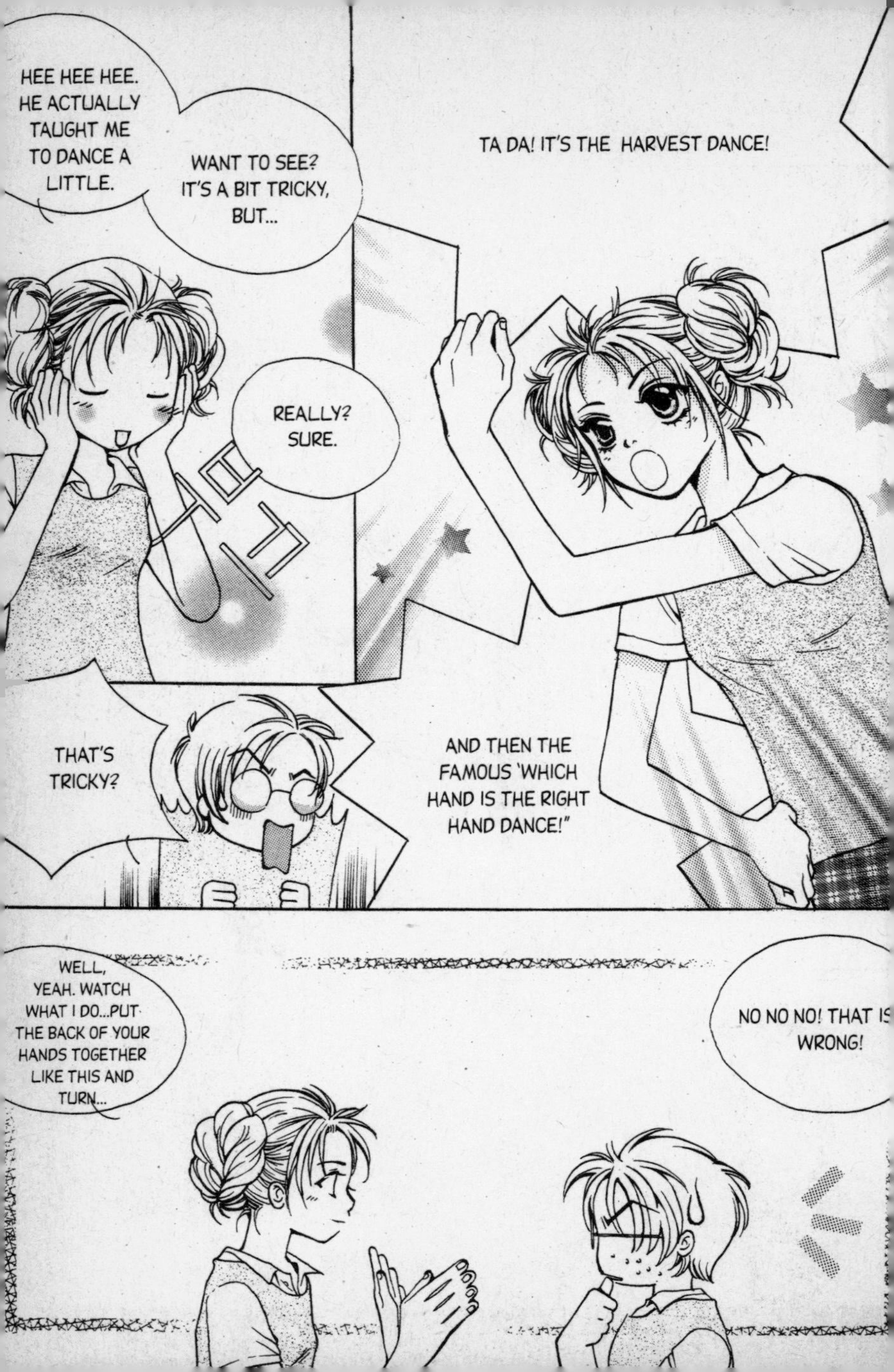

HEE HEE HEE. HE ACTUALLY TAUGHT ME TO DANCE A LITTLE.
WANT TO SEE? IT'S A BIT TRICKY, BUT...
REALLY? SURE.
TA DA! IT'S THE HARVEST DANCE!
AND THEN THE FAMOUS 'WHICH HAND IS THE RIGHT HAND DANCE!"
THAT'S TRICKY?
WELL, YEAH. WATCH WHAT I DO...PUT THE BACK OF YOUR HANDS TOGETHER LIKE THIS AND TURN...
NO NO NO! THAT IS WRONG!

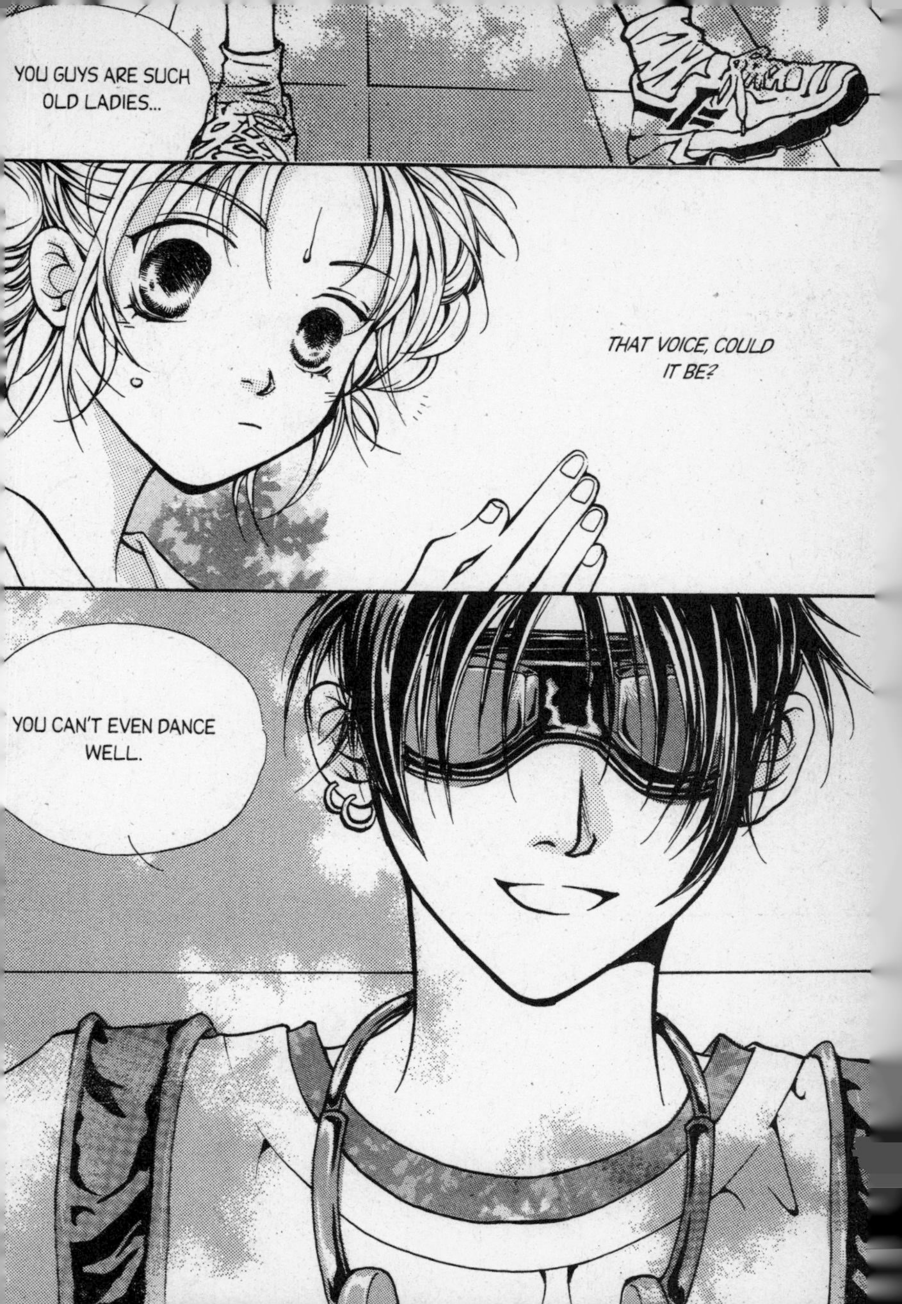
YOU GUYS ARE SUCH OLD LADIES...
THAT VOICE, COULD IT BE?
YOU CAN'T EVEN DANCE WELL.

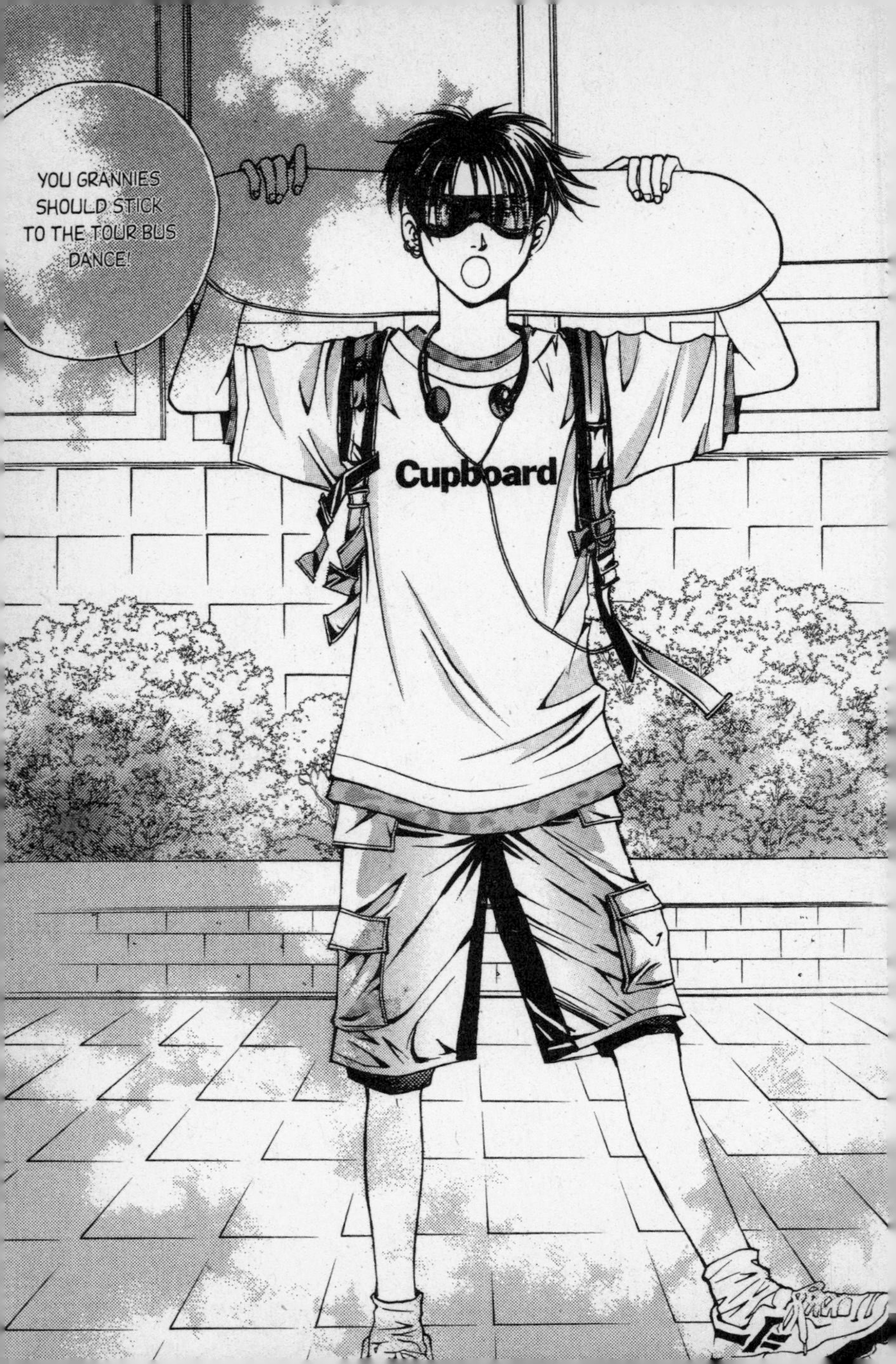
YOU GRANNIES SHOULD STICK TO THE TOUR BUS DANCE!
Cupboard

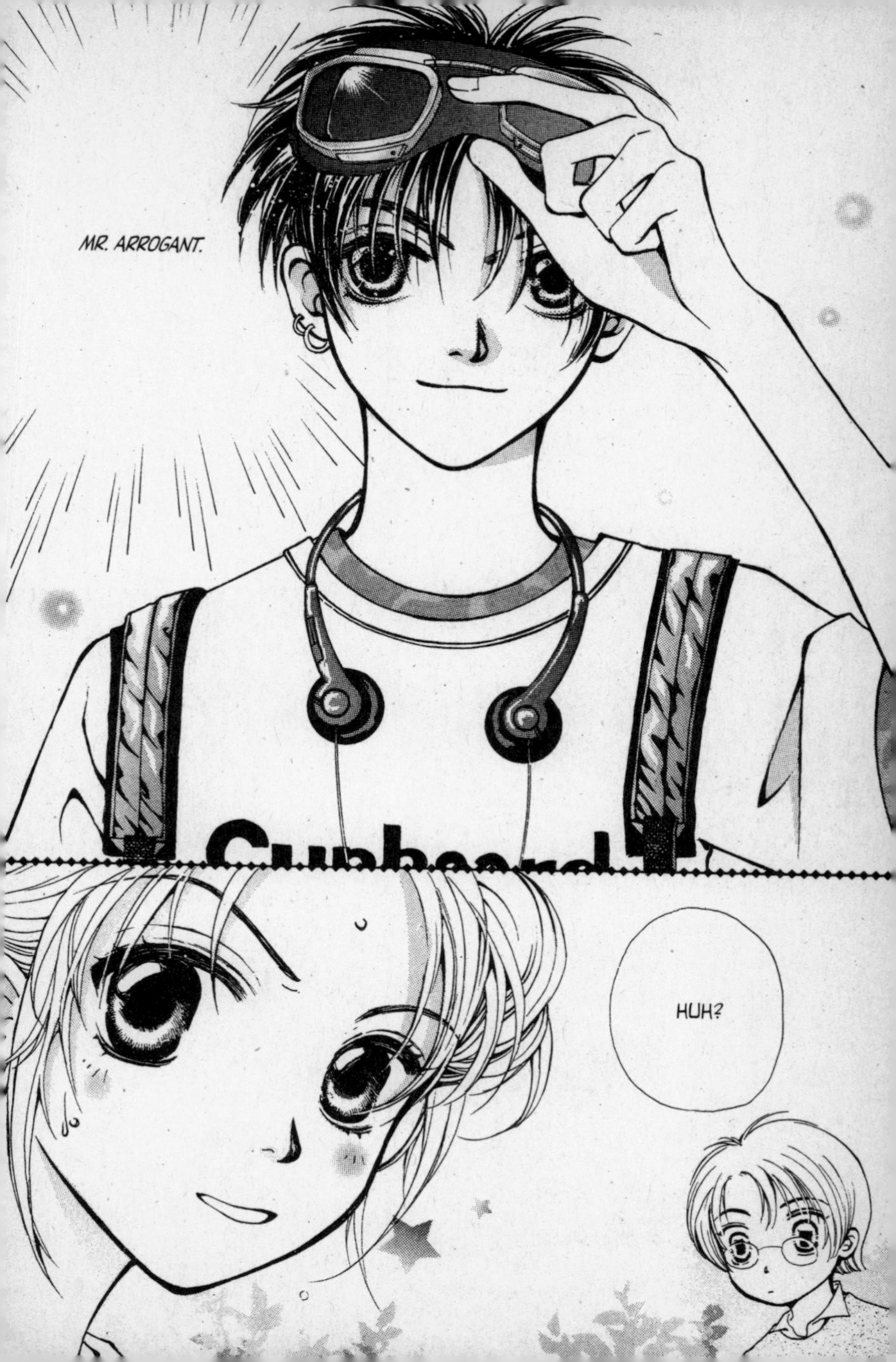
MR. ARROGANT.
HUH?

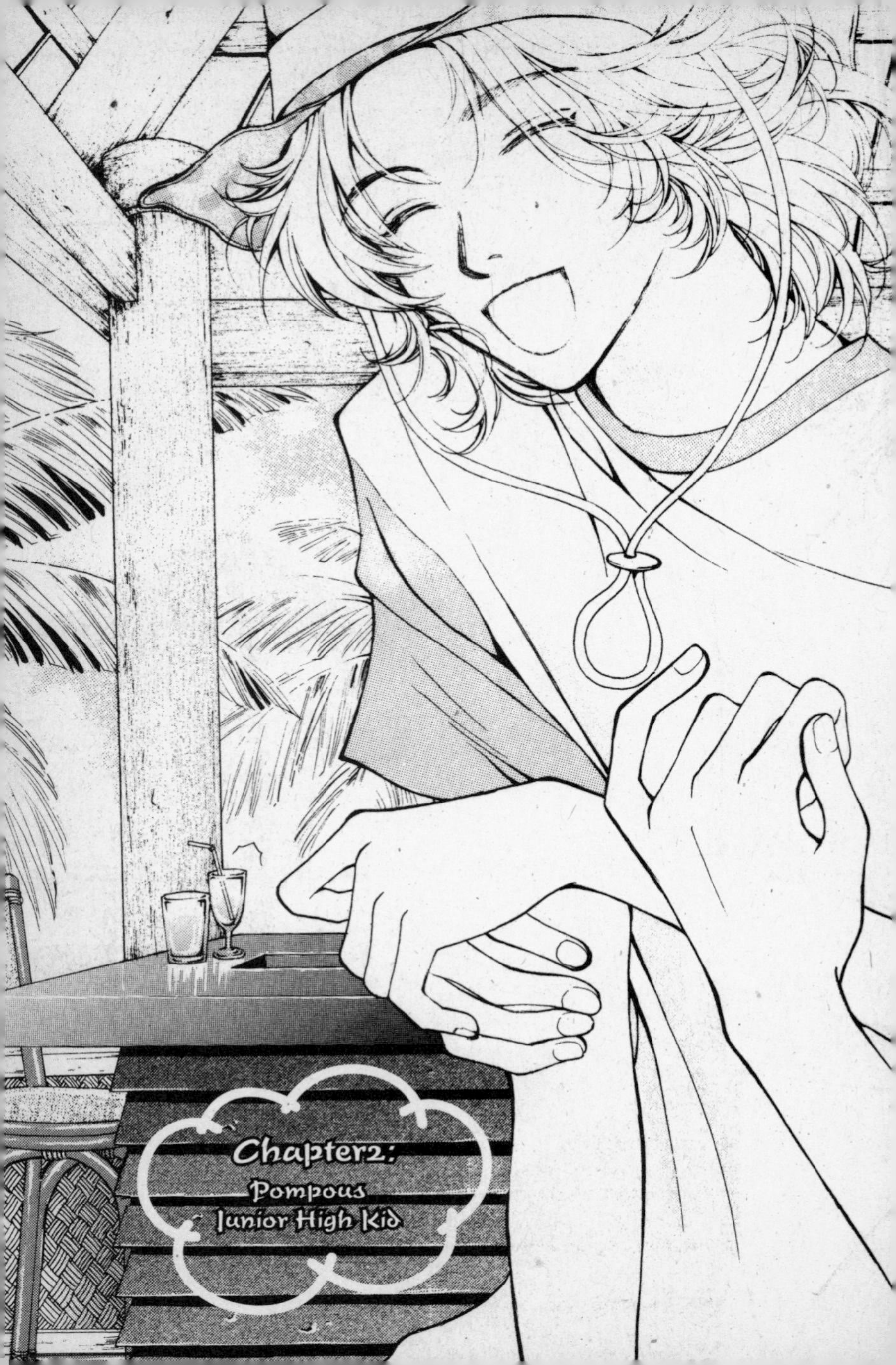
Chapter2:
Pompous
Junior High Kid

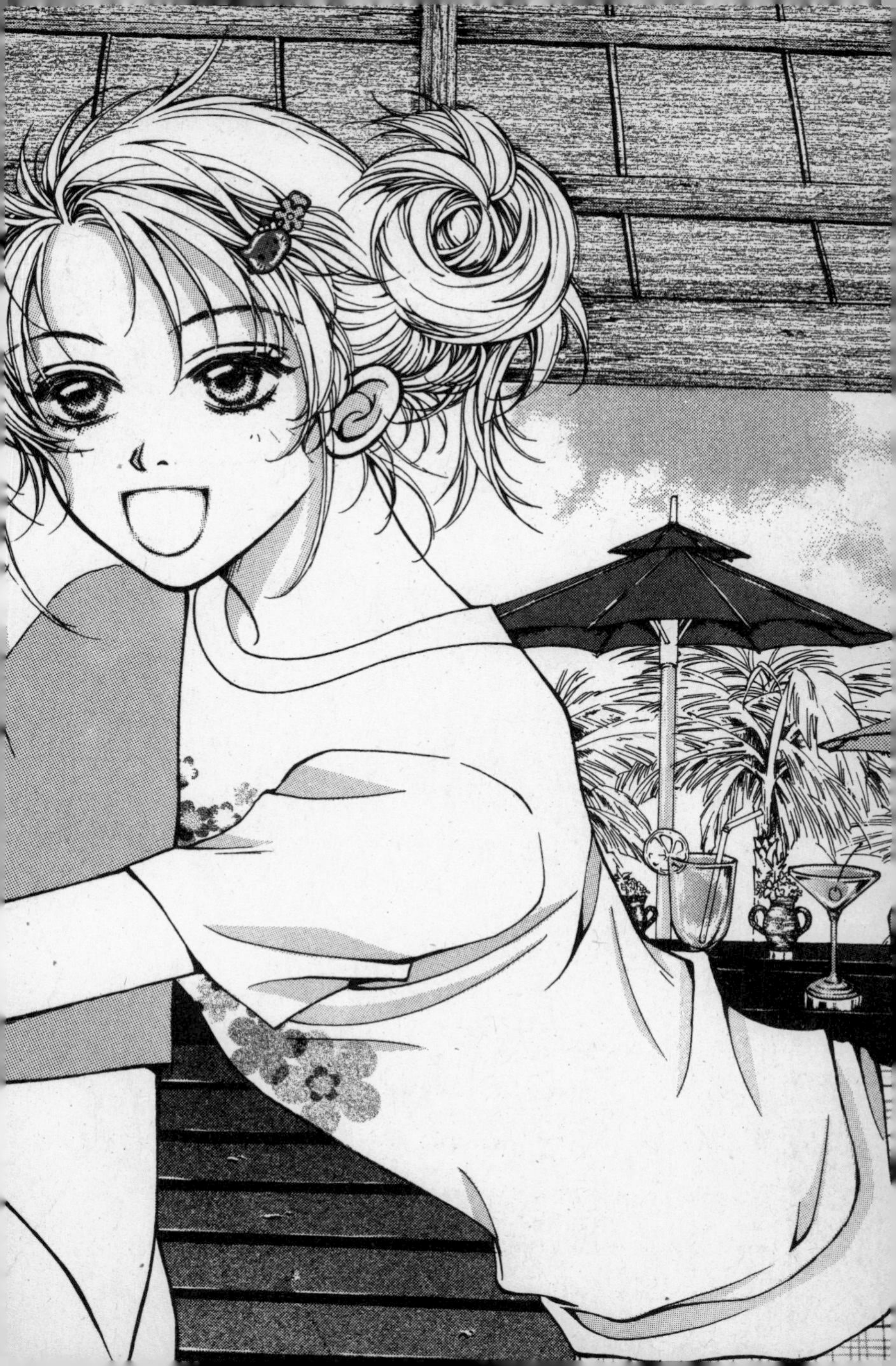

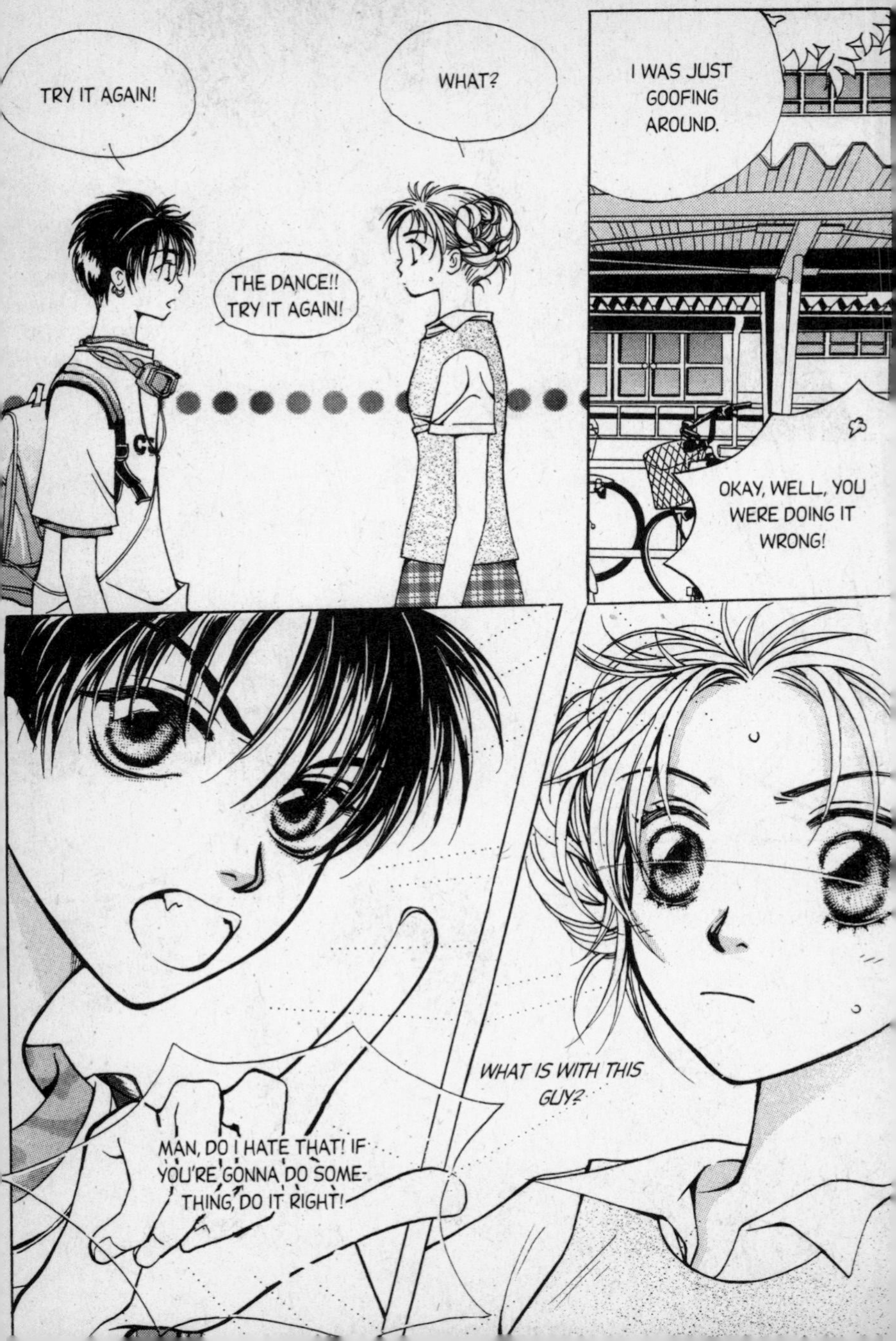
TRY IT AGAIN!
WHAT?
THE DANCE!! TRY IT AGAIN!
I WAS JUST GOOFING AROUND.
OKAY, WELL, YOU WERE DOING IT WRONG!
MAN, DO I HATE THAT! IF YOU'RE GONNA DO SOME-THING, DO IT RIGHT!
WHAT IS WITH THIS GUY?

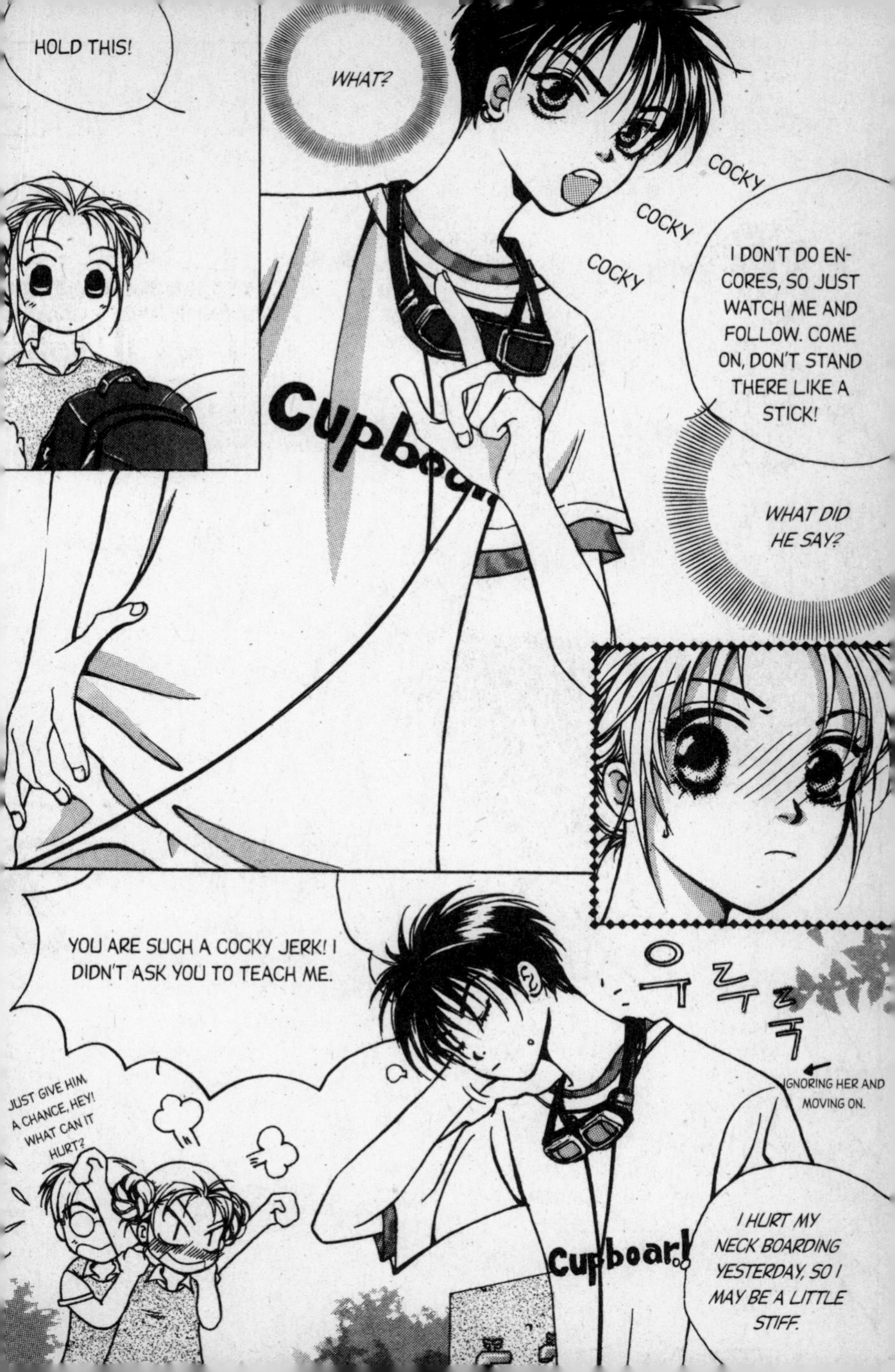

HOLD THIS!
WHAT?
Cupboar!
COCKY
COCKY
COCKY
I DON'T DO EN-CORES, SO JUST WATCH ME AND FOLLOW. COME ON, DON'T STAND THERE LIKE A STICK!
WHAT DID HE SAY?
YOU ARE SUCH A COCKY JERK! I DIDN'T ASK YOU TO TEACH ME.
IGNORING HER AND MOVING ON.
Cupboar!
I HURT MY NECK BOARDING YESTERDAY, SO I MAY BE A LITTLE STIFF.
JUST GIVE HIM A CHANCE, HEY! WHAT CAN IT HURT?

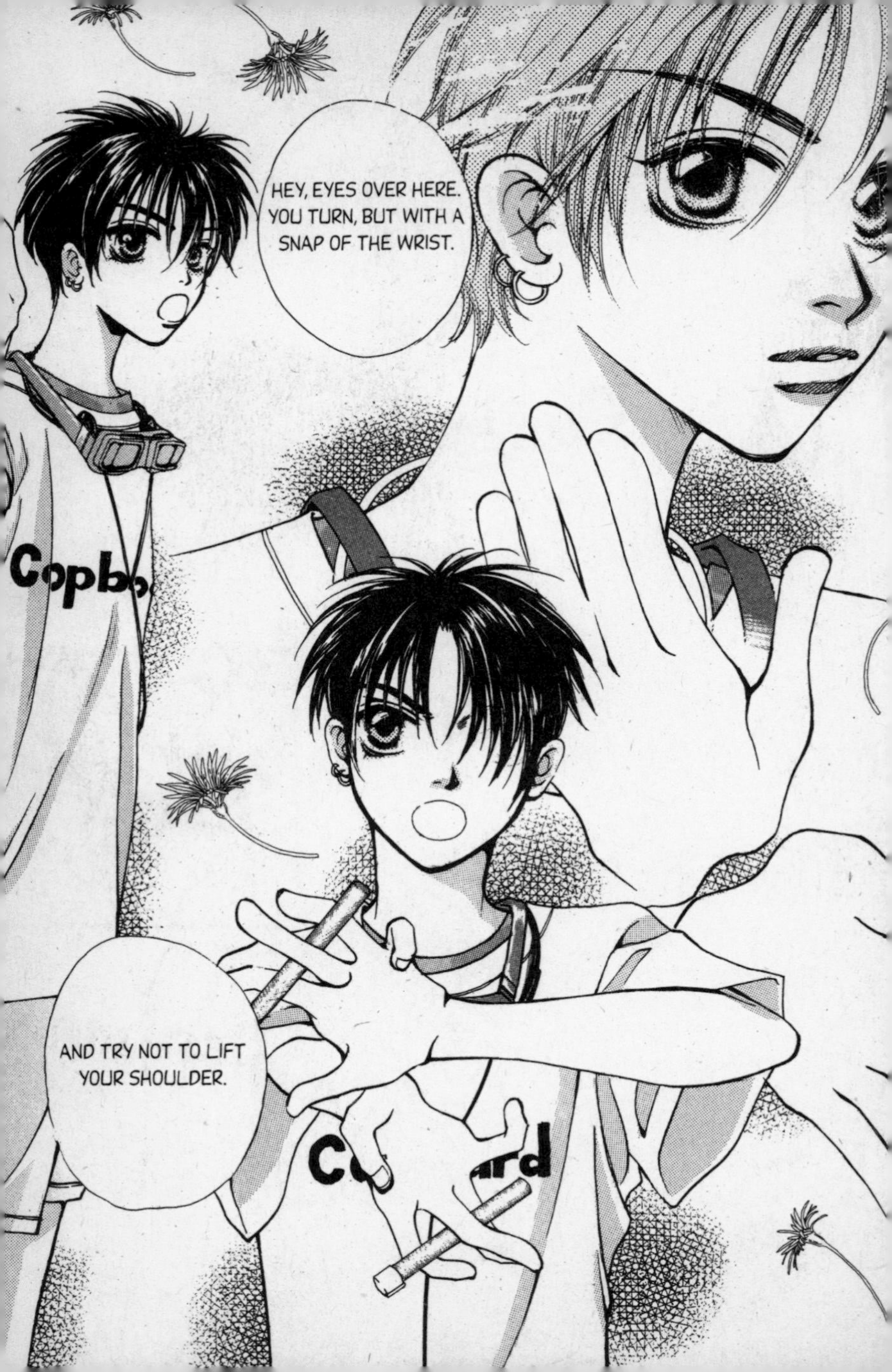
HEY, EYES OVER HERE. YOU TURN, BUT WITH A SNAP OF THE WRIST.
AND TRY NOT TO LIFT YOUR SHOULDER.

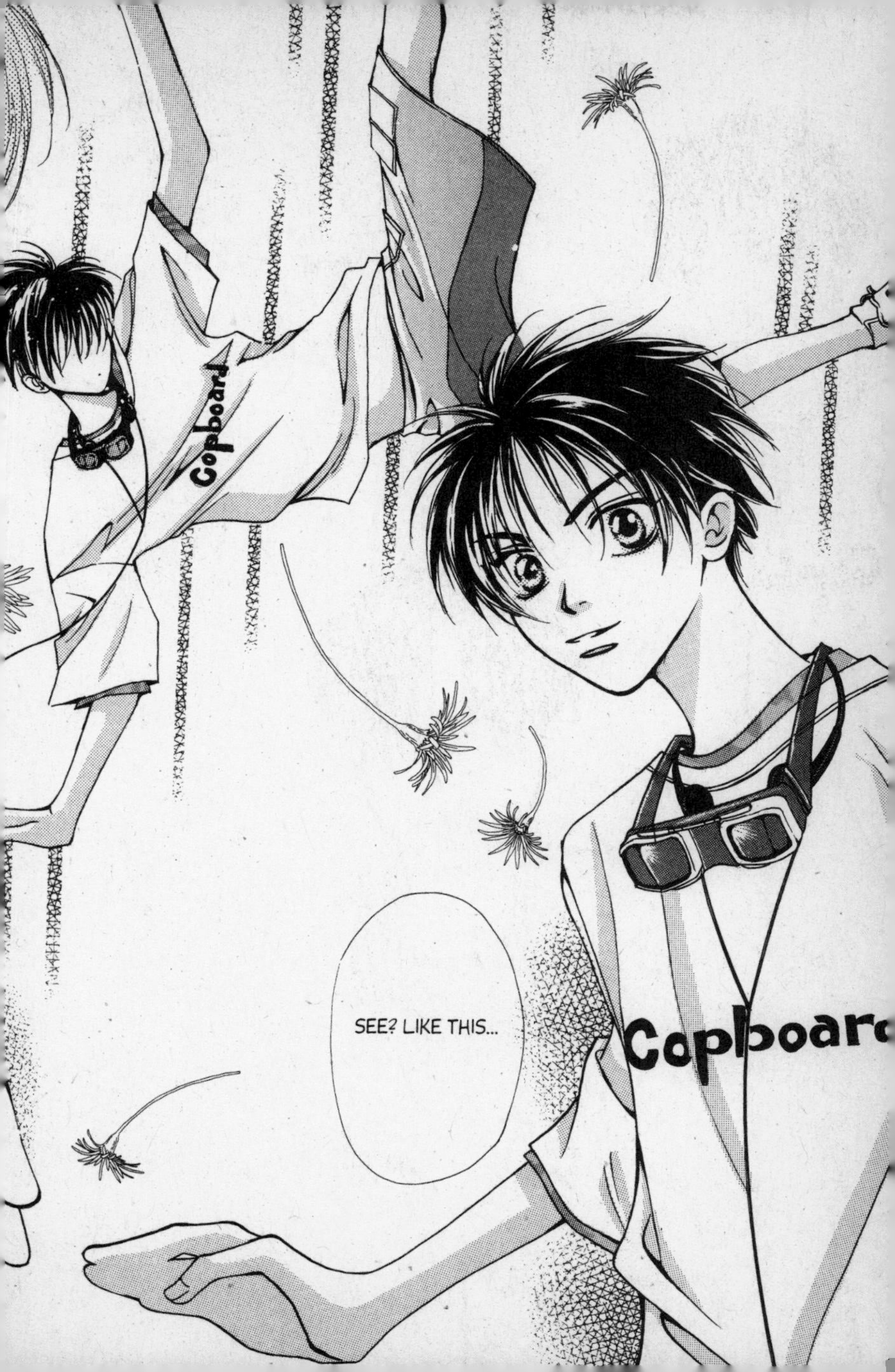
Copboard
SEE? LIKE THIS...
Copboard

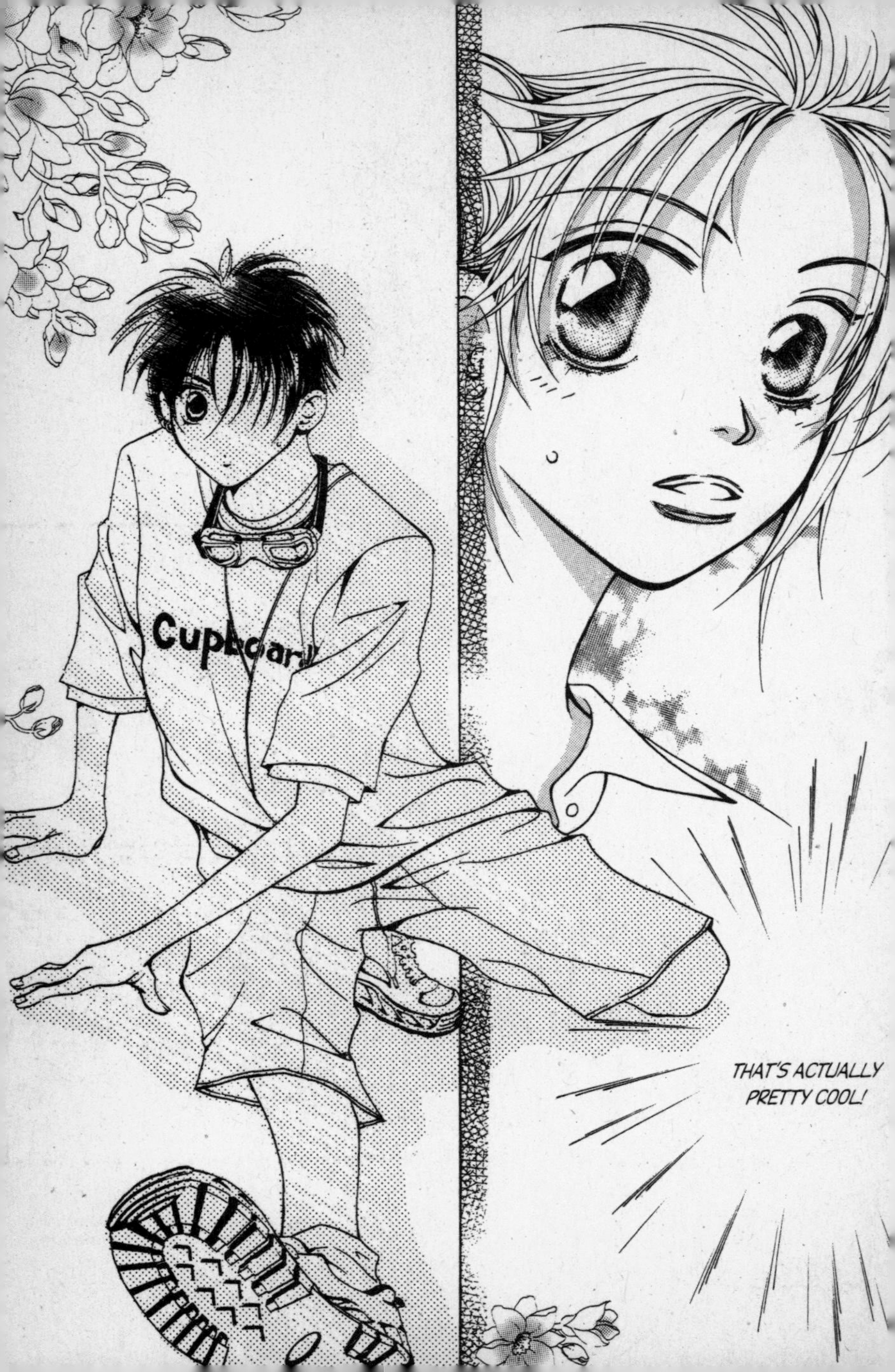
THAT'S ACTUALLY PRETTY COOL!

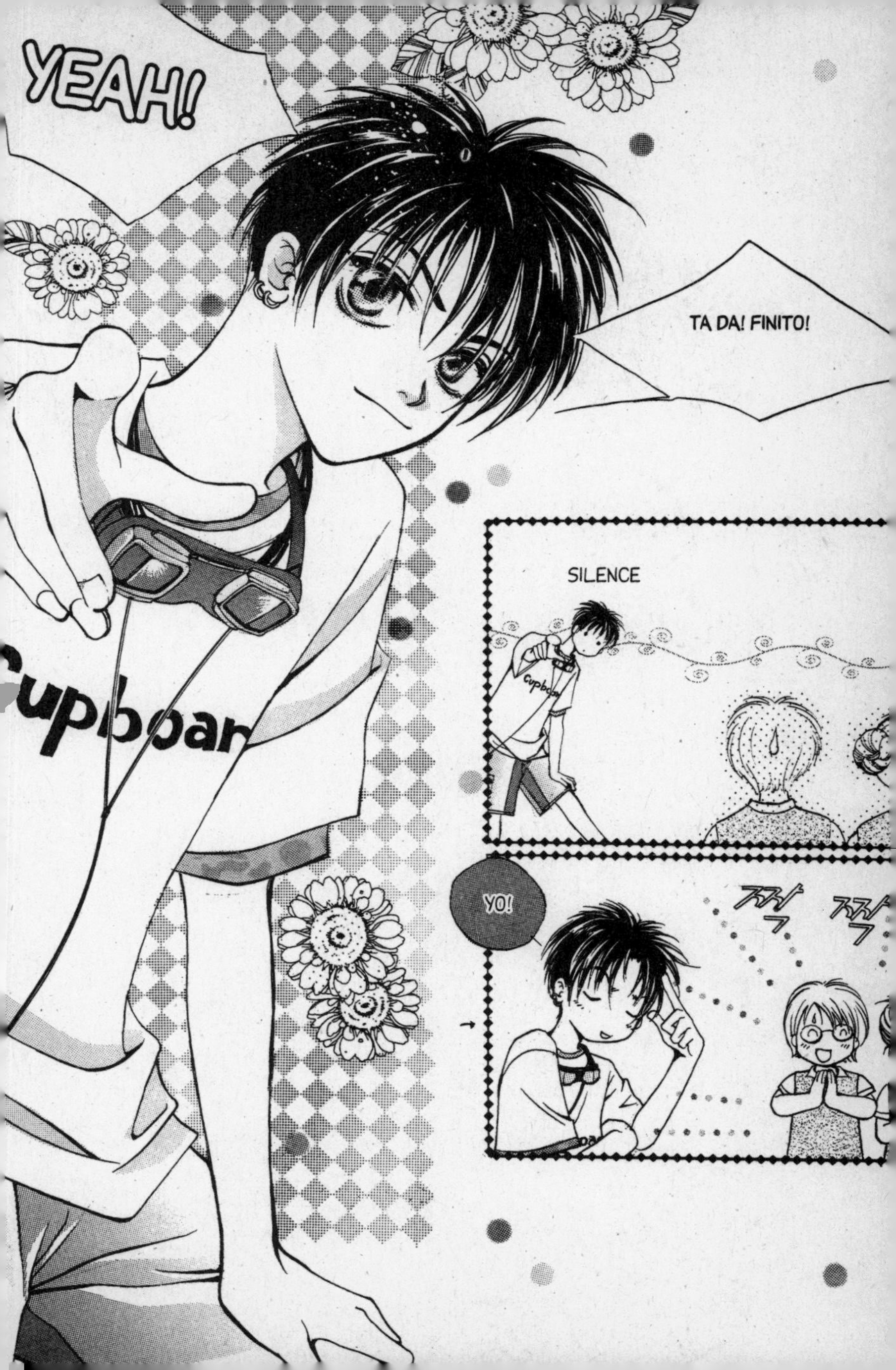
YEAH!
TA DA! FINITO!
Cupboar
SILENCE
YO!

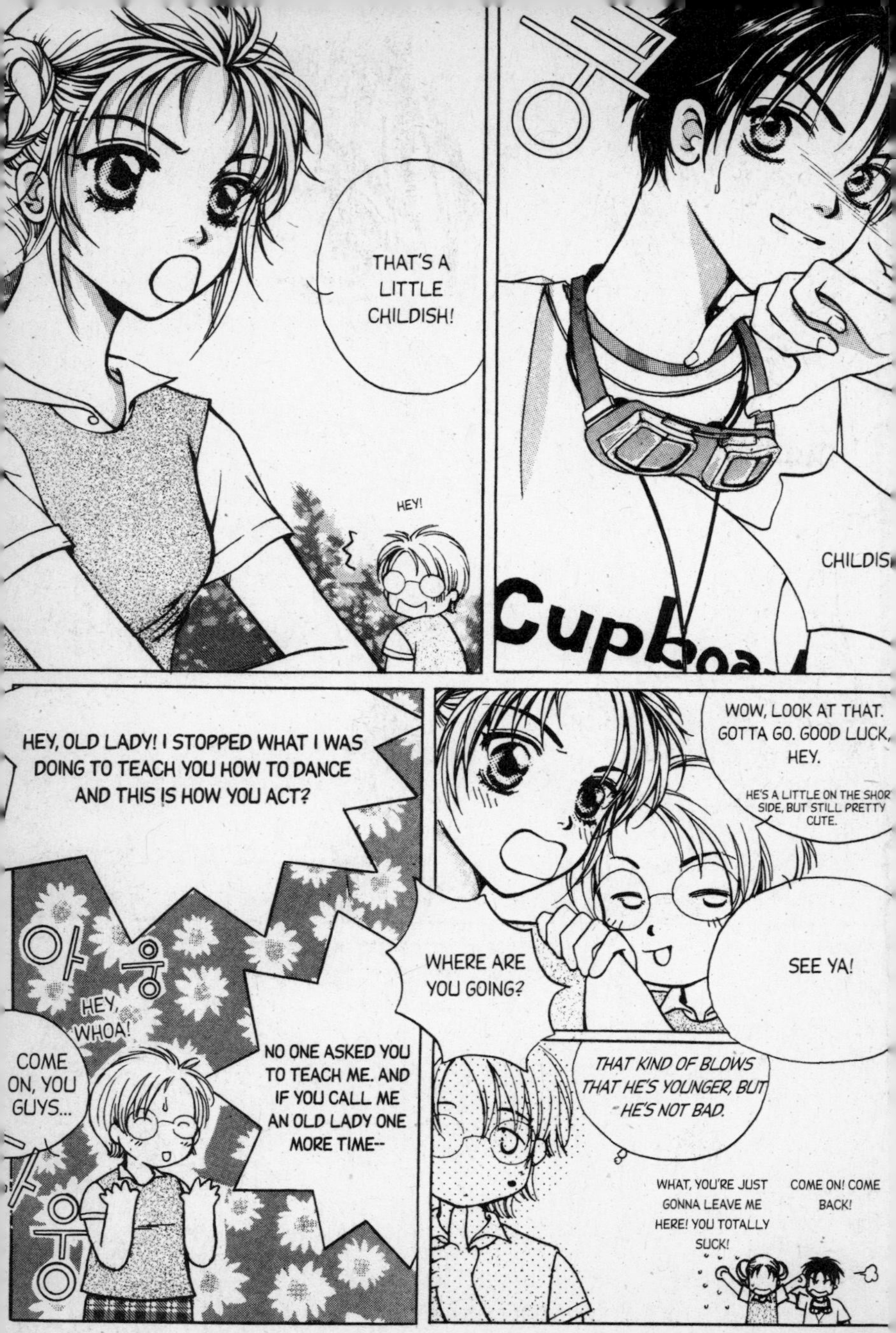
THAT'S A LITTLE CHILDISH!
HEY!
CHILDIS
Cupboa
HEY, OLD LADY! I STOPPED WHAT I WAS DOING TO TEACH YOU HOW TO DANCE AND THIS IS HOW YOU ACT?
HEY, WHOA!
COME ON, YOU GUYS...
NO ONE ASKED YOU TO TEACH ME. AND IF YOU CALL ME AN OLD LADY ONE MORE TIME--
WOW, LOOK AT THAT. GOTTA GO. GOOD LUCK, HEY.
HE'S A LITTLE ON THE SHOR SIDE, BUT STILL PRETTY CUTE.
WHERE ARE YOU GOING?
SEE YA!
THAT KIND OF BLOWS THAT HE'S YOUNGER, BUT HE'S NOT BAD.
WHAT, YOU'RE JUST GONNA LEAVE ME HERE! YOU TOTALLY SUCK!
COME ON! COME BACK!

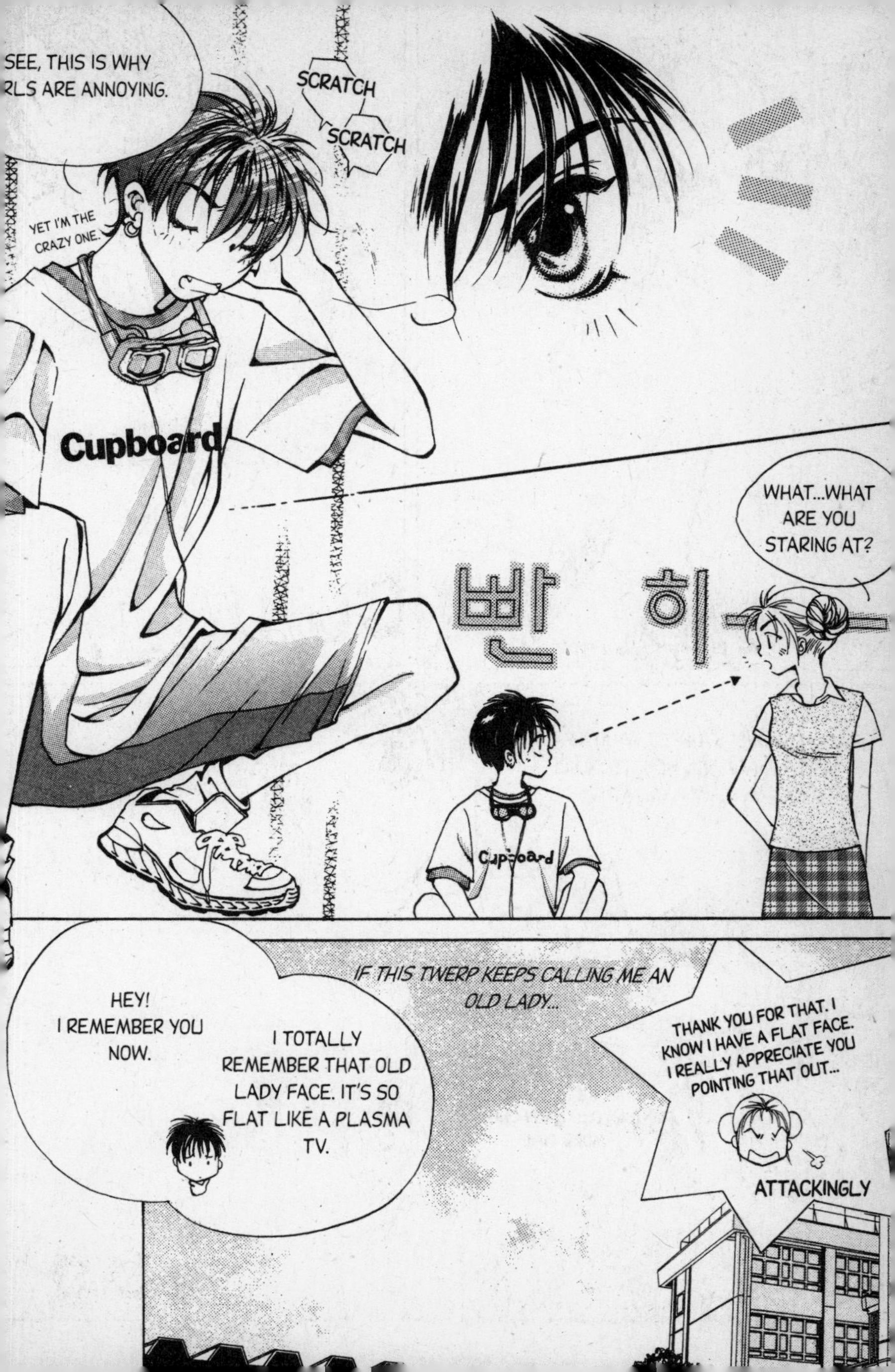
SEE, THIS IS WHY
RLS ARE ANNOYING.
YET I'M THE CRAZY ONE.
SCRATCH
SCRATCH
빤 히
WHAT...WHAT ARE YOU STARING AT?
HEY! I REMEMBER YOU NOW.
I TOTALLY REMEMBER THAT OLD LADY FACE. IT'S SO FLAT LIKE A PLASMA TV.
IF THIS TWERP KEEPS CALLING ME AN OLD LADY...
THANK YOU FOR THAT. I KNOW I HAVE A FLAT FACE. I REALLY APPRECIATE YOU POINTING THAT OUT...
ATTACKINGLY

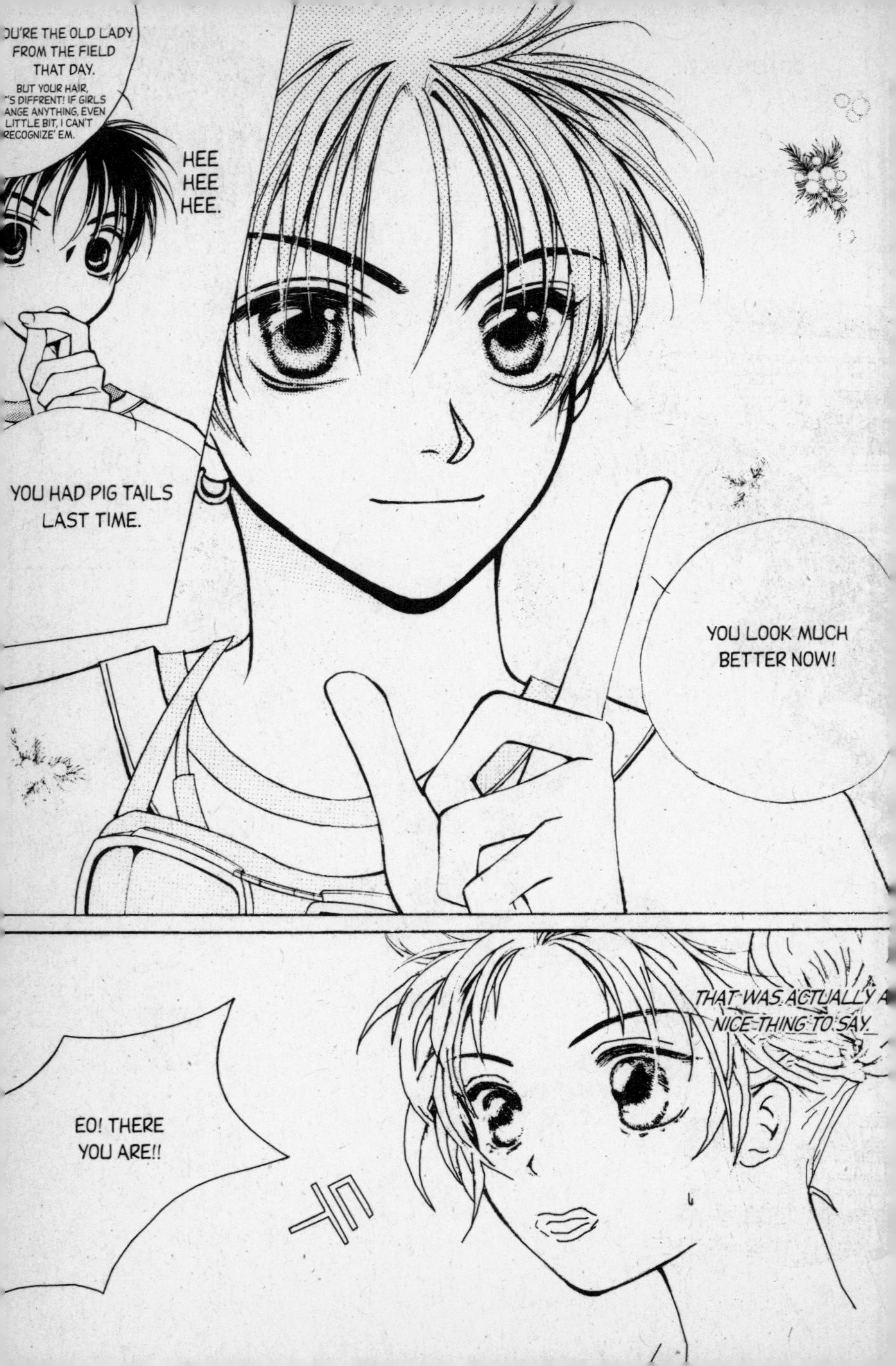
OU'RE THE OLD LADY FROM THE FIELD THAT DAY.
BUT YOUR HAIR, 'S DIFFRENT! IF GIRLS ANGE ANYTHING, EVEN LITTLE BIT, I CAN'T RECOGNIZE' EM.
HEE HEE HEE.
YOU HAD PIG TAILS LAST TIME.
YOU LOOK MUCH BETTER NOW!
THAT WAS ACTUALLY A NICE THING TO SAY.
EO! THERE YOU ARE!!

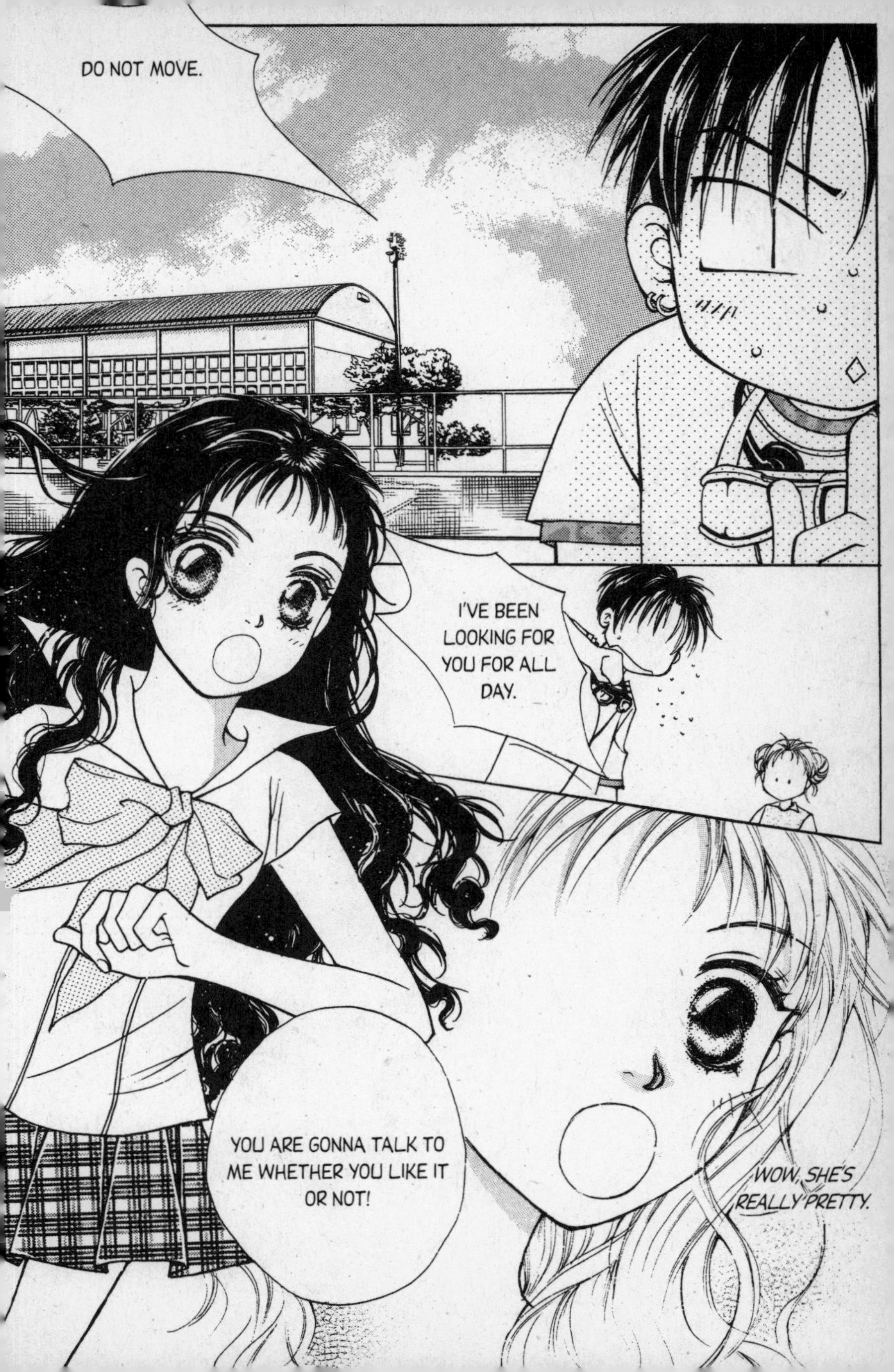
DO NOT MOVE.
I'VE BEEN LOOKING FOR YOU FOR ALL DAY.
YOU ARE GONNA TALK TO ME WHETHER YOU LIKE IT OR NOT!
WOW, SHE'S REALLY PRETTY.

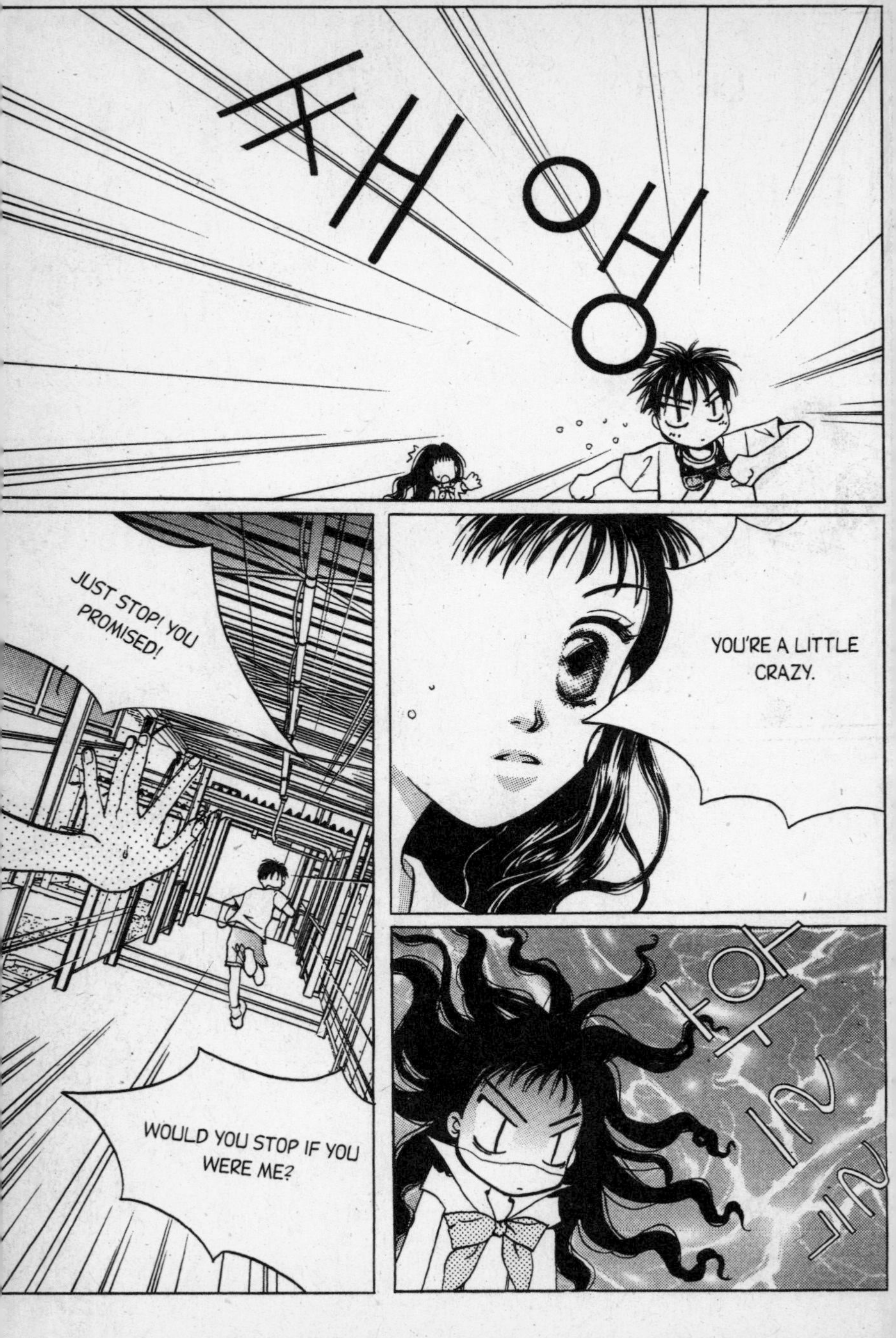
YOU'RE A LITTLE CRAZY.
JUST STOP! YOU PROMISED!
WOULD YOU STOP IF YOU WERE ME?

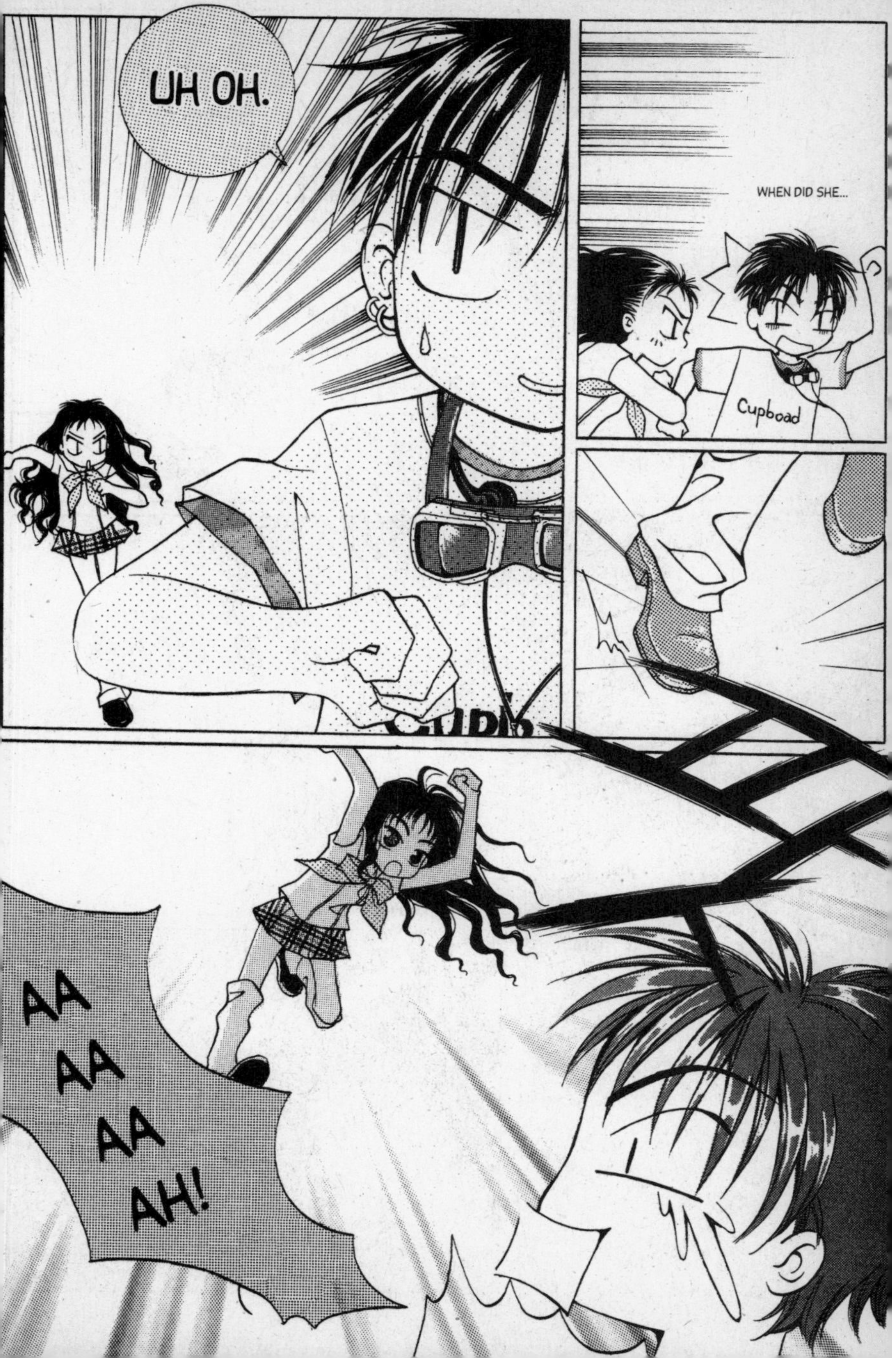
WHEN DID SHE...
Cupboad
UH OH.
AA AA AA AH!

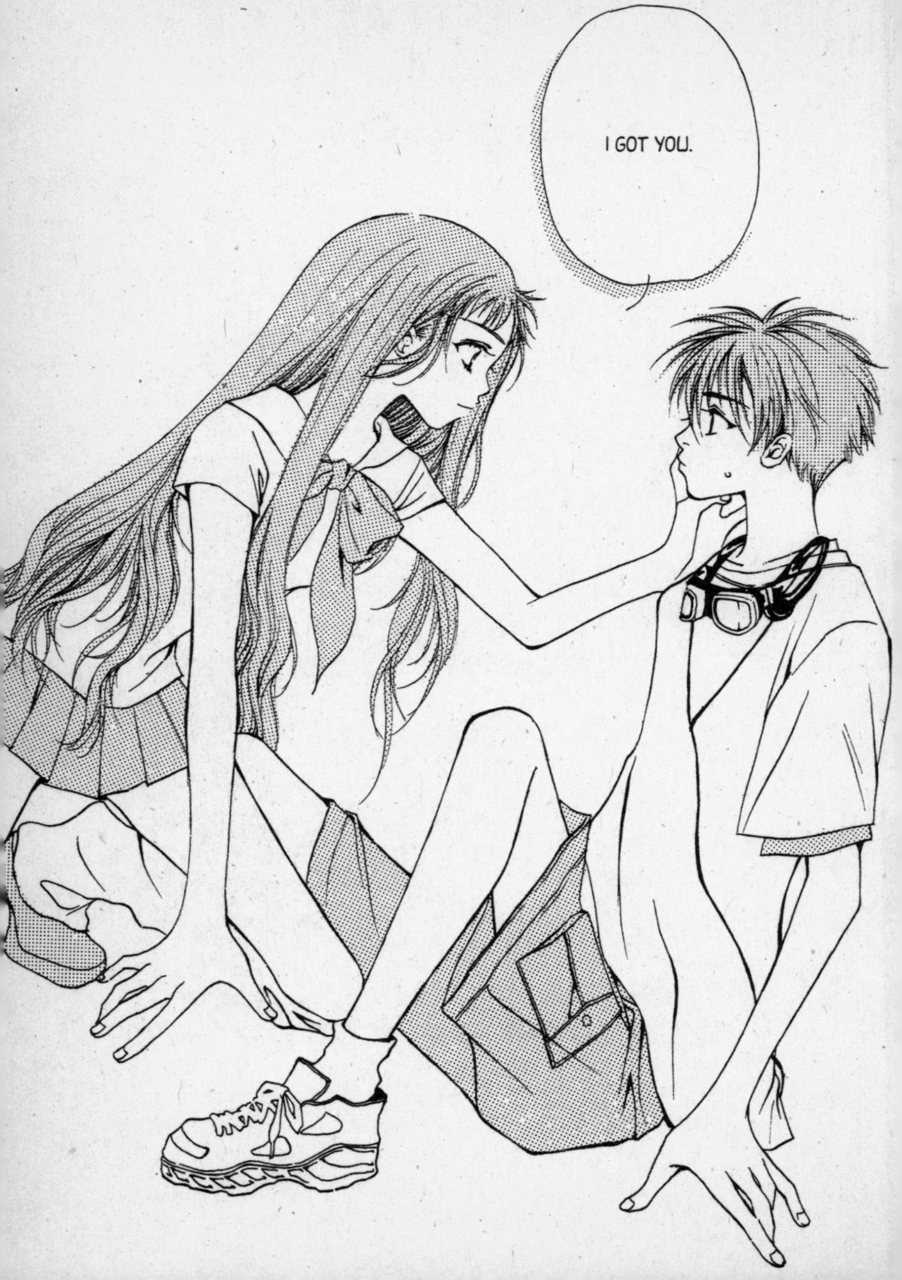
I GOT YOU.

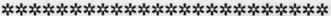

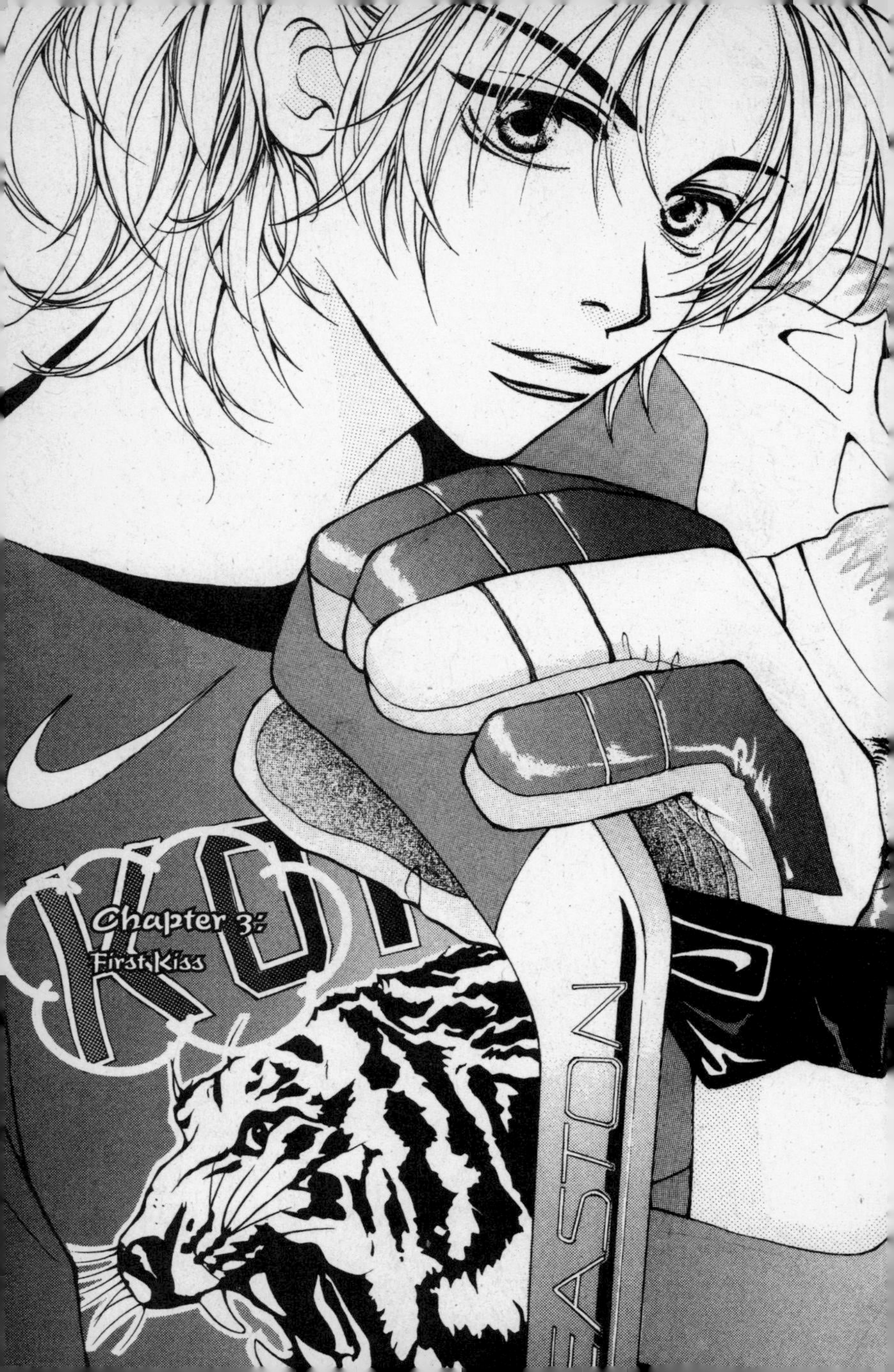
Chapter 3:
First Kiss
EASTON

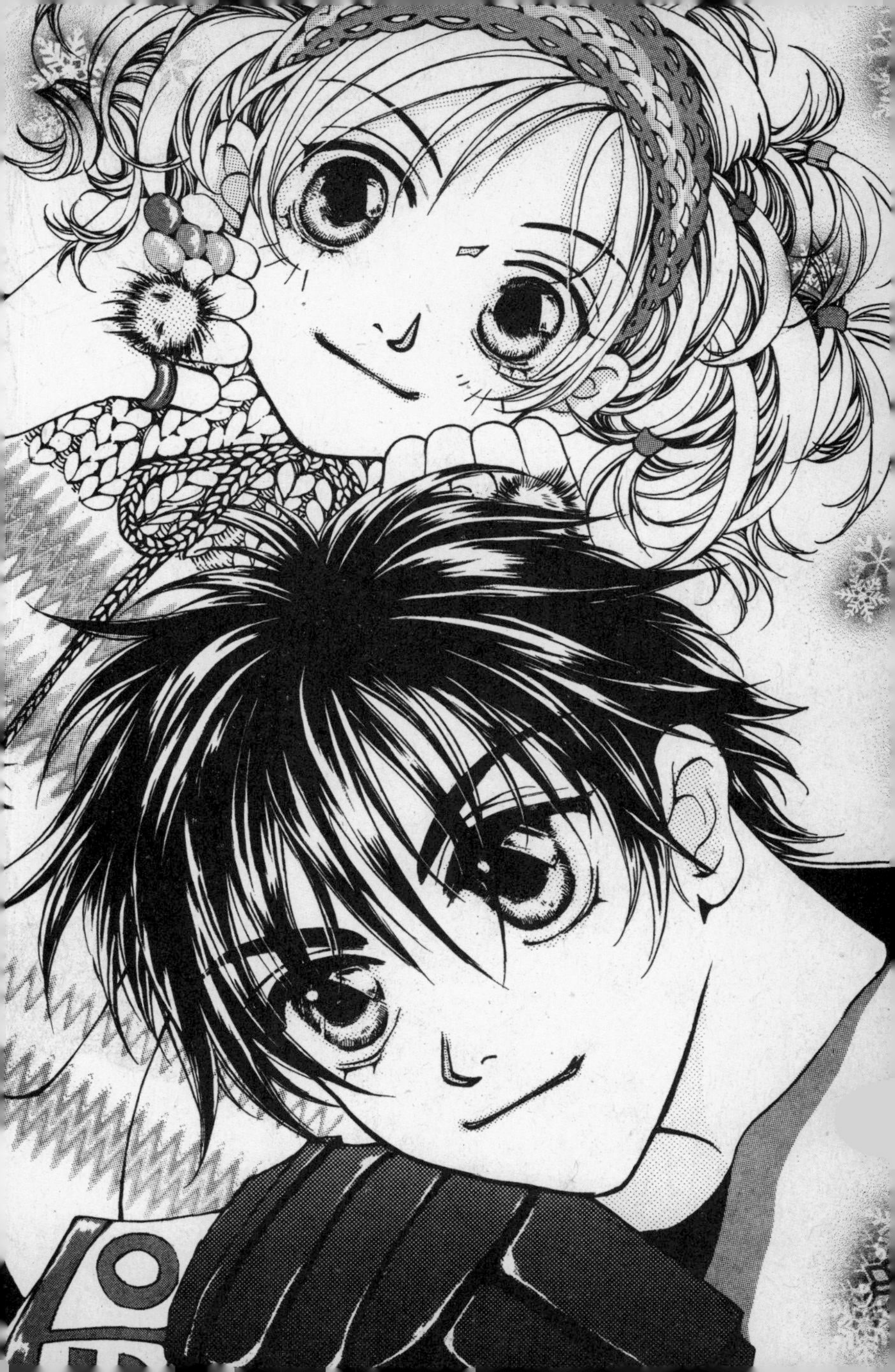

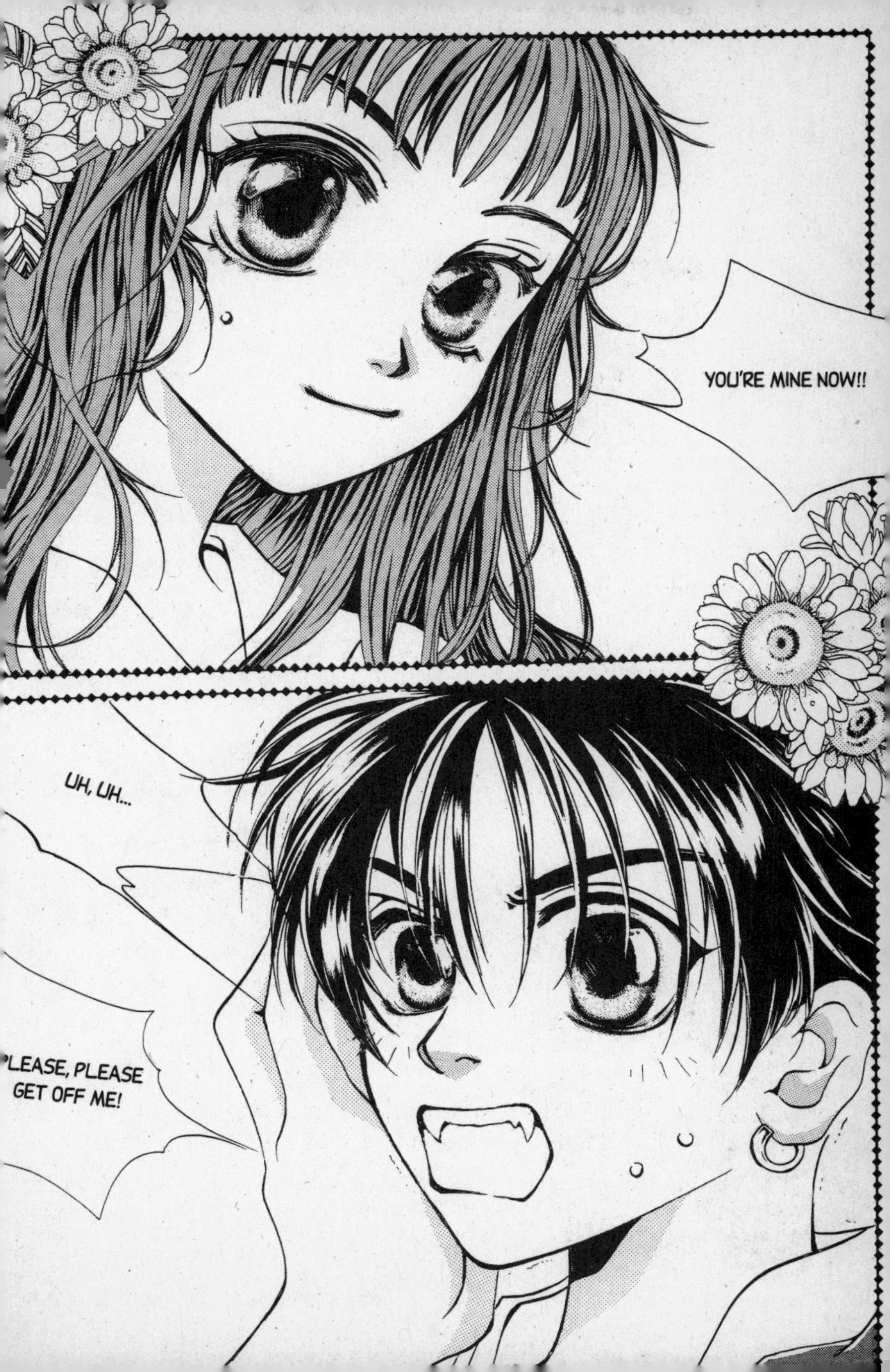
YOU'RE MINE NOW!!
UH, UH...
PLEASE, PLEASE GET OFF ME!

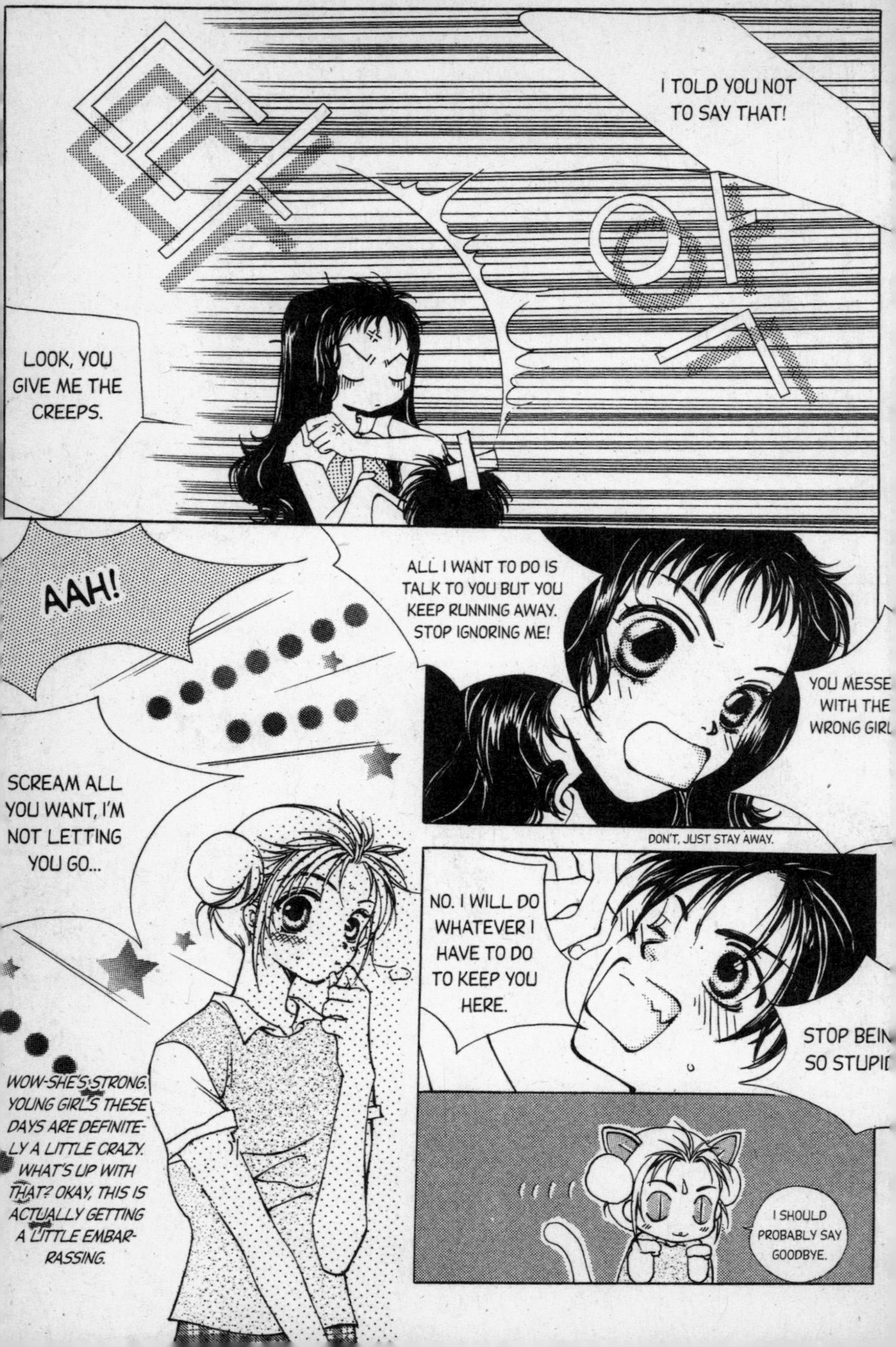
I TOLD YOU NOT TO SAY THAT!
LOOK, YOU GIVE ME THE CREEPS.
YOU MESSE WITH THE WRONG GIRL
ALL I WANT TO DO IS TALK TO YOU BUT YOU KEEP RUNNING AWAY. STOP IGNORING ME!
AAH!
DON'T, JUST STAY AWAY.
STOP BEIN SO STUPID
NO. I WILL DO WHATEVER I HAVE TO DO TO KEEP YOU HERE.
I SHOULD PROBABLY SAY GOODBYE.
SCREAM ALL YOU WANT, I'M NOT LETTING YOU GO...
WOW-SHE'S STRONG. YOUNG GIRLS THESE DAYS ARE DEFINITE-LY A LITTLE CRAZY. WHAT'S UP WITH THAT? OKAY, THIS IS ACTUALLY GETTING A LITTLE EMBAR-RASSING.

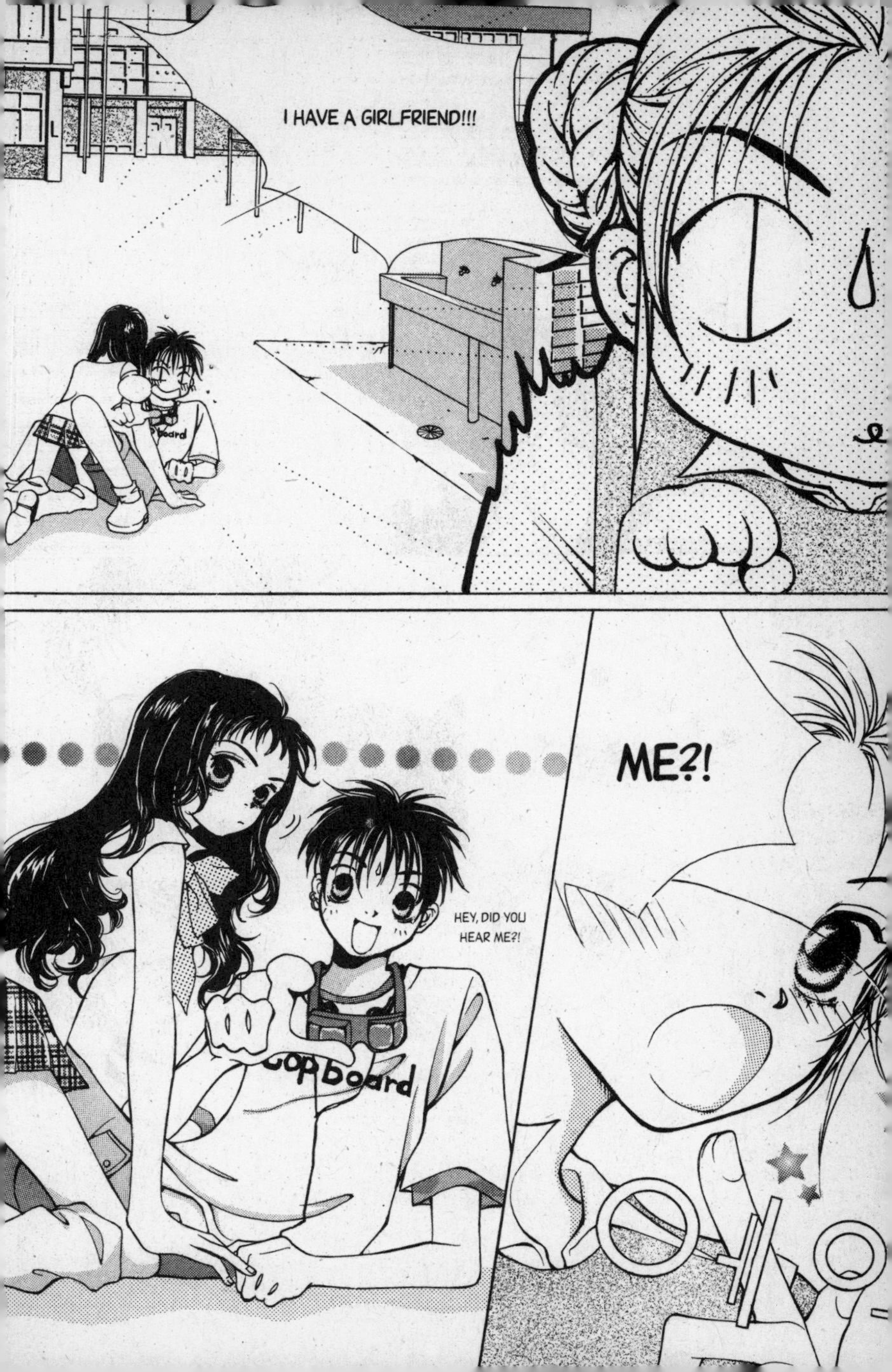
I HAVE A GIRLFRIEND!!!
ME?!
HEY, DID YOU HEAR ME?!

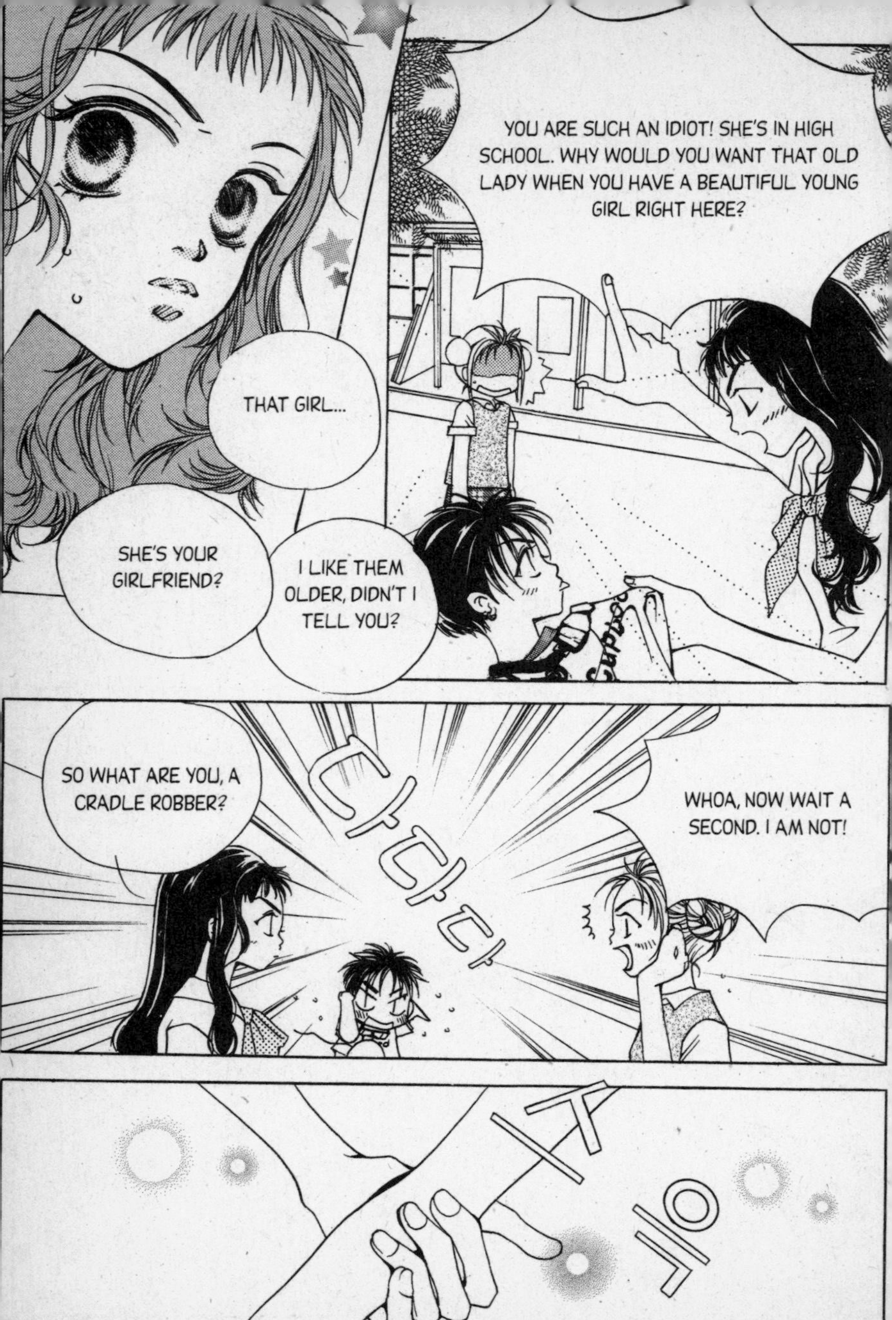
THAT GIRL...
SHE'S YOUR GIRLFRIEND?
I LIKE THEM OLDER, DIDN'T I TELL YOU?
YOU ARE SUCH AN IDIOT! SHE'S IN HIGH SCHOOL.. WHY WOULD YOU WANT THAT OLD LADY WHEN YOU HAVE A BEAUTIFUL YOUNG GIRL RIGHT HERE?
SO WHAT ARE YOU, A CRADLE ROBBER?
WHOA, NOW WAIT A SECOND. I AM NOT!

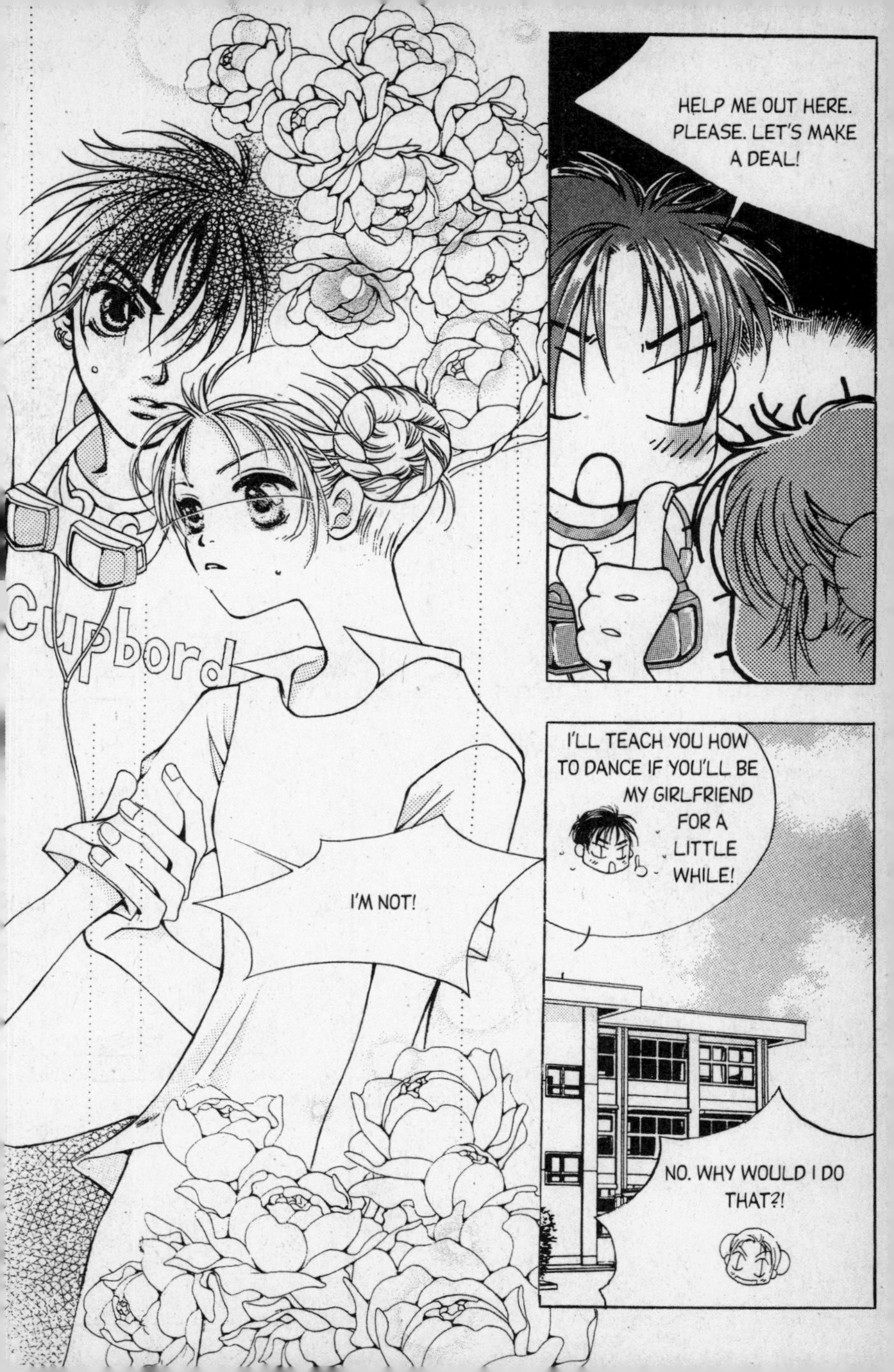
HELP ME OUT HERE. PLEASE. LET'S MAKE A DEAL!
I'LL TEACH YOU HOW TO DANCE IF YOU'LL BE MY GIRLFRIEND FOR A LITTLE WHILE!
NO. WHY WOULD I DO THAT?!
Cupbord
I'M NOT!

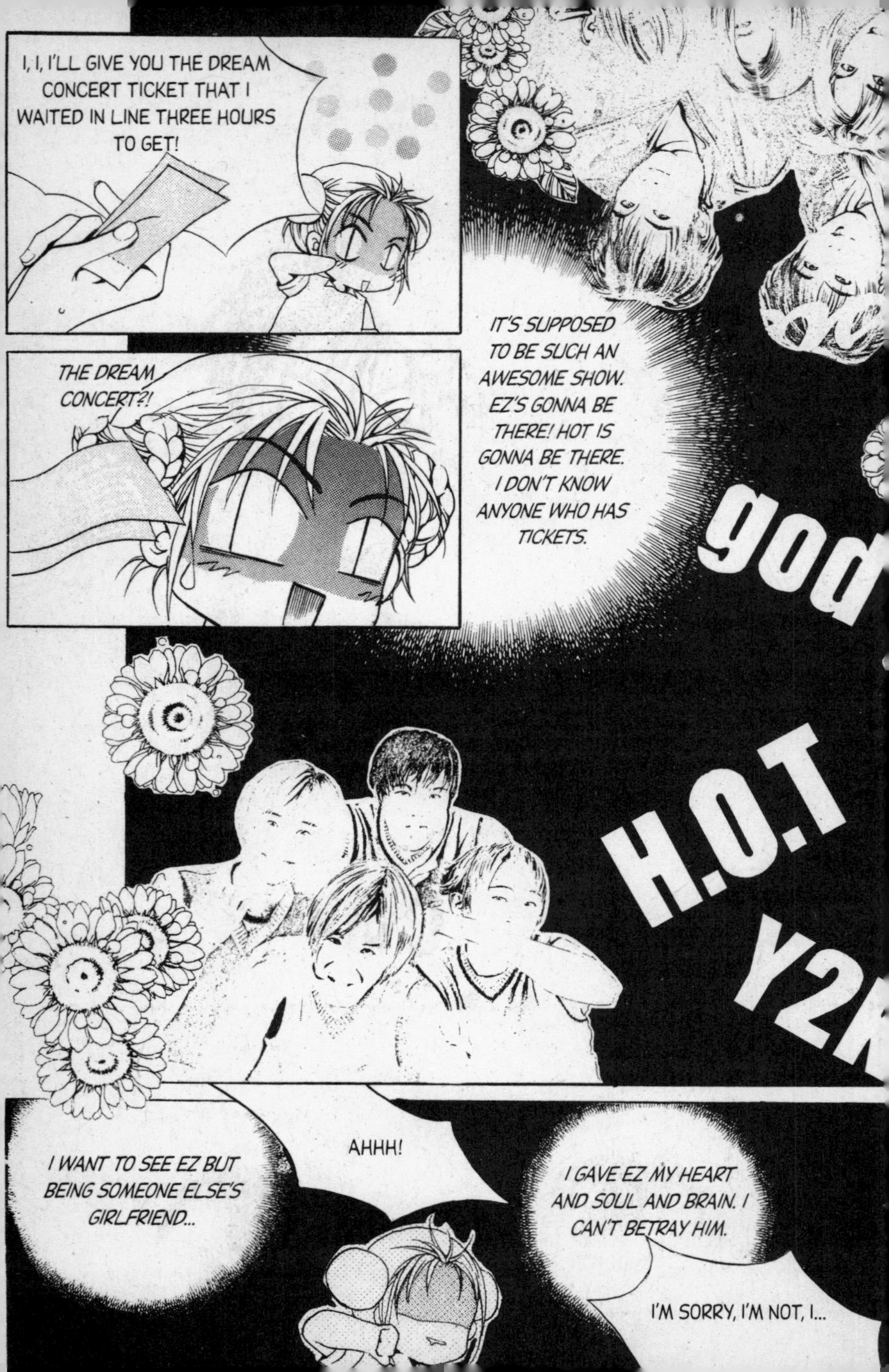
I, I, I'LL GIVE YOU THE DREAM CONCERT TICKET THAT I WAITED IN LINE THREE HOURS TO GET!
THE DREAM CONCERT?!
IT'S SUPPOSED TO BE SUCH AN AWESOME SHOW. EZ'S GONNA BE THERE! HOT IS GONNA BE THERE. I DON'T KNOW ANYONE WHO HAS TICKETS.
god
H.O.T
I WANT TO SEE EZ BUT BEING SOMEONE ELSE'S GIRLFRIEND...
AHHH!
I GAVE EZ MY HEART AND SOUL AND BRAIN. I CAN'T BETRAY HIM.
I'M SORRY, I'M NOT, I...

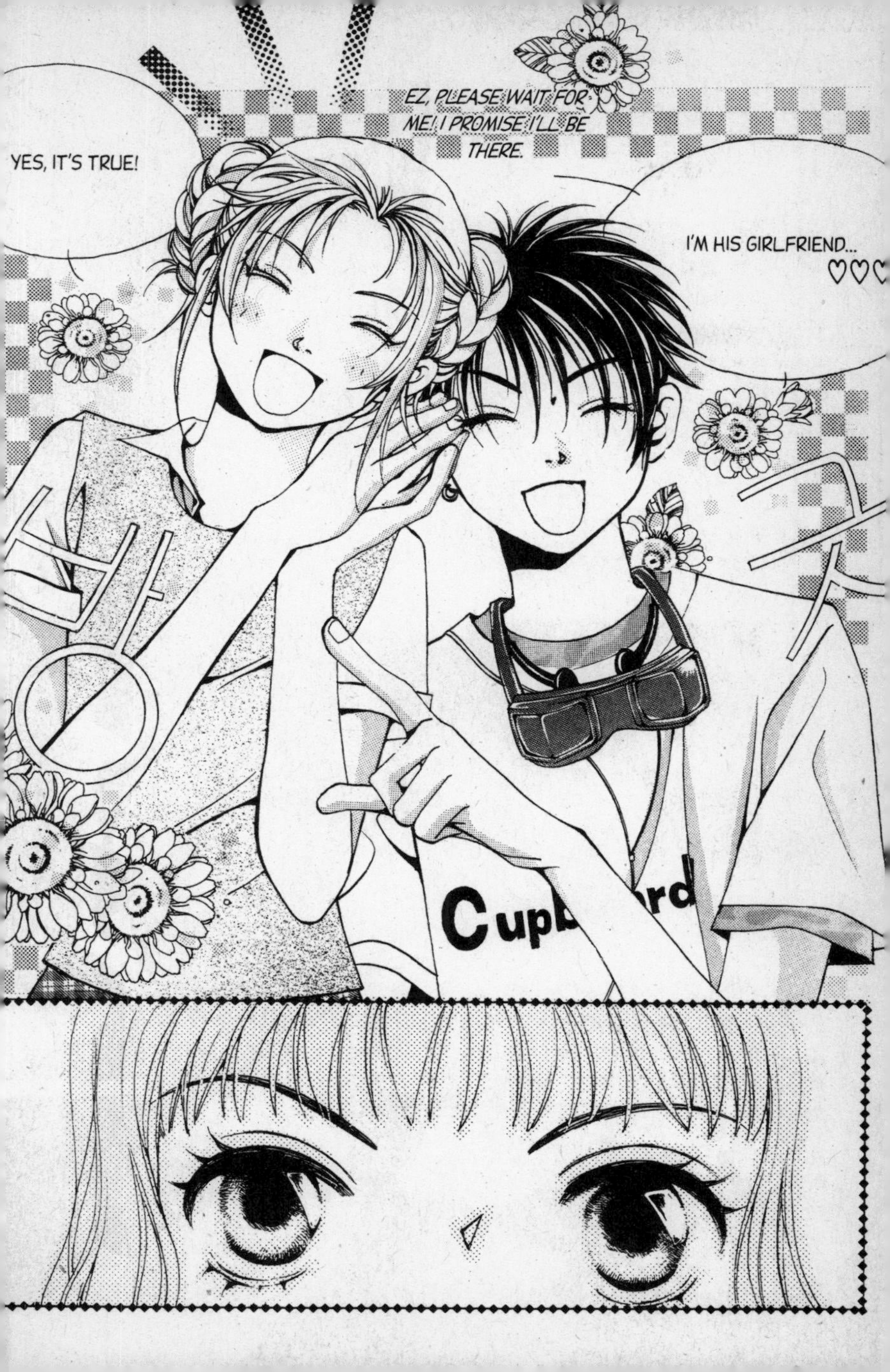
EZ, PLEASE WAIT FOR ME! I PROMISE I'LL BE THERE.
I'M HIS GIRLFRIEND... ♡♡♡
YES, IT'S TRUE!

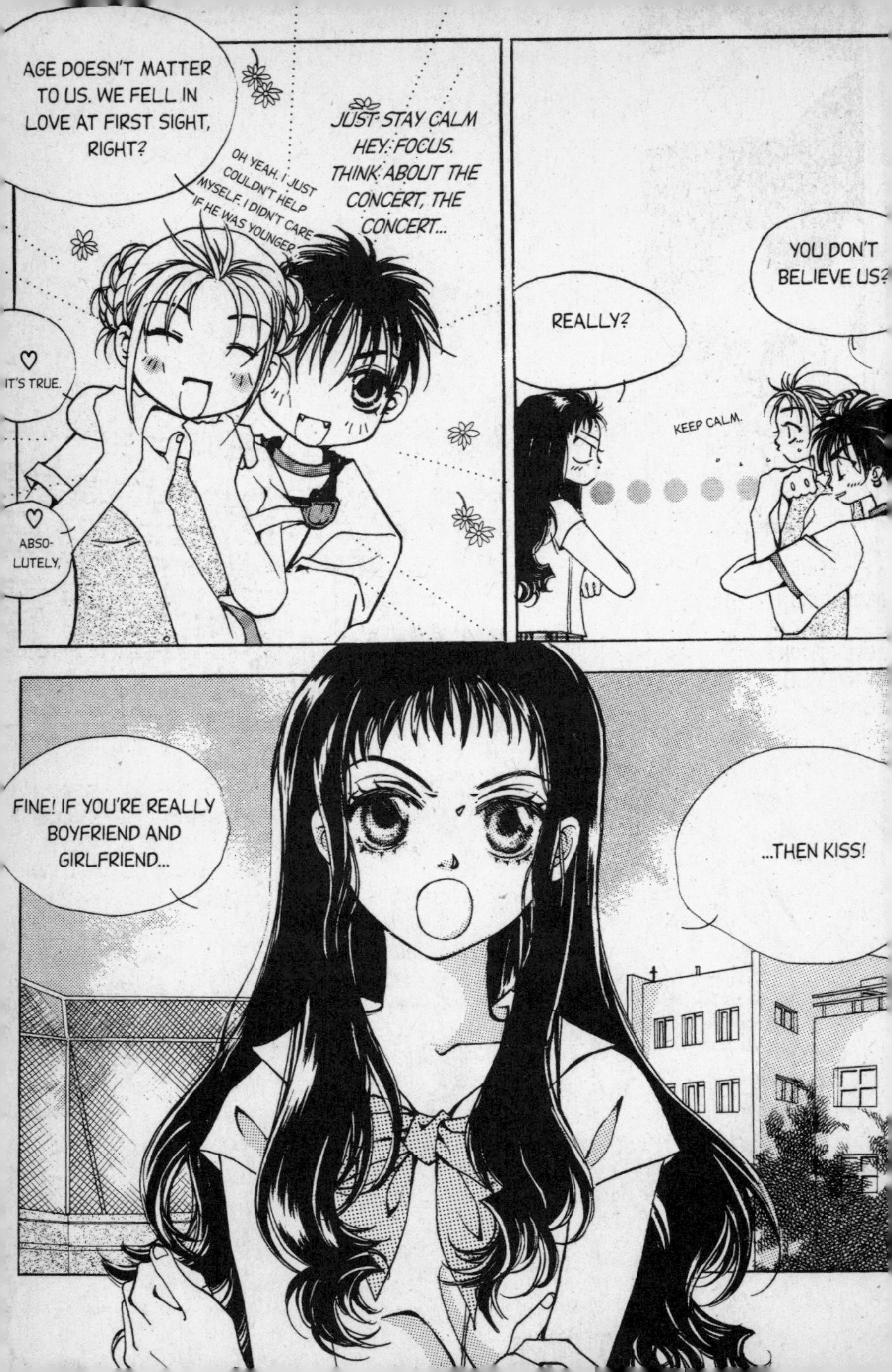

AGE DOESN'T MATTER TO US. WE FELL IN LOVE AT FIRST SIGHT, RIGHT?
OH YEAH. I JUST COULDN'T HELP MYSELF. I DIDN'T CARE IF HE WAS YOUNGER.
JUST STAY CALM HEY. FOCUS. THINK ABOUT THE CONCERT, THE CONCERT...
♡ IT'S TRUE.
♡ ABSO-LUTELY,
REALLY?
YOU DON'T BELIEVE US?
KEEP CALM.
FINE! IF YOU'RE REALLY BOYFRIEND AND GIRLFRIEND...
...THEN KISS!

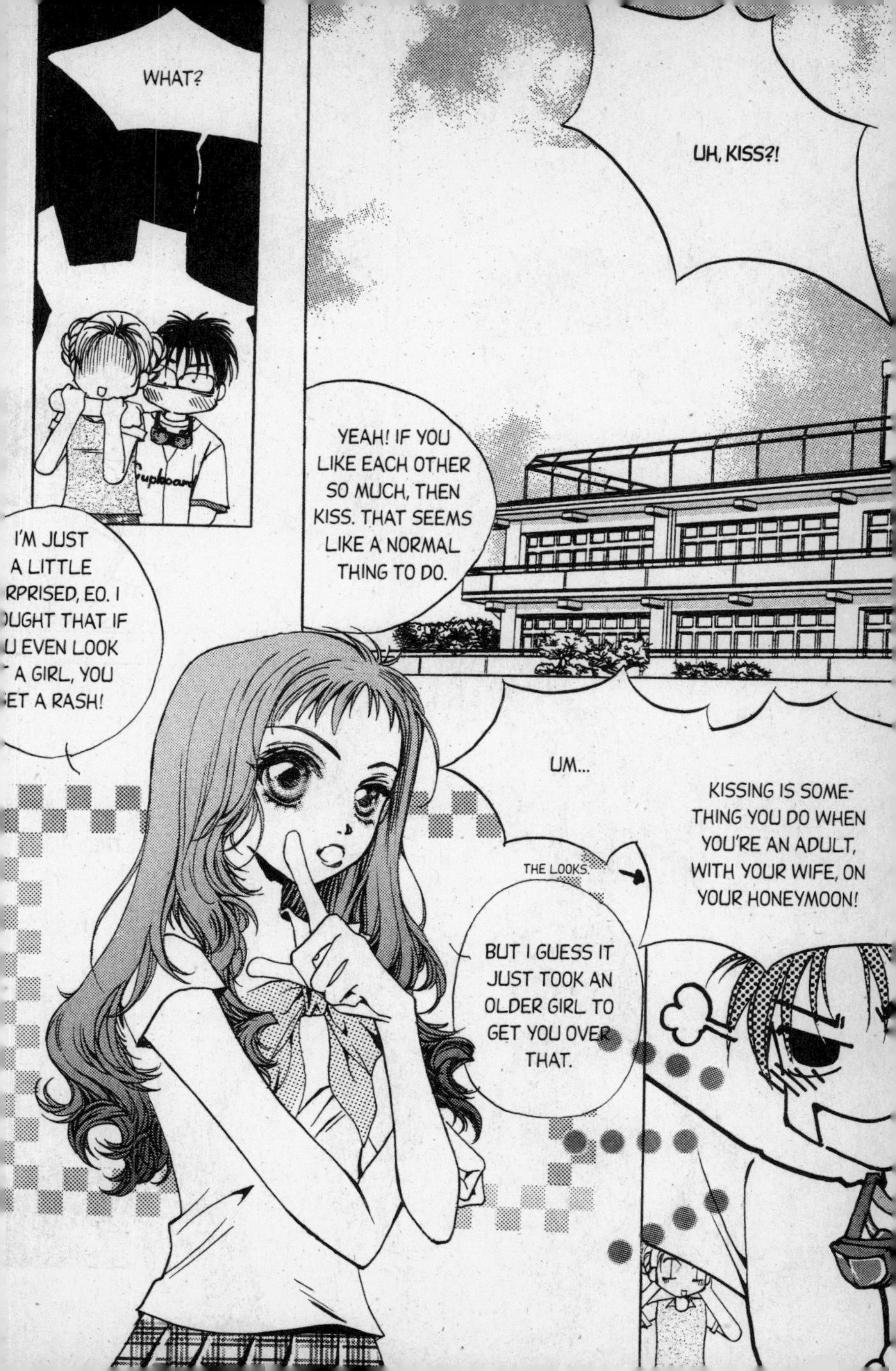
UH, KISS?!
YEAH! IF YOU LIKE EACH OTHER SO MUCH, THEN KISS. THAT SEEMS LIKE A NORMAL THING TO DO.
WHAT?
KISSING IS SOME-THING YOU DO WHEN YOU'RE AN ADULT, WITH YOUR WIFE, ON YOUR HONEYMOON!
UM...
THE LOOKS.
BUT I GUESS IT JUST TOOK AN OLDER GIRL TO GET YOU OVER THAT.
I'M JUST A LITTLE RPRISED, ED. I OUGHT THAT IF U EVEN LOOK T A GIRL, YOU ET A RASH!

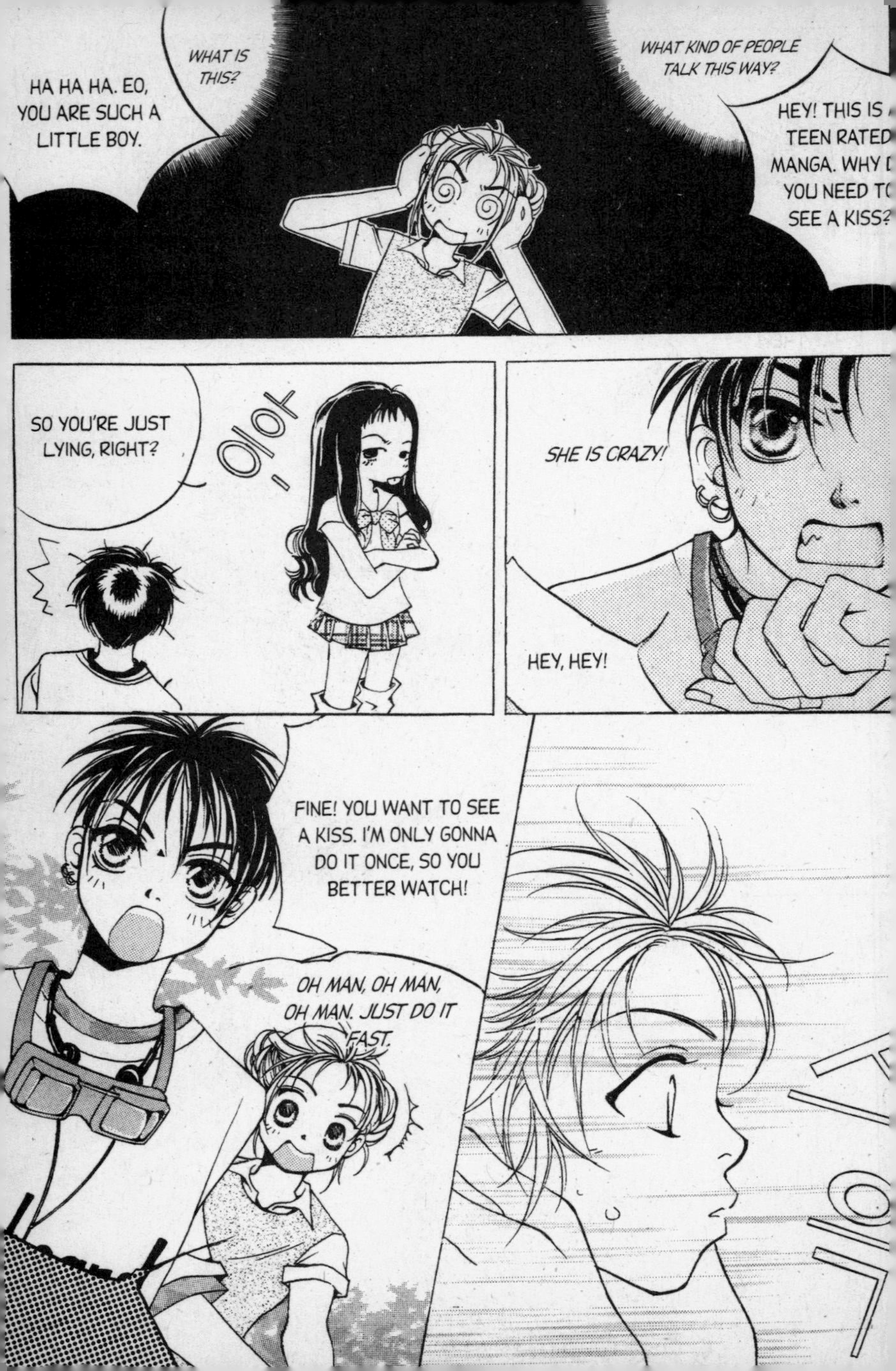
HA HA HA. EO, YOU ARE SUCH A LITTLE BOY.
WHAT IS THIS?
WHAT KIND OF PEOPLE TALK THIS WAY?
HEY! THIS IS TEEN RATED MANGA. WHY YOU NEED T SEE A KISS?
SO YOU'RE JUST LYING, RIGHT?
SHE IS CRAZY!
HEY, HEY!
FINE! YOU WANT TO SEE A KISS. I'M ONLY GONNA DO IT ONCE, SO YOU BETTER WATCH!
OH MAN, OH MAN, OH MAN. JUST DO IT FAST.

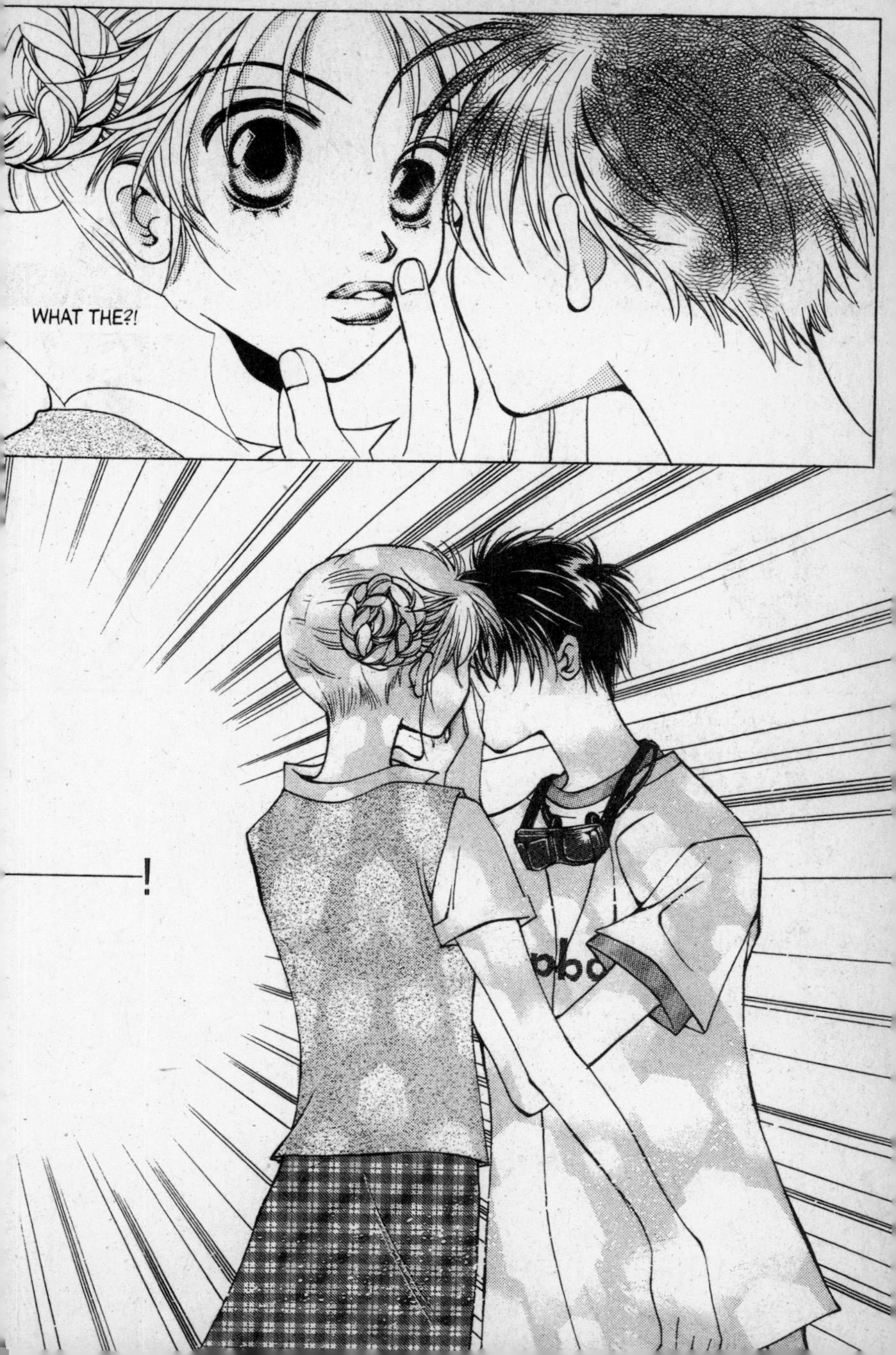
WHAT THE?!
——!

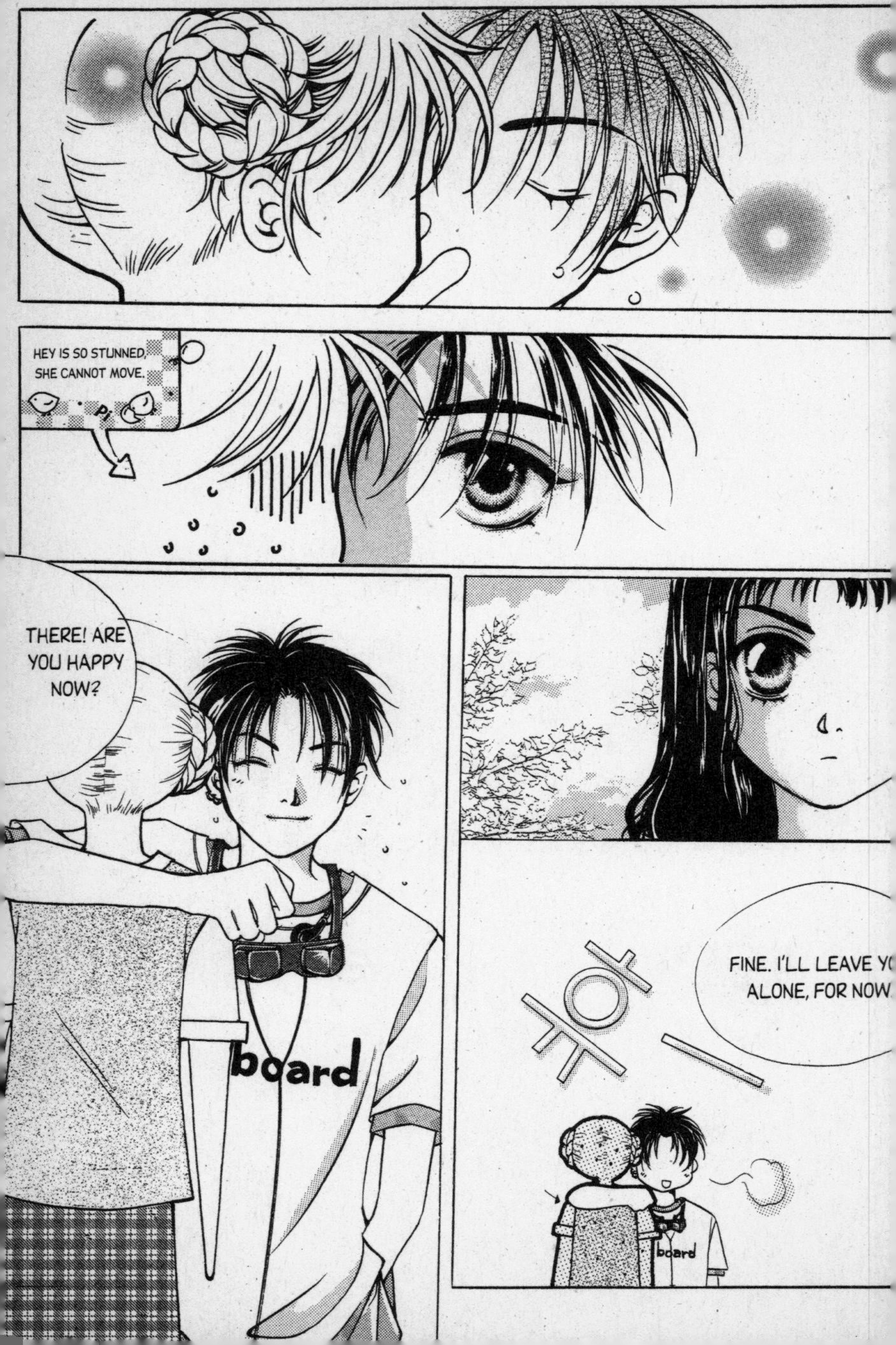
HEY IS SO STUNNED, SHE CANNOT MOVE.
Pi
THERE! ARE YOU HAPPY NOW?
board
FINE. I'LL LEAVE Y
ALONE, FOR NOW.
board

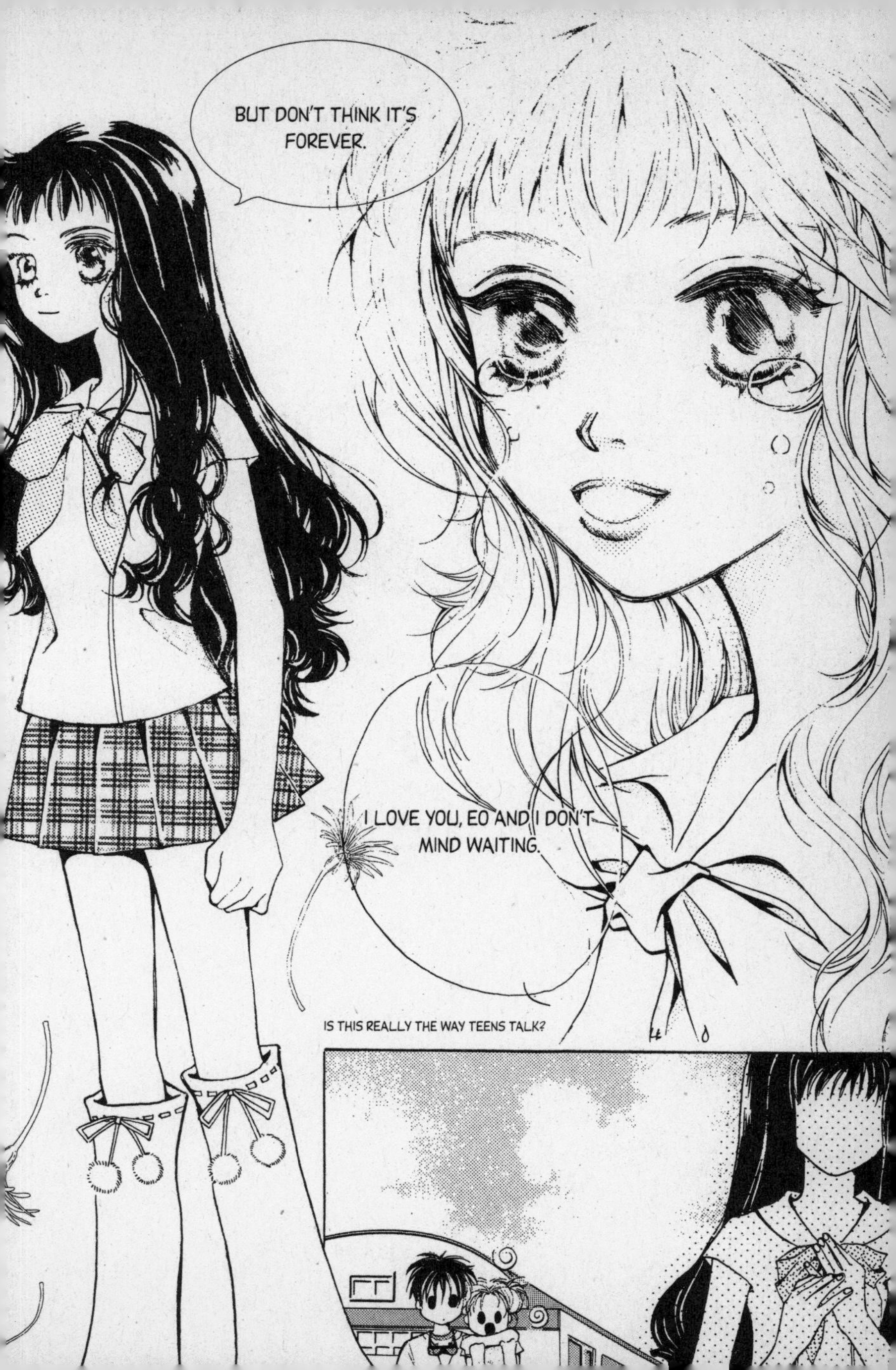
BUT DON'T THINK IT'S FOREVER.
I LOVE YOU, EO AND I DON'T MIND WAITING.
IS THIS REALLY THE WAY TEENS TALK?

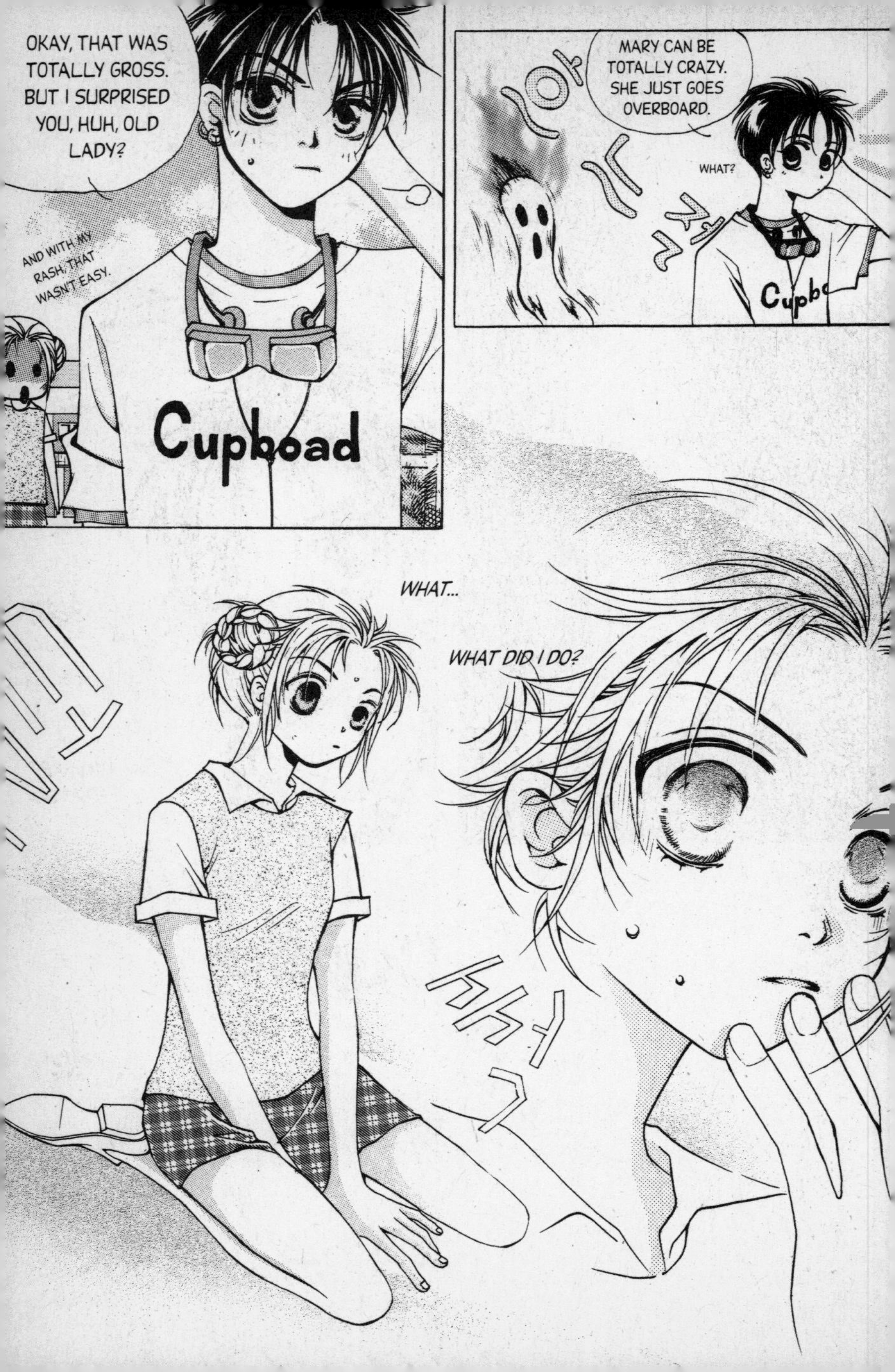
OKAY, THAT WAS TOTALLY GROSS. BUT I SURPRISED YOU, HUH, OLD LADY?
AND WITH MY RASH, THAT WASN'T EASY.
Cupboad
MARY CAN BE TOTALLY CRAZY. SHE JUST GOES OVERBOARD.
WHAT?
Cupbo
WHAT...
WHAT DID I DO?

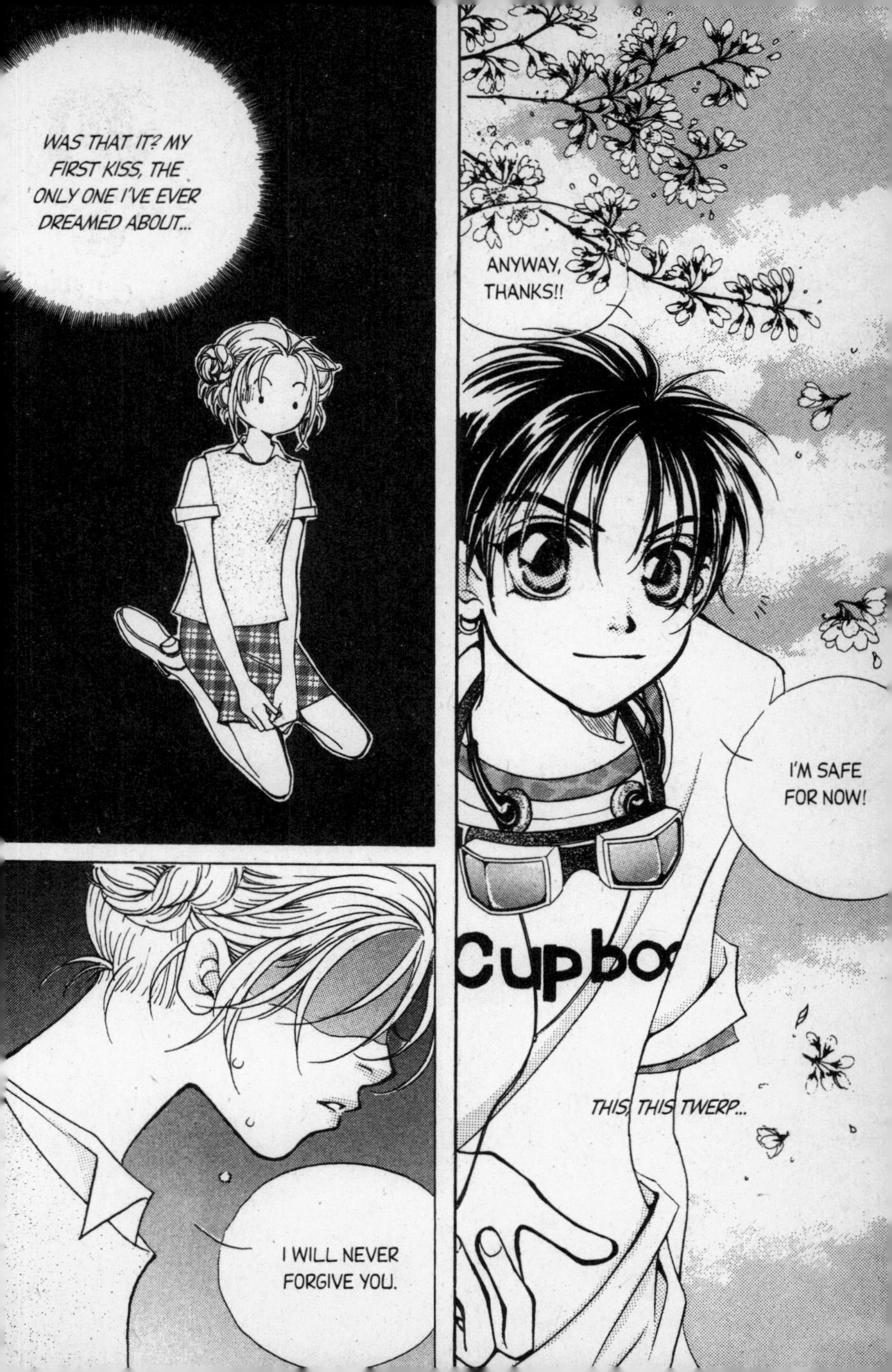
ANYWAY, THANKS!!
I'M SAFE FOR NOW!
Cupbo
THIS, THIS TWERP...
WAS THAT IT? MY FIRST KISS, THE ONLY ONE I'VE EVER DREAMED ABOUT...
I WILL NEVER FORGIVE YOU.

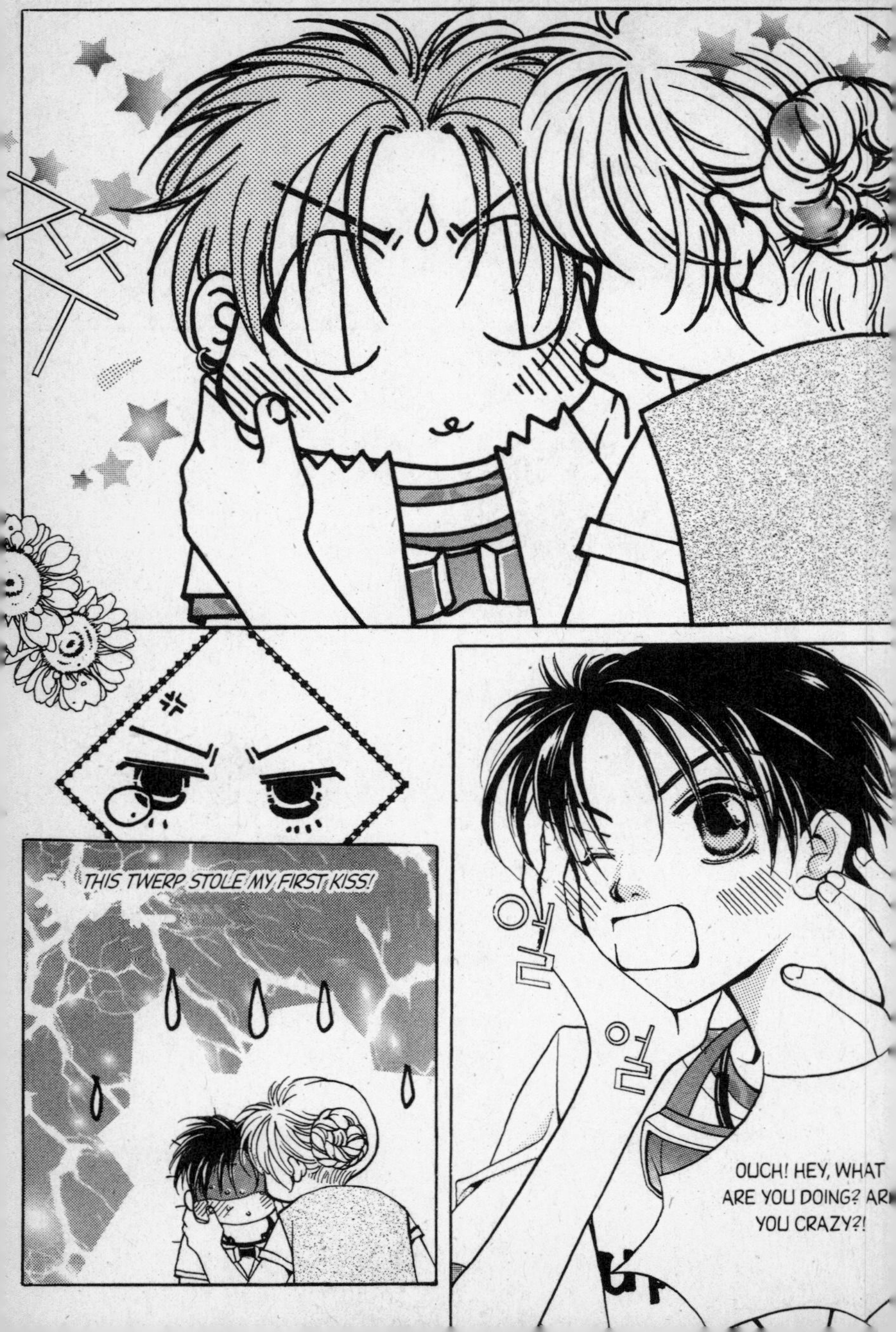
OUCH! HEY, WHAT ARE YOU DOING? AR YOU CRAZY?!
THIS TWERP STOLE MY FIRST KISS!

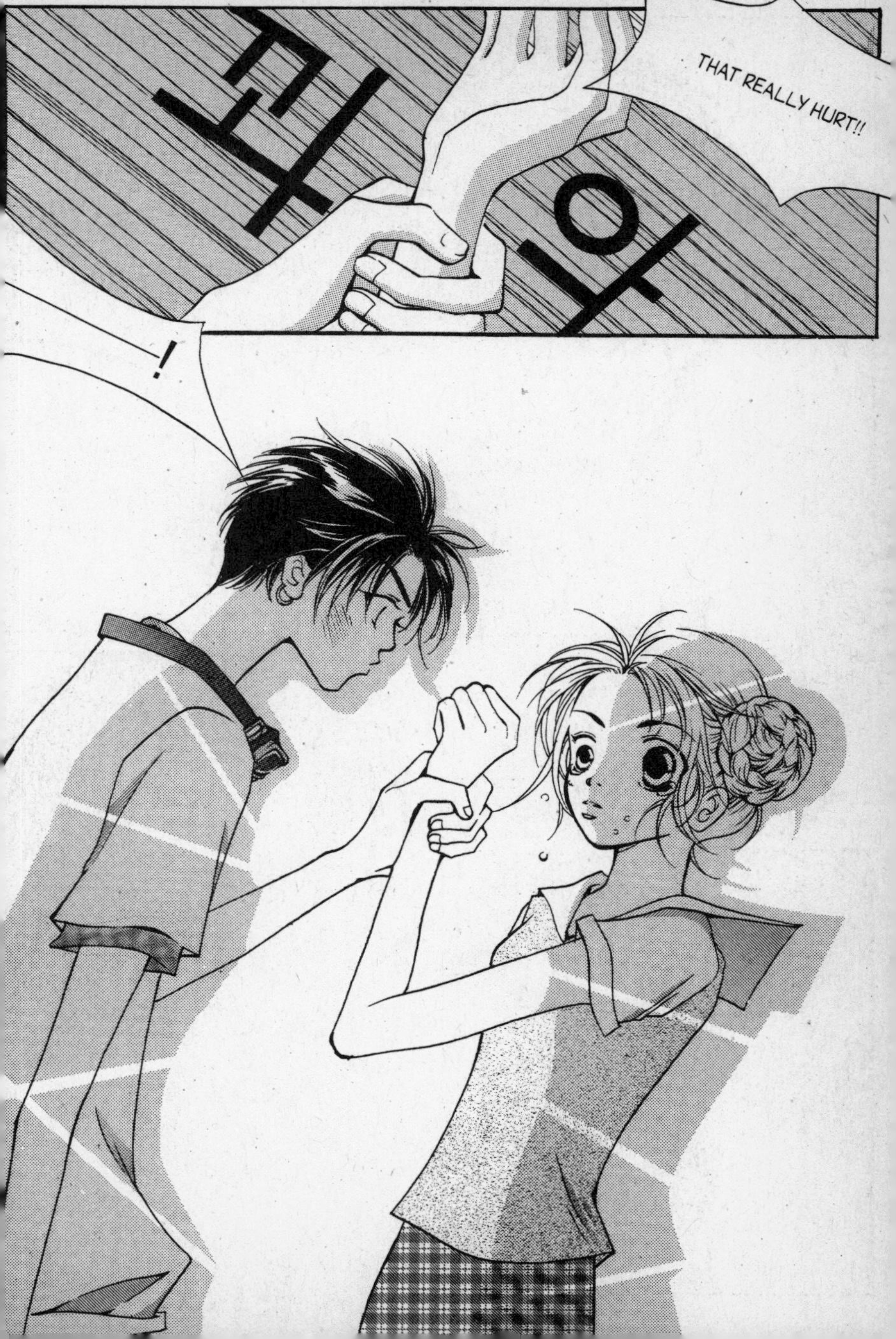
THAT REALLY HURT!!
!

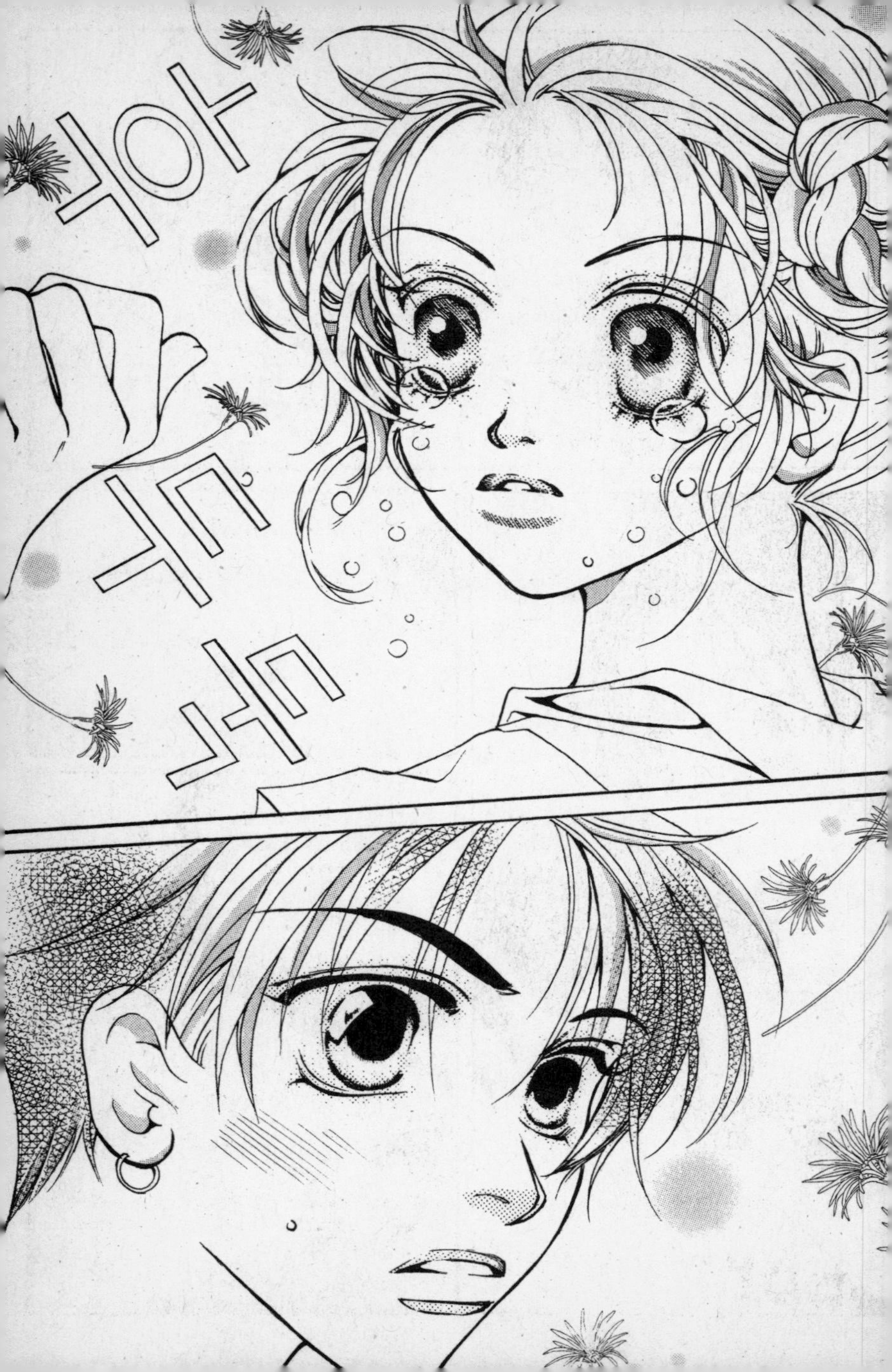

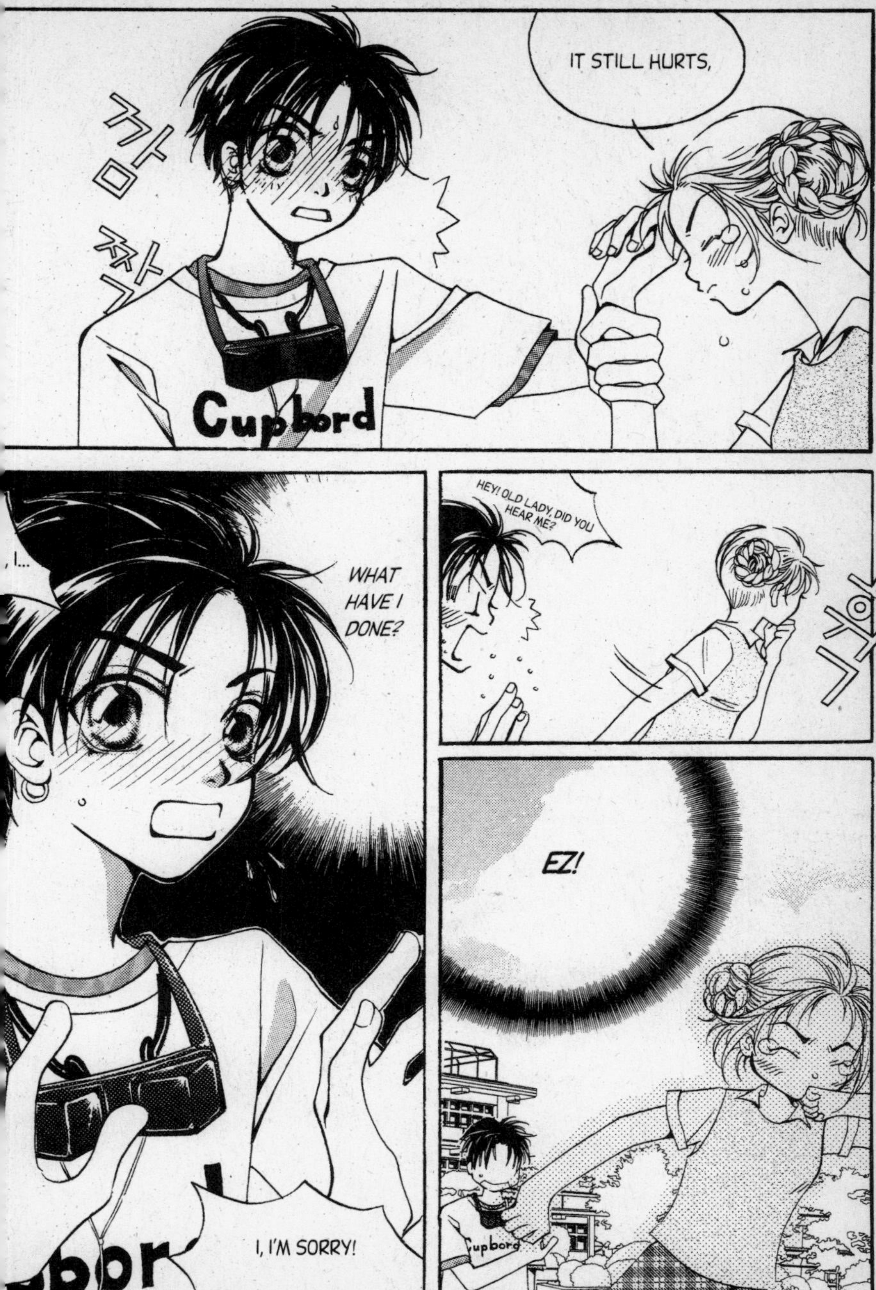
IT STILL HURTS,
깜짝
Cupbord
WHAT HAVE I DONE?
I, I'M SORRY!
HEY! OLD LADY, DID YOU HEAR ME?
EZ!
Cupbord

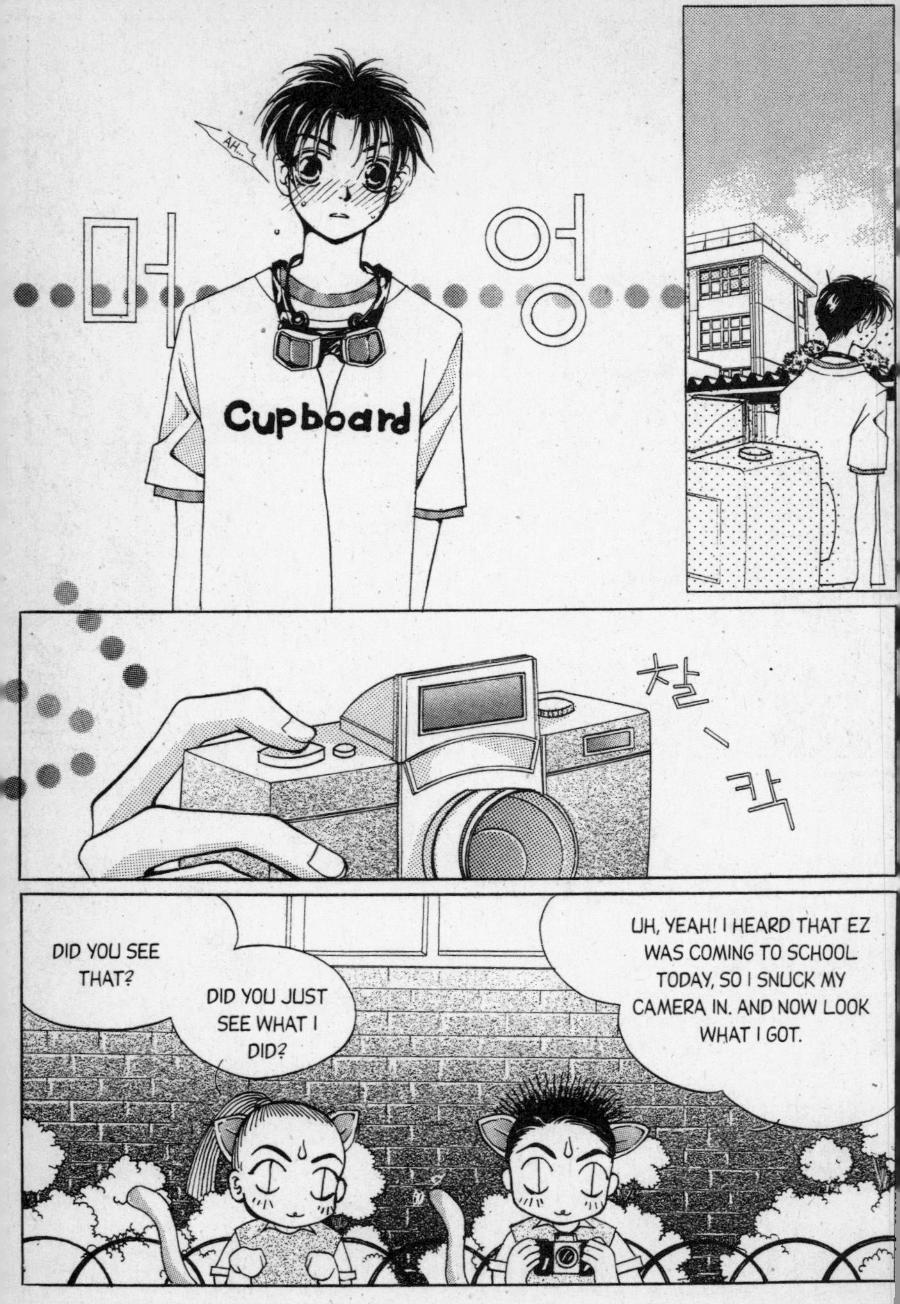

AH...
머
엉
찰 - 칵
DID YOU SEE THAT?
DID YOU JUST SEE WHAT I DID?
UH, YEAH! I HEARD THAT EZ WAS COMING TO SCHOOL TODAY, SO I SNUCK MY CAMERA IN. AND NOW LOOK WHAT I GOT.

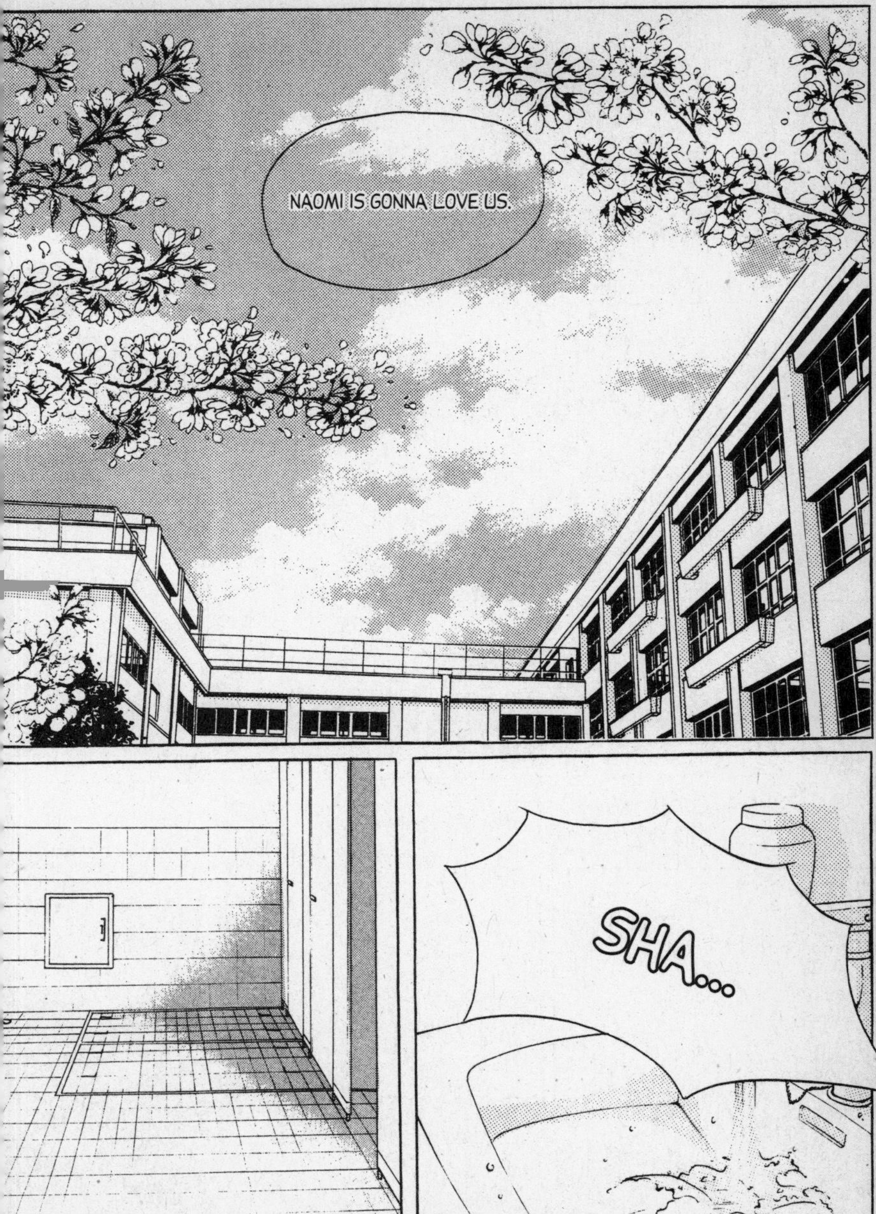
NAOMI IS GONNA LOVE US.
SHA...

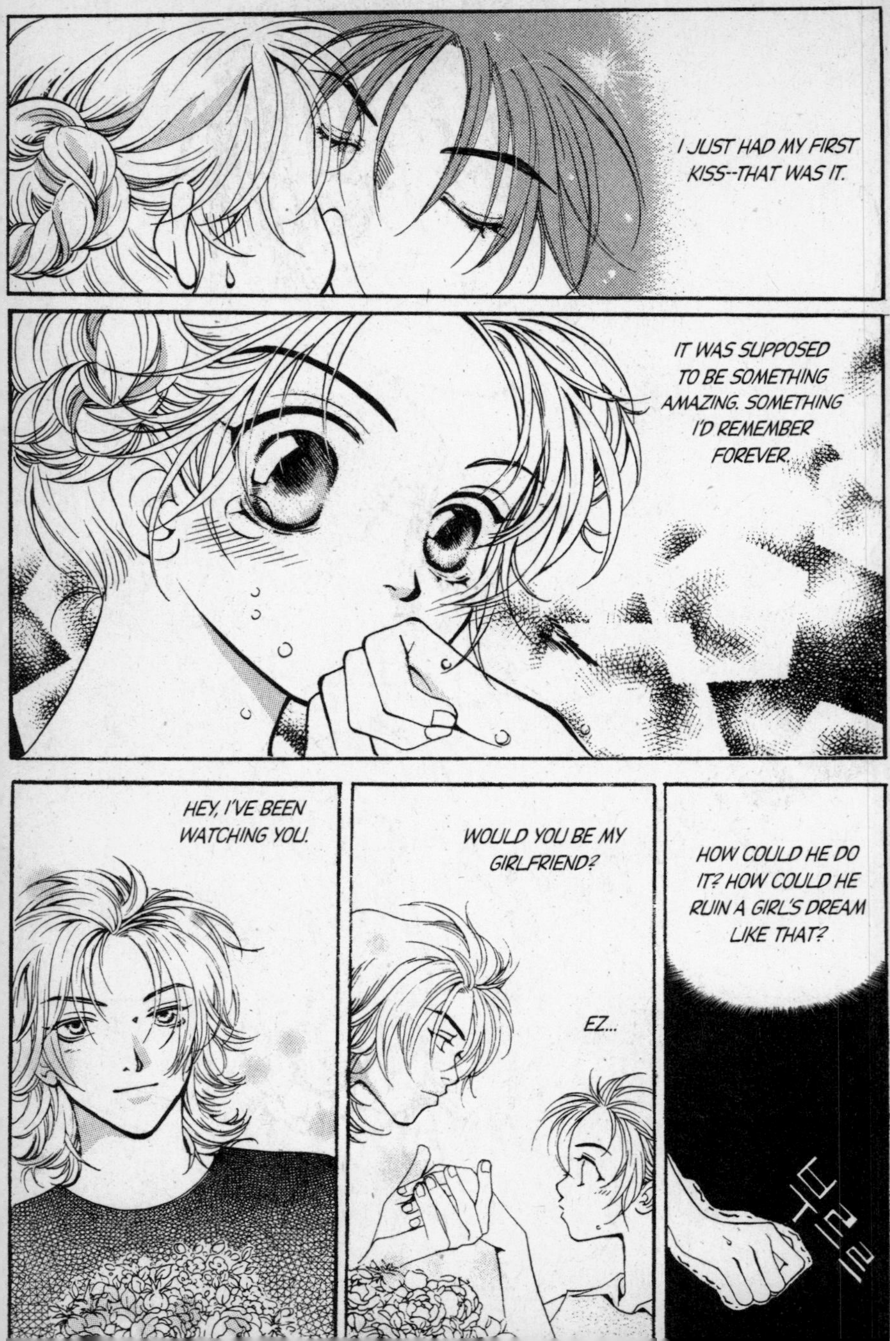
I JUST HAD MY FIRST KISS--THAT WAS IT.
IT WAS SUPPOSED TO BE SOMETHING AMAZING. SOMETHING I'D REMEMBER FOREVER.
HEY, I'VE BEEN WATCHING YOU.
WOULD YOU BE MY GIRLFRIEND?
EZ...
HOW COULD HE DO IT? HOW COULD HE RUIN A GIRL'S DREAM LIKE THAT?

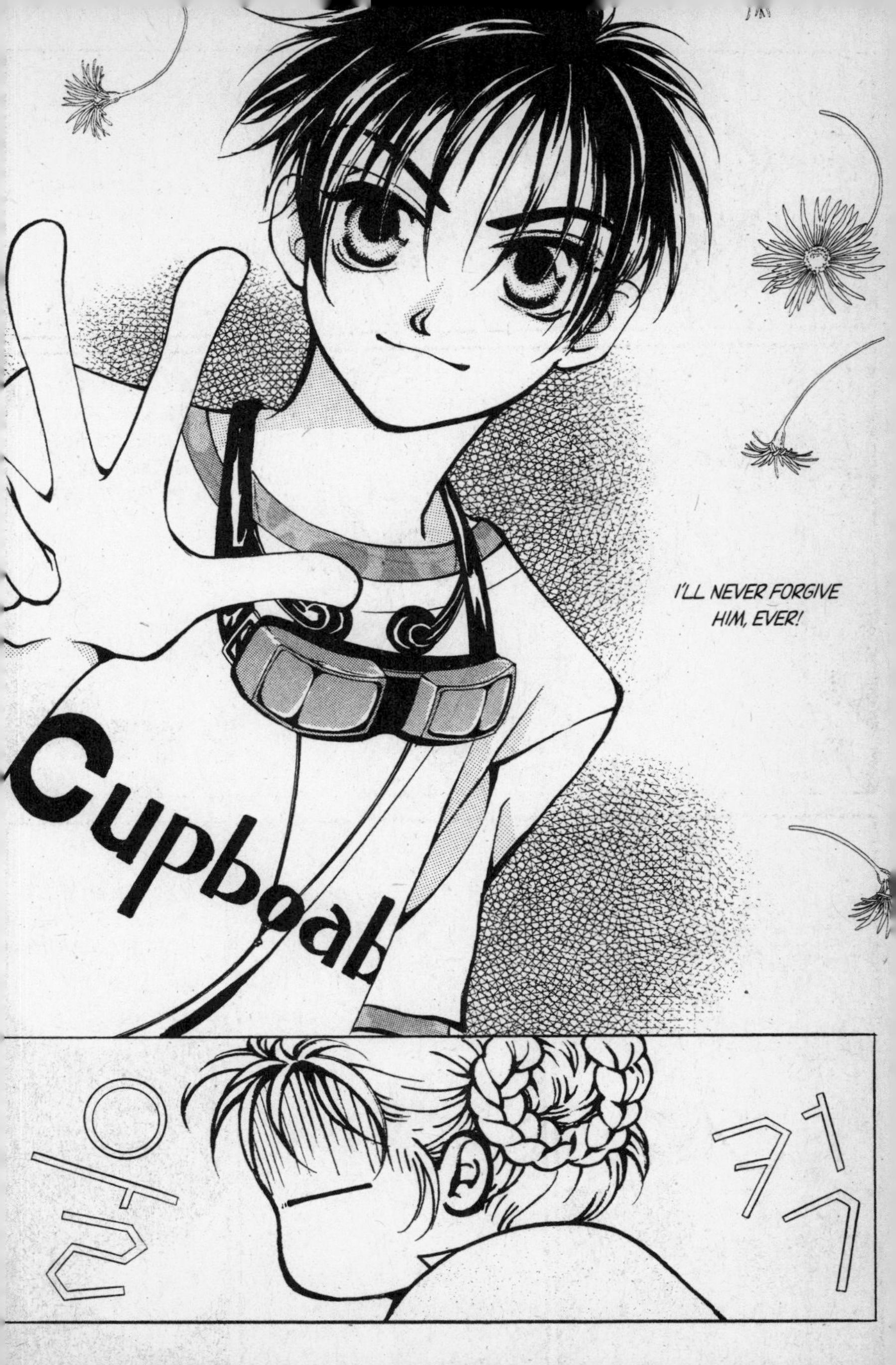
I'LL NEVER FORGIVE HIM, EVER!
Cupboab

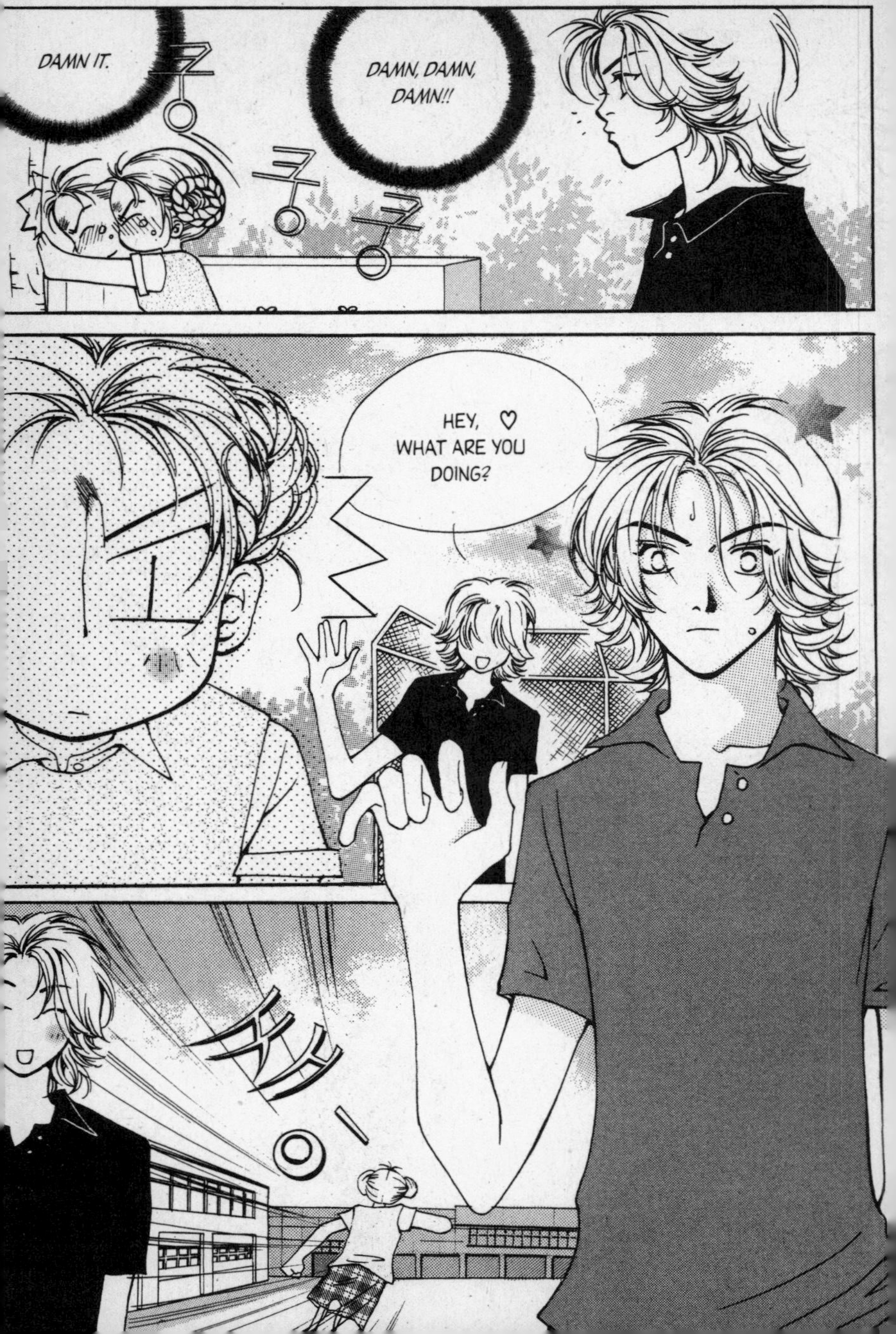
DAMN IT.
DAMN, DAMN, DAMN!!
HEY, ♡ WHAT ARE YOU DOING?

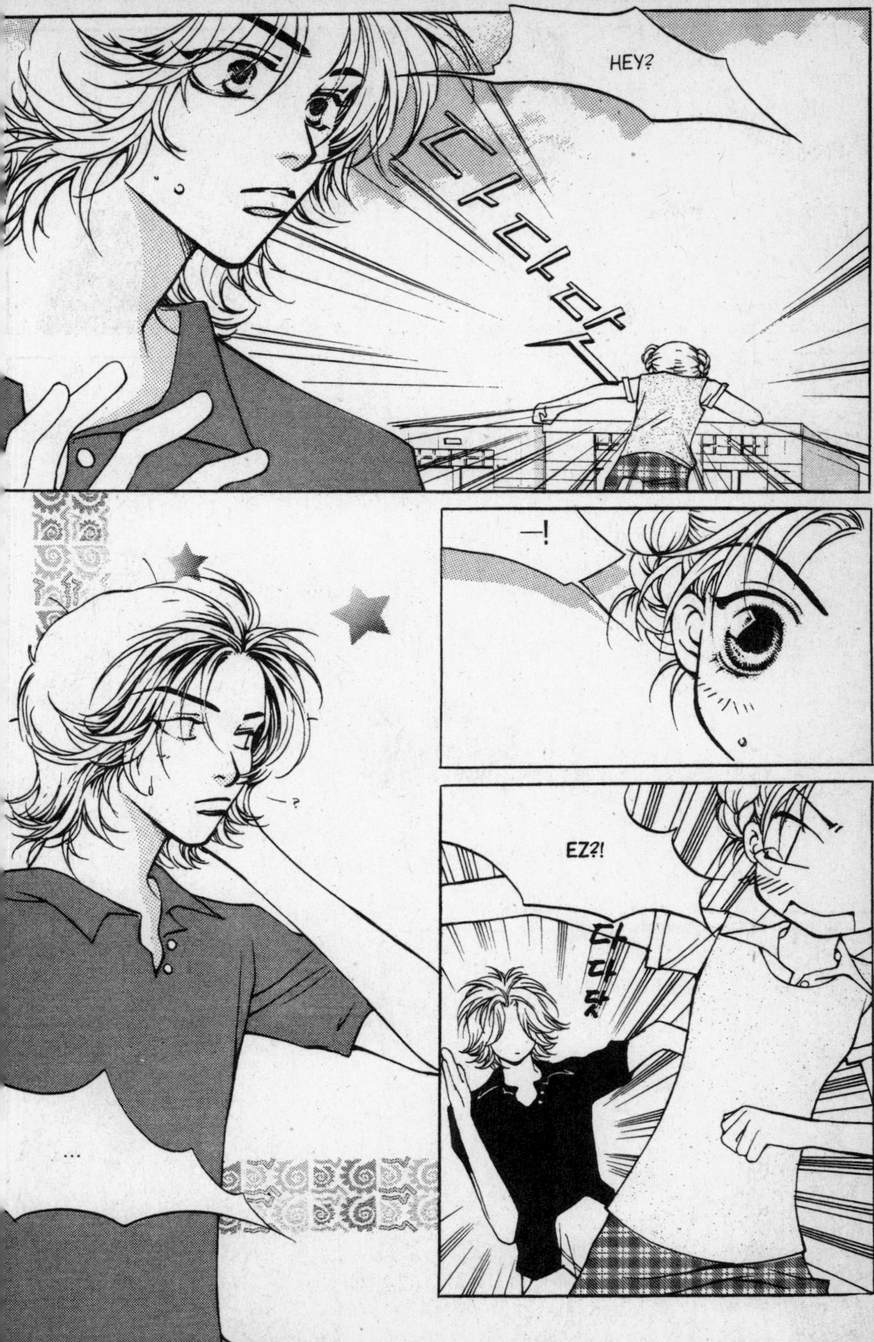
HEY?
—?
...
—!
EZ?!
다다닥

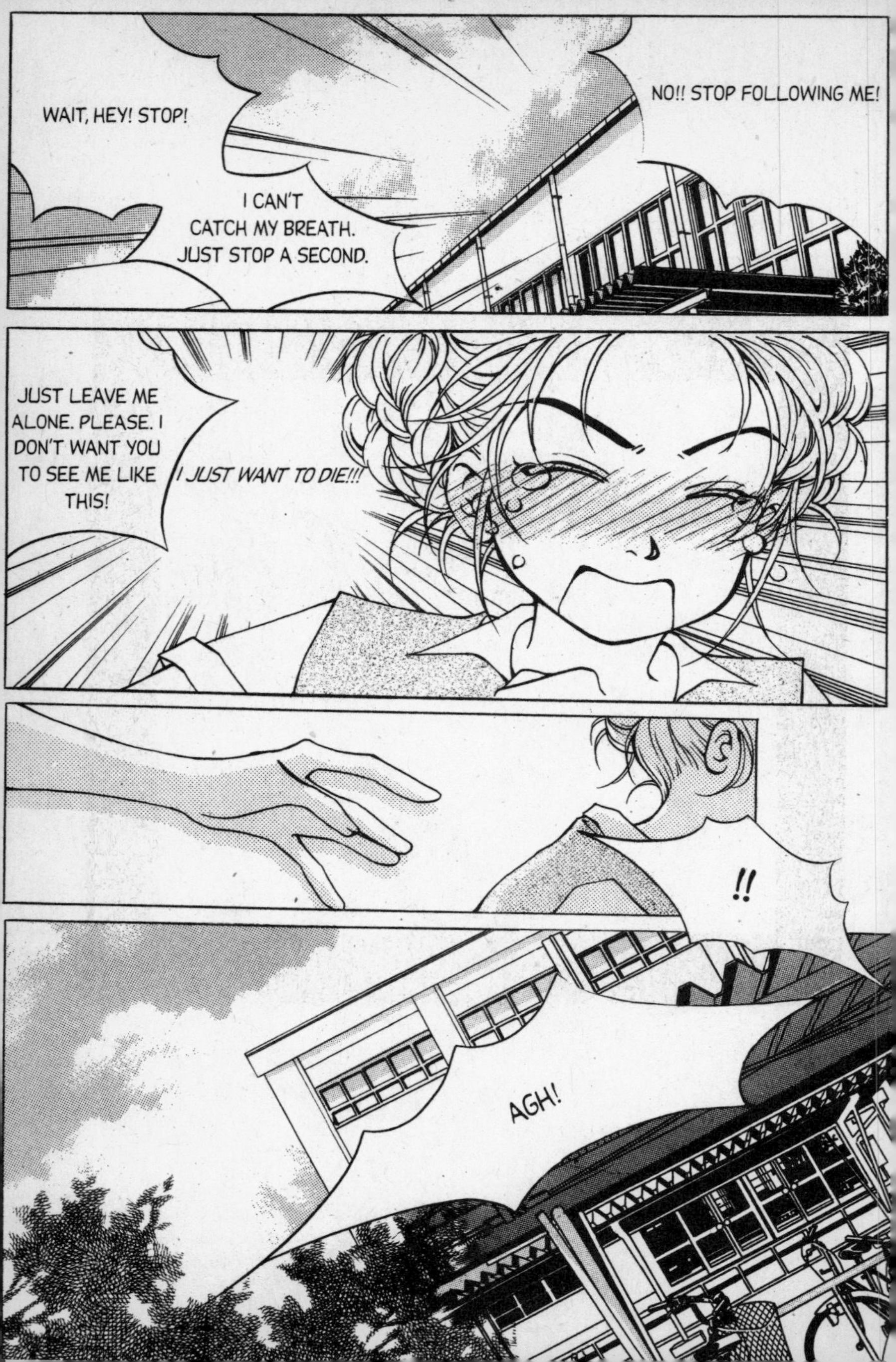
NO!! STOP FOLLOWING ME!
WAIT, HEY! STOP!
I CAN'T CATCH MY BREATH. JUST STOP A SECOND.
JUST LEAVE ME ALONE. PLEASE. I DON'T WANT YOU TO SEE ME LIKE THIS!
I JUST WANT TO DIE!!!
!!
AGH!

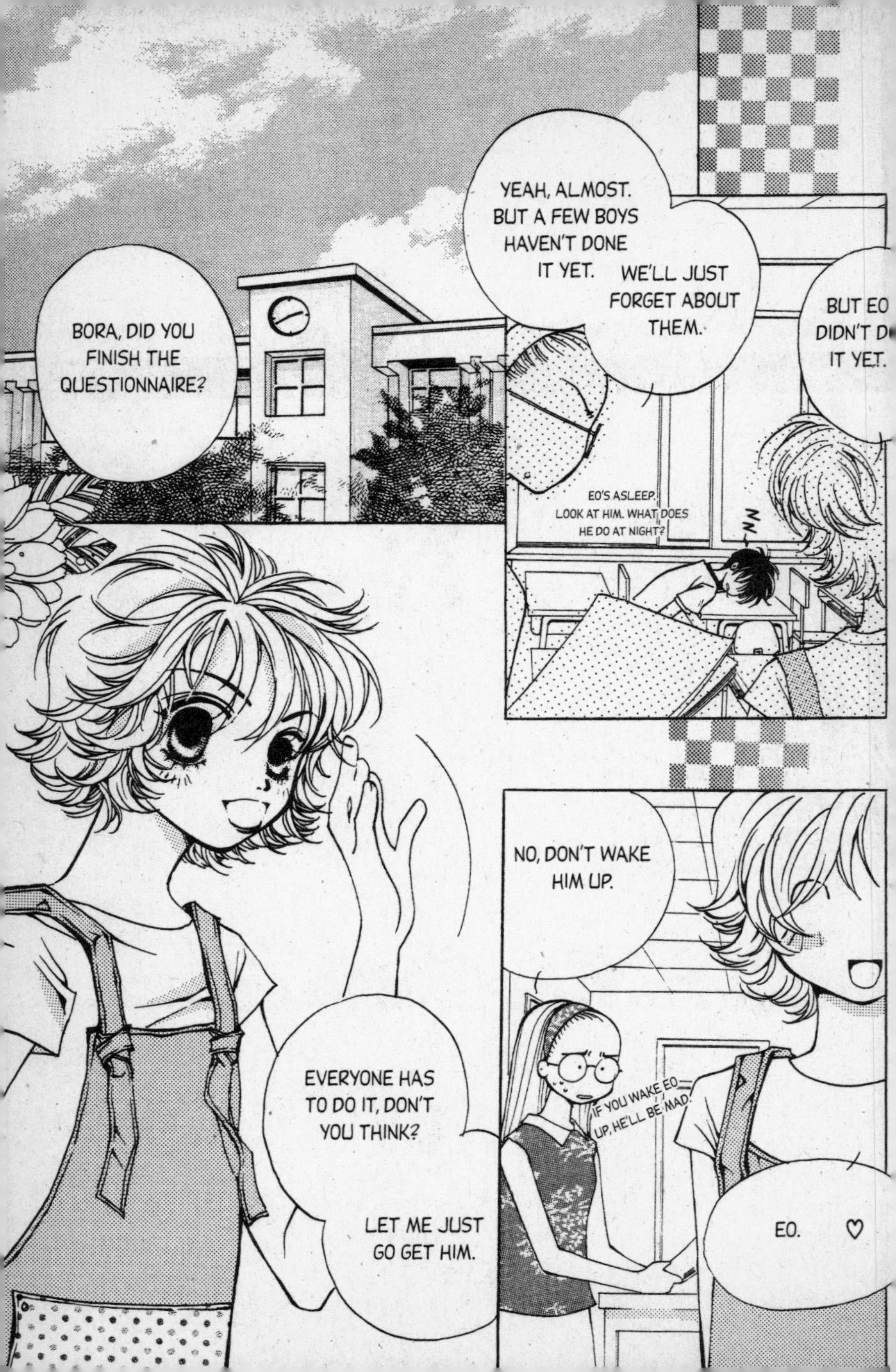
BORA, DID YOU FINISH THE QUESTIONNAIRE?
YEAH, ALMOST. BUT A FEW BOYS HAVEN'T DONE IT YET.
WE'LL JUST FORGET ABOUT THEM.
BUT EO DIDN'T D IT YET.
EO'S ASLEEP. LOOK AT HIM. WHAT DOES HE DO AT NIGHT?
EVERYONE HAS TO DO IT, DON'T YOU THINK?
LET ME JUST GO GET HIM.
NO, DON'T WAKE HIM UP.
IF YOU WAKE EO UP, HE'LL BE MAD.
EO. ♡

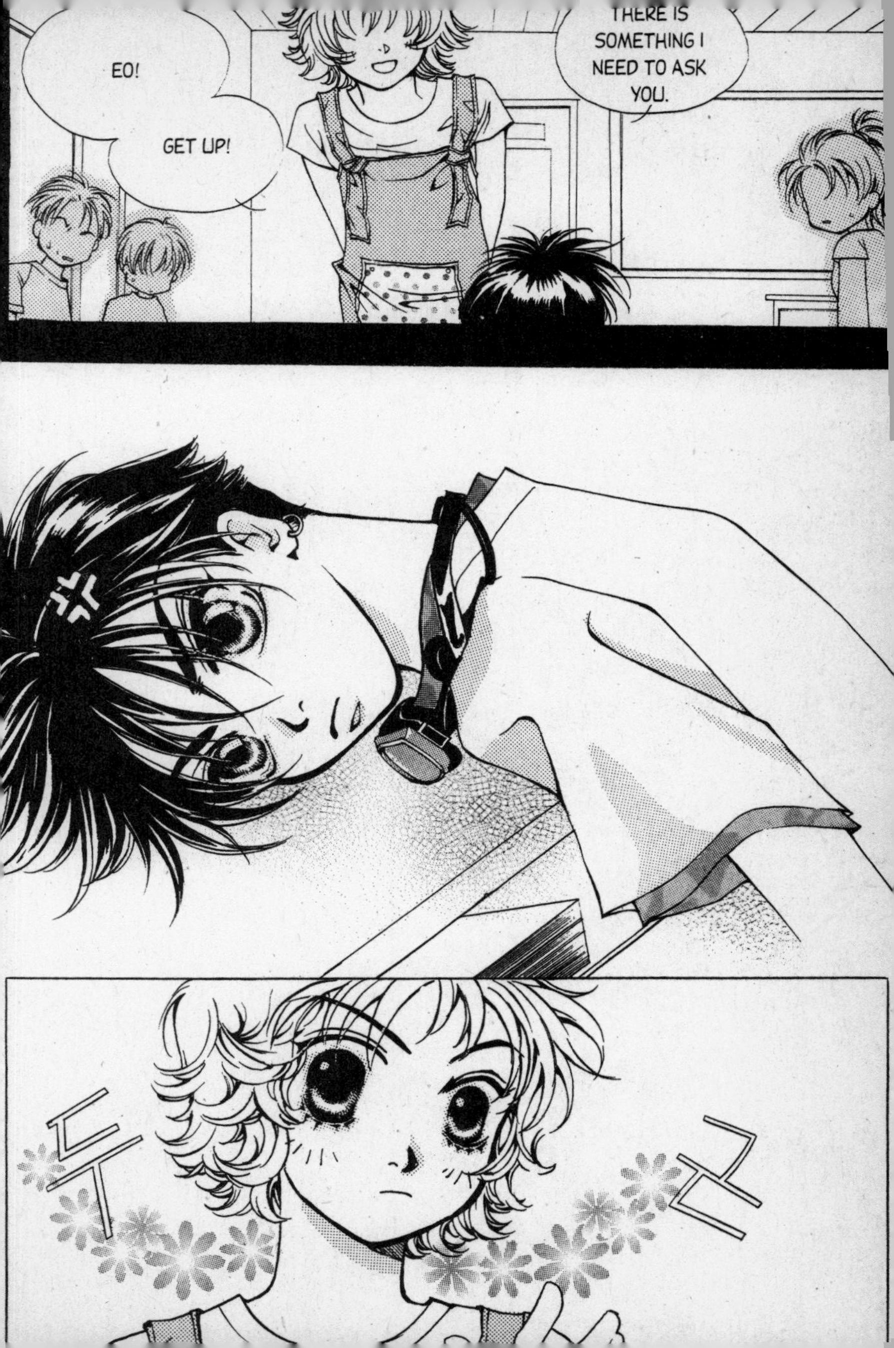
EO!
GET UP!
THERE IS SOMETHING I NEED TO ASK YOU.

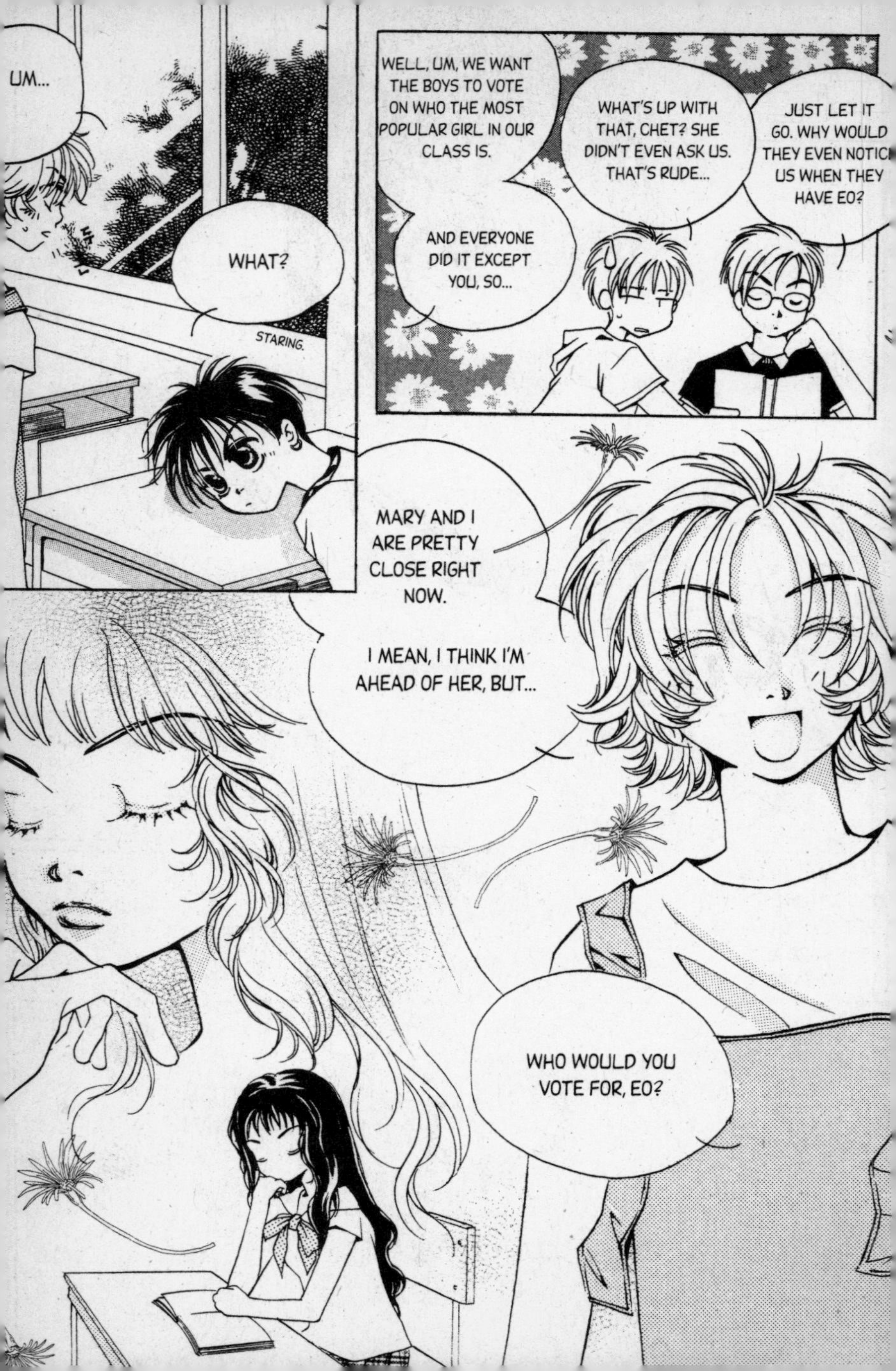
UM...
WHAT?
STARING.
WELL, UM, WE WANT THE BOYS TO VOTE ON WHO THE MOST POPULAR GIRL IN OUR CLASS IS.
AND EVERYONE DID IT EXCEPT YOU, SO...
WHAT'S UP WITH THAT, CHET? SHE DIDN'T EVEN ASK US. THAT'S RUDE...
JUST LET IT GO. WHY WOULD THEY EVEN NOTIC US WHEN THEY HAVE EO?
MARY AND I ARE PRETTY CLOSE RIGHT NOW.
I MEAN, I THINK I'M AHEAD OF HER, BUT...
WHO WOULD YOU VOTE FOR, EO?

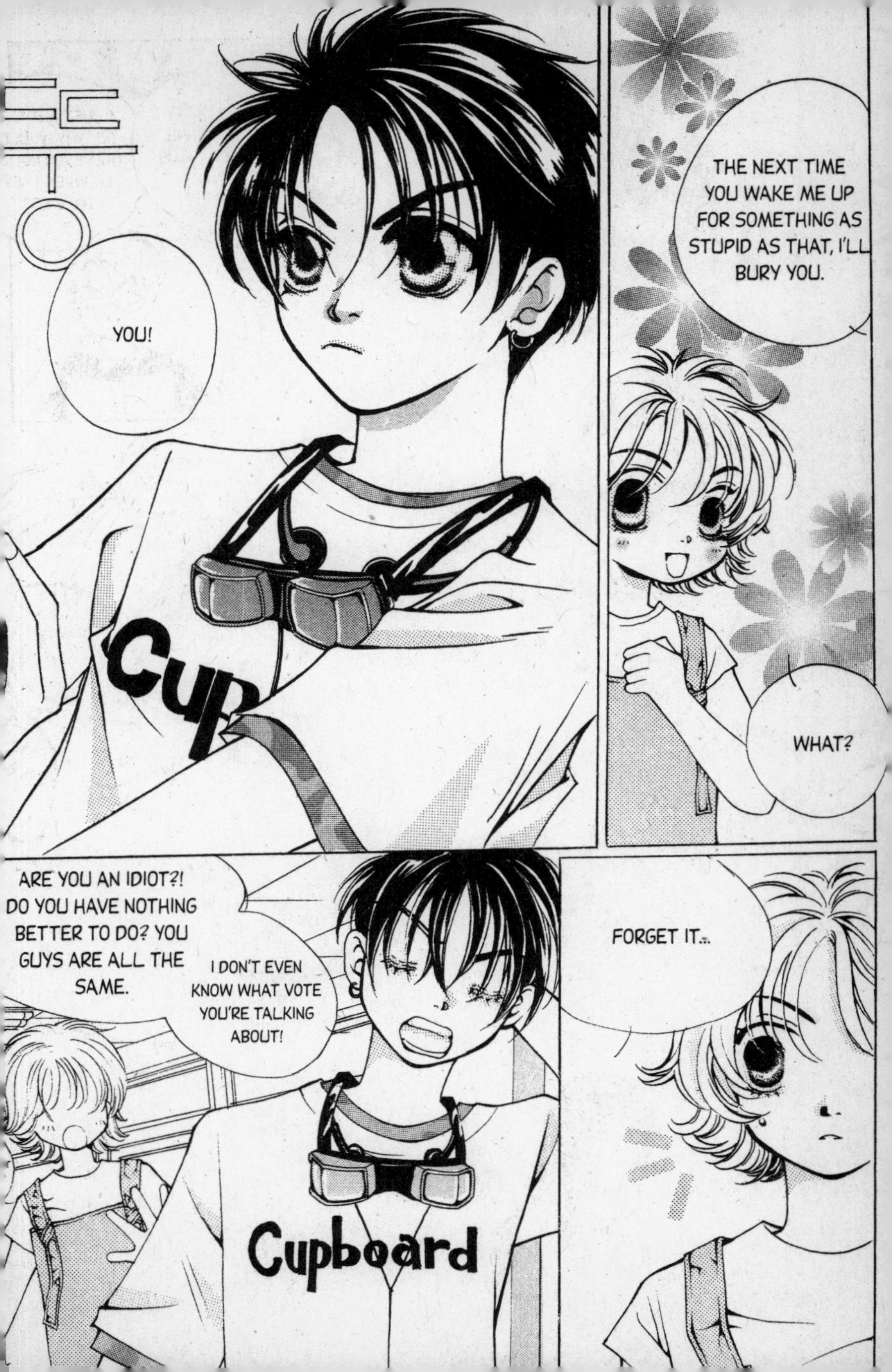
YOU!
THE NEXT TIME YOU WAKE ME UP FOR SOMETHING AS STUPID AS THAT, I'LL BURY YOU.
WHAT?
ARE YOU AN IDIOT?! DO YOU HAVE NOTHING BETTER TO DO? YOU GUYS ARE ALL THE SAME.
I DON'T EVEN KNOW WHAT VOTE YOU'RE TALKING ABOUT!
FORGET IT...
Cupboard

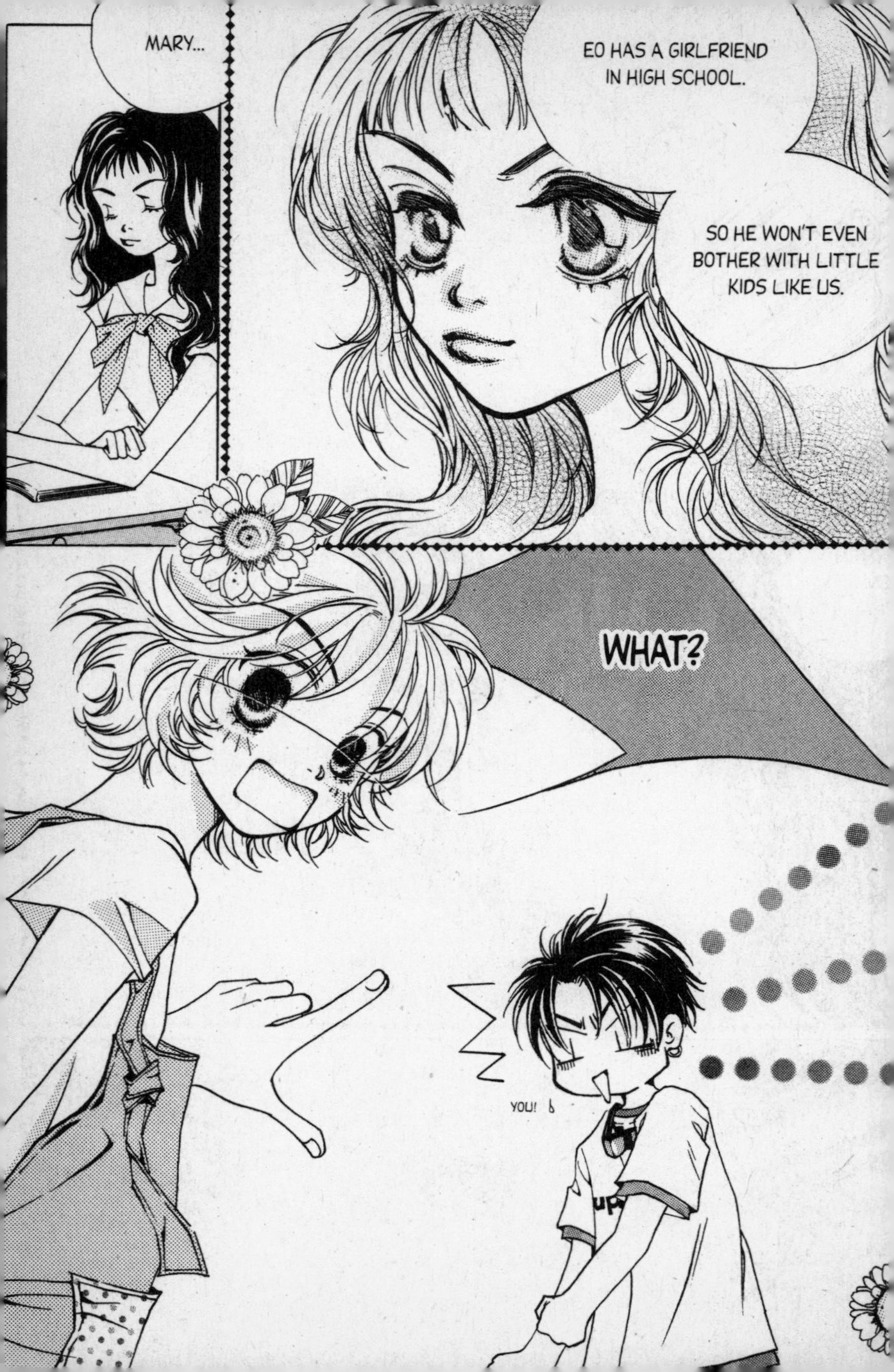
EO HAS A GIRLFRIEND IN HIGH SCHOOL.
SO HE WON'T EVEN BOTHER WITH LITTLE KIDS LIKE US.
MARY...
WHAT?
YOU!

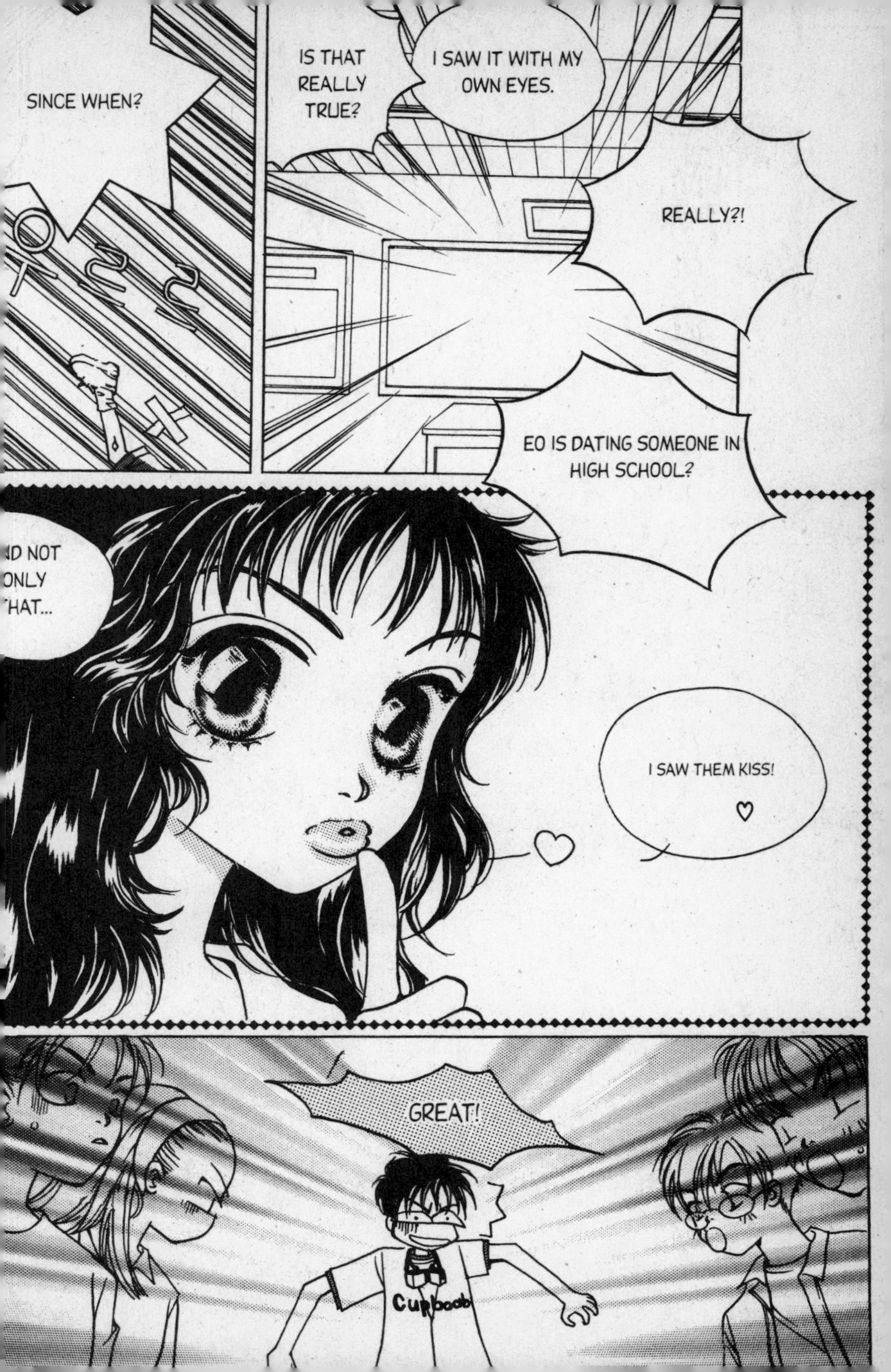
SINCE WHEN?
IS THAT REALLY TRUE?
I SAW IT WITH MY OWN EYES.
REALLY?!
EO IS DATING SOMEONE IN HIGH SCHOOL?
ND NOT ONLY THAT...
I SAW THEM KISS!
GREAT!
Cupboob

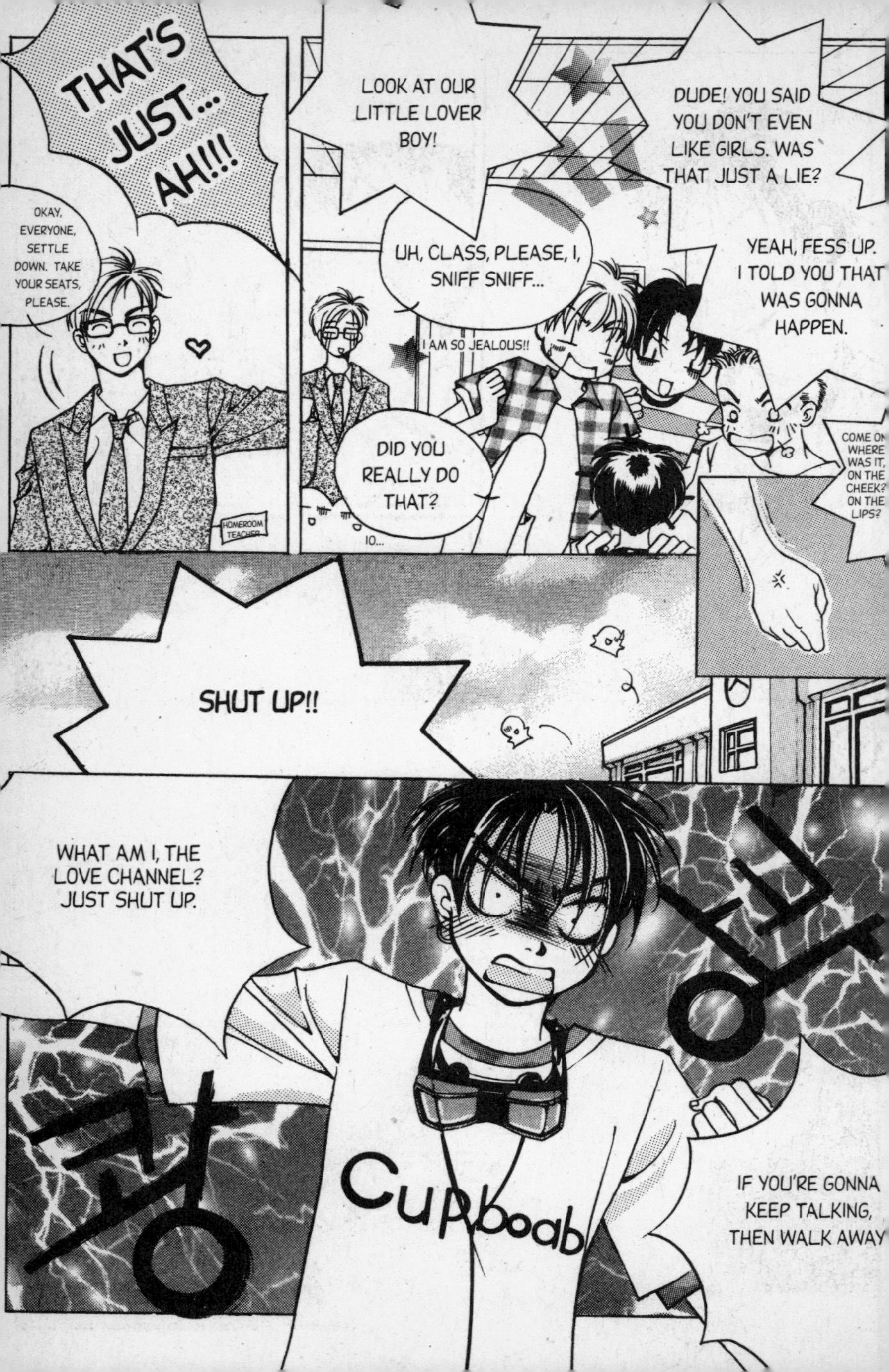
THAT'S JUST... AH!!!
OKAY, EVERYONE, SETTLE DOWN. TAKE YOUR SEATS, PLEASE.
HOMEROOM TEACHER
LOOK AT OUR LITTLE LOVER BOY!
DUDE! YOU SAID YOU DON'T EVEN LIKE GIRLS. WAS THAT JUST A LIE?
UH, CLASS, PLEASE, I, SNIFF SNIFF...
I AM SO JEALOUS!!
YEAH, FESS UP. I TOLD YOU THAT WAS GONNA HAPPEN.
DID YOU REALLY DO THAT?
IO...
COME ON WHERE WAS IT, ON THE CHEEK? ON THE LIPS?
SHUT UP!!
WHAT AM I, THE LOVE CHANNEL? JUST SHUT UP.
Cupboab
IF YOU'RE GONNA KEEP TALKING, THEN WALK AWAY

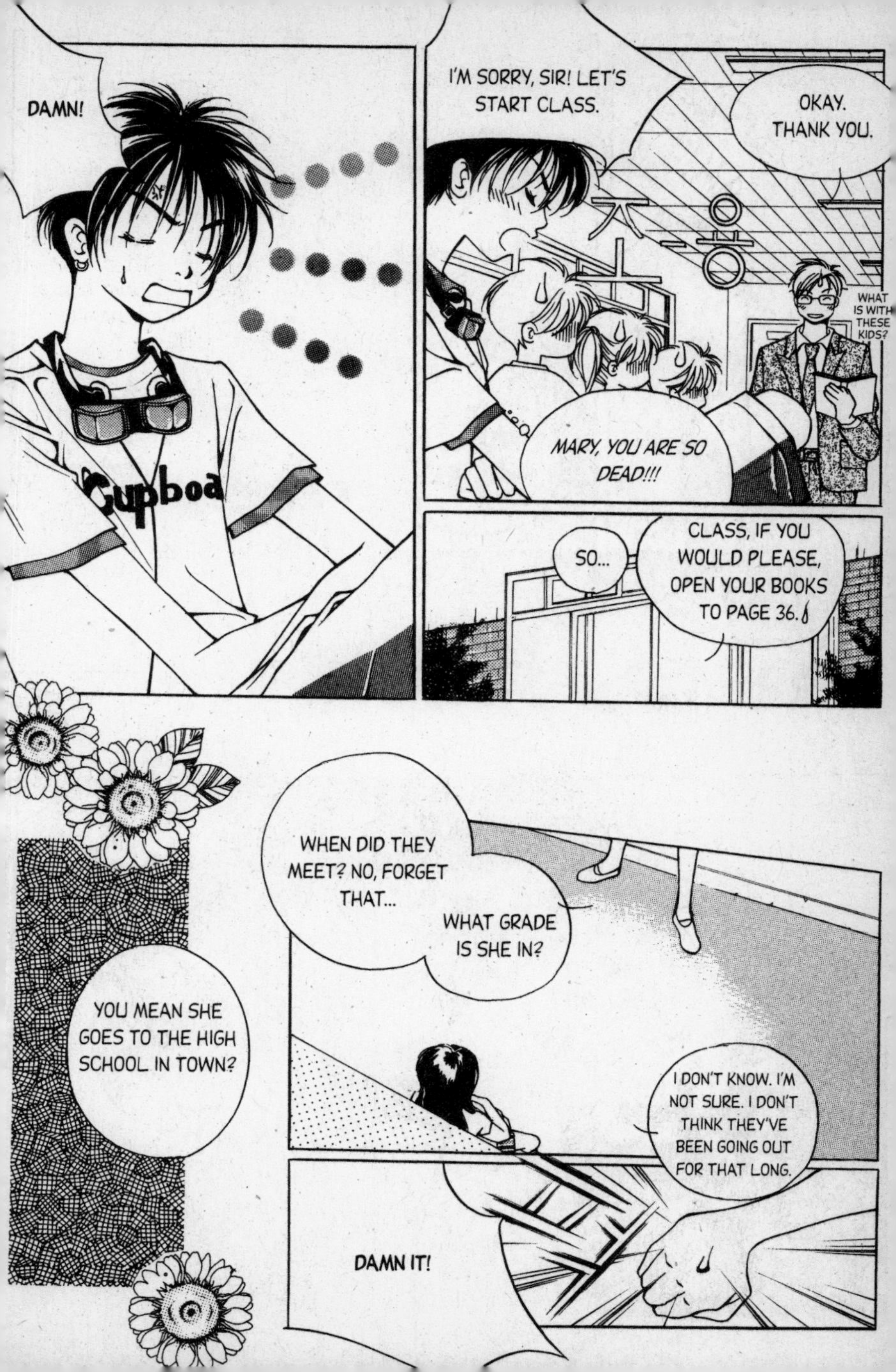
DAMN!
I'M SORRY, SIR! LET'S START CLASS.
OKAY. THANK YOU.
WHAT IS WITH THESE KIDS?
MARY, YOU ARE SO DEAD!!!
SO...
CLASS, IF YOU WOULD PLEASE, OPEN YOUR BOOKS TO PAGE 36.
WHEN DID THEY MEET? NO, FORGET THAT...
WHAT GRADE IS SHE IN?
YOU MEAN SHE GOES TO THE HIGH SCHOOL IN TOWN?
I DON'T KNOW. I'M NOT SURE. I DON'T THINK THEY'VE BEEN GOING OUT FOR THAT LONG.
DAMN IT!

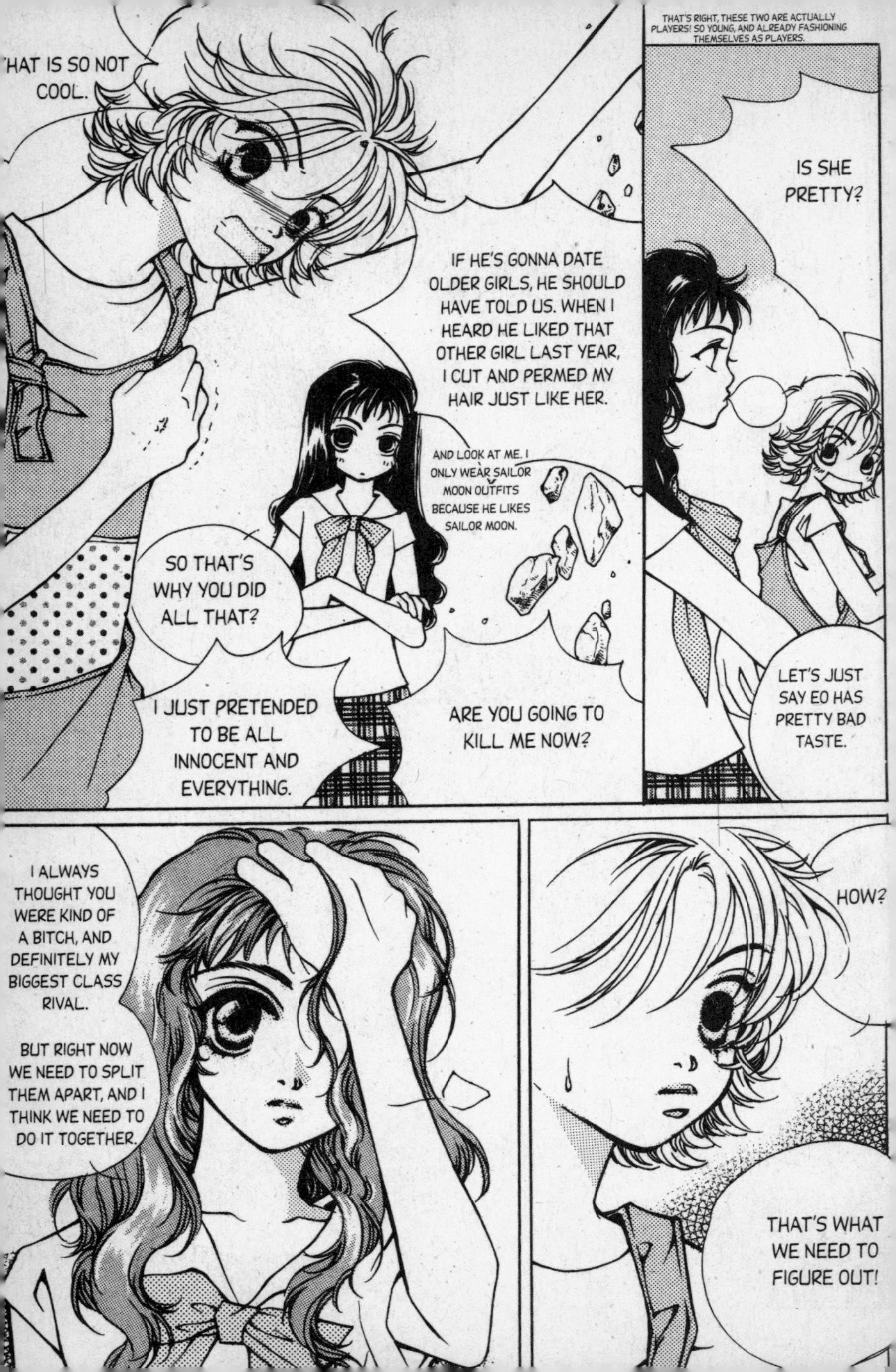
THAT IS SO NOT COOL.
IF HE'S GONNA DATE OLDER GIRLS, HE SHOULD HAVE TOLD US. WHEN I HEARD HE LIKED THAT OTHER GIRL LAST YEAR, I CUT AND PERMED MY HAIR JUST LIKE HER.
AND LOOK AT ME. I ONLY WEAR SAILOR MOON OUTFITS BECAUSE HE LIKES SAILOR MOON.
SO THAT'S WHY YOU DID ALL THAT?
I JUST PRETENDED TO BE ALL INNOCENT AND EVERYTHING.
ARE YOU GOING TO KILL ME NOW?
THAT'S RIGHT, THESE TWO ARE ACTUALLY PLAYERS! SO YOUNG, AND ALREADY FASHIONING THEMSELVES AS PLAYERS.
IS SHE PRETTY?
LET'S JUST SAY EO HAS PRETTY BAD TASTE.
I ALWAYS THOUGHT YOU WERE KIND OF A BITCH, AND DEFINITELY MY BIGGEST CLASS RIVAL.
BUT RIGHT NOW WE NEED TO SPLIT THEM APART, AND I THINK WE NEED TO DO IT TOGETHER.
HOW?
THAT'S WHAT WE NEED TO FIGURE OUT!

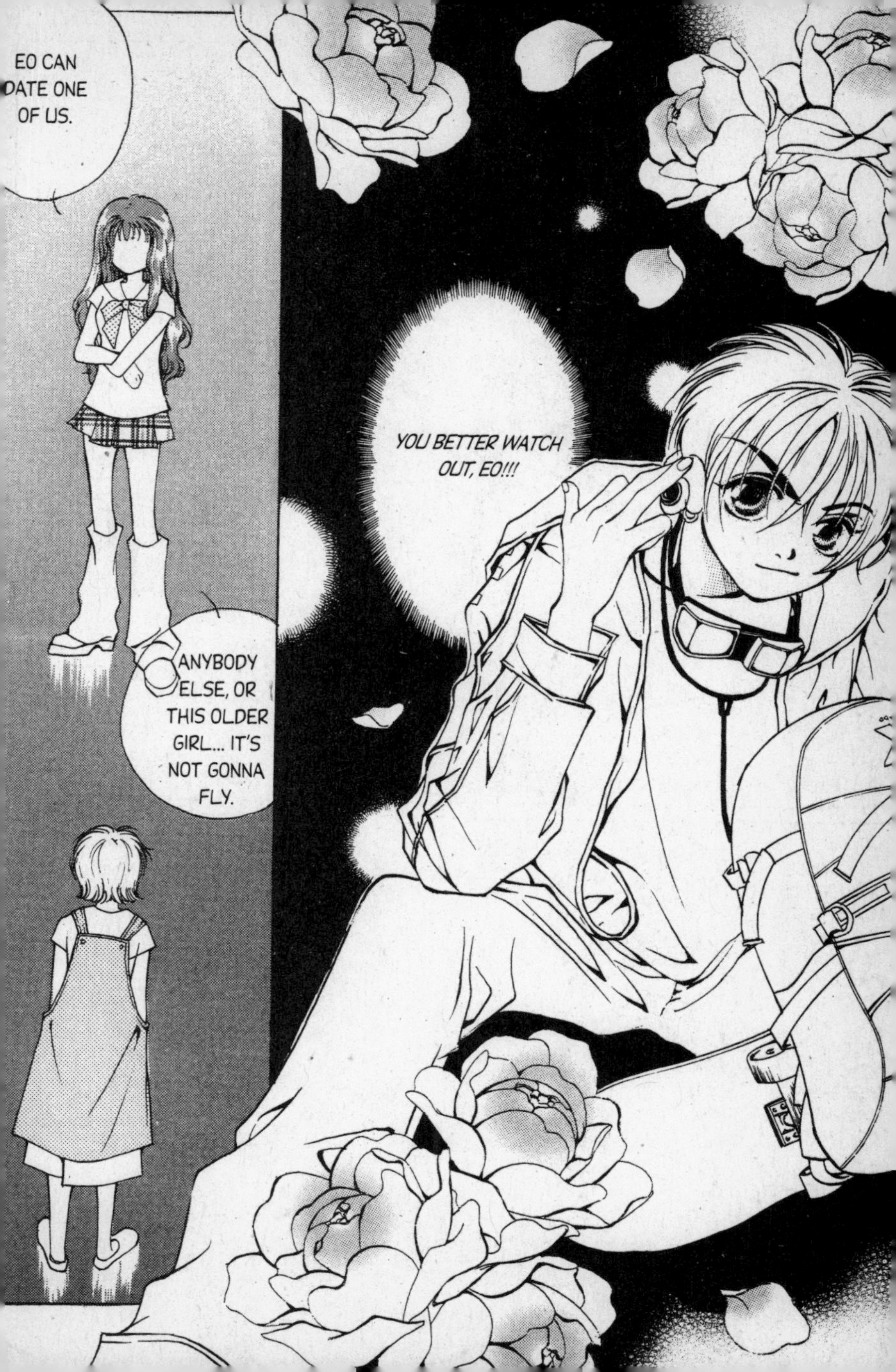
EO CAN DATE ONE OF US.
ANYBODY ELSE, OR THIS OLDER GIRL... IT'S NOT GONNA FLY.
YOU BETTER WATCH OUT, EO!!!

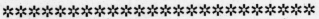

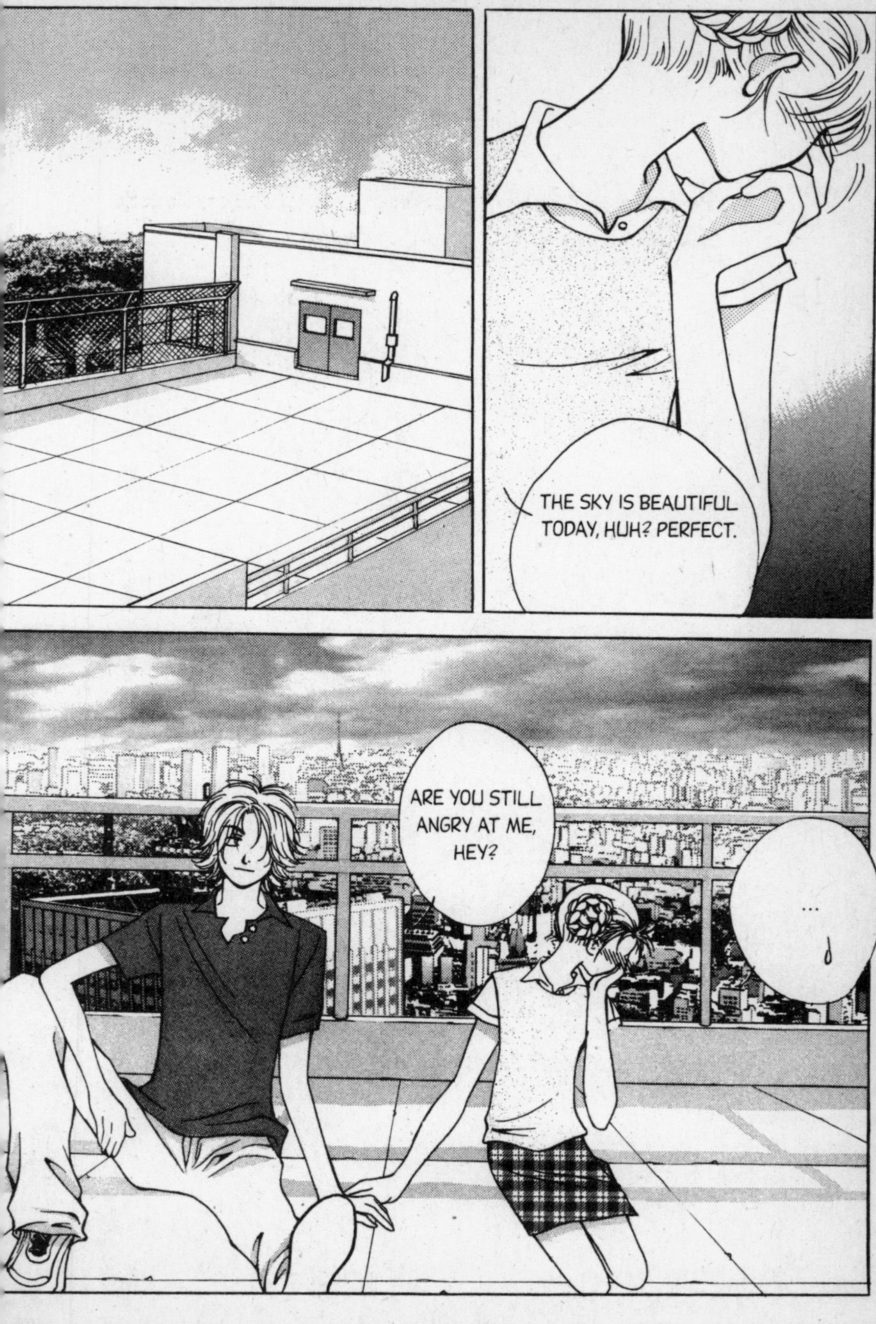
THE SKY IS BEAUTIFUL TODAY, HUH? PERFECT.
ARE YOU STILL ANGRY AT ME, HEY?
...

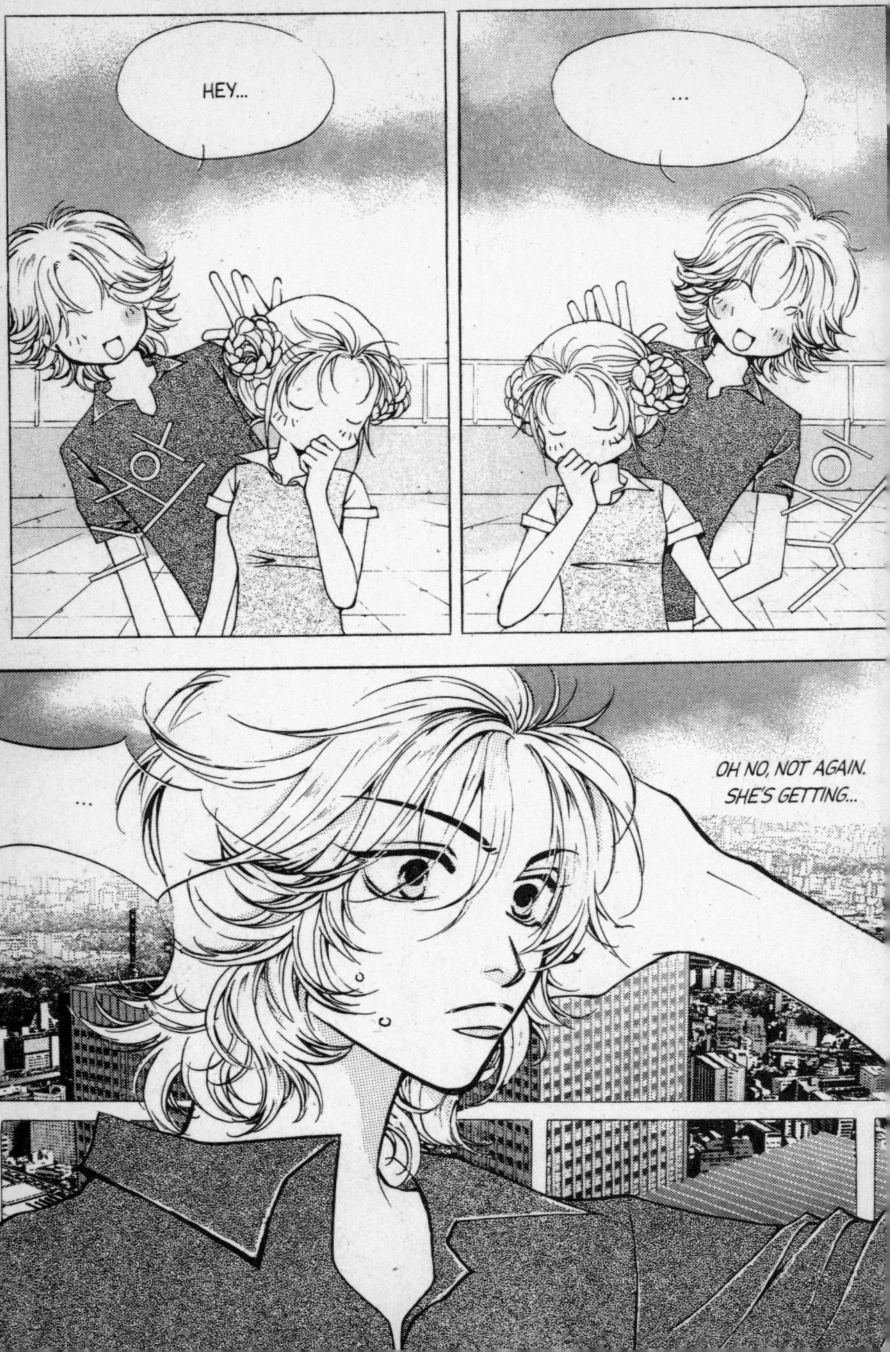
...
HEY...
OH NO, NOT AGAIN.
SHE'S GETTING...
...

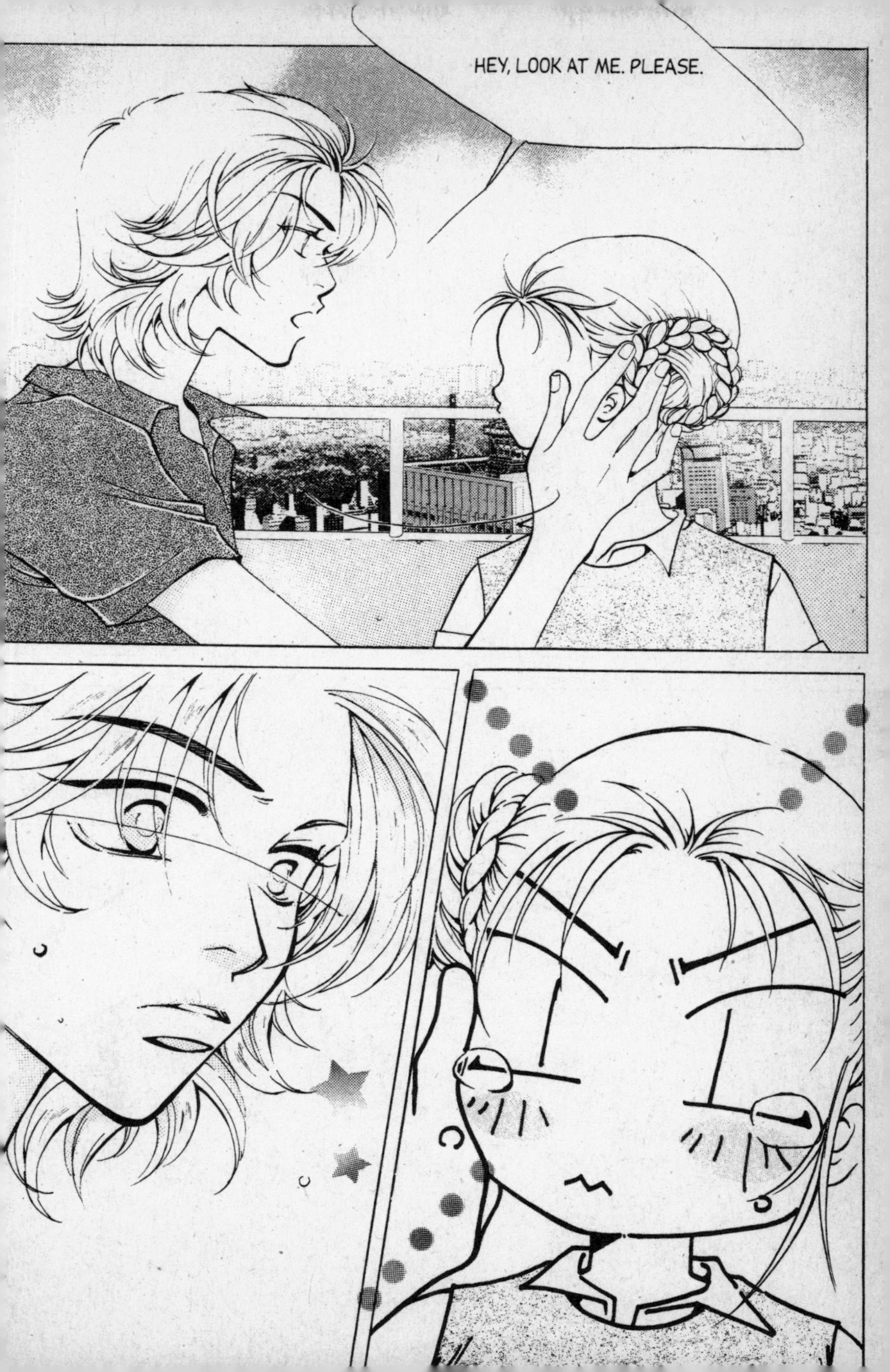
HEY, LOOK AT ME. PLEASE.

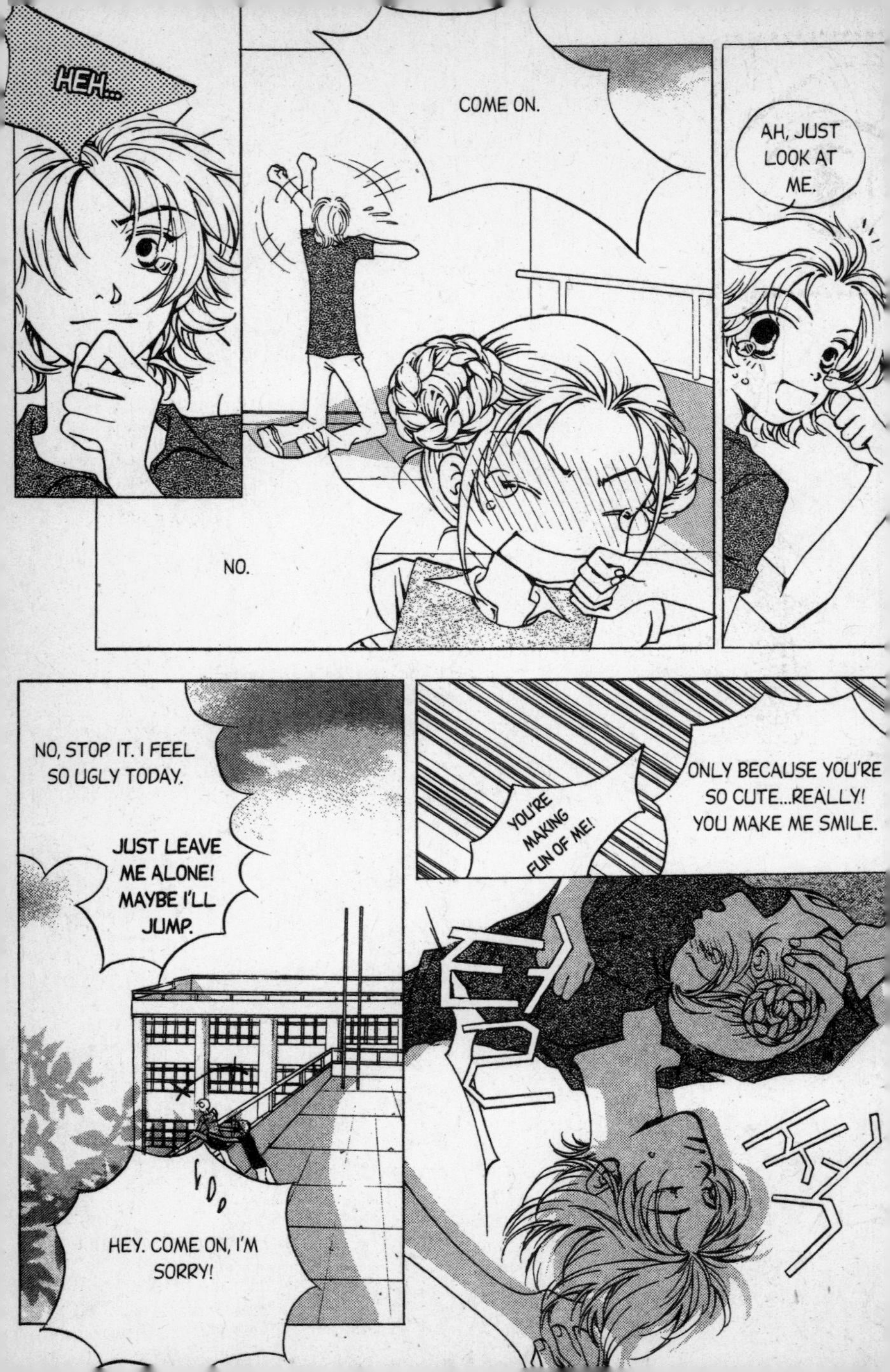
AH, JUST LOOK AT ME.
COME ON.
HEH...
NO.
ONLY BECAUSE YOU'RE SO CUTE...REALLY! YOU MAKE ME SMILE.
YOU'RE MAKING FUN OF ME!
NO, STOP IT. I FEEL SO UGLY TODAY.
JUST LEAVE ME ALONE! MAYBE I'LL JUMP.
HEY. COME ON, I'M SORRY!

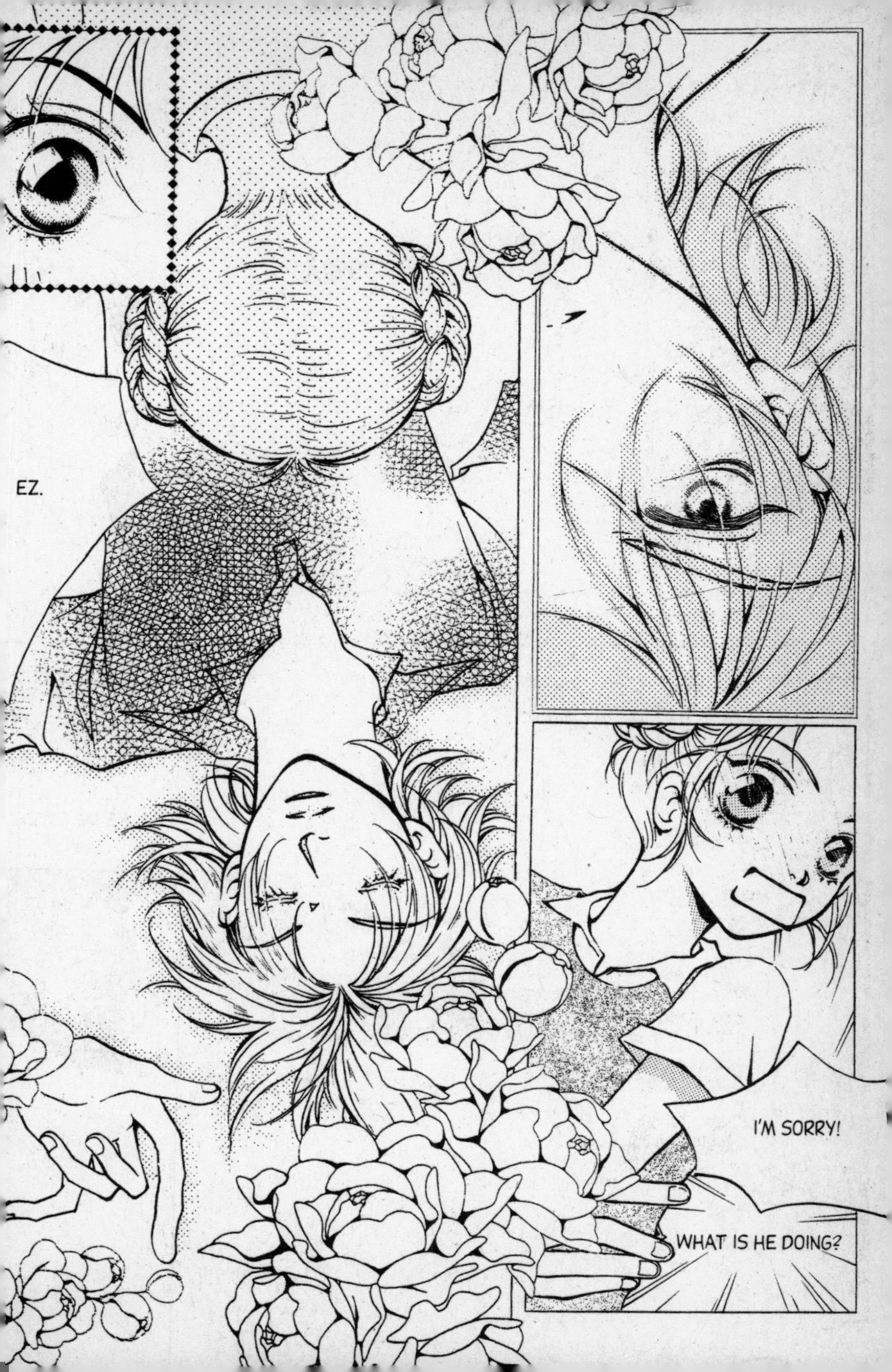
I'M SORRY!
WHAT IS HE DOING?
EZ.

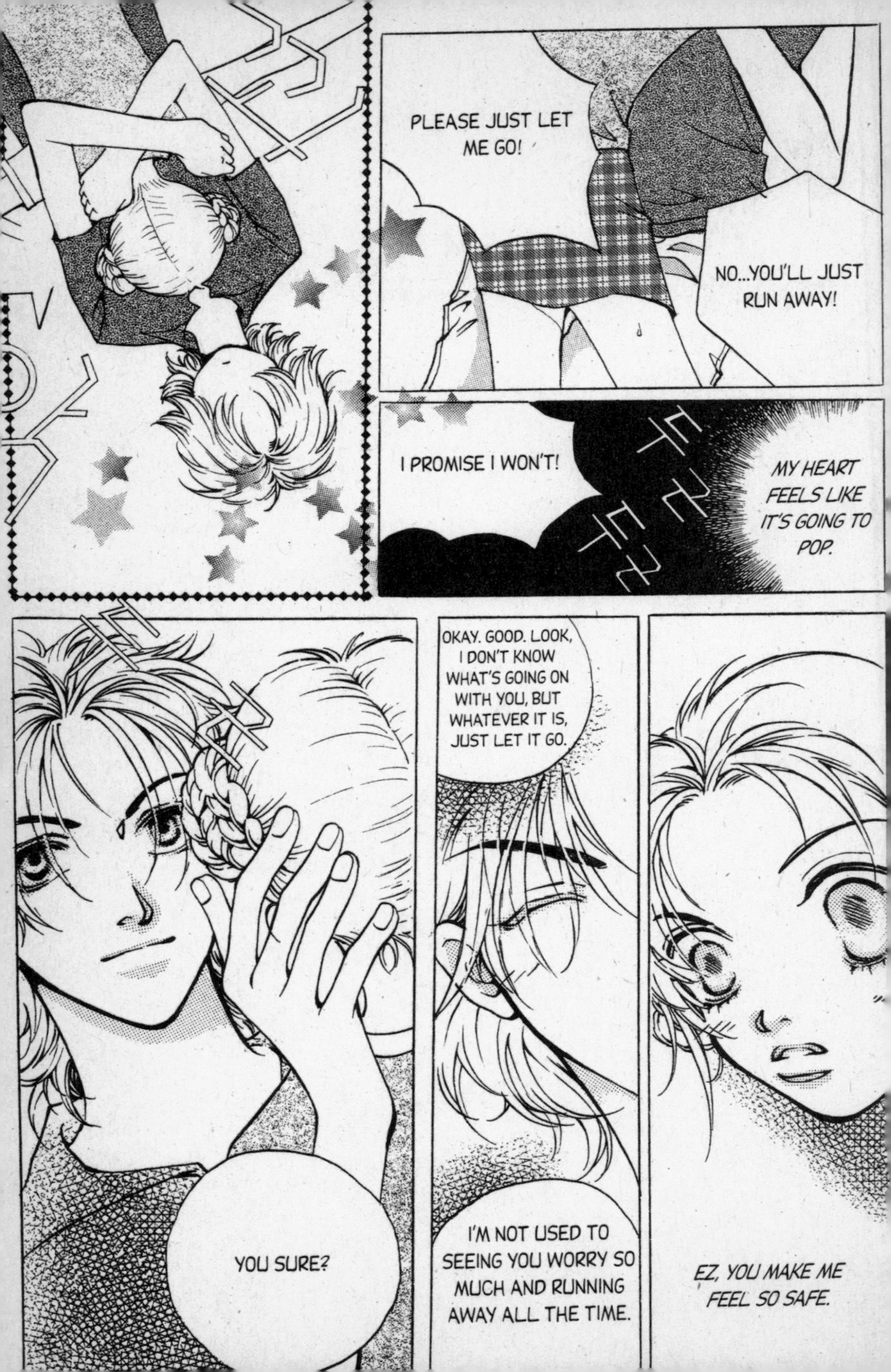
PLEASE JUST LET ME GO!
NO...YOU'LL JUST RUN AWAY!
I PROMISE I WON'T!
MY HEART FEELS LIKE IT'S GOING TO POP.
YOU SURE?
OKAY. GOOD. LOOK, I DON'T KNOW WHAT'S GOING ON WITH YOU, BUT WHATEVER IT IS, JUST LET IT GO.
I'M NOT USED TO SEEING YOU WORRY SO MUCH AND RUNNING AWAY ALL THE TIME.
EZ, YOU MAKE ME FEEL SO SAFE.

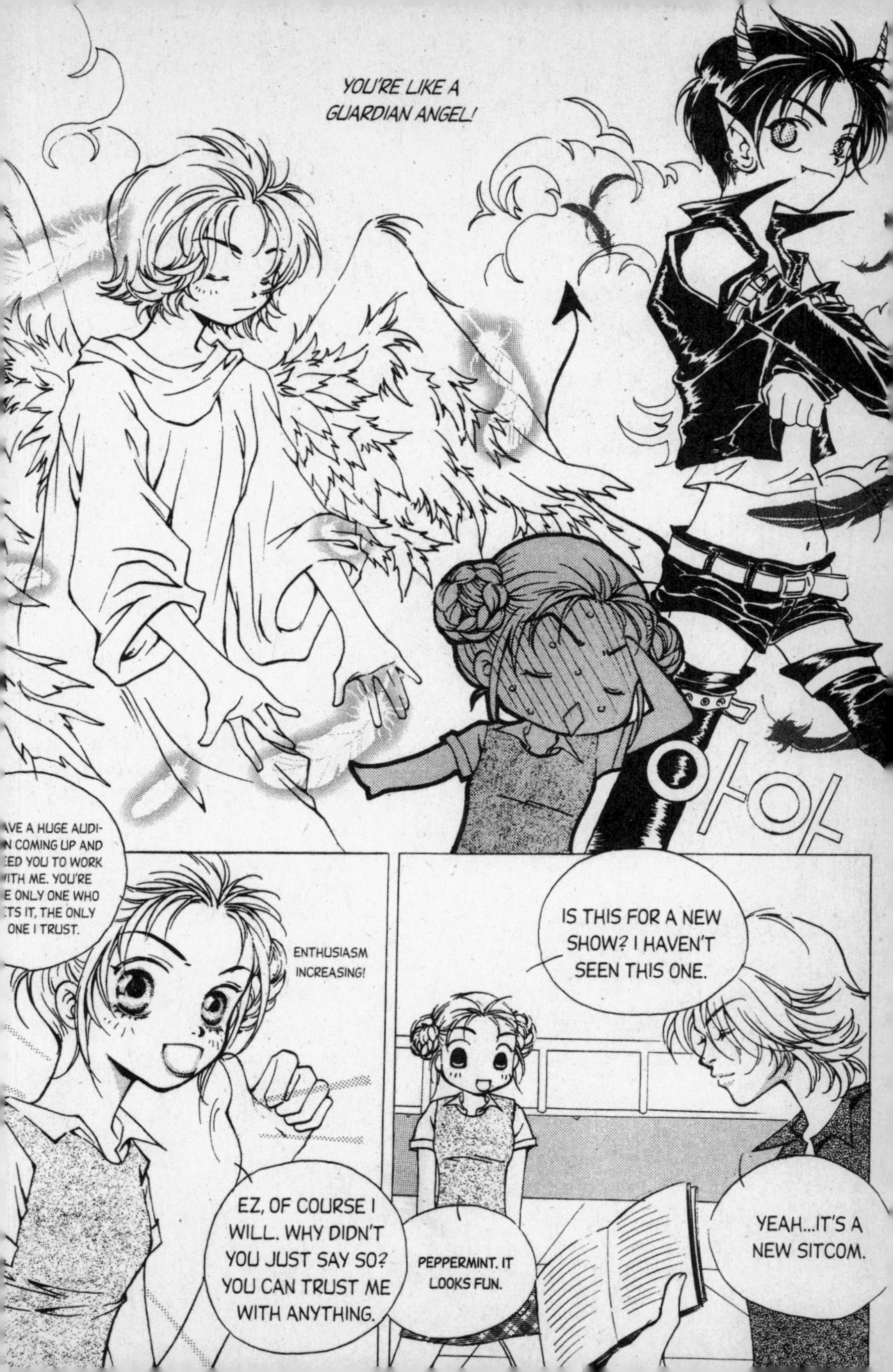
YOU'RE LIKE A GUARDIAN ANGEL!
AVE A HUGE AUDI- N COMING UP AND EED YOU TO WORK VITH ME. YOU'RE E ONLY ONE WHO ETS IT, THE ONLY ONE I TRUST.
ENTHUSIASM INCREASING!
EZ, OF COURSE I WILL. WHY DIDN'T YOU JUST SAY SO? YOU CAN TRUST ME WITH ANYTHING.
IS THIS FOR A NEW SHOW? I HAVEN'T SEEN THIS ONE.
PEPPERMINT. IT LOOKS FUN.
YEAH...IT'S A NEW SITCOM.

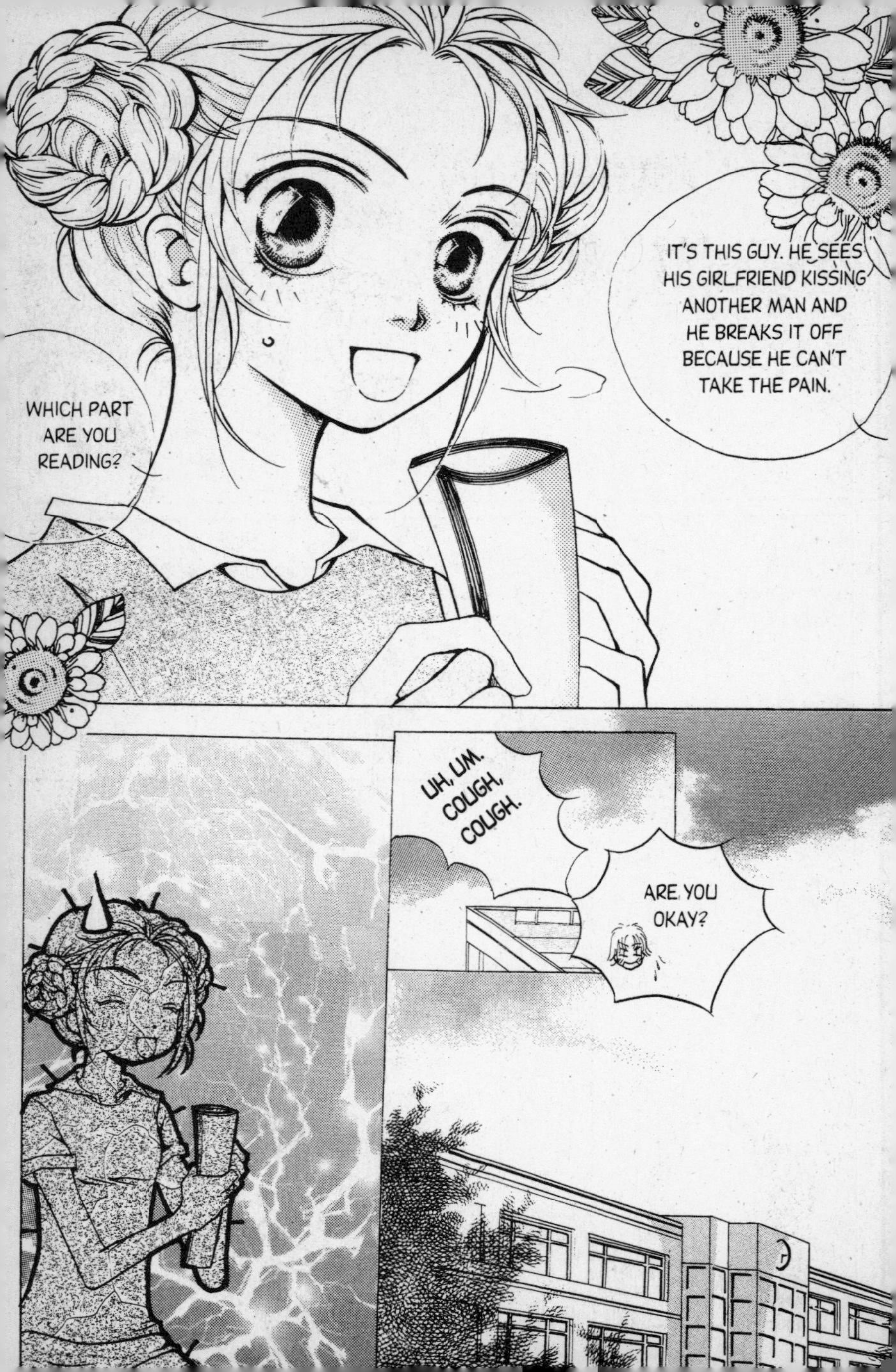
WHICH PART ARE YOU READING?
IT'S THIS GUY. HE SEES HIS GIRLFRIEND KISSING ANOTHER MAN AND HE BREAKS IT OFF BECAUSE HE CAN'T TAKE THE PAIN.
UH, UM. COUGH, COUGH.
ARE YOU OKAY?

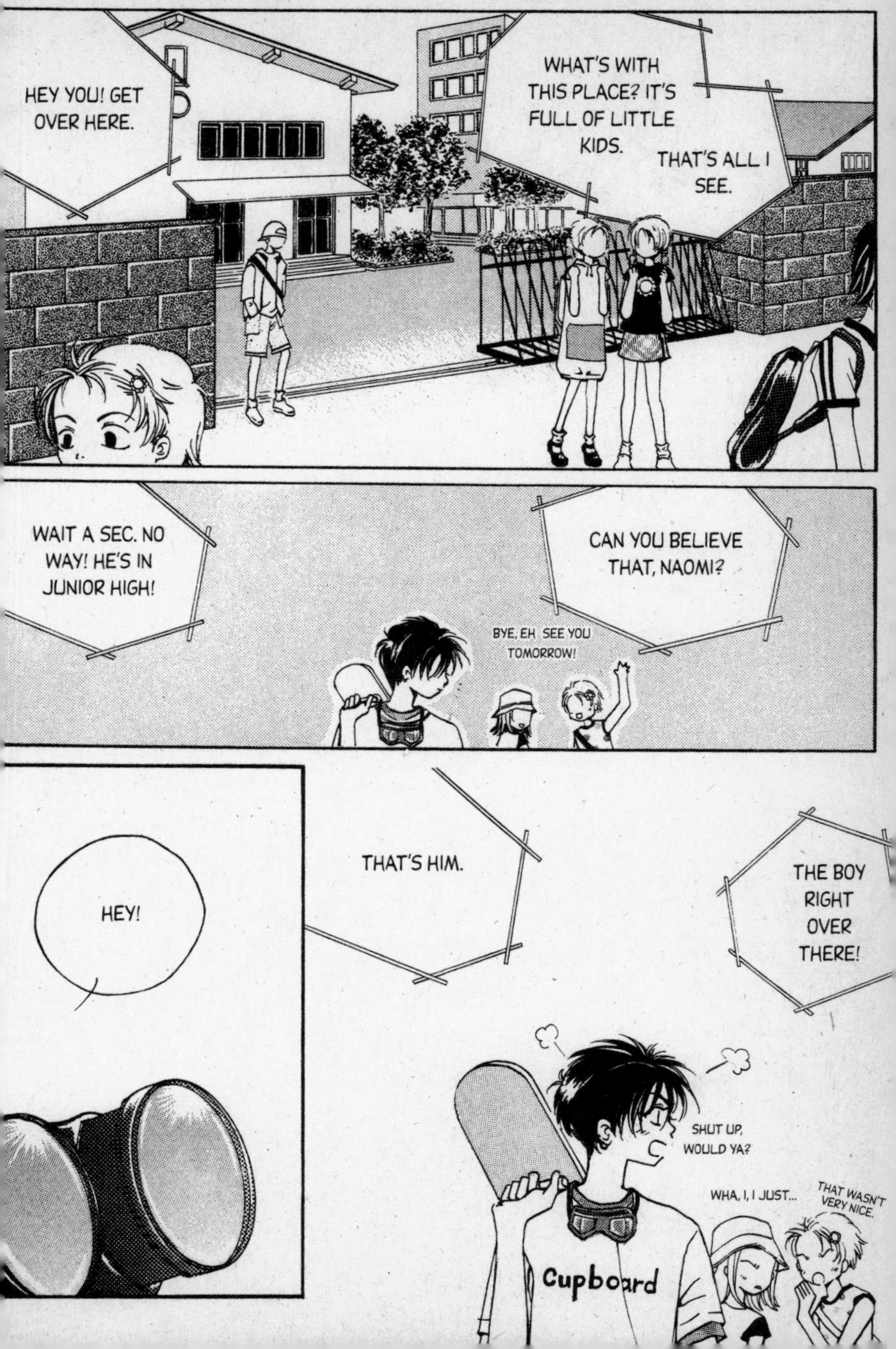
WHAT'S WITH THIS PLACE? IT'S FULL OF LITTLE KIDS.
THAT'S ALL I SEE.
HEY YOU! GET OVER HERE.
CAN YOU BELIEVE THAT, NAOMI?
WAIT A SEC. NO WAY! HE'S IN JUNIOR HIGH!
BYE, EH SEE YOU TOMORROW!
THE BOY RIGHT OVER THERE!
THAT'S HIM.
SHUT UP, WOULD YA?
THAT WASN'T VERY NICE.
WHA, I, I JUST...
Cupboard
HEY!

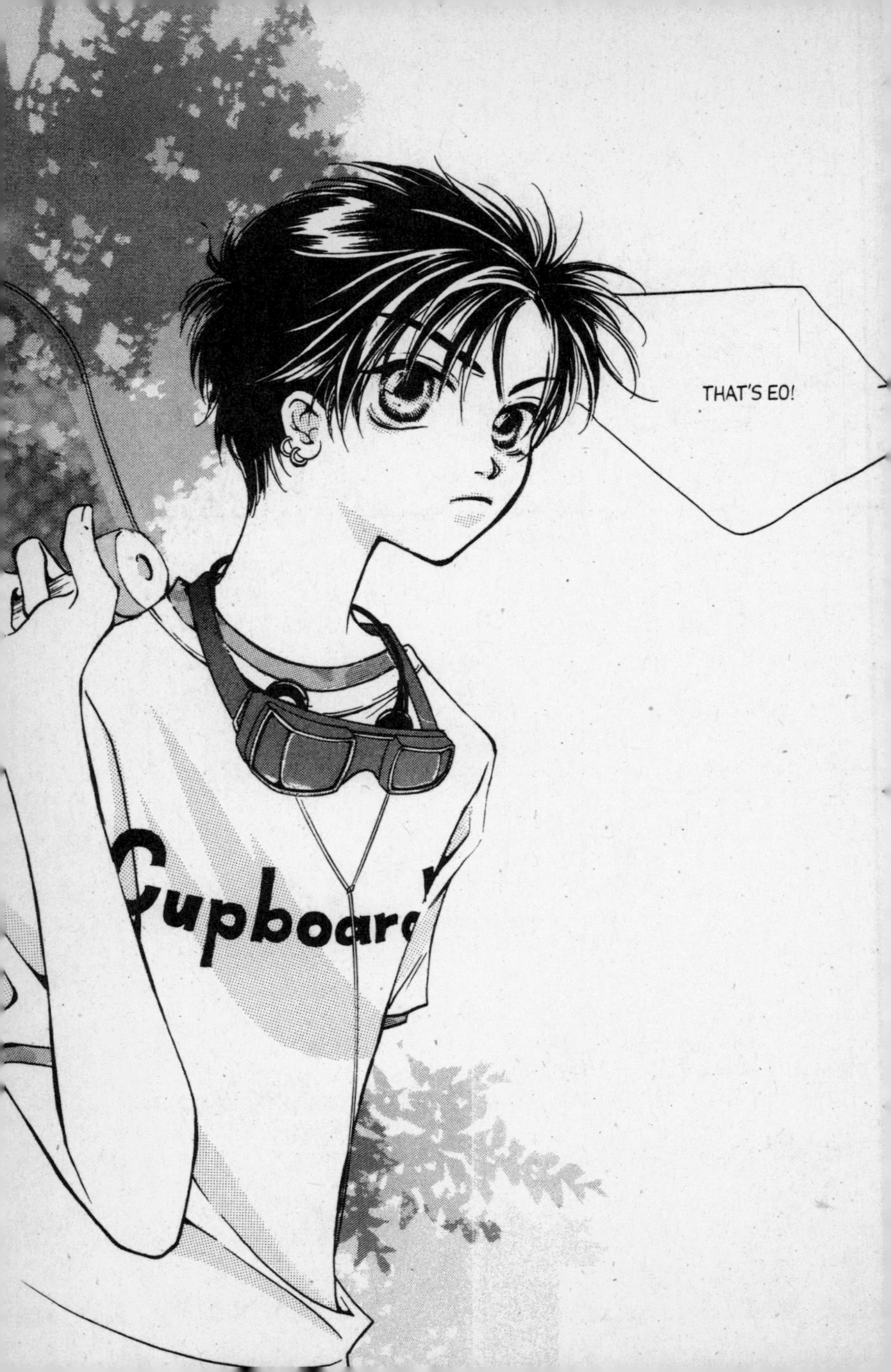
THAT'S EO!
Cupboard

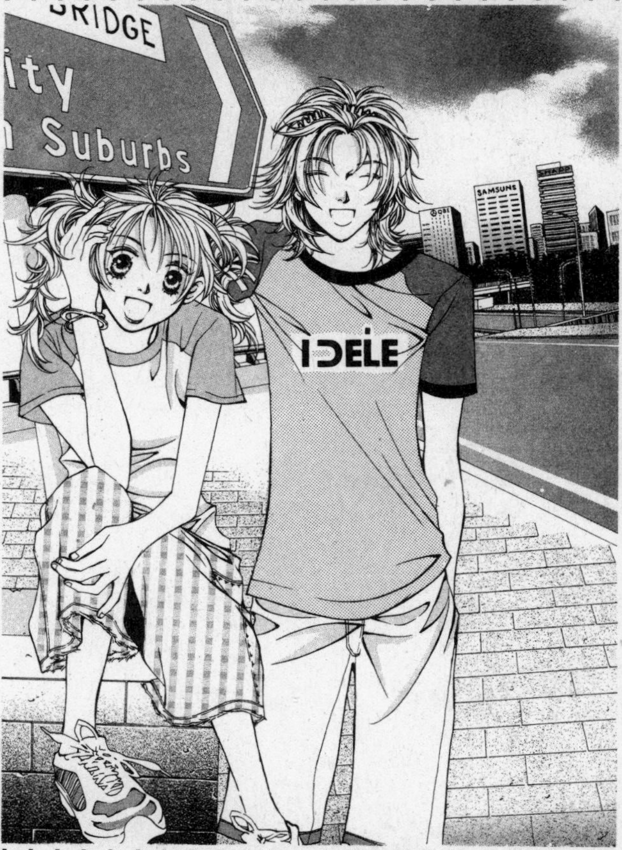
Suburbs

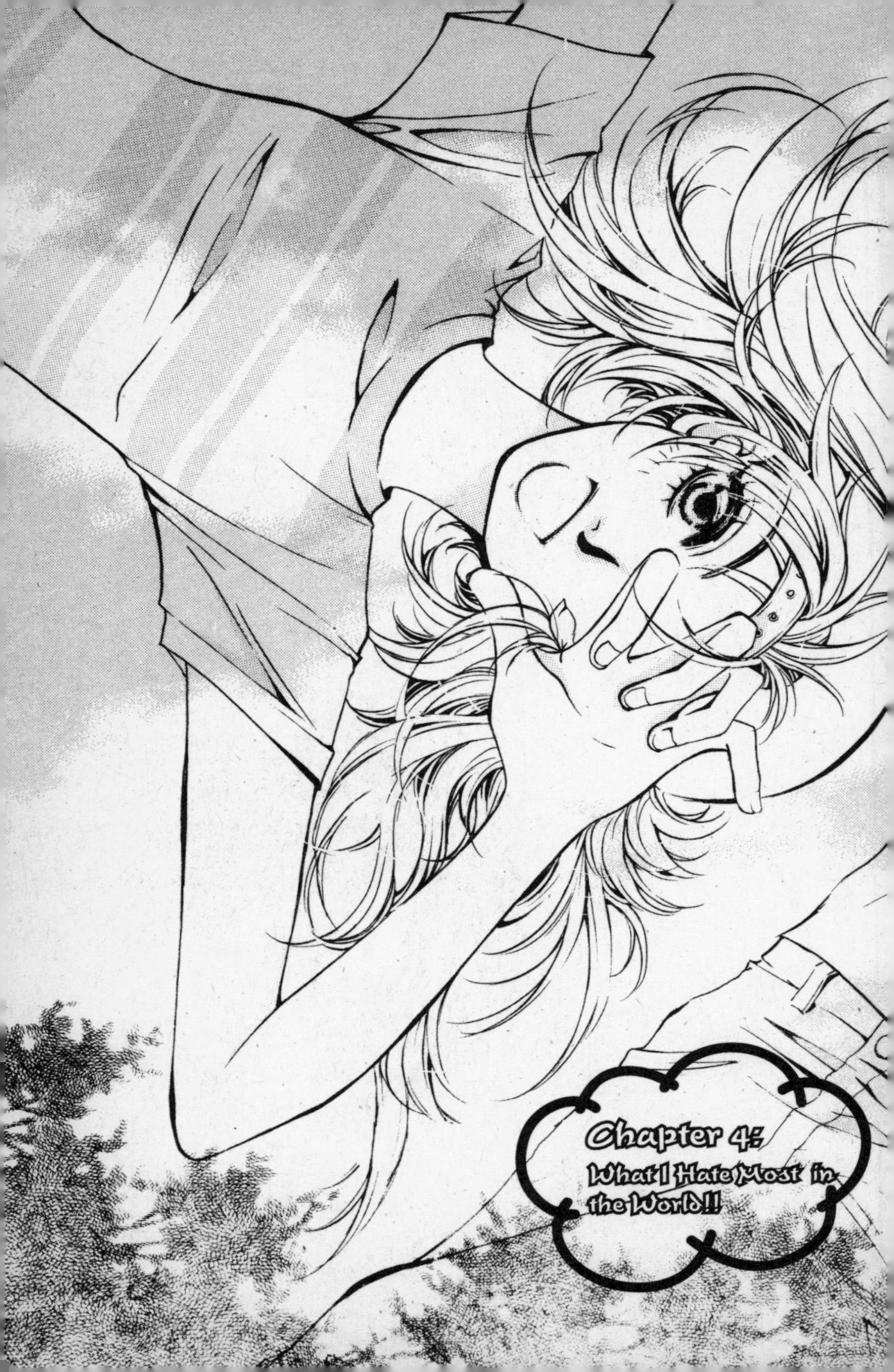
Chapter 4:
What I Hate Most in the World!!

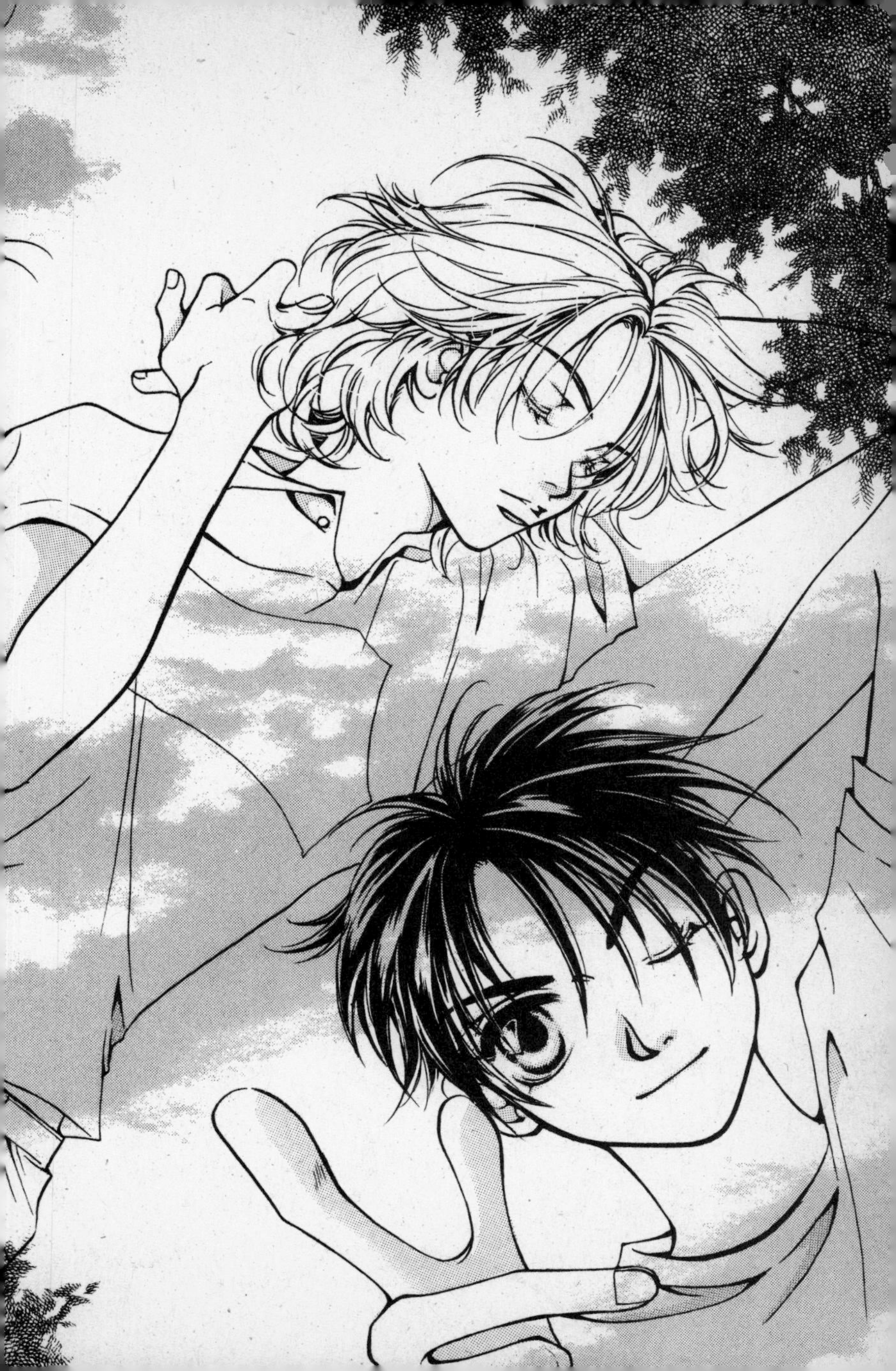

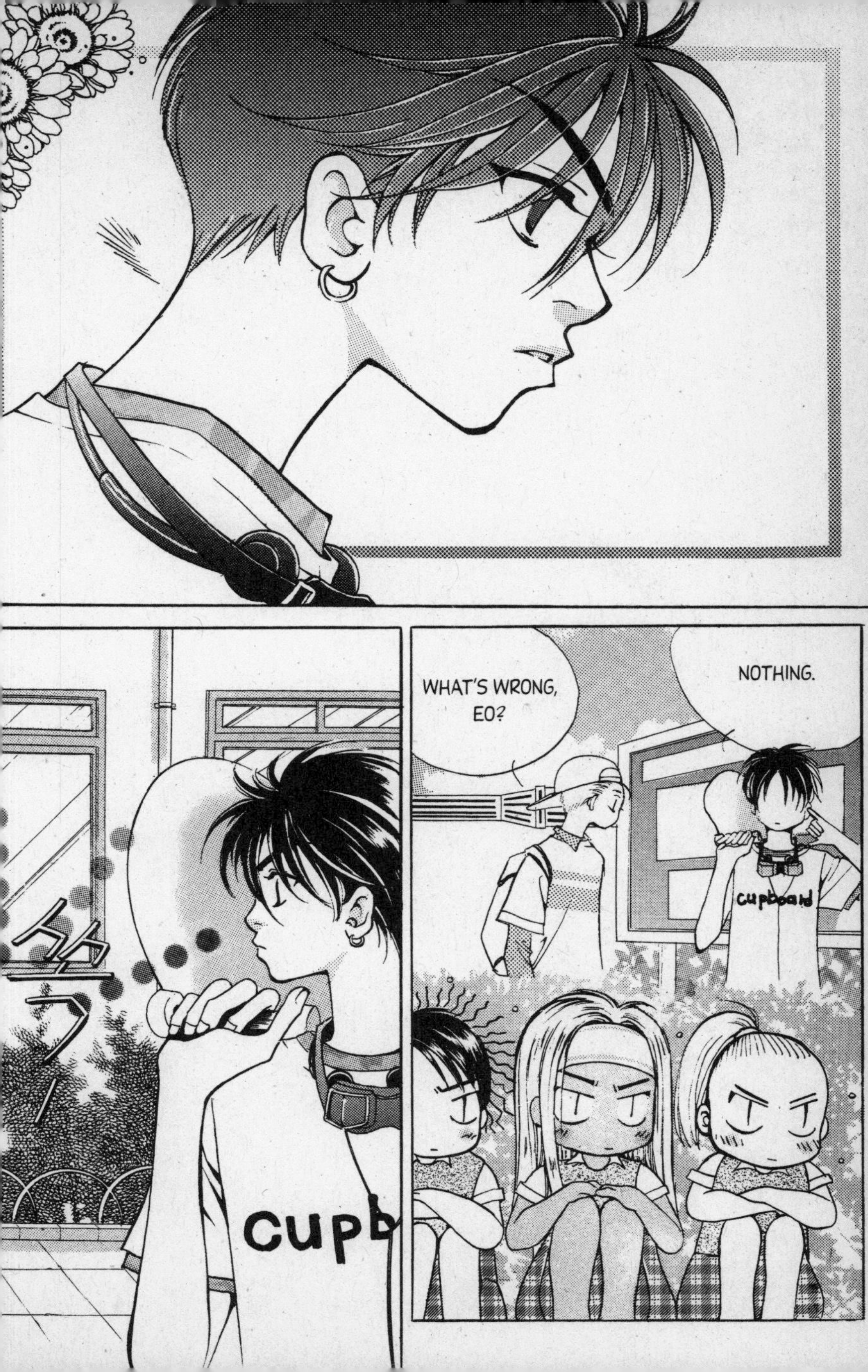
WHAT'S WRONG, EO?
NOTHING.

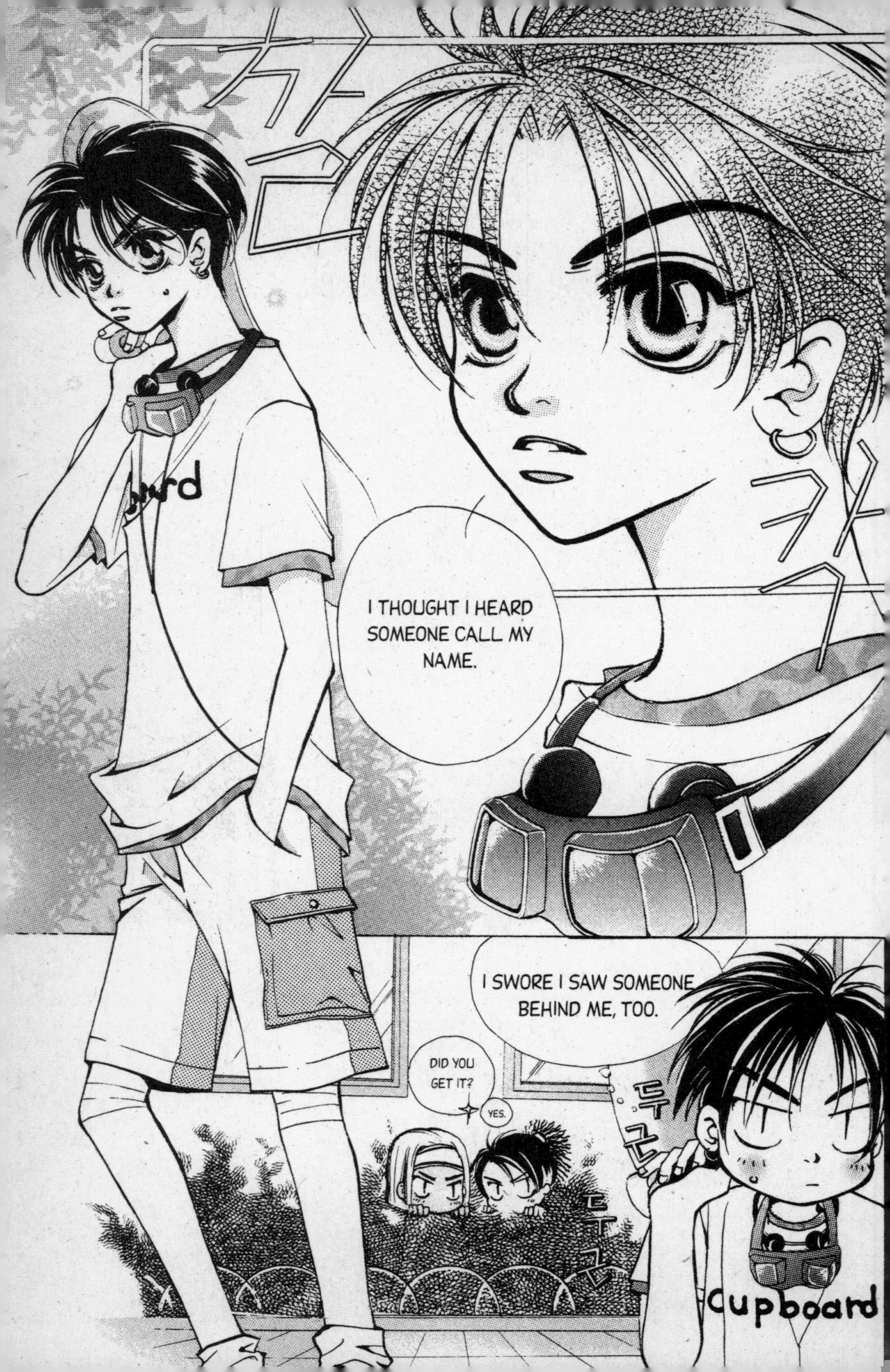
I THOUGHT I HEARD SOMEONE CALL MY NAME.
I SWORE I SAW SOMEONE BEHIND ME, TOO.
DID YOU GET IT?
YES.
Cupboard

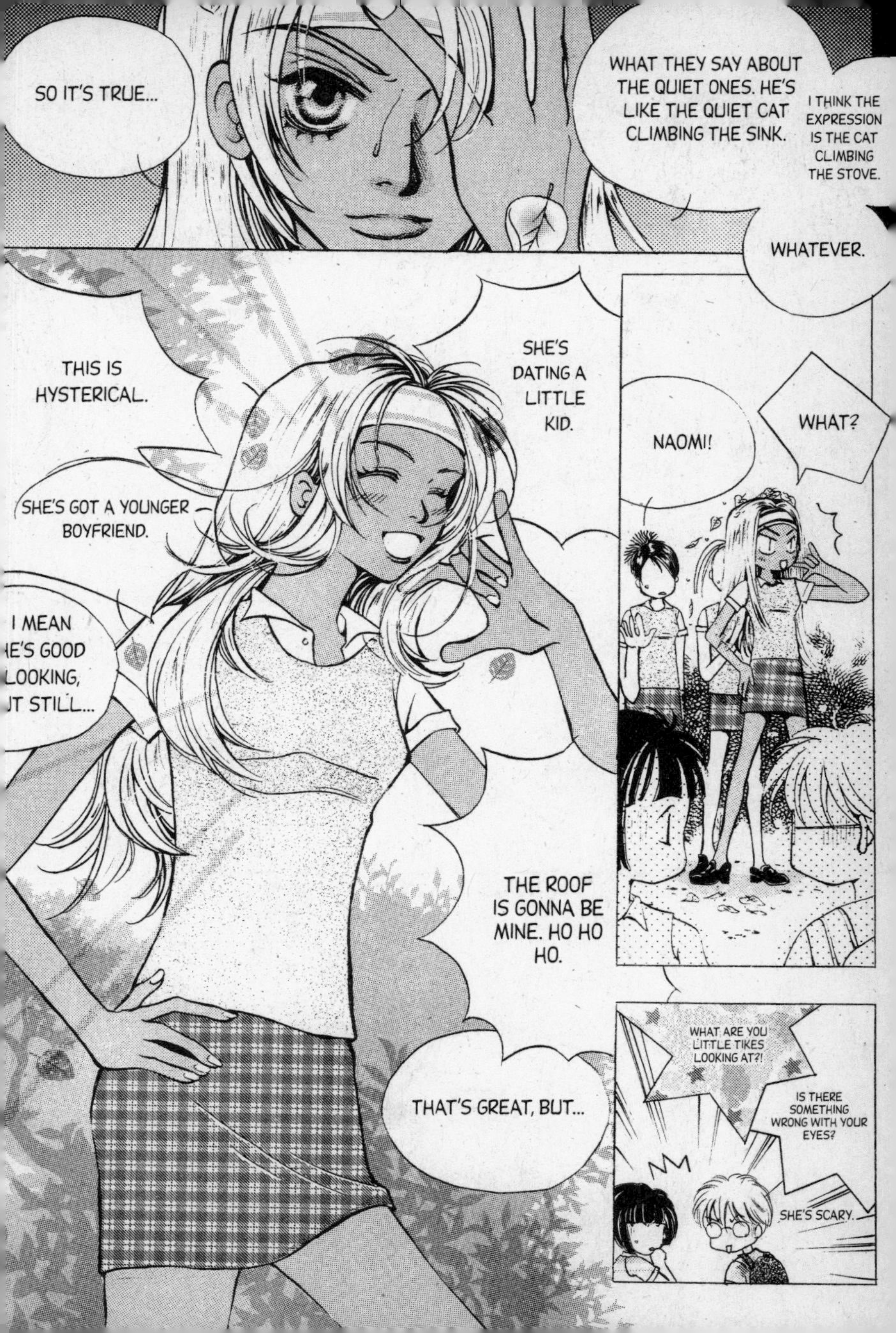
SO IT'S TRUE...
WHAT THEY SAY ABOUT THE QUIET ONES. HE'S LIKE THE QUIET CAT CLIMBING THE SINK.
I THINK THE EXPRESSION IS THE CAT CLIMBING THE STOVE.
WHATEVER.
THIS IS HYSTERICAL.
SHE'S DATING A LITTLE KID.
SHE'S GOT A YOUNGER BOYFRIEND.
I MEAN HE'S GOOD LOOKING, BUT STILL...
THE ROOF IS GONNA BE MINE. HO HO HO.
THAT'S GREAT, BUT...
NAOMI!
WHAT?
WHAT ARE YOU LITTLE TIKES LOOKING AT?!
IS THERE SOMETHING WRONG WITH YOUR EYES?
SHE'S SCARY.

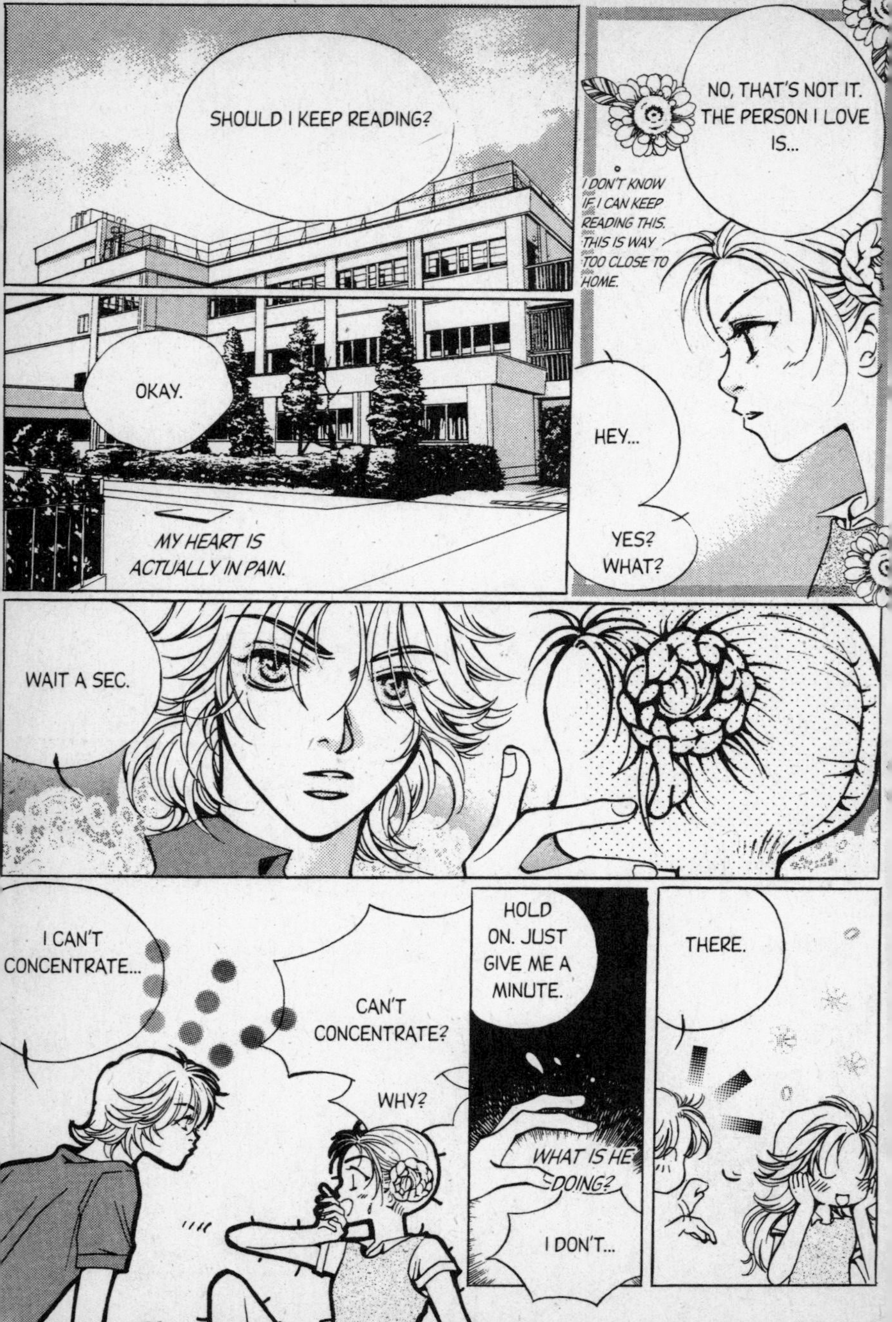
SHOULD I KEEP READING?
OKAY.
MY HEART IS ACTUALLY IN PAIN.
NO, THAT'S NOT IT. THE PERSON I LOVE IS...
I DON'T KNOW IF I CAN KEEP READING THIS. THIS IS WAY TOO CLOSE TO HOME.
HEY...
YES? WHAT?
WAIT A SEC.
I CAN'T CONCENTRATE...
CAN'T CONCENTRATE?
WHY?
HOLD ON. JUST GIVE ME A MINUTE.
WHAT IS HE DOING?
I DON'T...
THERE.

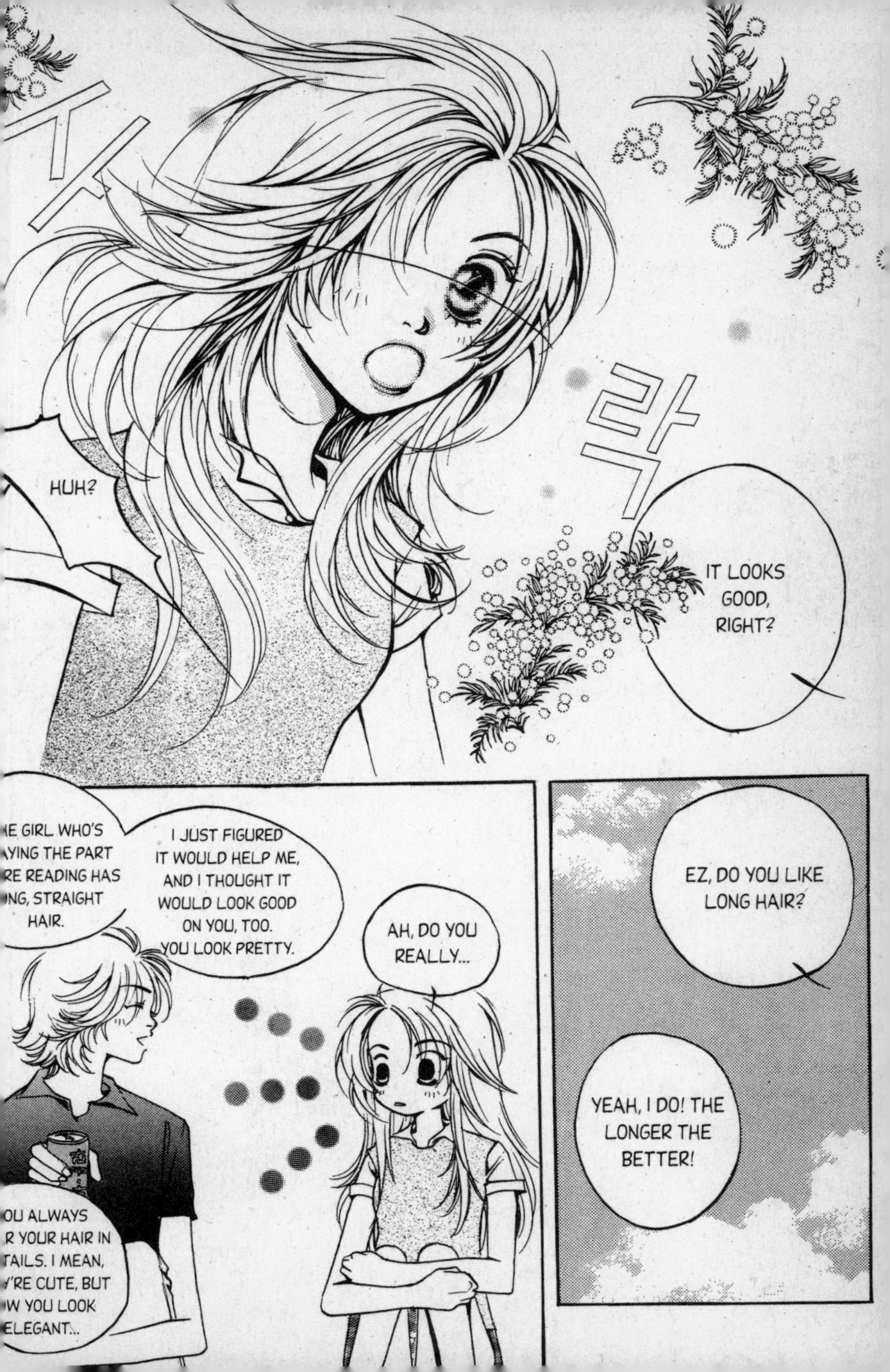

HUH?
IT LOOKS GOOD, RIGHT?
HE GIRL WHO'S AYING THE PART RE READING HAS NG, STRAIGHT HAIR.
I JUST FIGURED IT WOULD HELP ME, AND I THOUGHT IT WOULD LOOK GOOD ON YOU, TOO. YOU LOOK PRETTY.
AH, DO YOU REALLY...
OU ALWAYS R YOUR HAIR IN TAILS. I MEAN, Y'RE CUTE, BUT W YOU LOOK ELEGANT...
EZ, DO YOU LIKE LONG HAIR?
YEAH, I DO! THE LONGER THE BETTER!

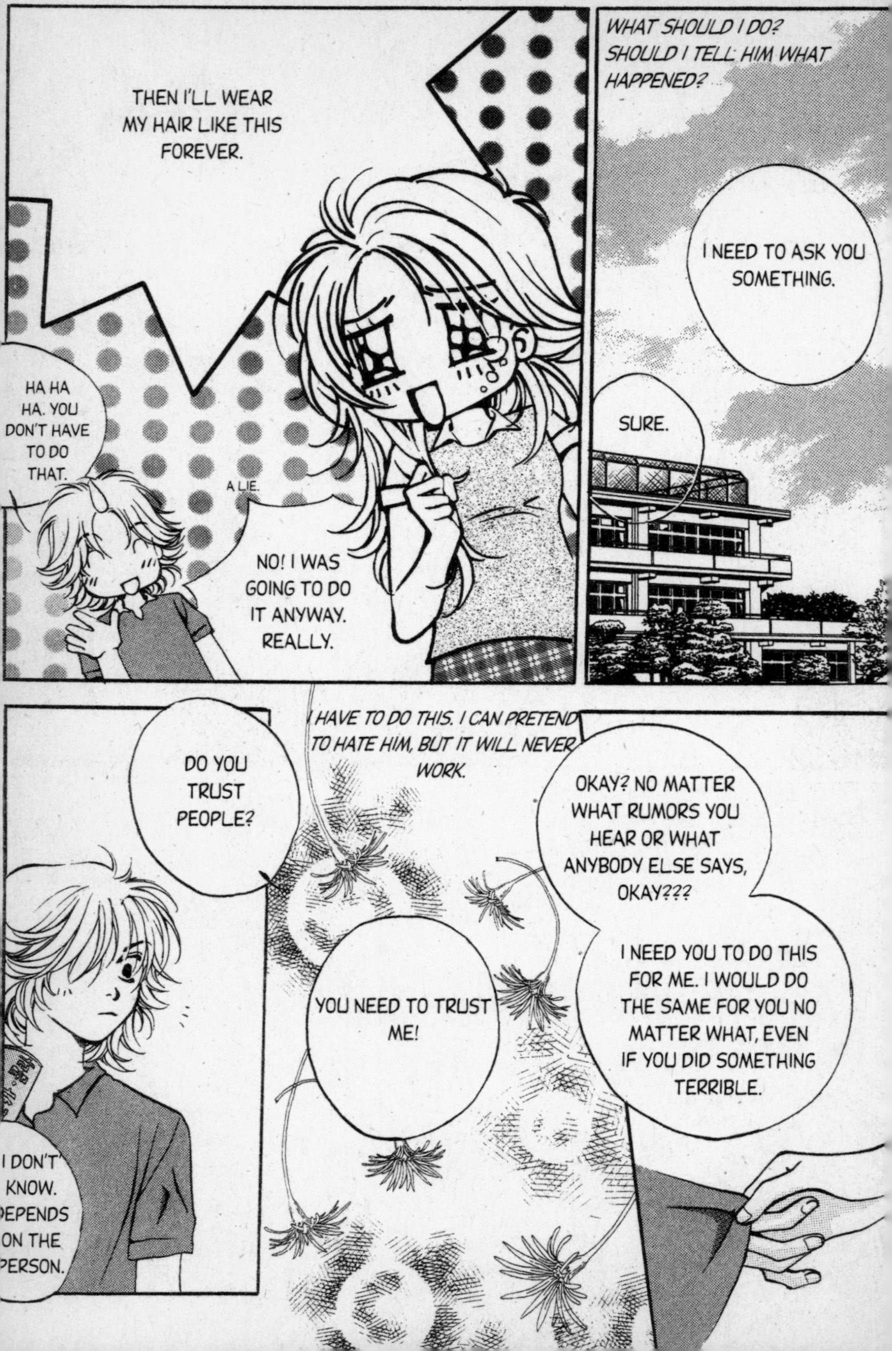
THEN I'LL WEAR MY HAIR LIKE THIS FOREVER.
HA HA HA. YOU DON'T HAVE TO DO THAT.
A LIE.
NO! I WAS GOING TO DO IT ANYWAY. REALLY.
WHAT SHOULD I DO? SHOULD I TELL HIM WHAT HAPPENED?
I NEED TO ASK YOU SOMETHING.
SURE.
DO YOU TRUST PEOPLE?
I DON'T KNOW. EPENDS ON THE ERSON.
I HAVE TO DO THIS. I CAN PRETEND TO HATE HIM, BUT IT WILL NEVER WORK.
YOU NEED TO TRUST ME!
OKAY? NO MATTER WHAT RUMORS YOU HEAR OR WHAT ANYBODY ELSE SAYS, OKAY???
I NEED YOU TO DO THIS FOR ME. I WOULD DO THE SAME FOR YOU NO MATTER WHAT, EVEN IF YOU DID SOMETHING TERRIBLE.

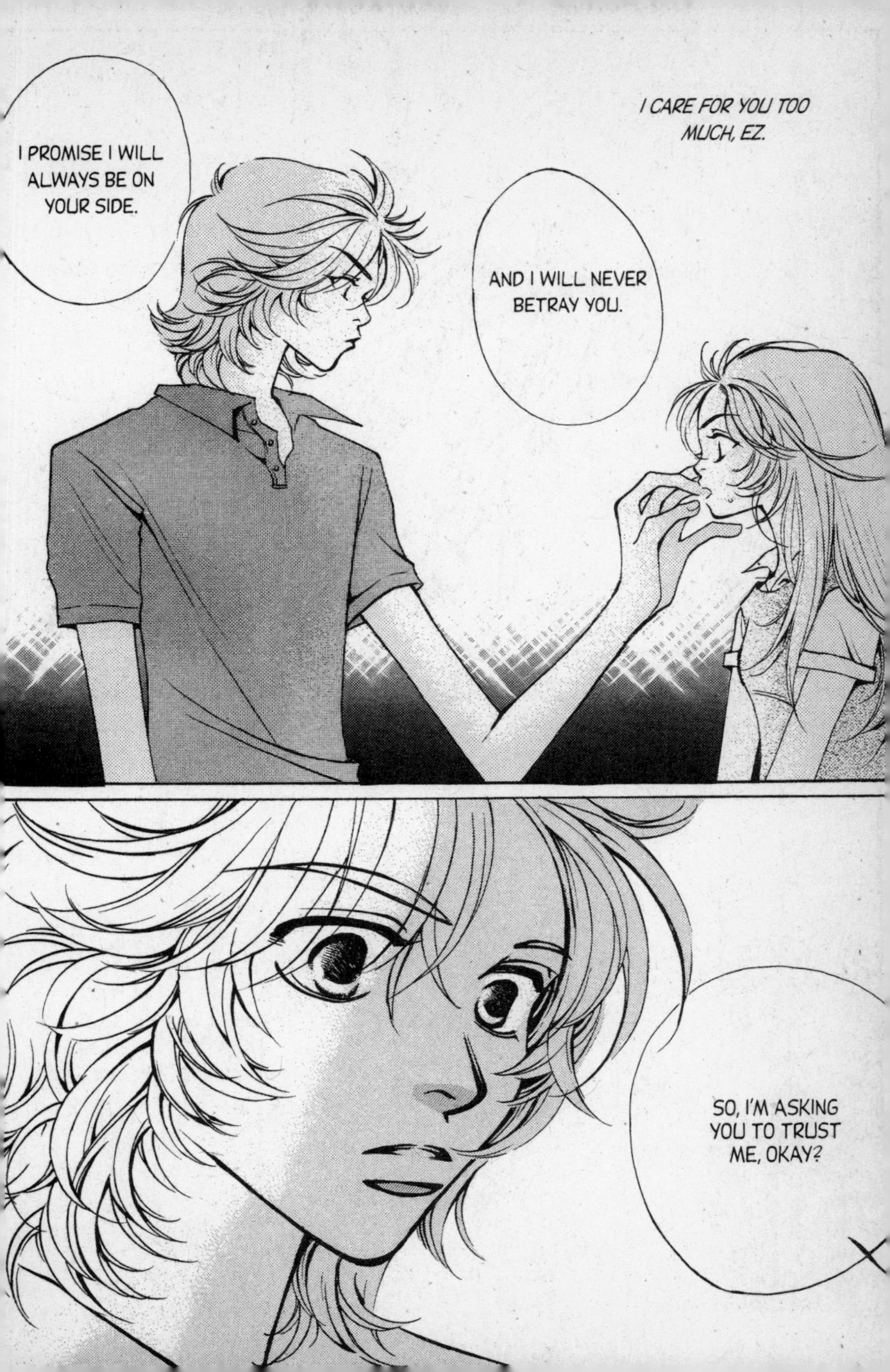
I PROMISE I WILL ALWAYS BE ON YOUR SIDE.
AND I WILL NEVER BETRAY YOU.
I CARE FOR YOU TOO MUCH, EZ.
SO, I'M ASKING YOU TO TRUST ME, OKAY?

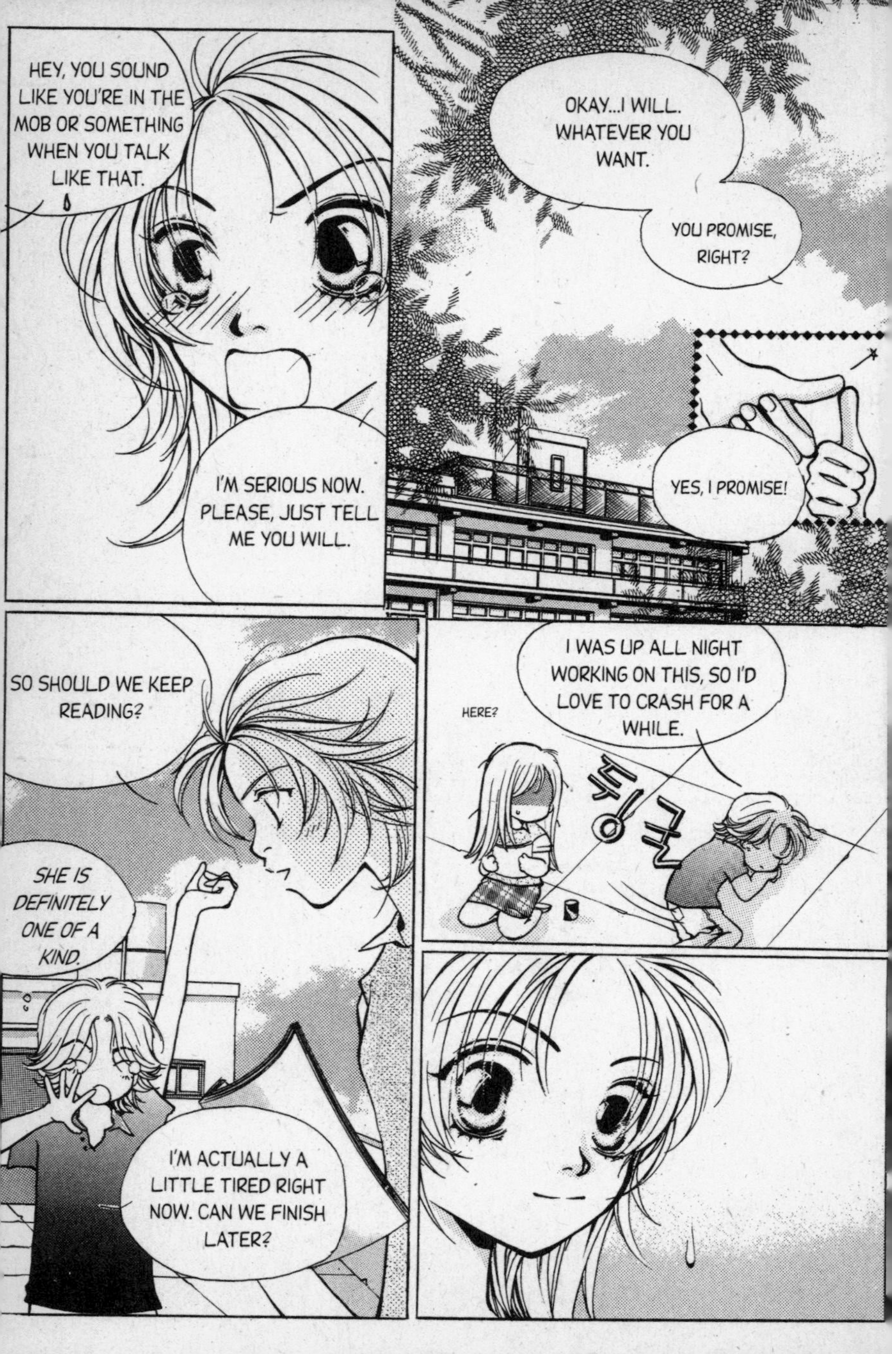
HEY, YOU SOUND LIKE YOU'RE IN THE MOB OR SOMETHING WHEN YOU TALK LIKE THAT.
I'M SERIOUS NOW. PLEASE, JUST TELL ME YOU WILL.
OKAY...I WILL. WHATEVER YOU WANT.
YOU PROMISE, RIGHT?
YES, I PROMISE!
SO SHOULD WE KEEP READING?
SHE IS DEFINITELY ONE OF A KIND.
I'M ACTUALLY A LITTLE TIRED RIGHT NOW. CAN WE FINISH LATER?
I WAS UP ALL NIGHT WORKING ON THIS, SO I'D LOVE TO CRASH FOR A WHILE.
HERE?
털썩

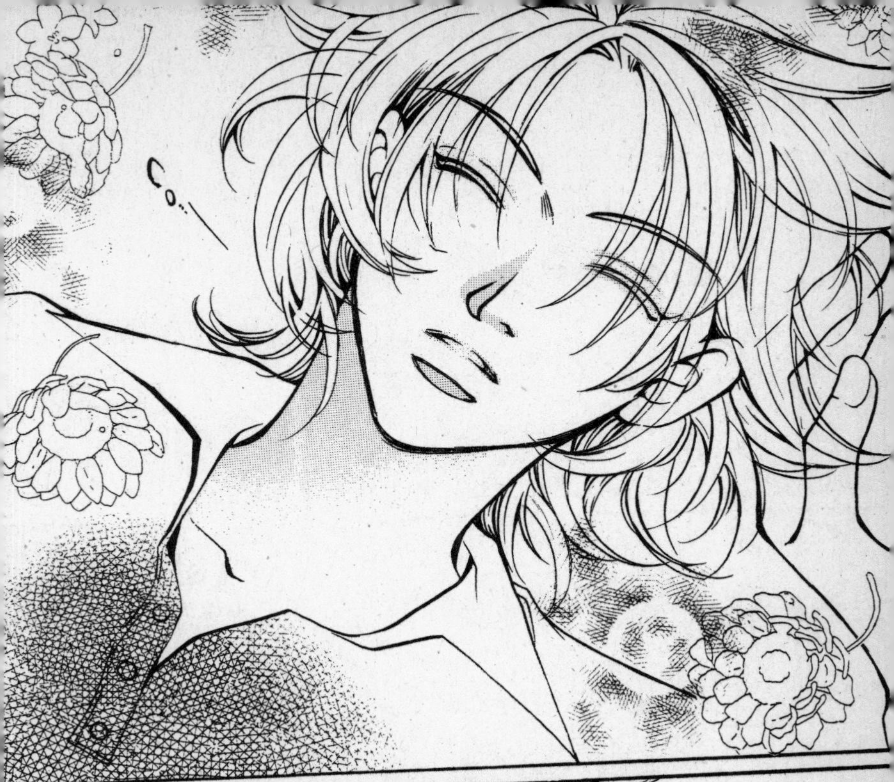
Co...

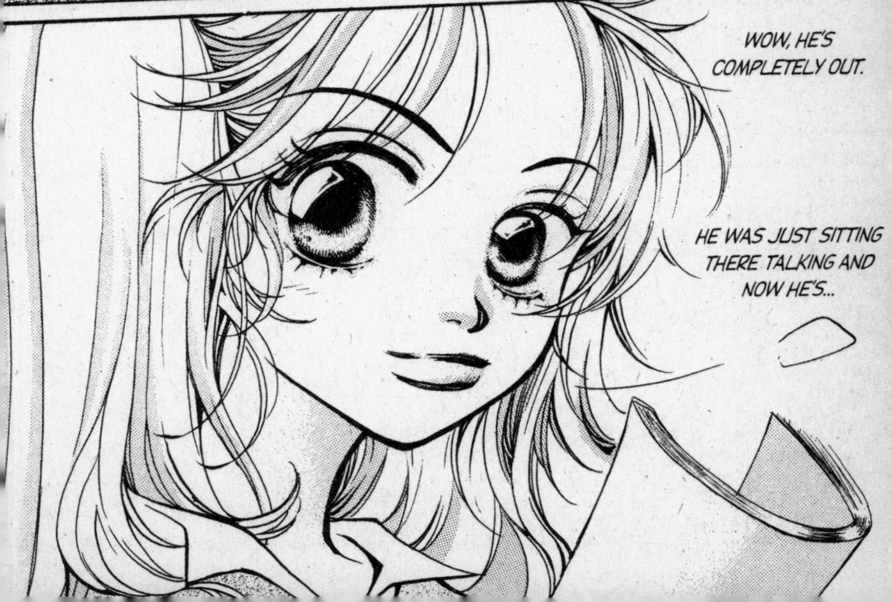
WOW, HE'S COMPLETELY OUT.
HE WAS JUST SITTING THERE TALKING AND NOW HE'S...

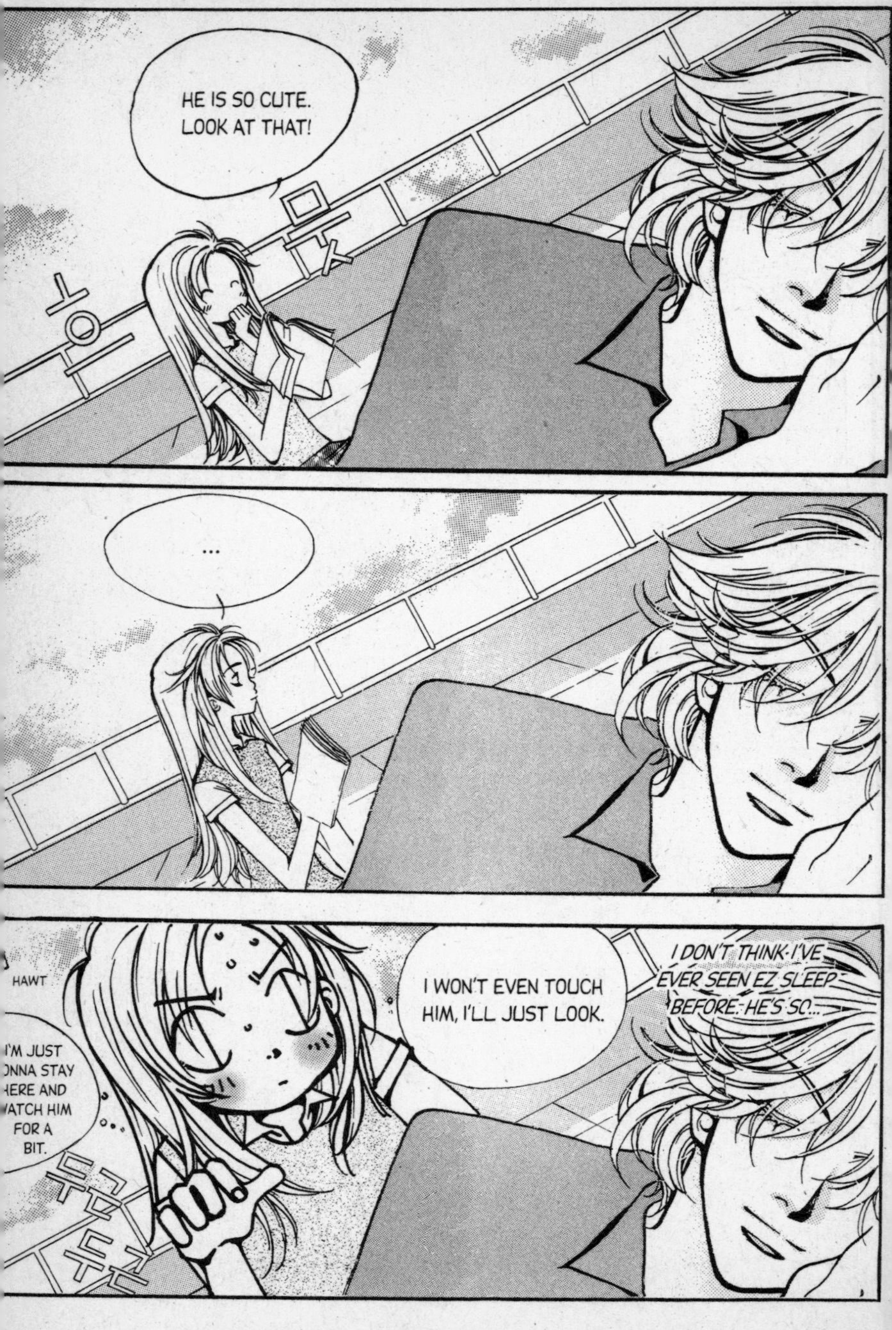
HE IS SO CUTE. LOOK AT THAT!
...
HAWT
I'M JUST ONNA STAY HERE AND ATCH HIM FOR A BIT.
I WON'T EVEN TOUCH HIM, I'LL JUST LOOK.
I DON'T THINK I'VE EVER SEEN EZ SLEEP BEFORE. HE'S SO...

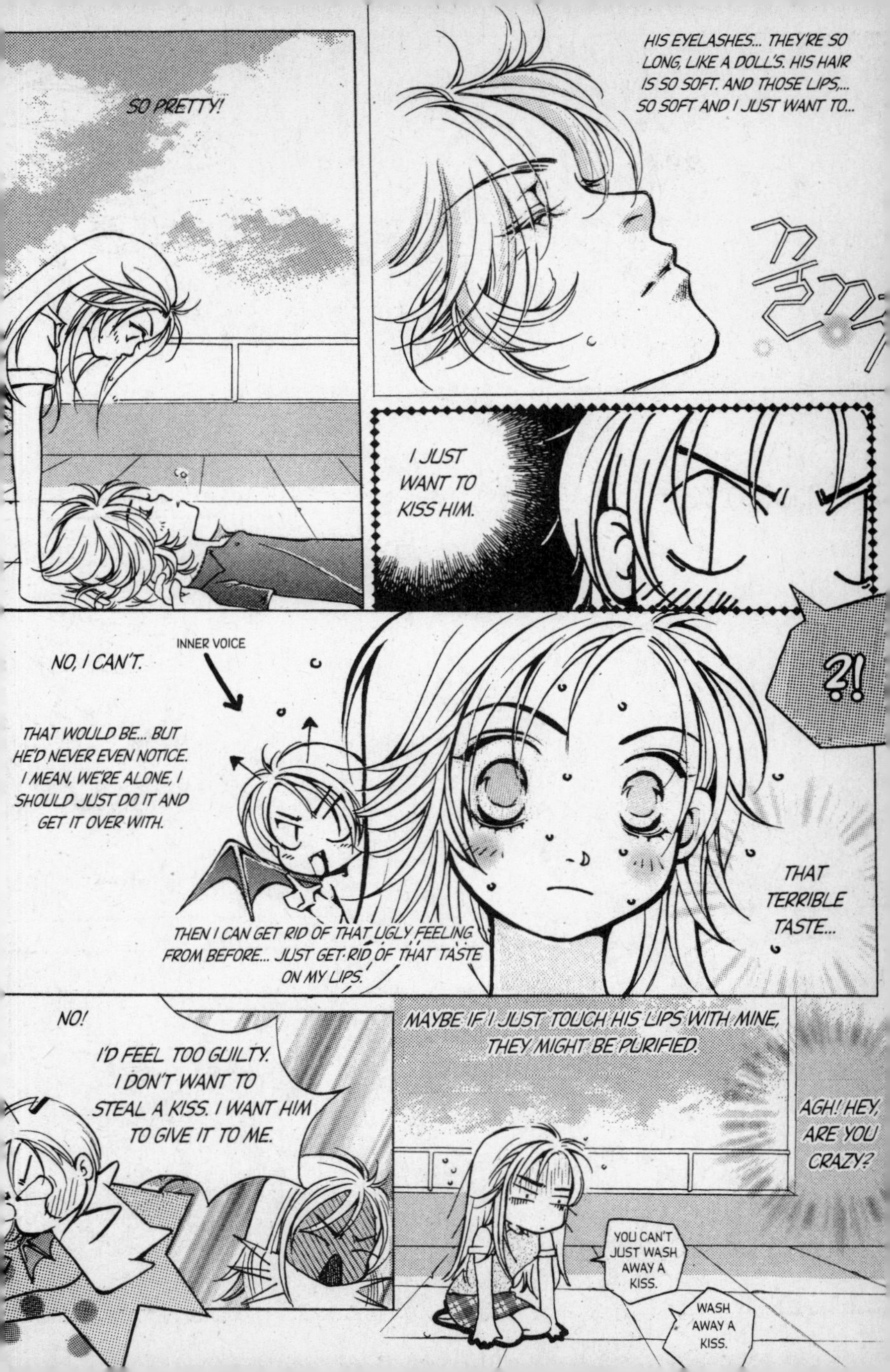
SO PRETTY!
HIS EYELASHES... THEY'RE SO LONG, LIKE A DOLL'S. HIS HAIR IS SO SOFT. AND THOSE LIPS,... SO SOFT AND I JUST WANT TO...
I JUST WANT TO KISS HIM.
?!
THAT TERRIBLE TASTE...
NO, I CAN'T.
INNER VOICE
THAT WOULD BE... BUT HE'D NEVER EVEN NOTICE. I MEAN, WE'RE ALONE, I SHOULD JUST DO IT AND GET IT OVER WITH.
THEN I CAN GET RID OF THAT UGLY FEELING FROM BEFORE... JUST GET RID OF THAT TASTE ON MY LIPS.
NO!
I'D FEEL TOO GUILTY. I DON'T WANT TO STEAL A KISS. I WANT HIM TO GIVE IT TO ME.
MAYBE IF I JUST TOUCH HIS LIPS WITH MINE, THEY MIGHT BE PURIFIED.
AGH! HEY, ARE YOU CRAZY?
YOU CAN'T JUST WASH AWAY A KISS.
WASH AWAY A KISS.

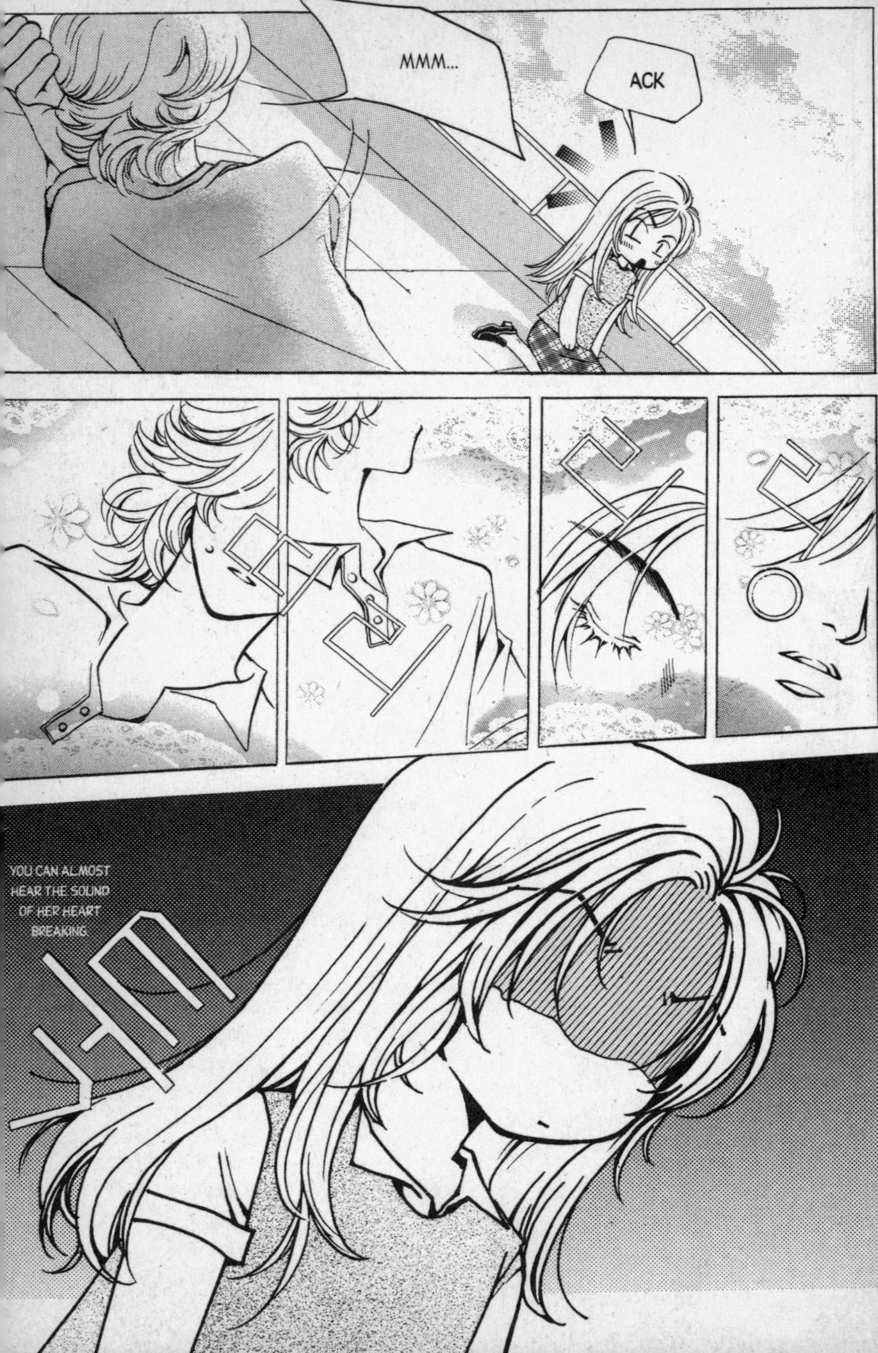
ACK
MMM...
YOU CAN ALMOST HEAR THE SOUND OF HER HEART BREAKING.

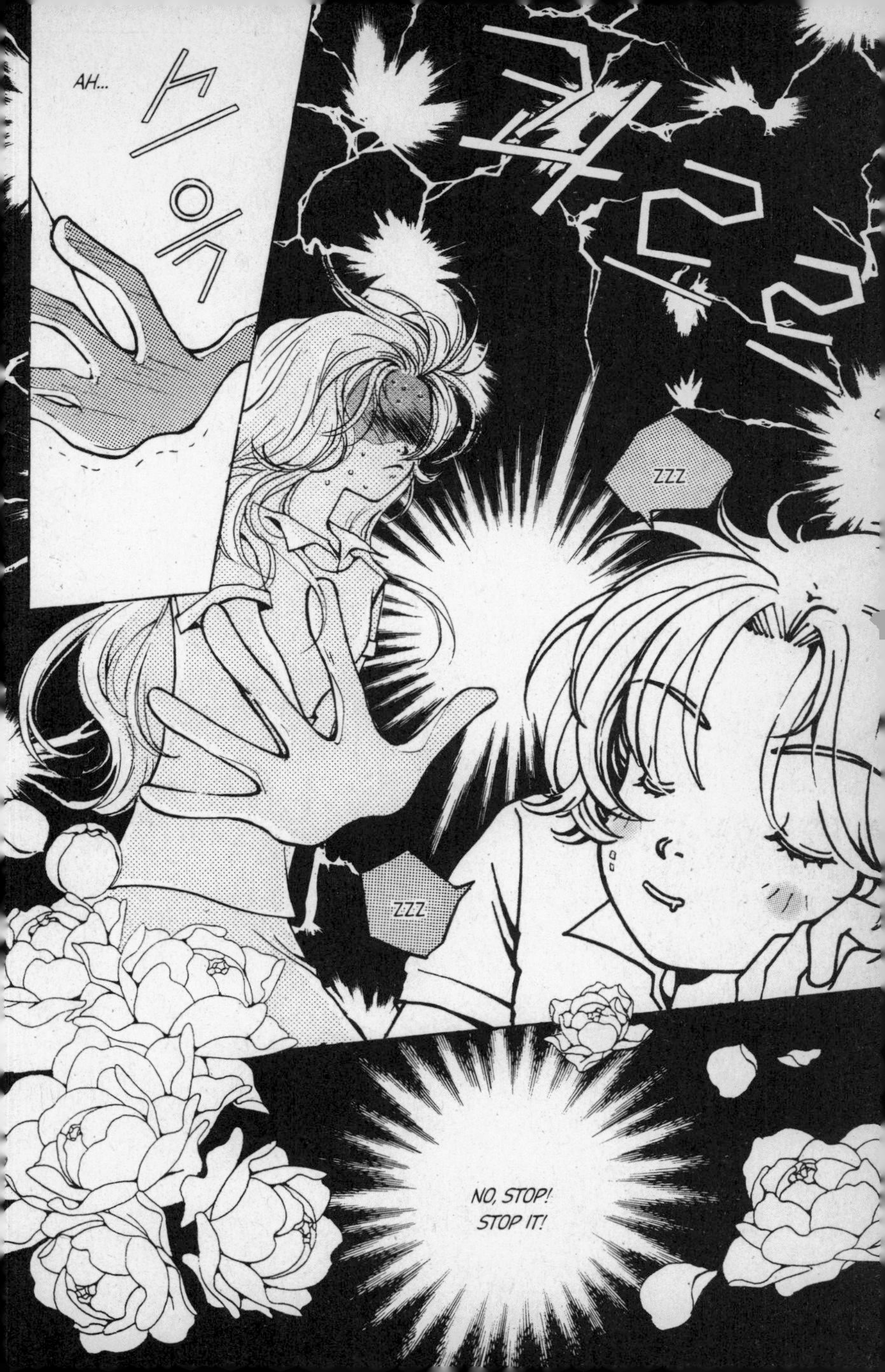
AH...
ZZZ
ZZZ
NO, STOP!
STOP IT!

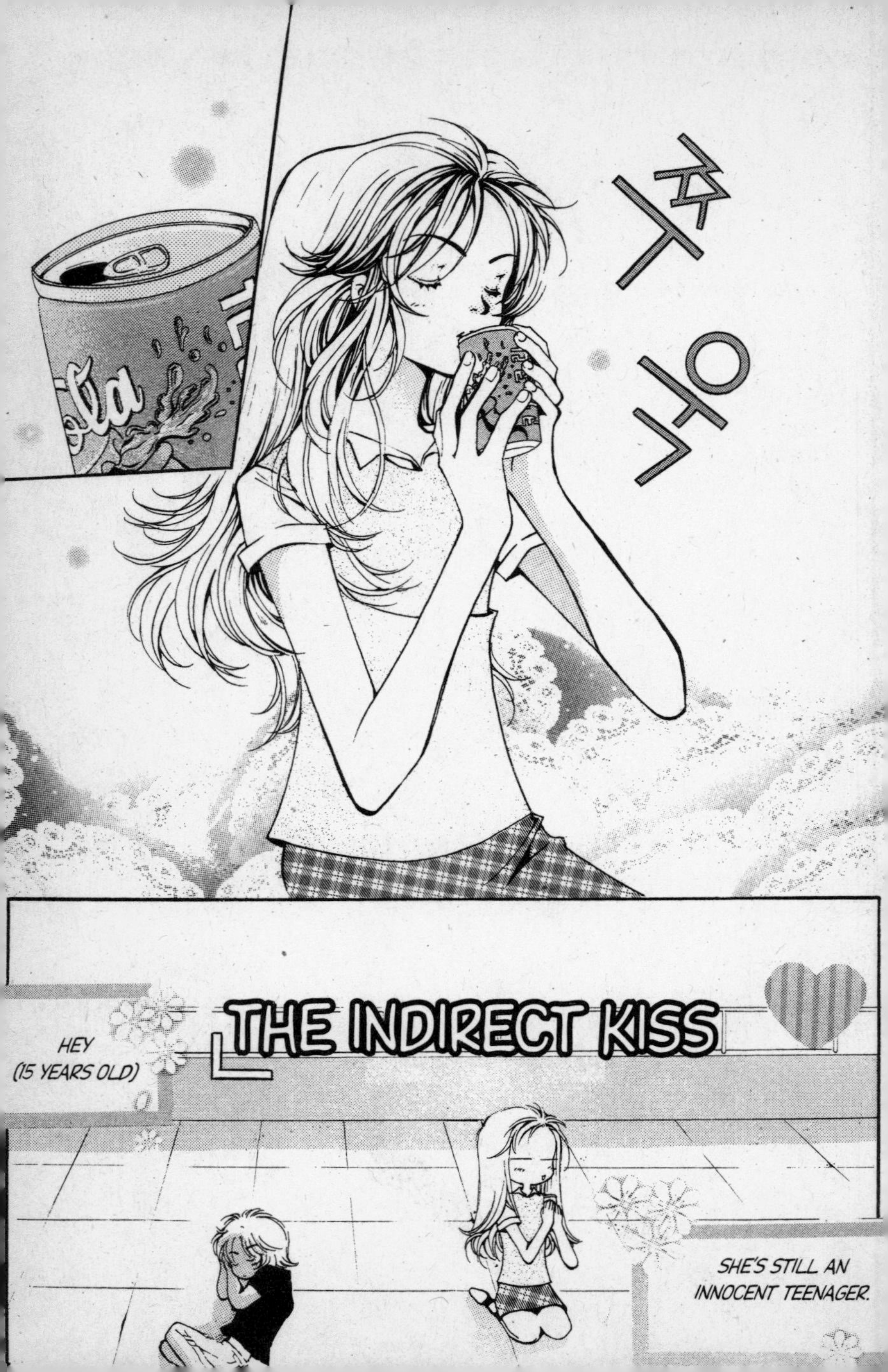
THE INDIRECT KISS
HEY
(15 YEARS OLD)
SHE'S STILL AN INNOCENT TEENAGER.

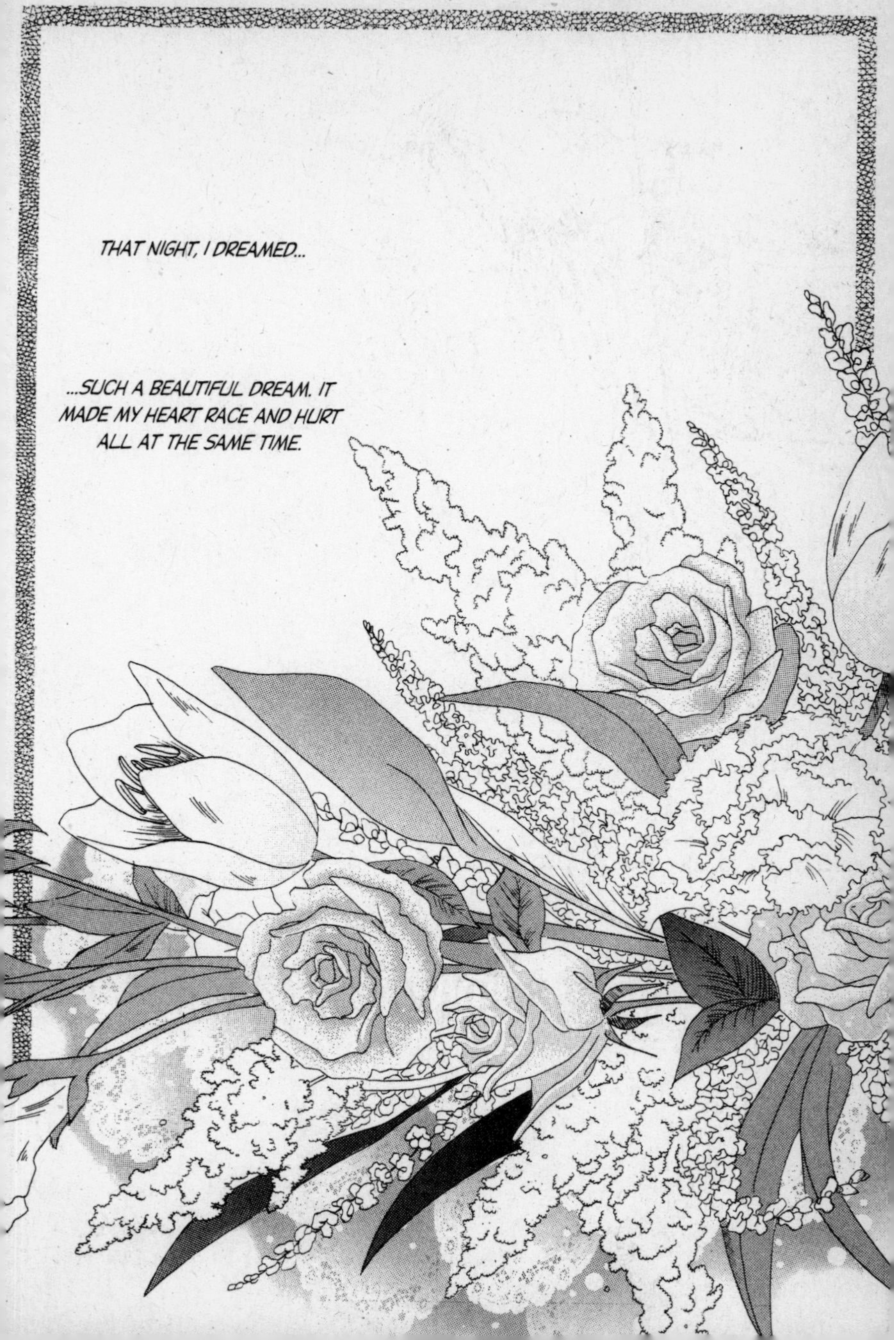
THAT NIGHT, I DREAMED...
...SUCH A BEAUTIFUL DREAM. IT MADE MY HEART RACE AND HURT ALL AT THE SAME TIME.

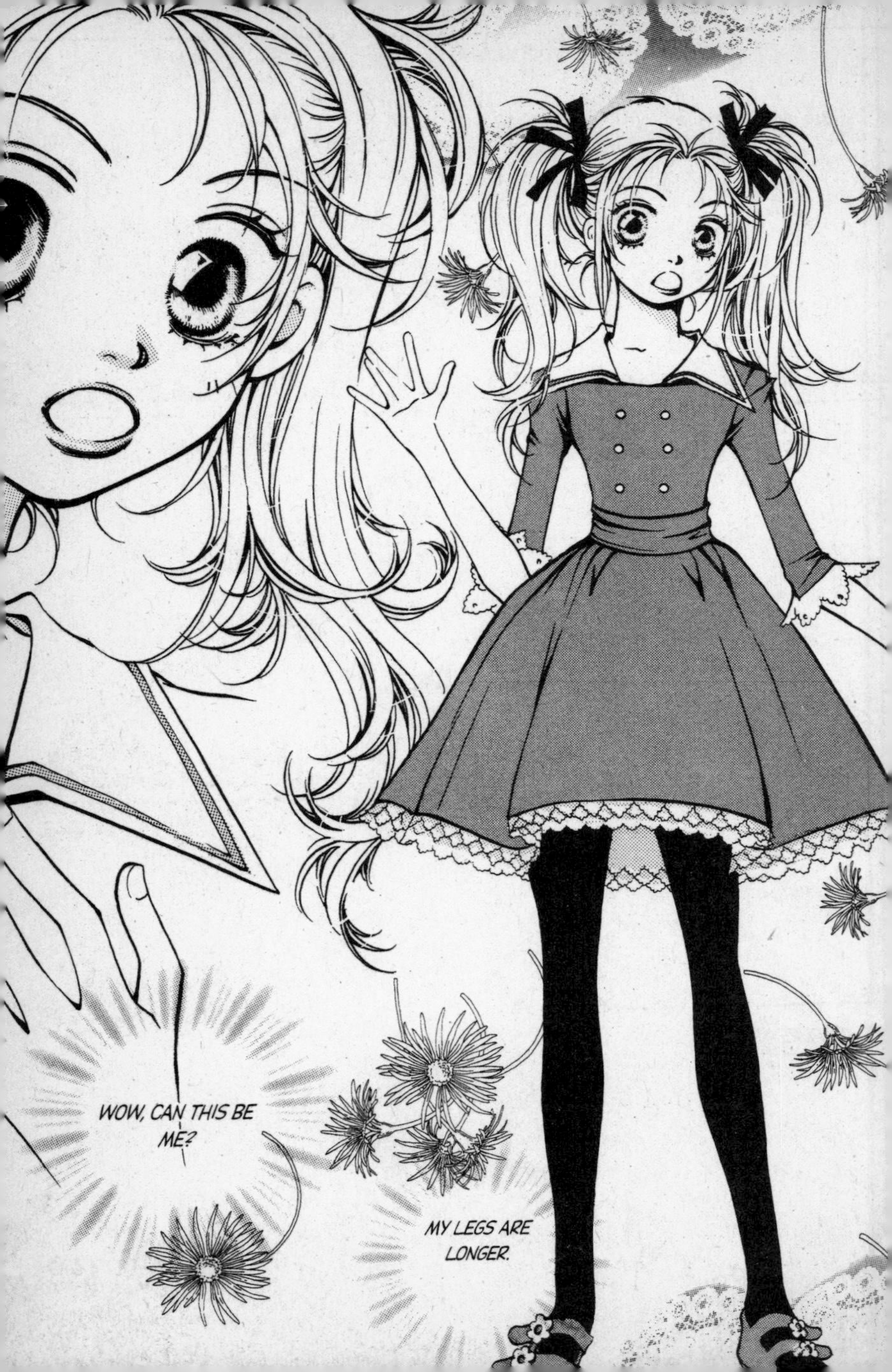
WOW, CAN THIS BE ME?
MY LEGS ARE LONGER.

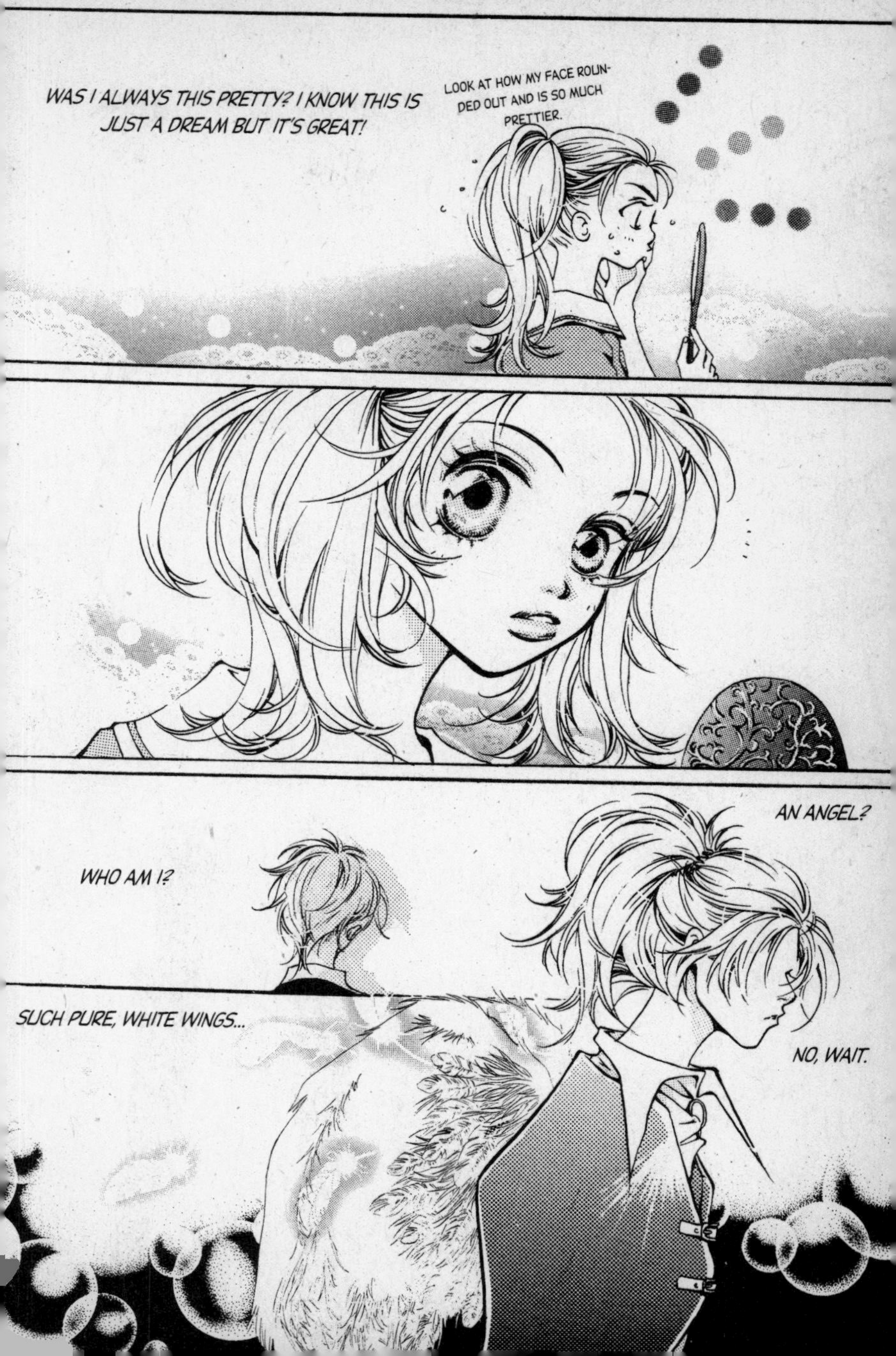
LOOK AT HOW MY FACE ROUNDED OUT AND IS SO MUCH PRETTIER.
WAS I ALWAYS THIS PRETTY? I KNOW THIS IS JUST A DREAM BUT IT'S GREAT!
AN ANGEL?
WHO AM I?
NO, WAIT.
SUCH PURE, WHITE WINGS...

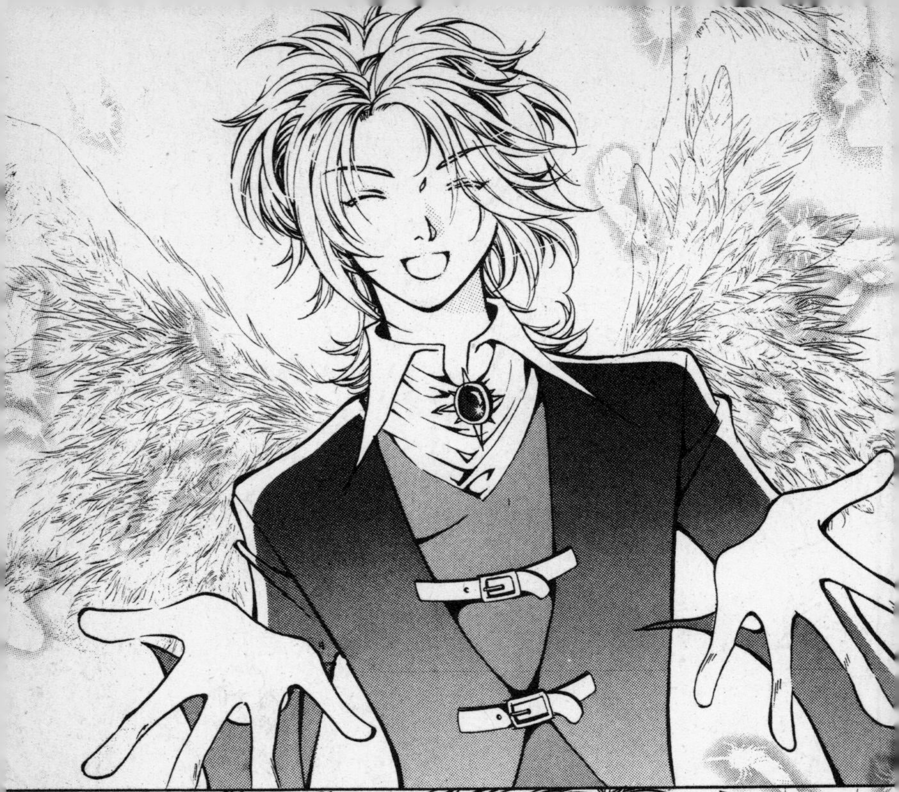
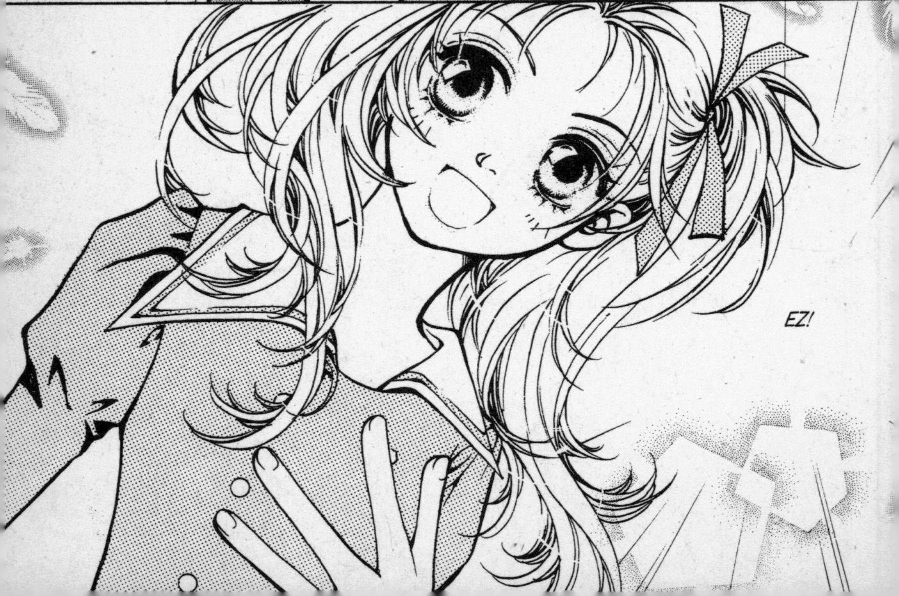
EZ!

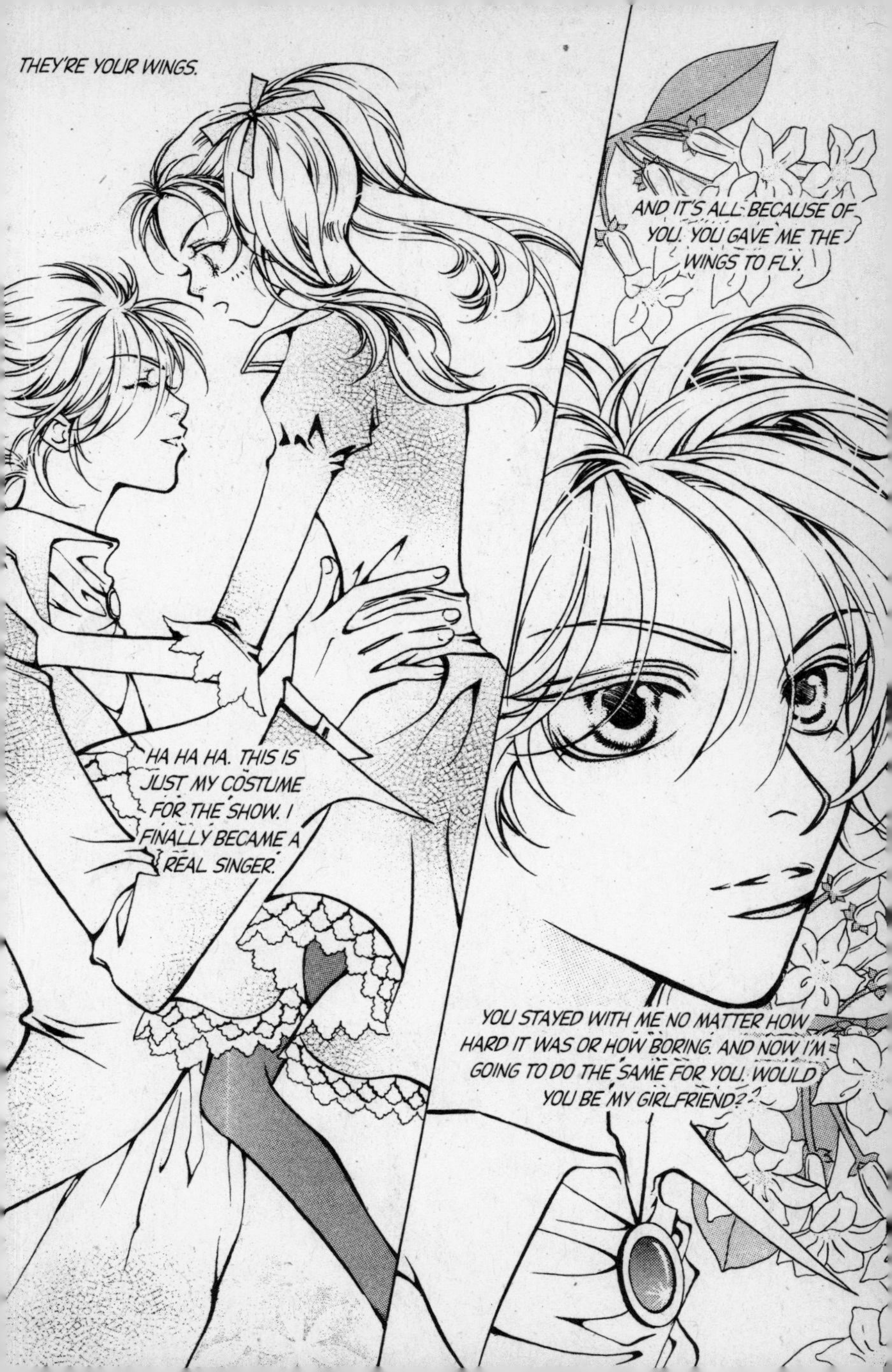
THEY'RE YOUR WINGS.
HA HA HA. THIS IS JUST MY COSTUME FOR THE SHOW. I FINALLY BECAME A REAL SINGER.
AND IT'S ALL BECAUSE OF YOU. YOU GAVE ME THE WINGS TO FLY.
YOU STAYED WITH ME NO MATTER HOW HARD IT WAS OR HOW BORING. AND NOW I'M GOING TO DO THE SAME FOR YOU. WOULD YOU BE MY GIRLFRIEND?

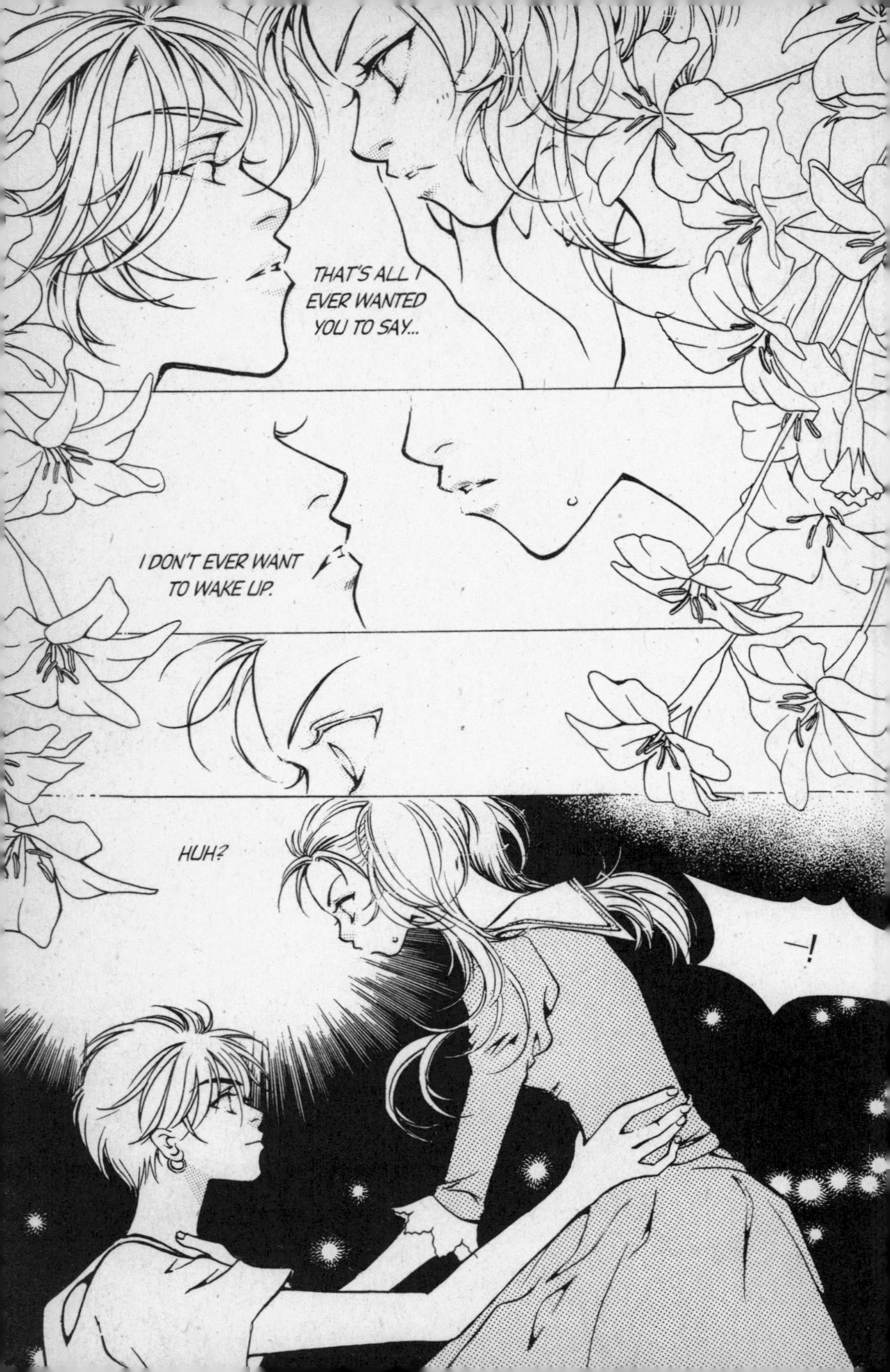
THAT'S ALL I EVER WANTED YOU TO SAY...
I DON'T EVER WANT TO WAKE UP.
HUH?
—!

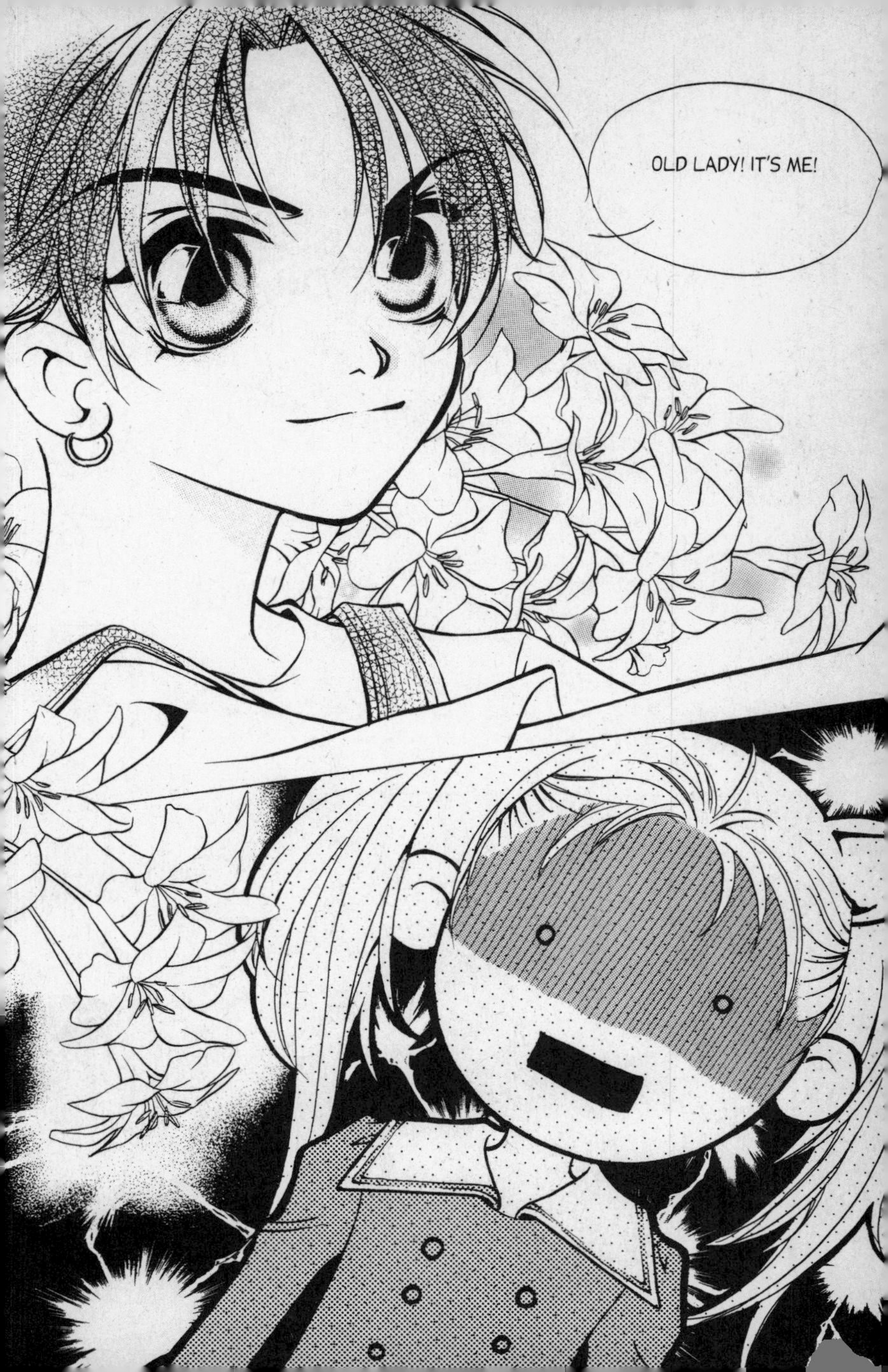
OLD LADY! IT'S ME!

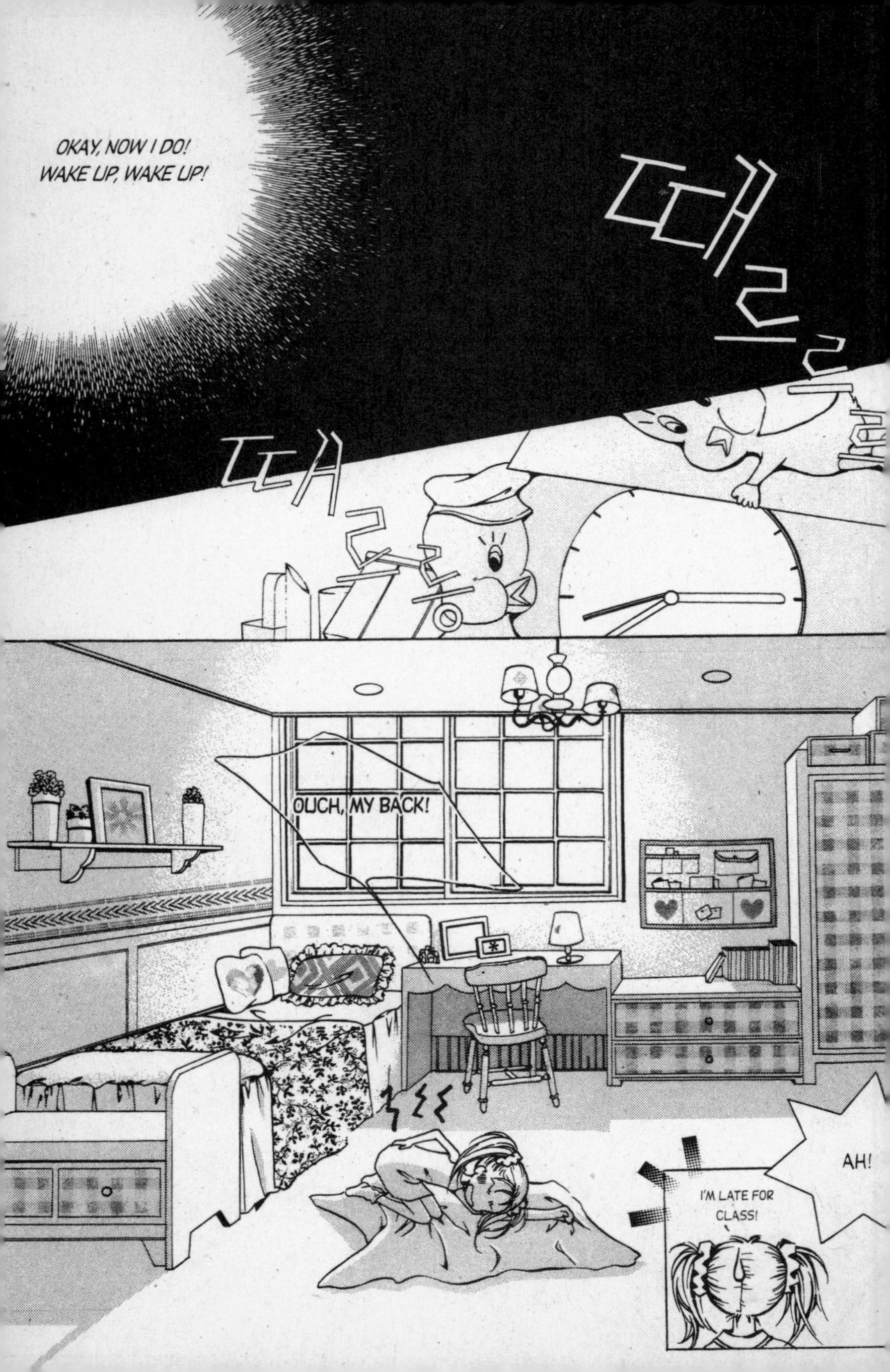
OKAY, NOW I DO!
WAKE UP, WAKE UP!
OUCH, MY BACK!
AH!
I'M LATE FOR CLASS!

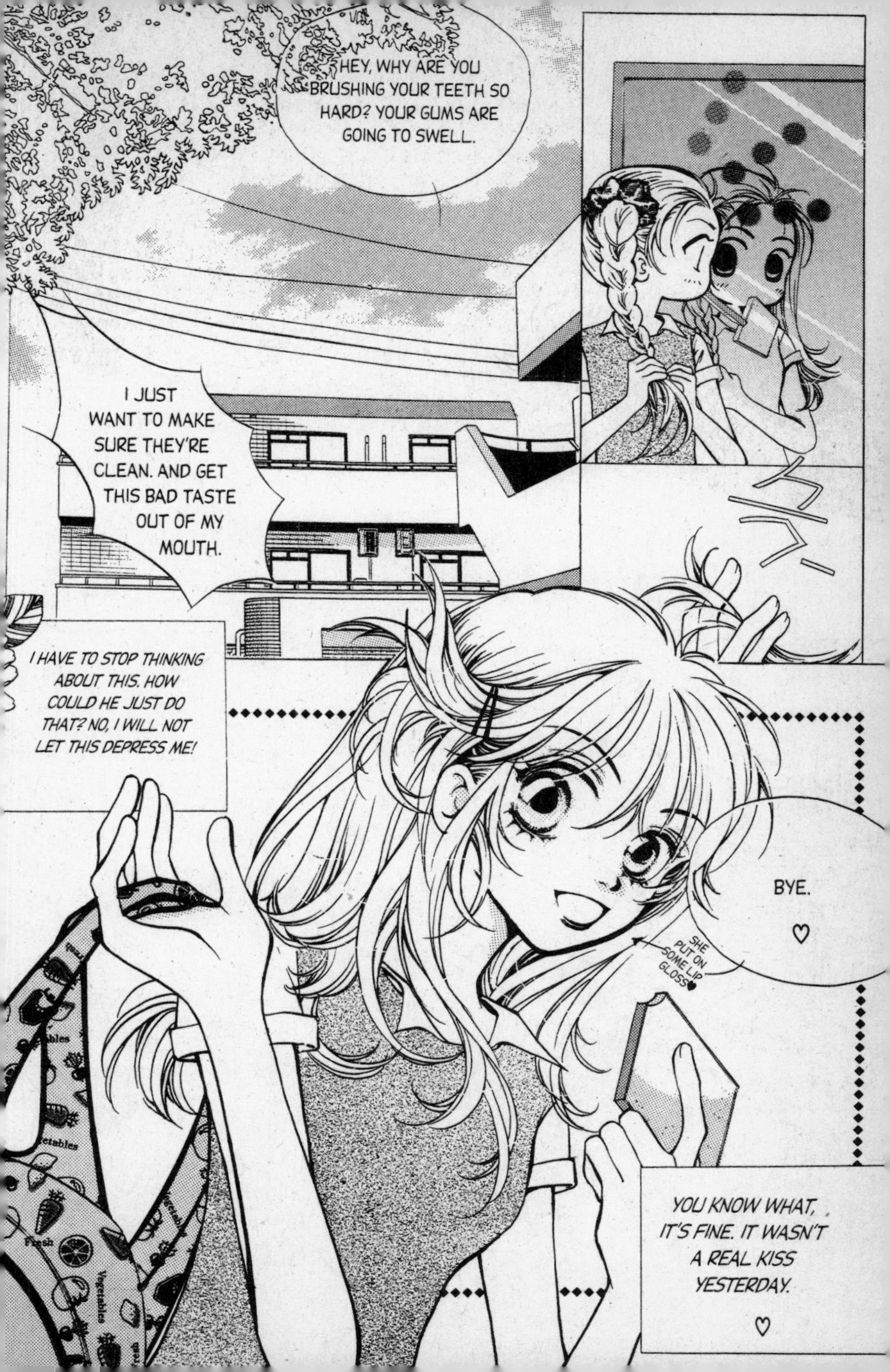
HEY, WHY ARE YOU BRUSHING YOUR TEETH SO HARD? YOUR GUMS ARE GOING TO SWELL.
I JUST WANT TO MAKE SURE THEY'RE CLEAN. AND GET THIS BAD TASTE OUT OF MY MOUTH.
I HAVE TO STOP THINKING ABOUT THIS. HOW COULD HE JUST DO THAT? NO, I WILL NOT LET THIS DEPRESS ME!
YOU KNOW WHAT, IT'S FINE. IT WASN'T A REAL KISS YESTERDAY. ♡
BYE. ♡
SHE PUT ON SOME LIP GLOSS♥

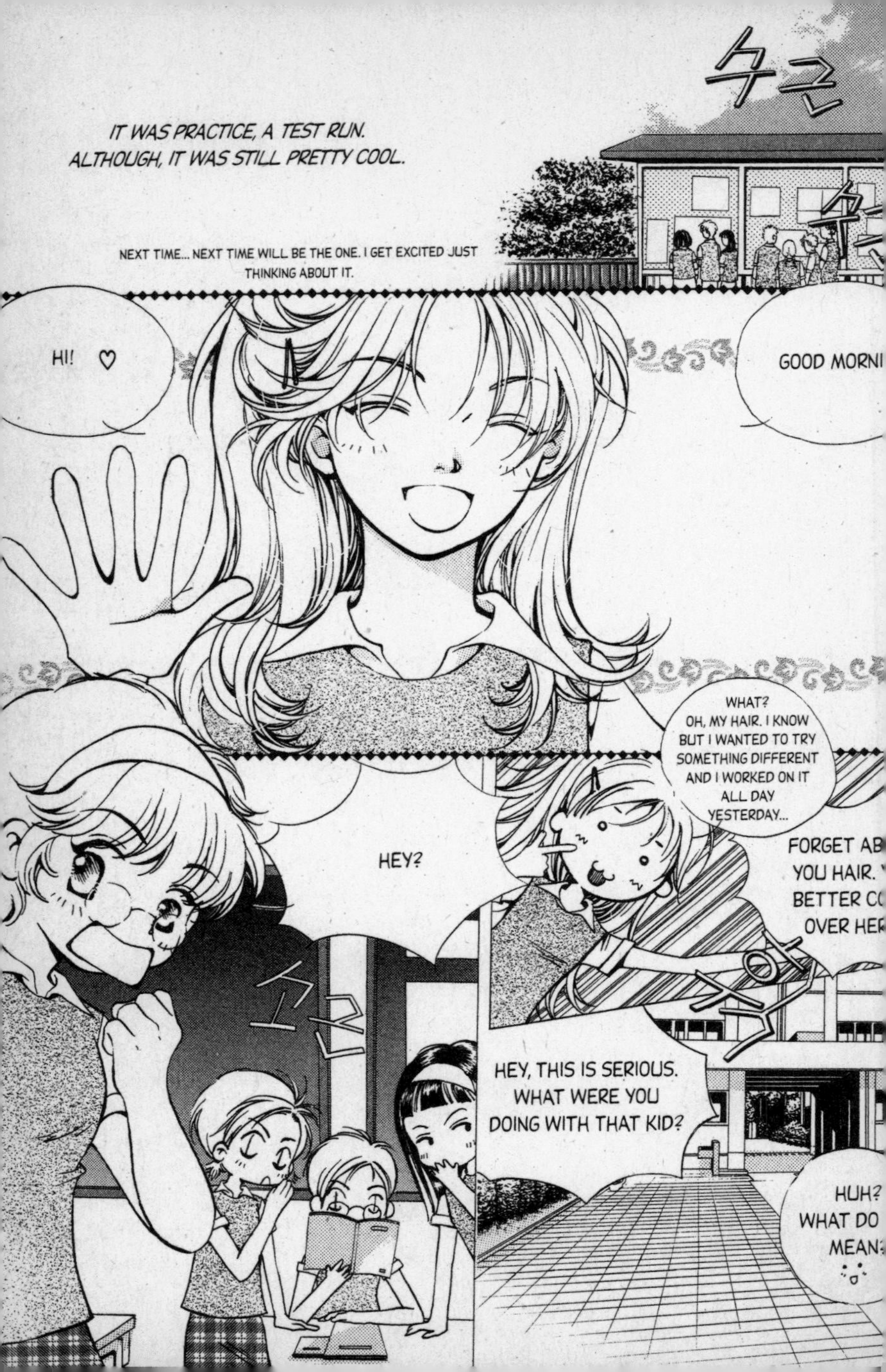
IT WAS PRACTICE, A TEST RUN.
ALTHOUGH, IT WAS STILL PRETTY COOL.
NEXT TIME... NEXT TIME WILL BE THE ONE. I GET EXCITED JUST THINKING ABOUT IT.
HI! ♡
GOOD MORNI
HEY?
WHAT? OH, MY HAIR. I KNOW BUT I WANTED TO TRY SOMETHING DIFFERENT AND I WORKED ON IT ALL DAY YESTERDAY...
FORGET AB YOU HAIR. BETTER CO OVER HER
HEY, THIS IS SERIOUS. WHAT WERE YOU DOING WITH THAT KID?
HUH? WHAT DO MEAN?

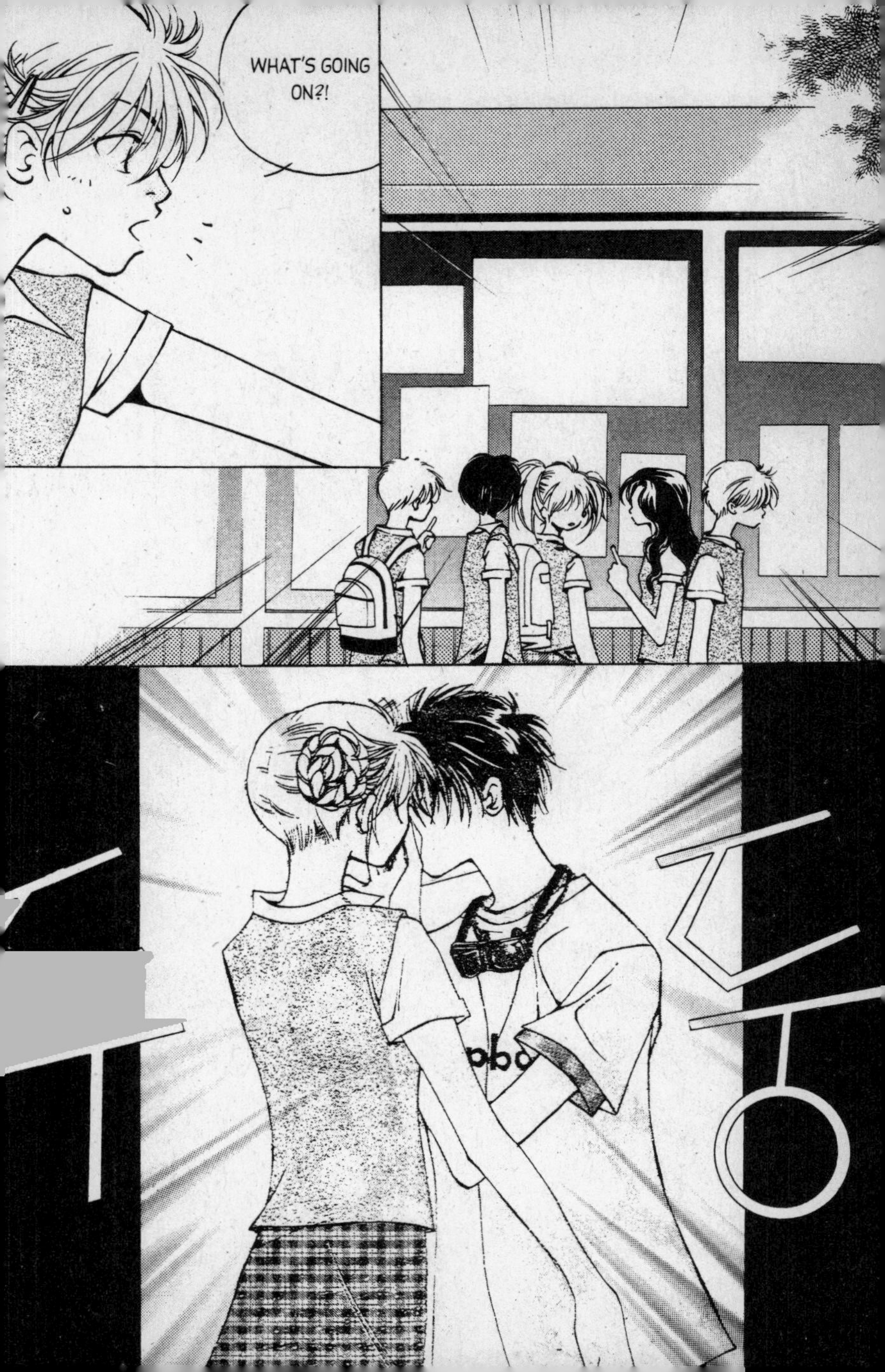
WHAT'S GOING ON?!

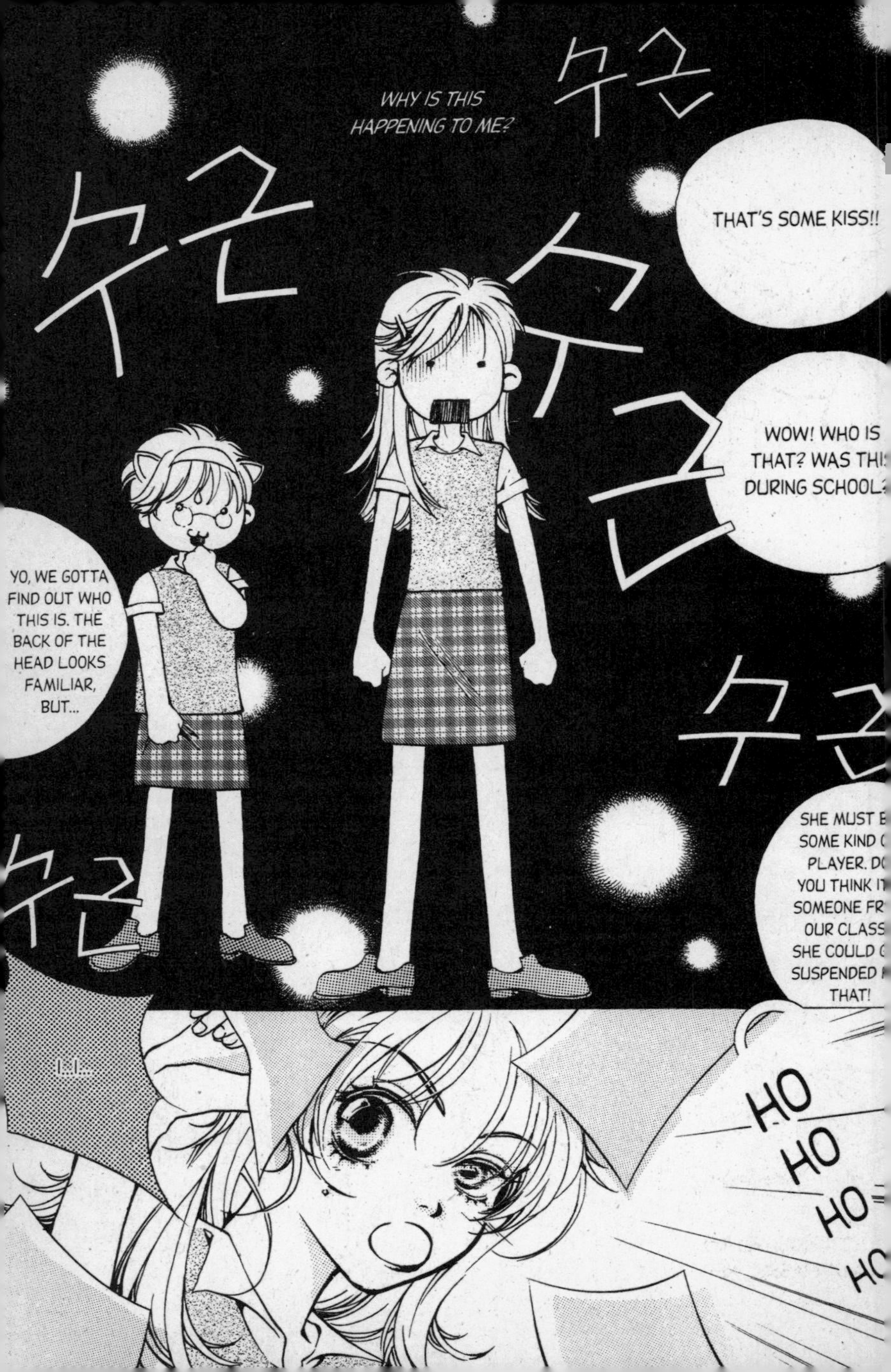
WHY IS THIS HAPPENING TO ME?
THAT'S SOME KISS!!
WOW! WHO IS THAT? WAS THI DURING SCHOOL
SHE MUST B SOME KIND PLAYER. D YOU THINK I SOMEONE FR OUR CLASS SHE COULD SUSPENDED THAT!
YO, WE GOTTA FIND OUT WHO THIS IS. THE BACK OF THE HEAD LOOKS FAMILIAR, BUT...
HO HO HO HO
I..I...

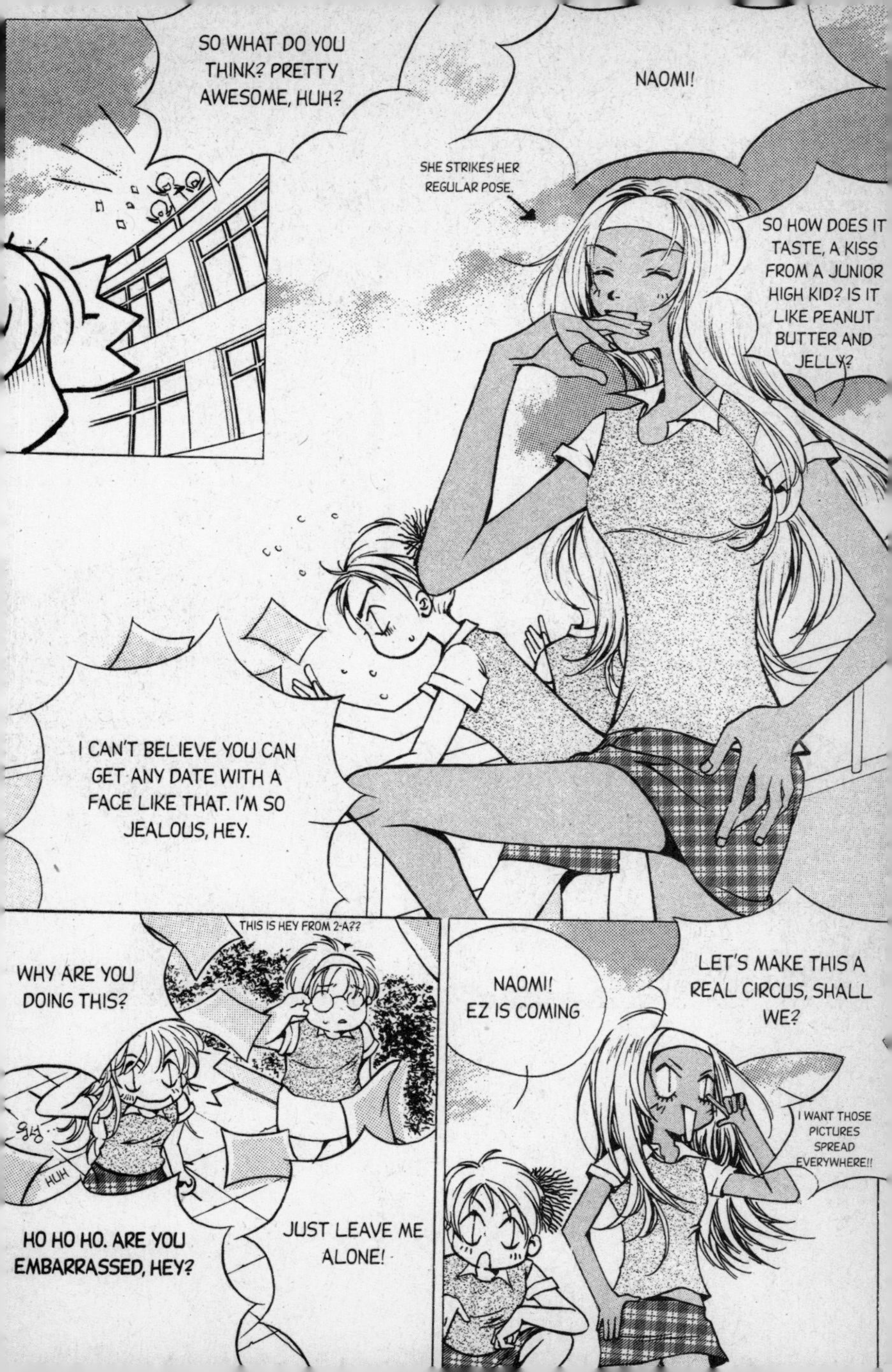
NAOMI!
SO WHAT DO YOU THINK? PRETTY AWESOME, HUH?
SHE STRIKES HER REGULAR POSE.
SO HOW DOES IT TASTE, A KISS FROM A JUNIOR HIGH KID? IS IT LIKE PEANUT BUTTER AND JELLY?
I CAN'T BELIEVE YOU CAN GET ANY DATE WITH A FACE LIKE THAT. I'M SO JEALOUS, HEY.
LET'S MAKE THIS A REAL CIRCUS, SHALL WE?
NAOMI! EZ IS COMING
I WANT THOSE PICTURES SPREAD EVERYWHERE!!
THIS IS HEY FROM 2-A??
WHY ARE YOU DOING THIS?
JUST LEAVE ME ALONE!
HUH
HO HO HO. ARE YOU EMBARRASSED, HEY?

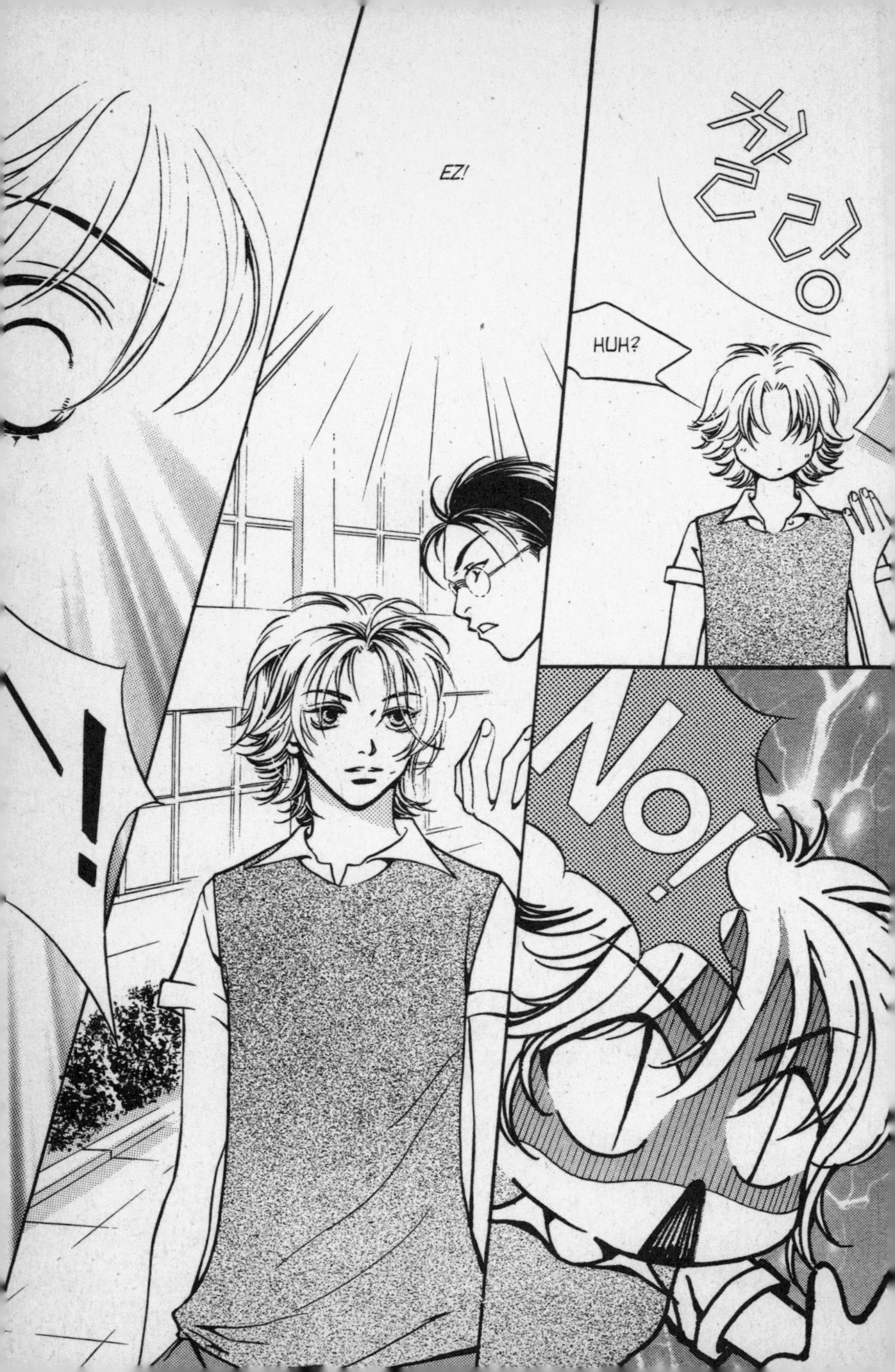
HUH?
NO!
EZ!
!

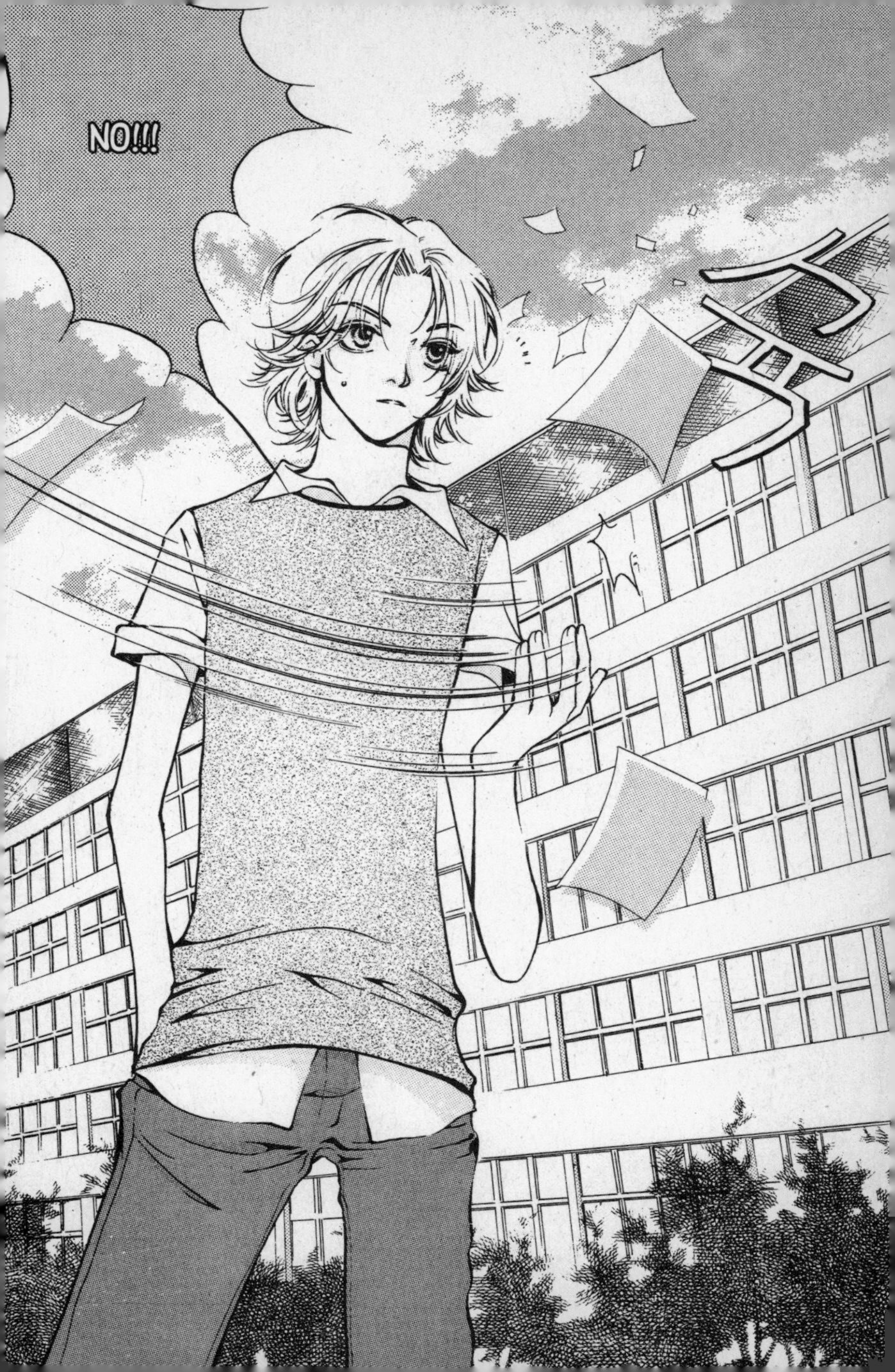
NO!!!

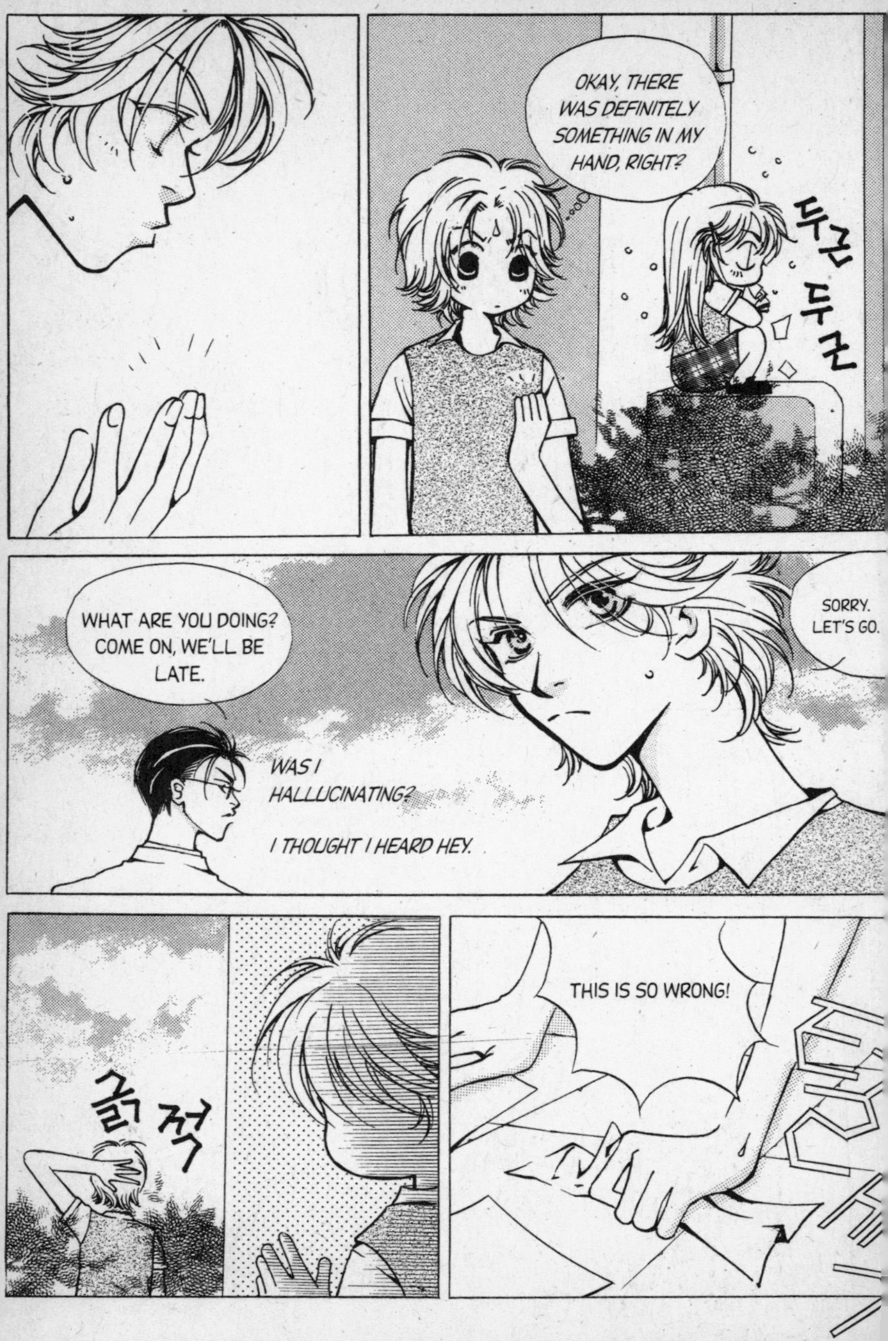
OKAY, THERE WAS DEFINITELY SOMETHING IN MY HAND, RIGHT?
두근 두근
WHAT ARE YOU DOING? COME ON, WE'LL BE LATE.
WAS I HALLUCINATING?
I THOUGHT I HEARD HEY.
SORRY. LET'S GO.
긁적
THIS IS SO WRONG!

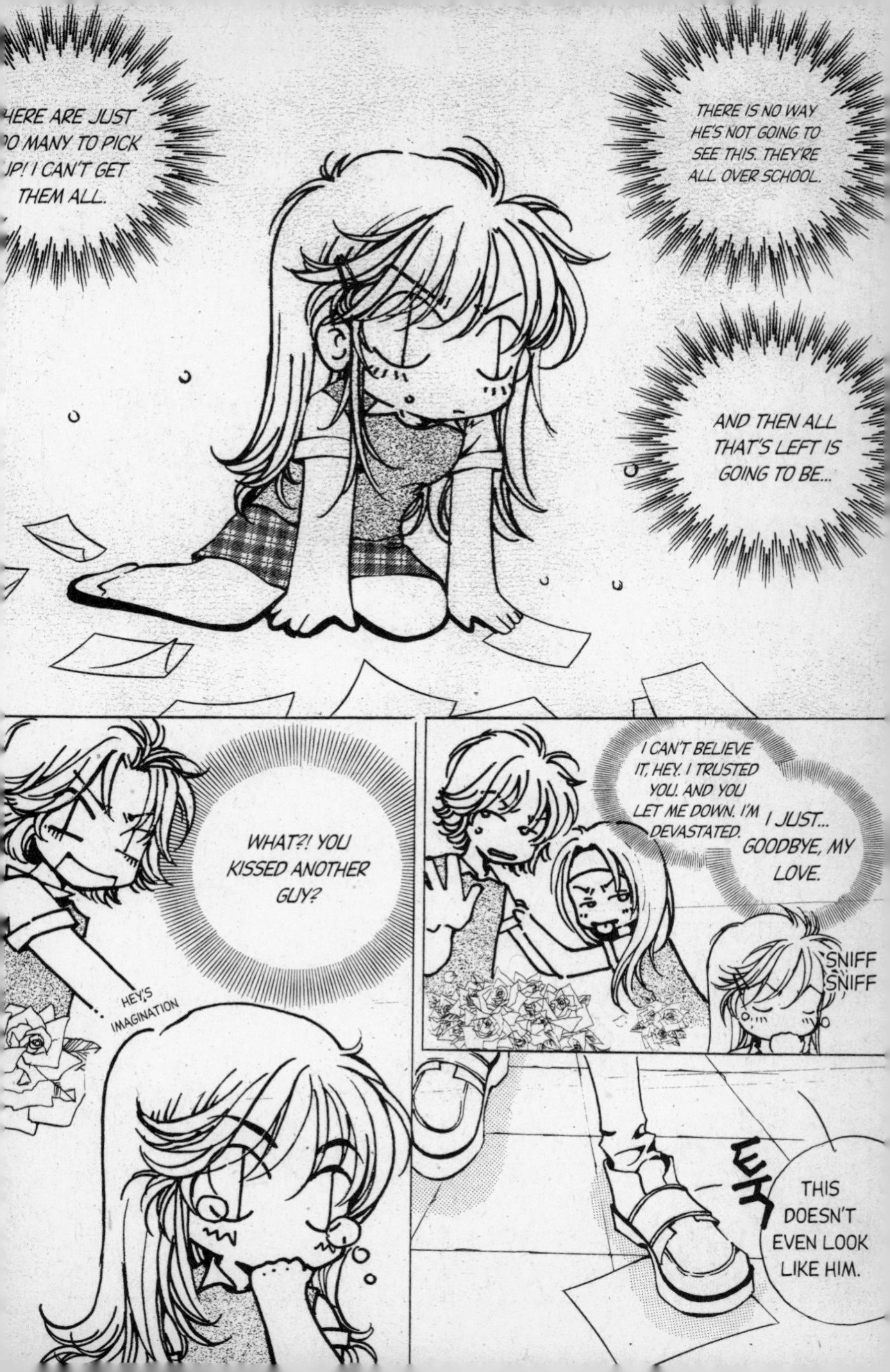
HERE ARE JUST OO MANY TO PICK UP! I CAN'T GET THEM ALL.
THERE IS NO WAY HE'S NOT GOING TO SEE THIS. THEY'RE ALL OVER SCHOOL.
AND THEN ALL THAT'S LEFT IS GOING TO BE...
WHAT?! YOU KISSED ANOTHER GUY?
HEY'S IMAGINATION
I CAN'T BELIEVE IT, HEY. I TRUSTED YOU. AND YOU LET ME DOWN. I'M DEVASTATED.
I JUST... GOODBYE, MY LOVE.
SNIFF SNIFF
THIS DOESN'T EVEN LOOK LIKE HIM.

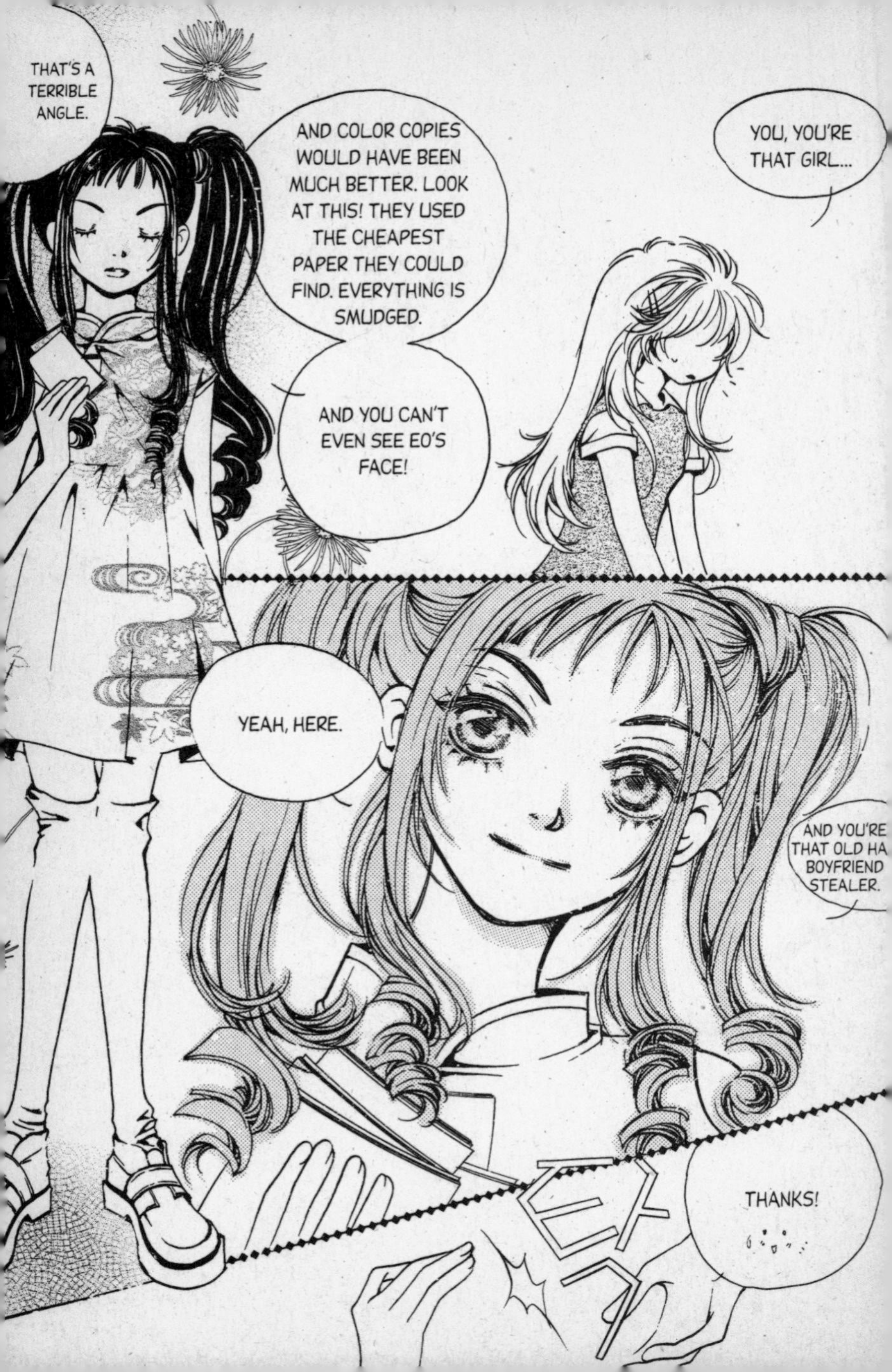
YOU, YOU'RE THAT GIRL...
AND YOU'RE THAT OLD HA BOYFRIEND STEALER.
YEAH, HERE.
THANKS!
THAT'S A TERRIBLE ANGLE.
AND COLOR COPIES WOULD HAVE BEEN MUCH BETTER. LOOK AT THIS! THEY USED THE CHEAPEST PAPER THEY COULD FIND. EVERYTHING IS SMUDGED.
AND YOU CAN'T EVEN SEE EO'S FACE!

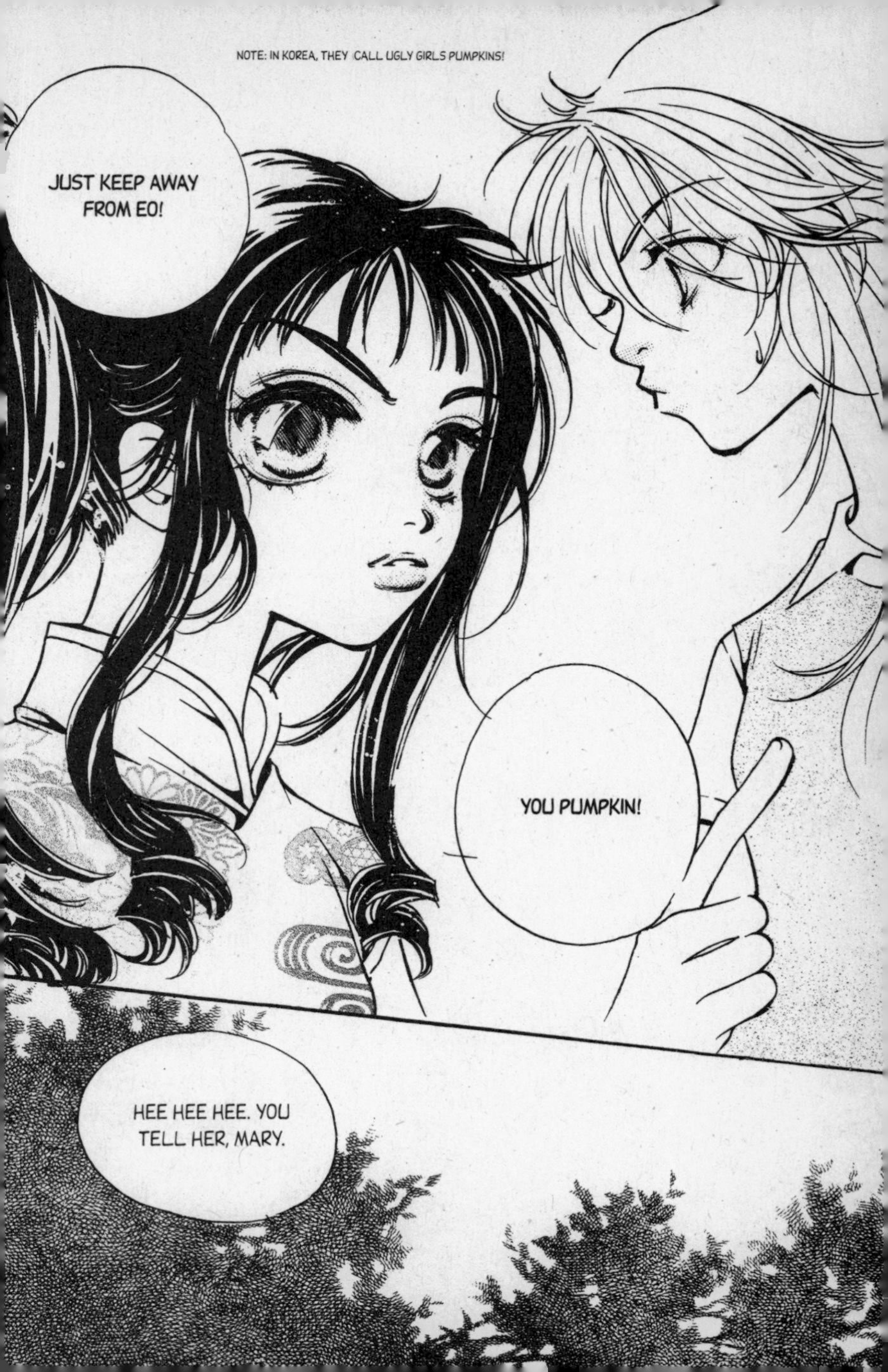
NOTE: IN KOREA, THEY CALL UGLY GIRLS PUMPKINS!
JUST KEEP AWAY FROM EO!
YOU PUMPKIN!
HEE HEE HEE. YOU TELL HER, MARY.

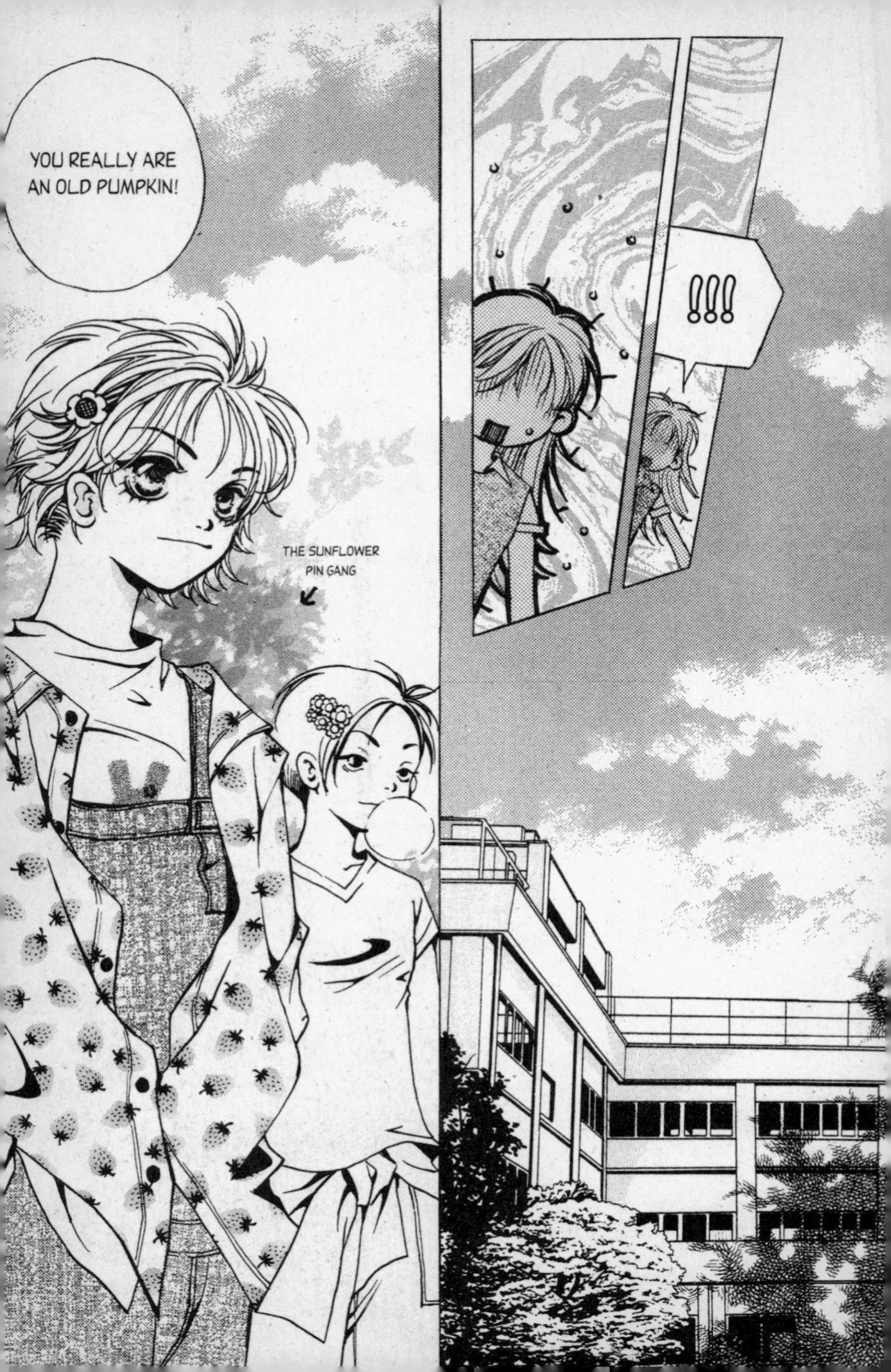
YOU REALLY ARE AN OLD PUMPKIN!
THE SUNFLOWER PIN GANG
!!!

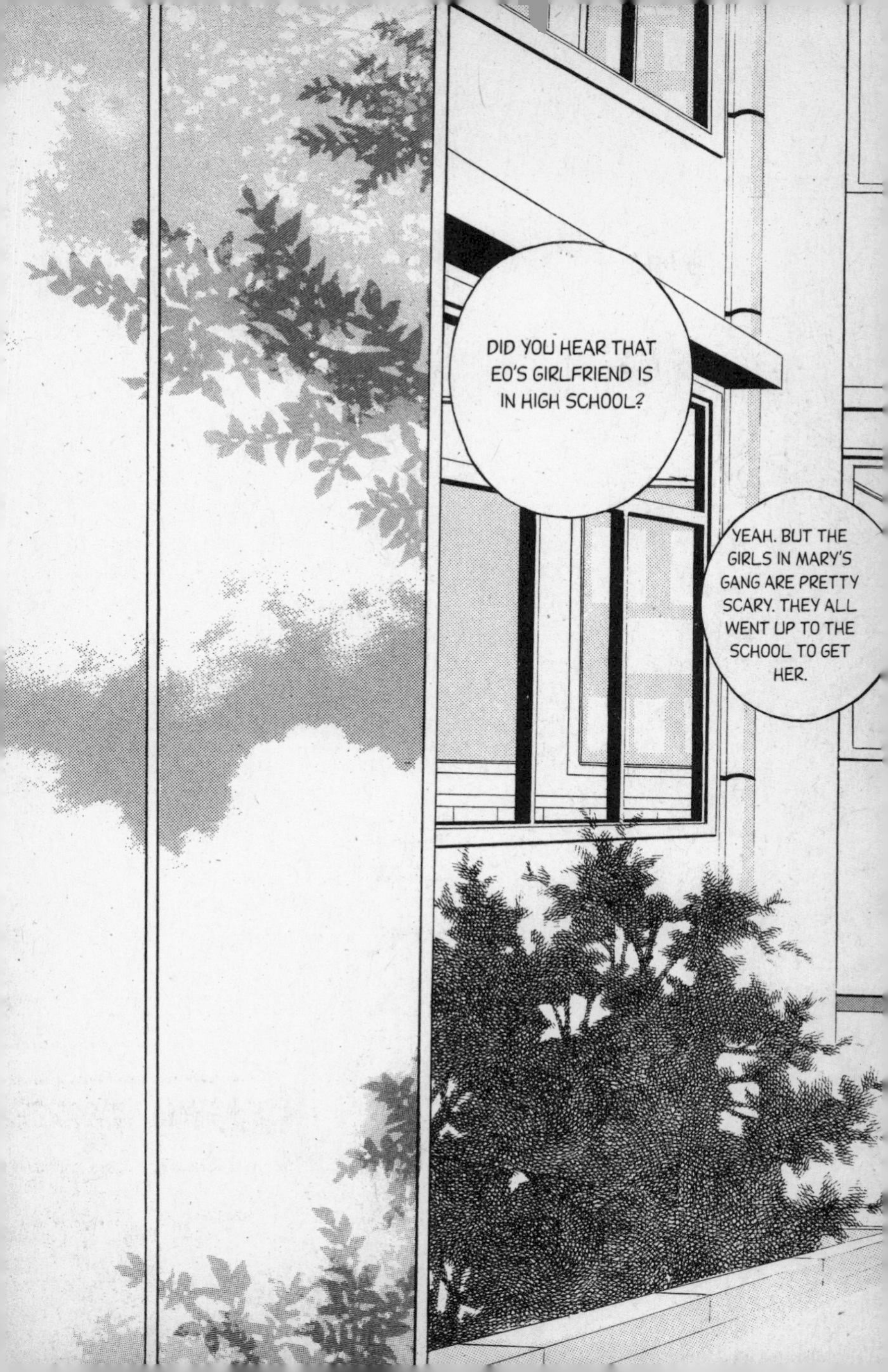
DID YOU HEAR THAT EO'S GIRLFRIEND IS IN HIGH SCHOOL?
YEAH. BUT THE GIRLS IN MARY'S GANG ARE PRETTY SCARY. THEY ALL WENT UP TO THE SCHOOL TO GET HER.

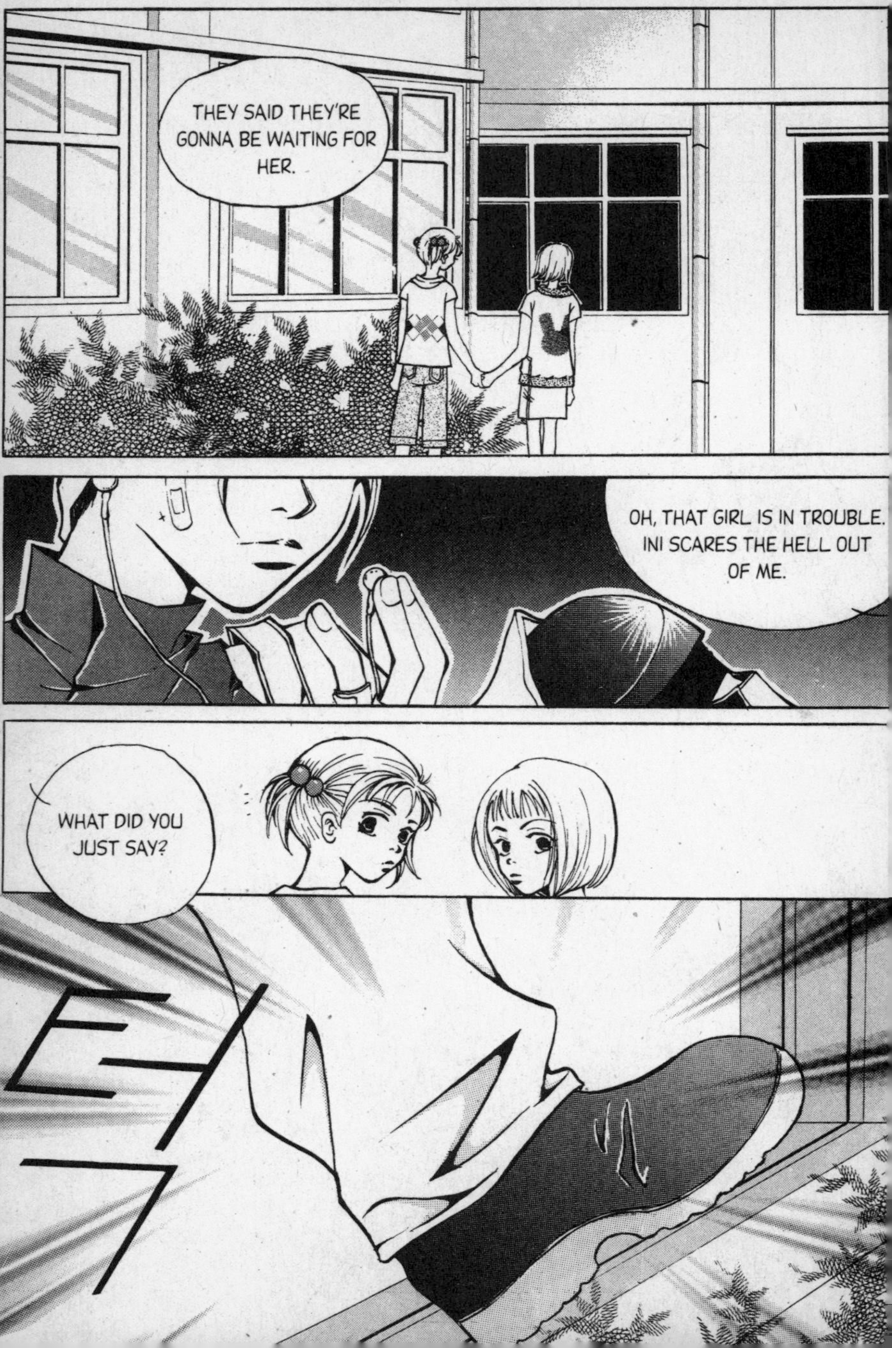
THEY SAID THEY'RE GONNA BE WAITING FOR HER.
OH, THAT GIRL IS IN TROUBLE. INI SCARES THE HELL OUT OF ME.
WHAT DID YOU JUST SAY?

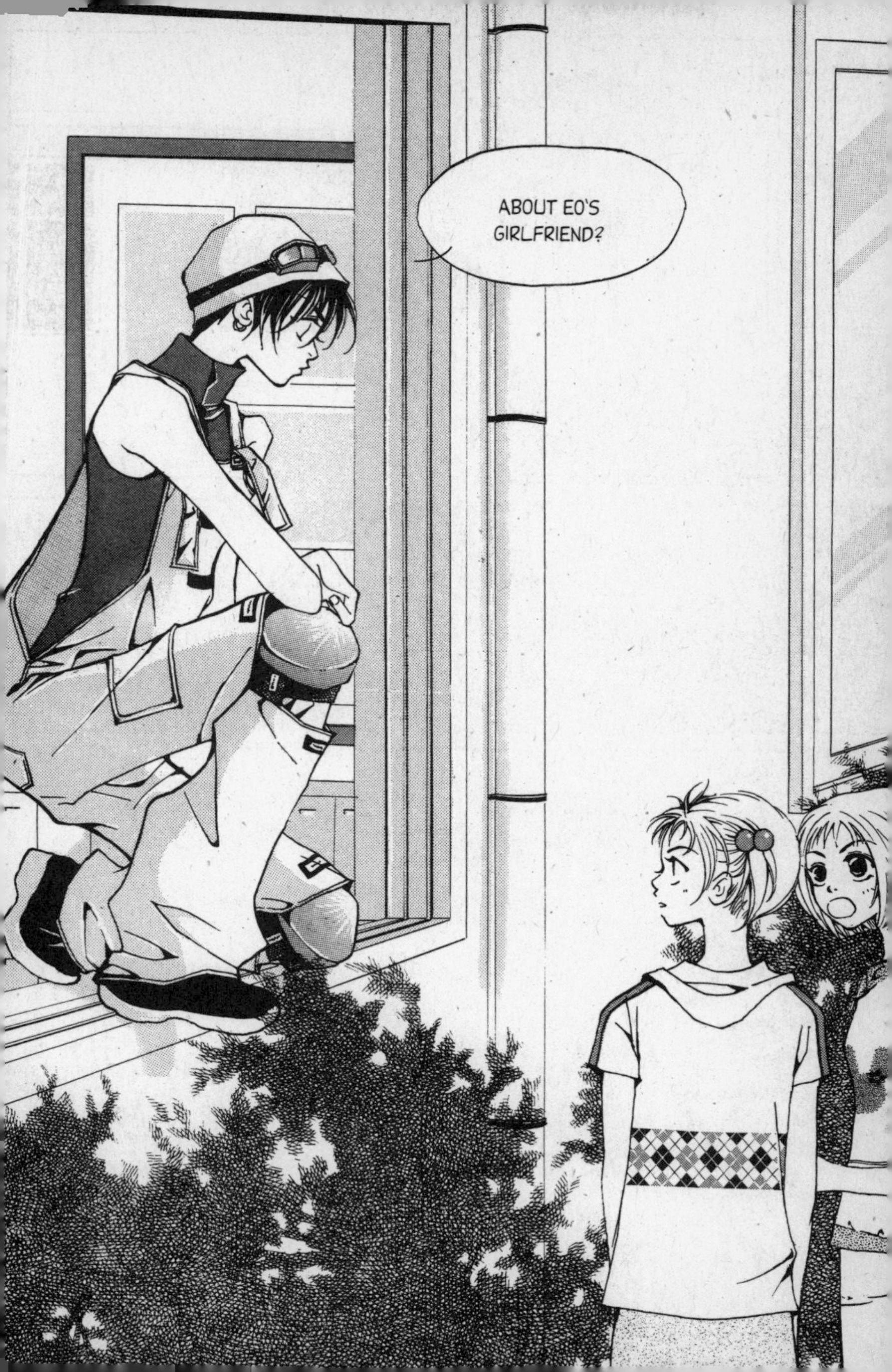
ABOUT EO'S
GIRLFRIEND?

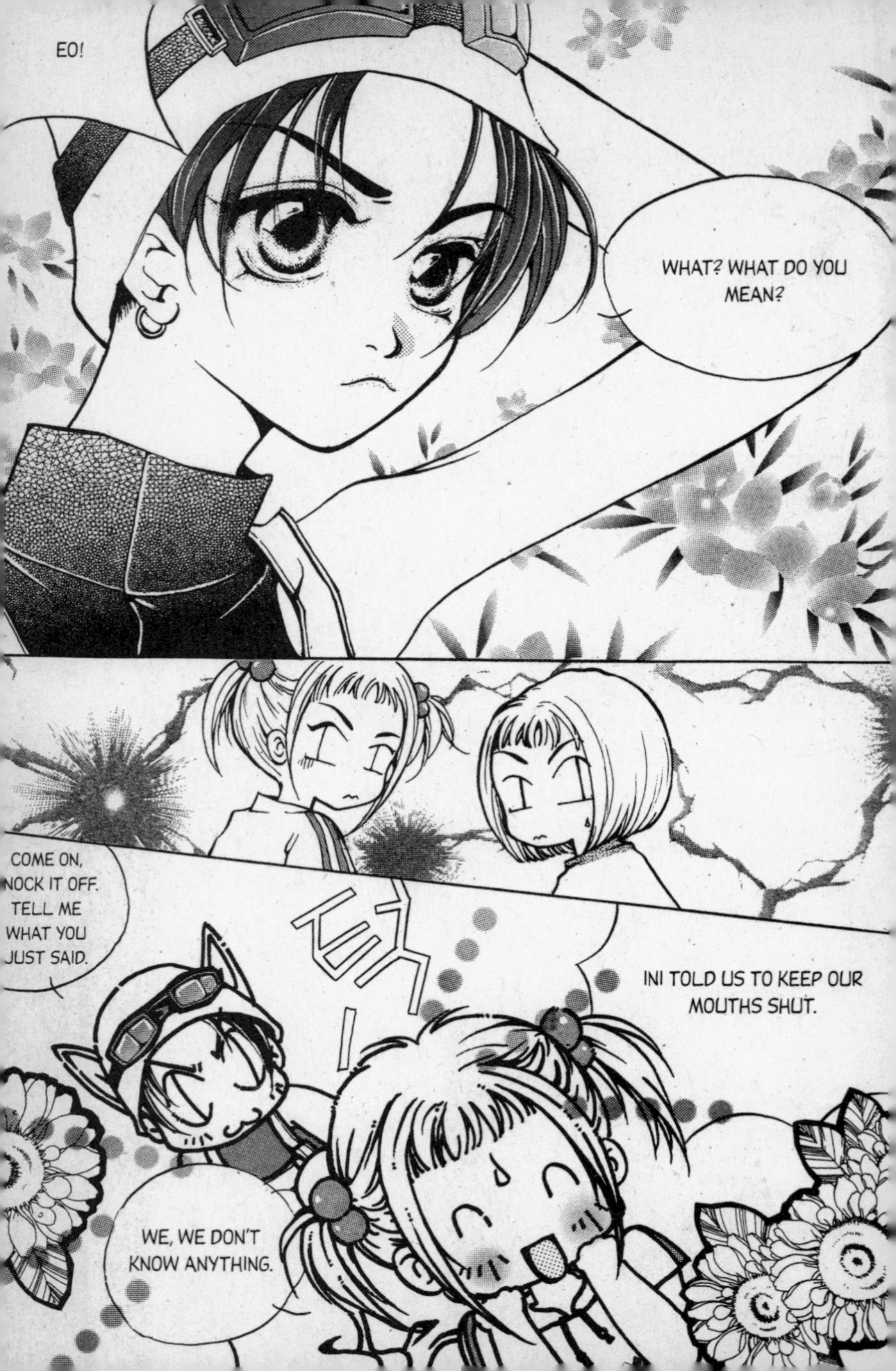
EO!
WHAT? WHAT DO YOU MEAN?
INI TOLD US TO KEEP OUR MOUTHS SHUT.
COME ON, NOCK IT OFF. TELL ME WHAT YOU JUST SAID.
KEK!
WE, WE DON'T KNOW ANYTHING.

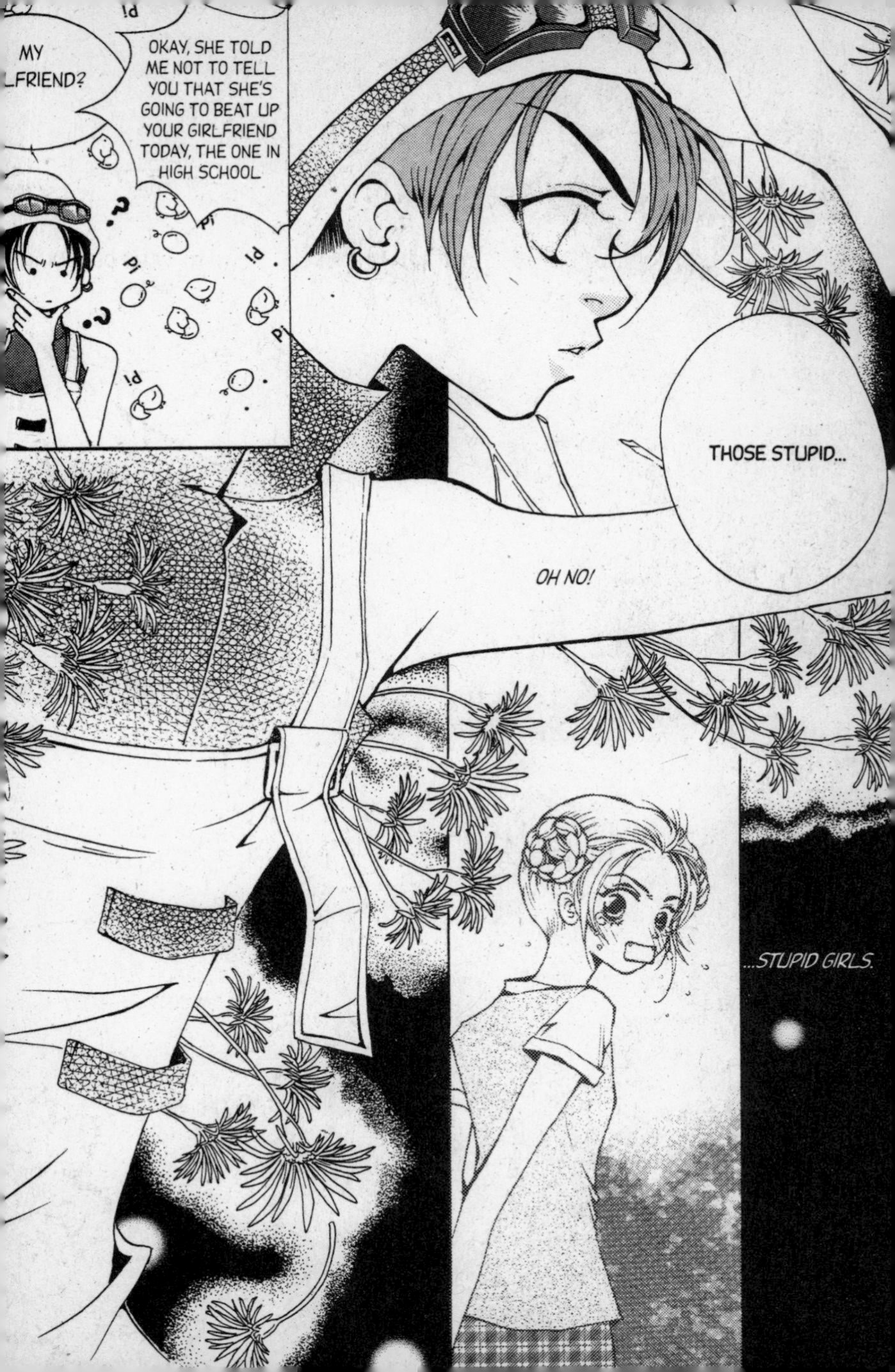

OKAY, SHE TOLD ME NOT TO TELL YOU THAT SHE'S GOING TO BEAT UP YOUR GIRLFRIEND TODAY, THE ONE IN HIGH SCHOOL.
MY
LFRIEND?
THOSE STUPID...
OH NO!
...STUPID GIRLS.

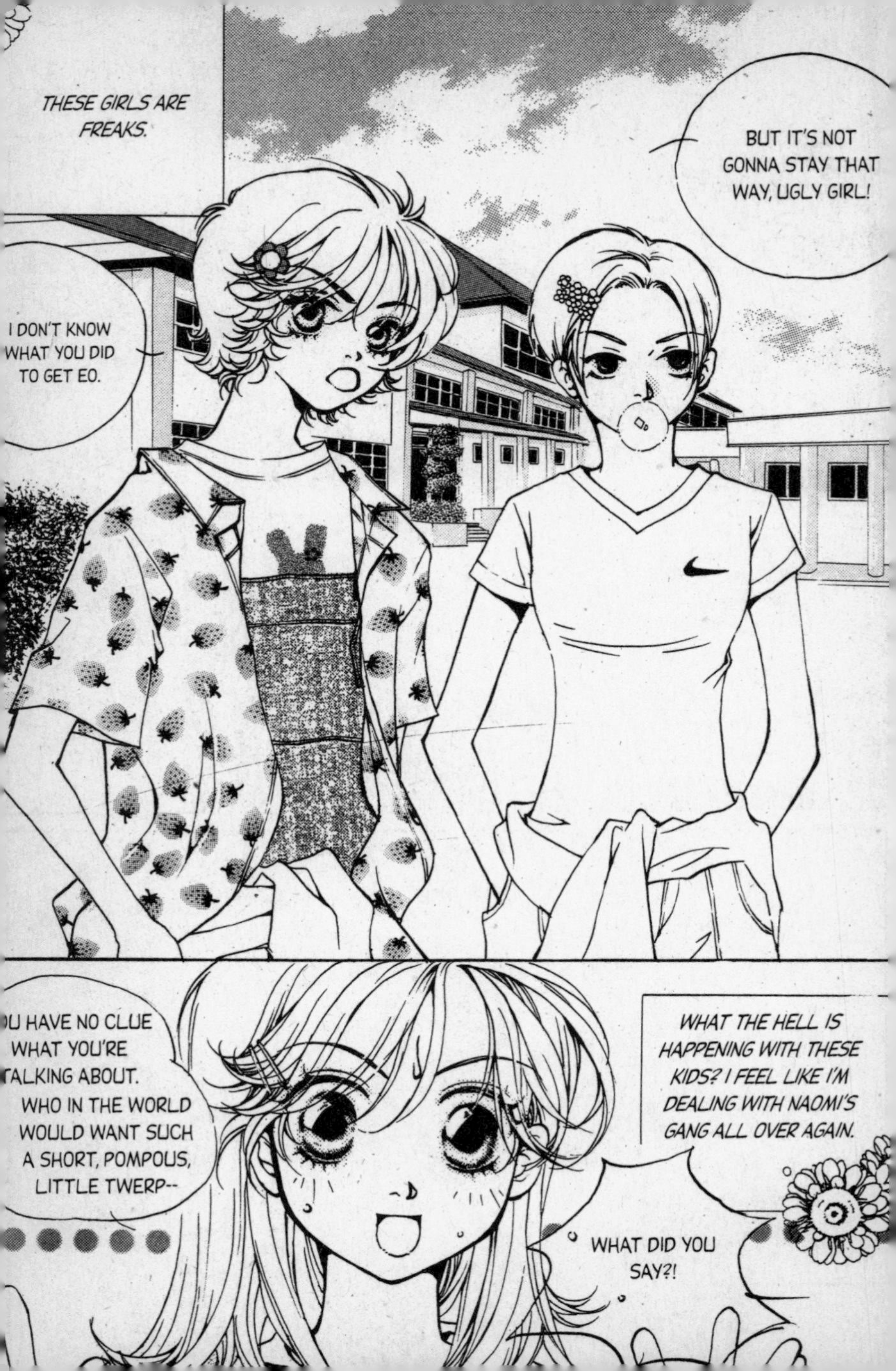
THESE GIRLS ARE FREAKS.
I DON'T KNOW WHAT YOU DID TO GET EO.
BUT IT'S NOT GONNA STAY THAT WAY, UGLY GIRL!
OU HAVE NO CLUE WHAT YOU'RE TALKING ABOUT. WHO IN THE WORLD WOULD WANT SUCH A SHORT, POMPOUS, LITTLE TWERP--
WHAT THE HELL IS HAPPENING WITH THESE KIDS? I FEEL LIKE I'M DEALING WITH NAOMI'S GANG ALL OVER AGAIN.
WHAT DID YOU SAY?!

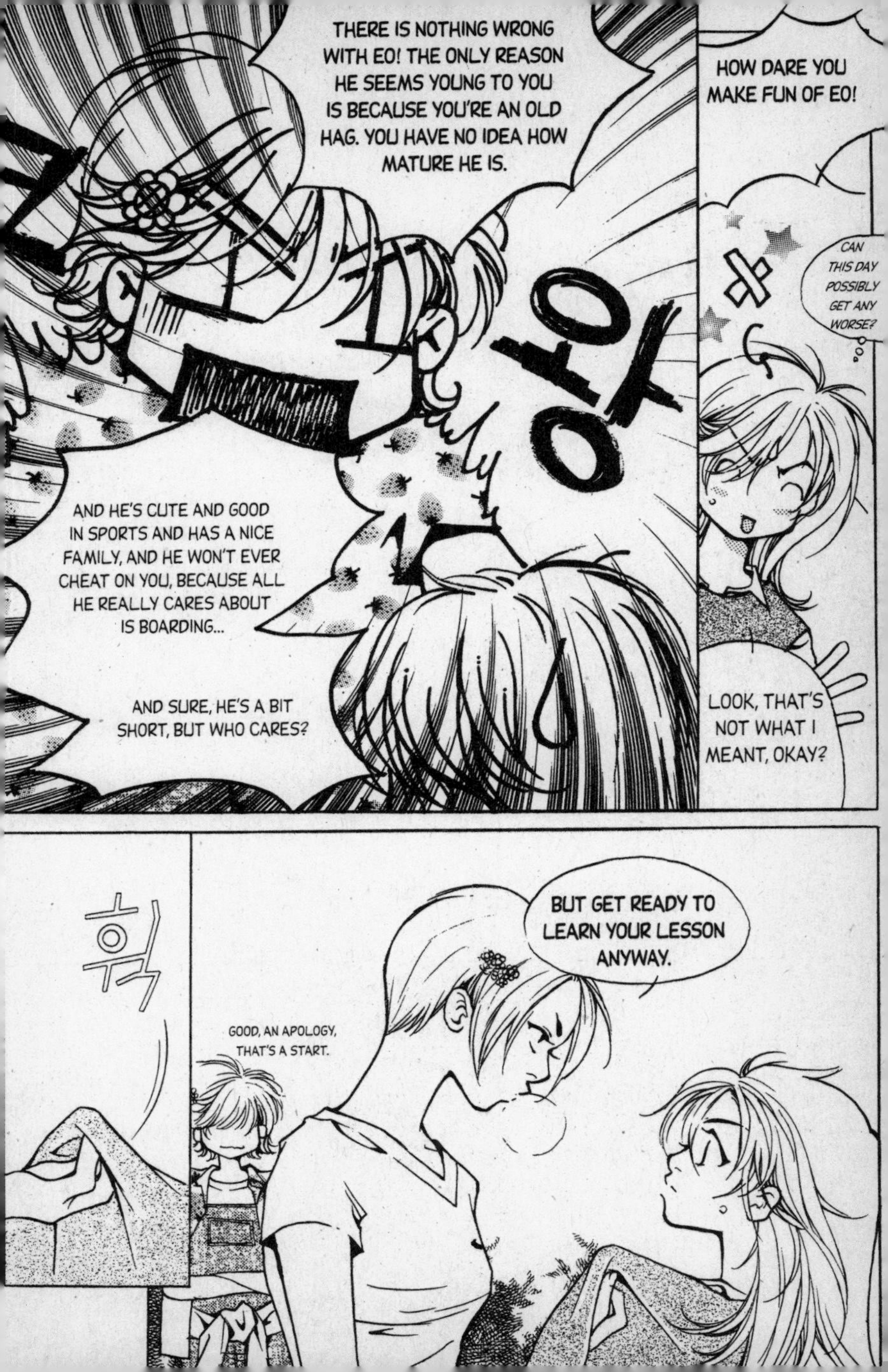
THERE IS NOTHING WRONG WITH EO! THE ONLY REASON HE SEEMS YOUNG TO YOU IS BECAUSE YOU'RE AN OLD HAG. YOU HAVE NO IDEA HOW MATURE HE IS.
AND HE'S CUTE AND GOOD IN SPORTS AND HAS A NICE FAMILY, AND HE WON'T EVER CHEAT ON YOU, BECAUSE ALL HE REALLY CARES ABOUT IS BOARDING...
AND SURE, HE'S A BIT SHORT, BUT WHO CARES?
HOW DARE YOU MAKE FUN OF EO!
CAN THIS DAY POSSIBLY GET ANY WORSE?
LOOK, THAT'S NOT WHAT I MEANT, OKAY?
휙
BUT GET READY TO LEARN YOUR LESSON ANYWAY.
GOOD, AN APOLOGY, THAT'S A START.

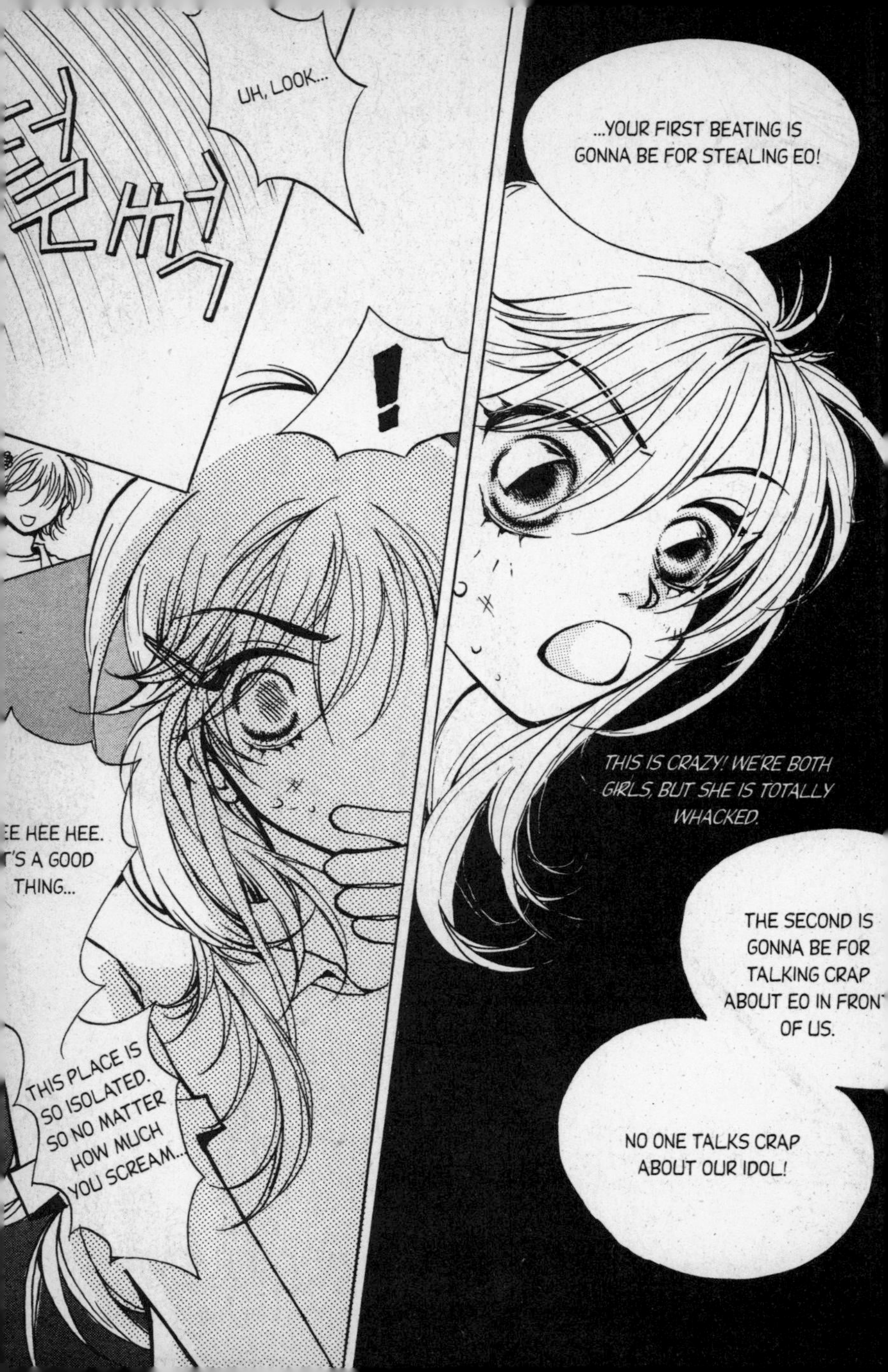
UH, LOOK...
!
EE HEE HEE.
T'S A GOOD THING...
THIS PLACE IS SO ISOLATED. SO NO MATTER HOW MUCH YOU SCREAM...
...YOUR FIRST BEATING IS GONNA BE FOR STEALING EO!
THIS IS CRAZY! WE'RE BOTH GIRLS, BUT SHE IS TOTALLY WHACKED.
THE SECOND IS GONNA BE FOR TALKING CRAP ABOUT EO IN FRON OF US.
NO ONE TALKS CRAP ABOUT OUR IDOL!

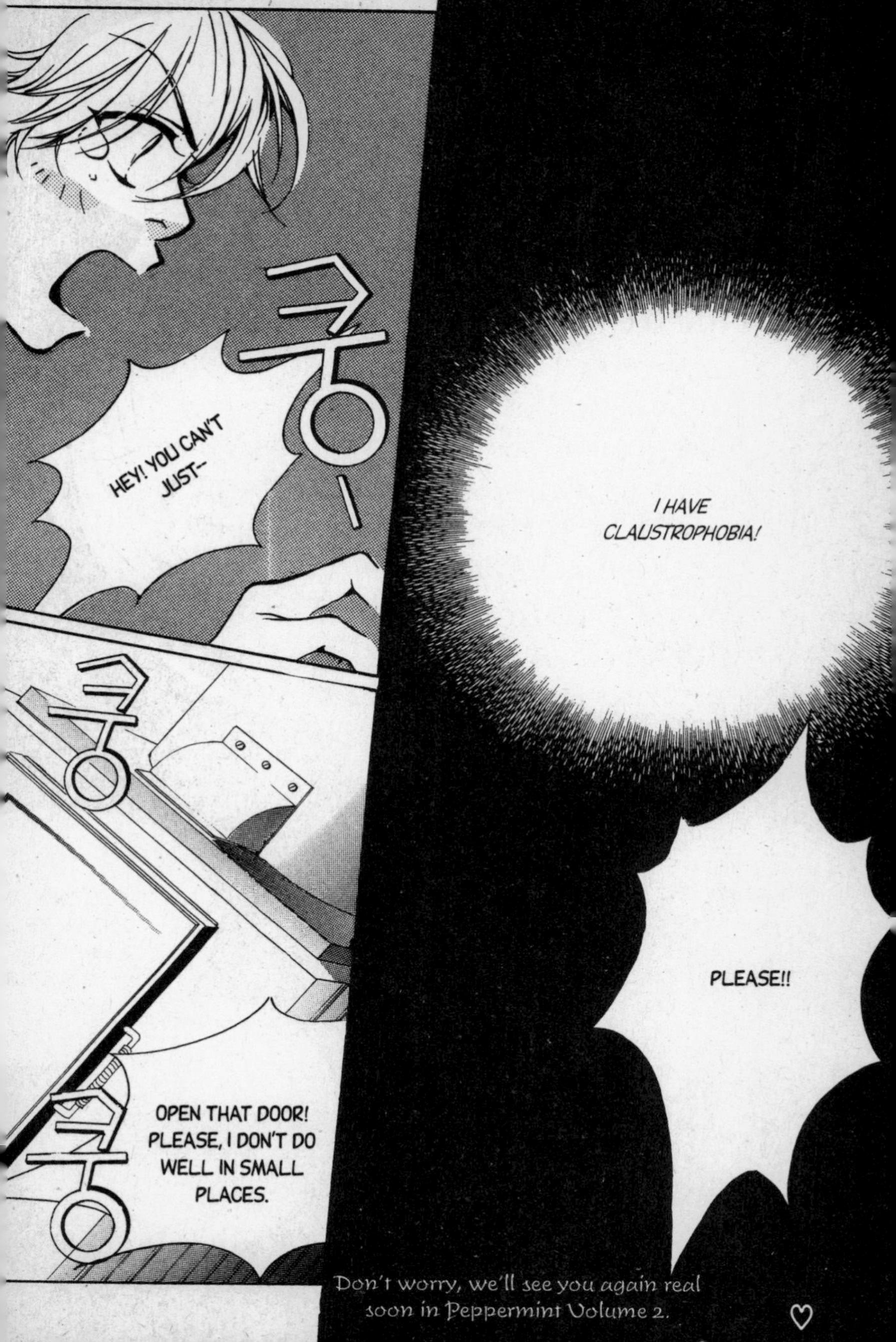
HEY! YOU CAN'T JUST-
OPEN THAT DOOR! PLEASE, I DON'T DO WELL IN SMALL PLACES.
I HAVE CLAUSTROPHOBIA!
PLEASE!!
Don't worry, we'll see you again real soon in Peppermint Volume 2.
♡

In the next volume of...

Peppermint

Who will save Hey from the terrors of the Sunflower Clip gang? And what's the bigger problem for Hey—that Naomi's gang would rather give her a false address than see her show up at EZ's birthday party or that EO, her fake boyfriend will be there?

Find out in
Peppermint Volume 2!

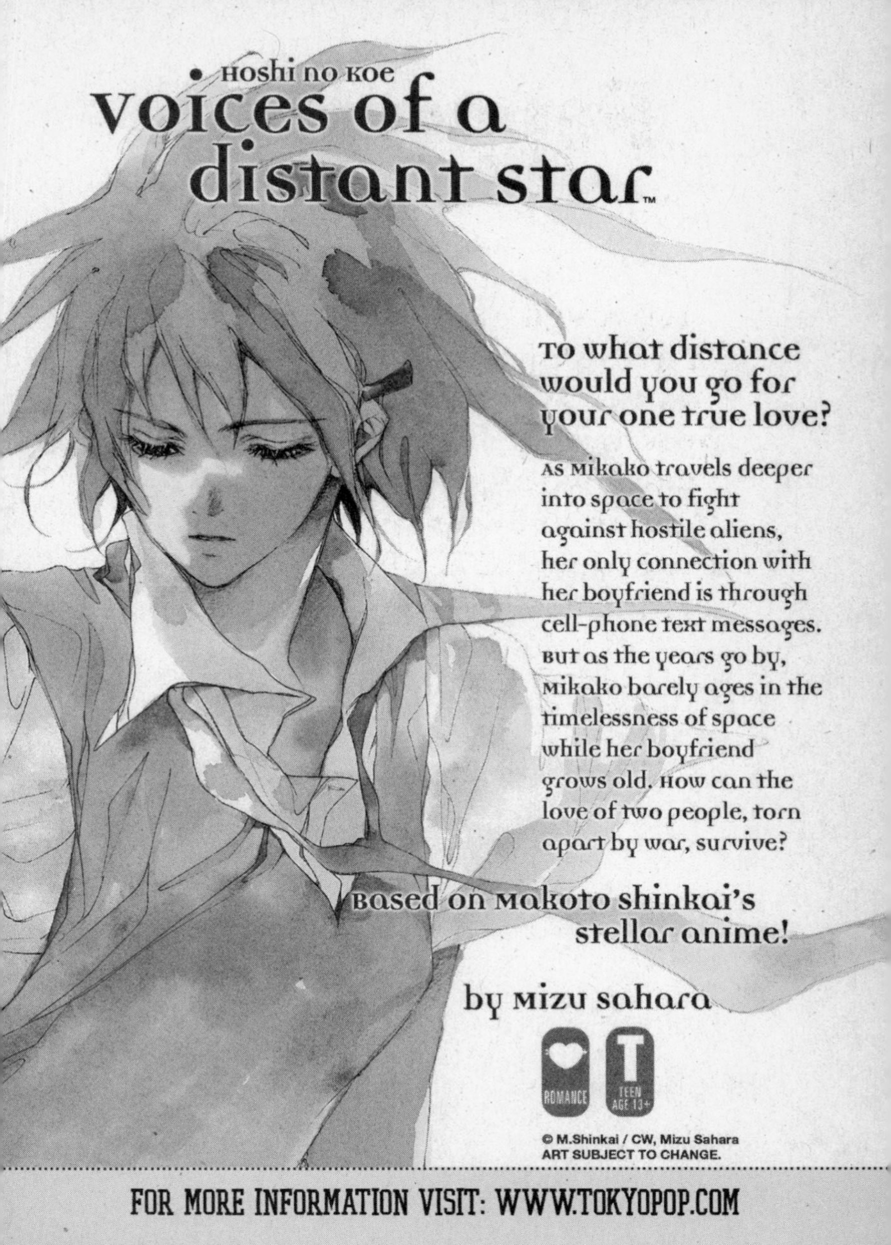
HOSHI NO KOE
voices of a distant star™
To what distance would you go for your one true love?
As Mikako travels deeper into space to fight against hostile aliens, her only connection with her boyfriend is through cell-phone text messages. But as the years go by, Mikako barely ages in the timelessness of space while her boyfriend grows old. How can the love of two people, torn apart by war, survive?
Based on Makoto Shinkai's stellar anime!
by Mizu Sahara
ROMANCE
T
TEEN AGE 13+
© M.Shinkai / CW, Mizu Sahara
ART SUBJECT TO CHANGE.

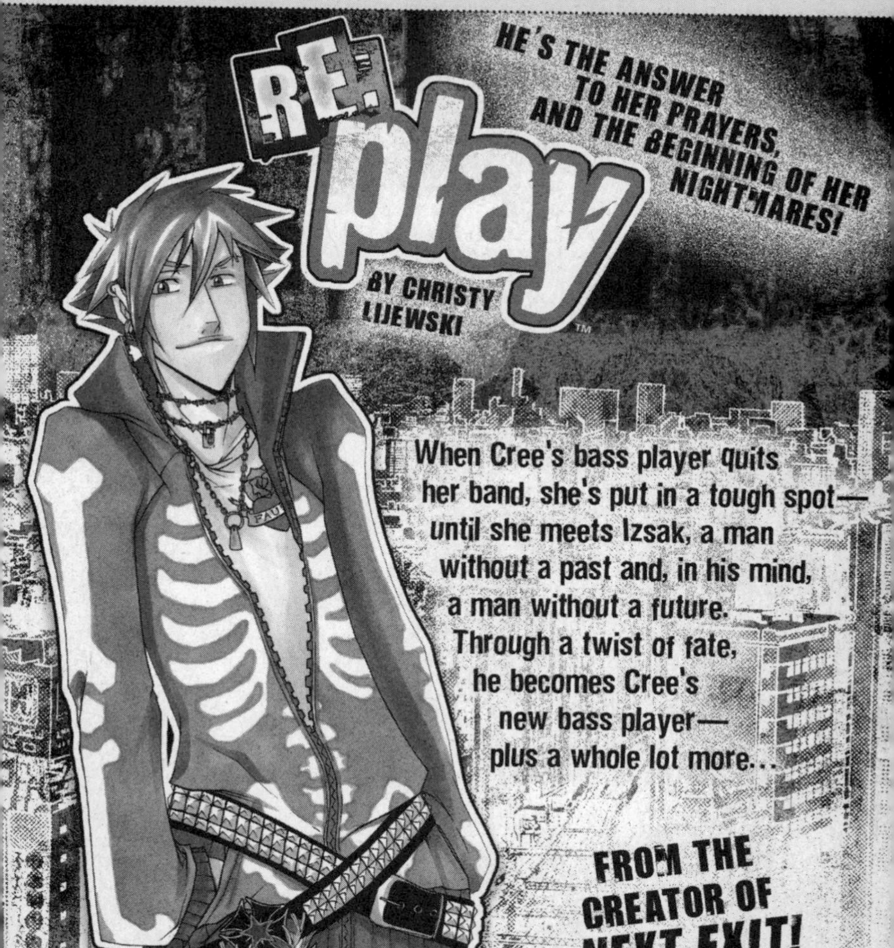
RE: play
HE'S THE ANSWER TO HER PRAYERS, AND THE BEGINNING OF HER NIGHTMARES!
BY CHRISTY LIJEWSKI
When Cree's bass player quits her band, she's put in a tough spot—until she meets Izsak, a man without a past and, in his mind, a man without a future. Through a twist of fate, he becomes Cree's new bass player—plus a whole lot more...
FROM THE CREATOR OF NEXT EXIT!
DRAMA
T TEEN AGE 13+
© Christy Lijewski and TOKYOPOP Inc.

TOKYOPOP SHOP

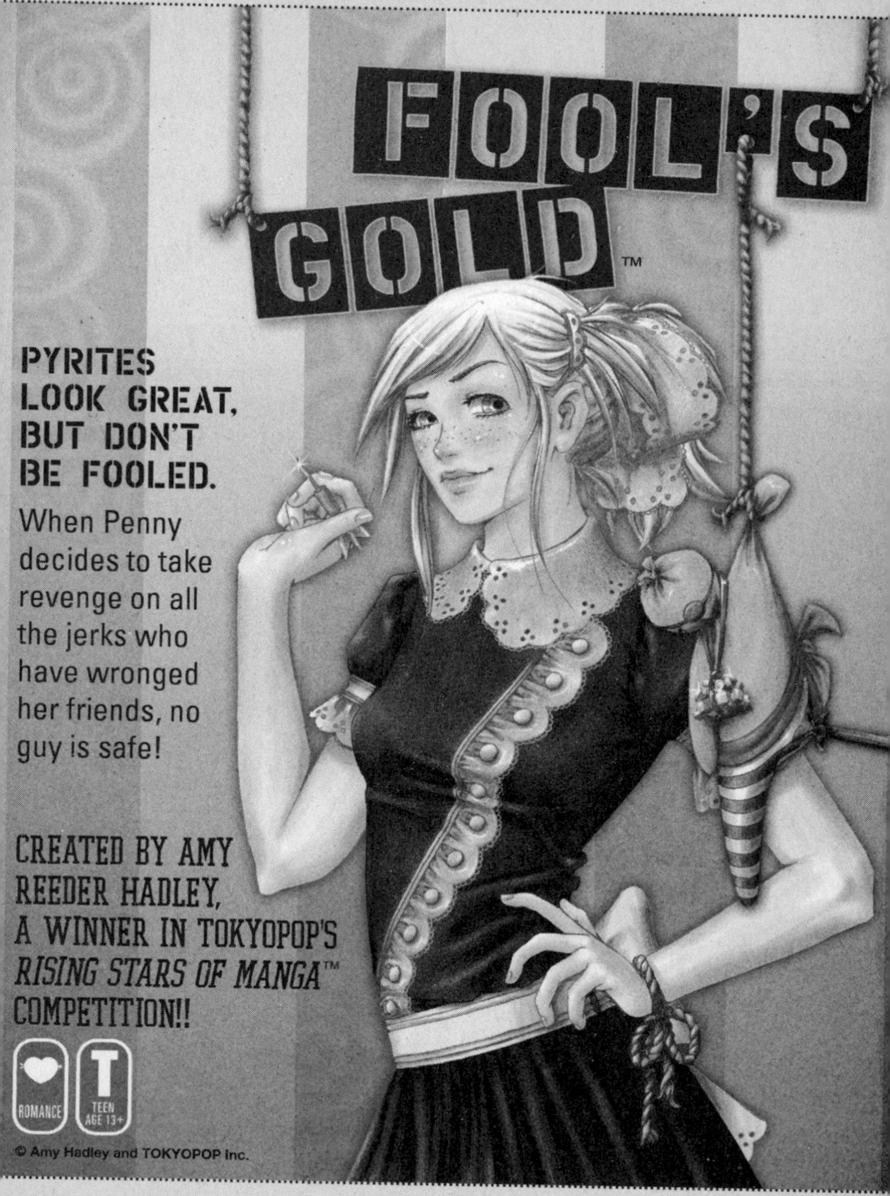
FOOL'S GOLD™
PYRITES LOOK GREAT, BUT DON'T BE FOOLED.
When Penny decides to take revenge on all the jerks who have wronged her friends, no guy is safe!
CREATED BY AMY REEDER HADLEY, A WINNER IN TOKYOPOP'S *RISING STARS OF MANGA*™ COMPETITION!!
ROMANCE
T
TEEN AGE 13+
© Amy Hadley and TOKYOPOP Inc.

DRAMACON™

Sometimes even two's a crowd.

When Christie settles in the Artist Alley of her first-ever anime convention, she only sees it as an opportunity to promote the comic she has started with her boyfriend. But conventions are never what you expect, and soon a whirlwind of events sweeps Christie off her feet and changes her life. Who is the mysterious cosplayer who won't even take off his sunglasses indoors? What do you do when you fall in love with a guy who is going to be miles away from you in just a couple of days?

CREATED BY SVETLANA CHMAKOVA!
"YOU CAN'T AVOID FALLING UNDER ITS CHARM." -IGN.COM

READ AN ENTIRE CHAPTER ONLINE FOR FREE:
WWW.TOKYOPOP.COM/MANGAONLINE

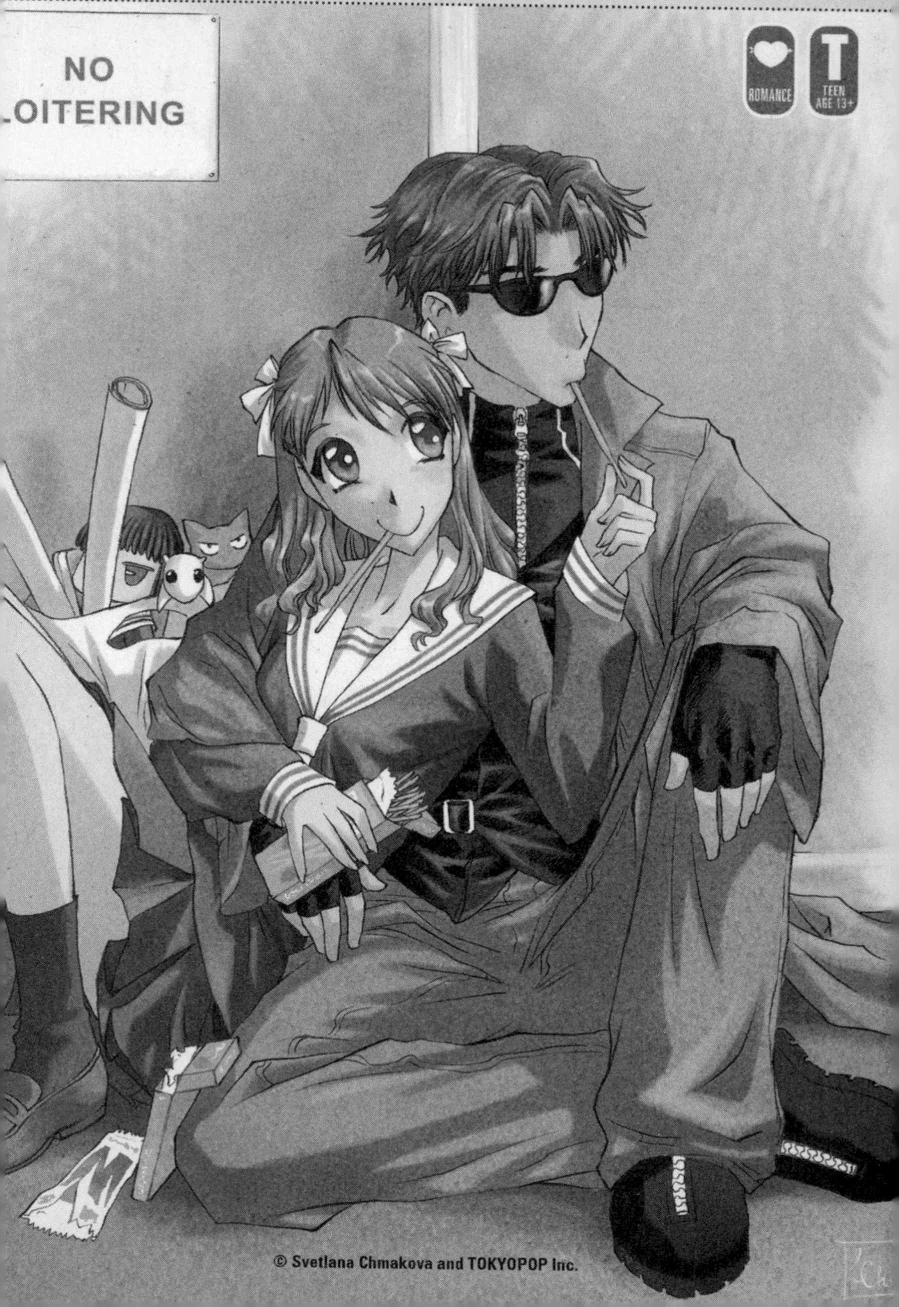
NO
LOITERING
ROMANCE
T
TEEN
AGE 13+

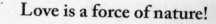

OTOGI ZOSHI
BY NARUMI SETO

An all-out samurai battle to retrieve the Magatama, the legendary gem that is said to hold the power to save the world!

Hot new prequel to the hit anime!

© NARUMI SETO. © IG/VAP/NTV.

STRAWBERRY MARSHMALLOW
BY BARASUI

Cute girls do cute things...in *very* cute ways.

A sweet slice of delight that launched the delicious anime series!

© Barasui.

TRASH
BY SANAMI MATOH

When your uncle is the biggest mob boss in New York, it's hard to stay out of the family business!

From the creator of the fan-favorite *Fake!*

© SANAMI MATOH.

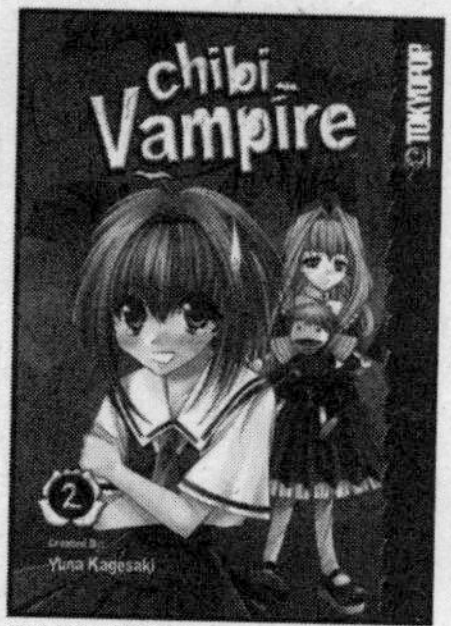
chibi
Vampire
TOKYOPOP
2
Yuna Kagesaki

CHIBI VAMPIRE VOLUME 2

BY YUNA KAGESAKI

This bloody-good vampire has a big crush on her prey!

COMEDY · OT OLDER TEEN AGE 16+

Inspired the hit anime!

DEVIL MAY CRY 3 VOLUME 2

BY SUGURO CHAYAMACHI

The secret of the seven seals will release the demon world unto the earth!

**It's good against evil...
and brother against brother!**

ACTION · OT OLDER TEEN AGE 16+

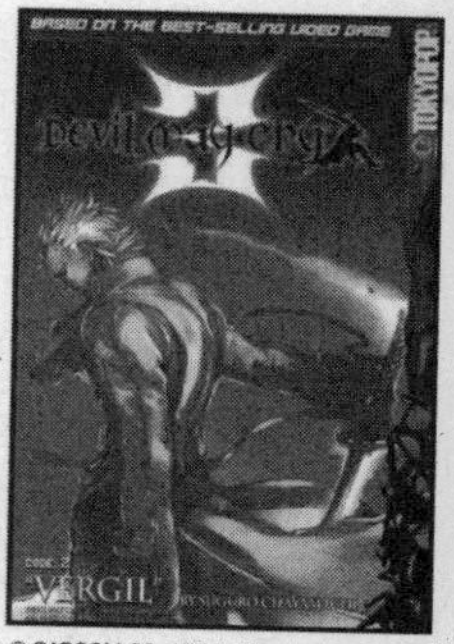
BASED ON THE BEST-SELLING VIDEO GAME
TOKYOPOP
VERGIL

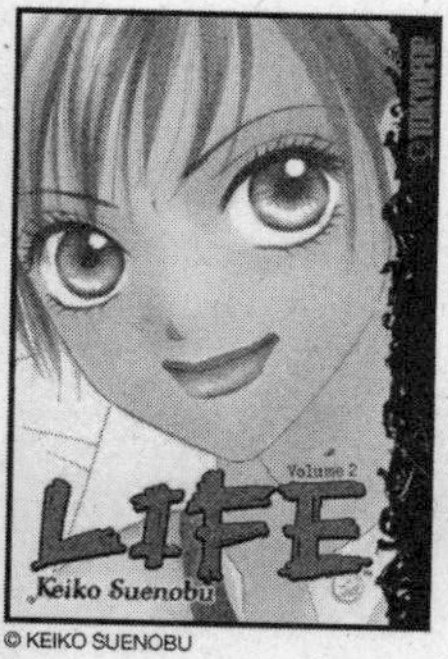
TOKYOPOP
Volume 2
LIFE
Keiko Suenobu

LIFE VOLUME 2

BY KEIKO SUENOBU

It's about real teenagers...
real high school...
real life!

DRAMA · OT OLDER TEEN AGE 16+

**Every life has a story...
Every story has a life of its own.**